A NOTE ON THE AUTHOR

KAREN CAMPBELL is a graduate of Glasgow University's
renowned Creative Writing Masters, and author of *The Twilight
Time*, *After the Fire*, *Shadowplay*, *Proof of Life* and, most recently,
This Is Where I Am, which was a BBC Radio 4 Book at Bedtime.
A former police officer, and council PR, Karen Campbell won
the Best New Scottish Writer Award in 2009. She lives in
Galloway, Scotland.

karencampbell.co.uk

RISE

KAREN CAMPBELL

BLOOMSBURY

LONDON · OXFORD · NEW YORK · NEW DELHI · SYDNEY

Bloomsbury Paperbacks
An imprint of Bloomsbury Publishing Plc

50 Bedford Square   1385 Broadway
London   New York
WC1B 3DP   NY 10018
UK   USA

www.bloomsbury.com

BLOOMSBURY and the Diana logo are trademarks of Bloomsbury Publishing Plc

First published in Great Britain 2015
This paperback edition first published in 2016

British Library Cataloguing-in-Publication Data
A catalogue record for this book is available from the British Library.

ISBN: HB: 978-1-4088-5792-2
PB: 978-1-4088-5675-8
ePub: 978-1-4088-5674-1

2 4 6 8 10 9 7 5 3 1

Typeset by Hewer Text UK Ltd, Edinburgh
Printed and bound in Great Britain by CPI Group (UK) Ltd, Croydon CR0 4YY

For Mum

Chapter One

Pin in a map, pin in a map. Anywhere at all. Don't care, as long as it's not here.

The sandstone tenements glare, crushing her, towering, toppling, full of lives and noise, and she doesn't want any part of this. They staunch air; it flows sickly through manky alleys. Great visionaries planned glass ceilings for these streets, to protect the air their children breathed; Justine has a clear picture of her teacher at school, showing plans for arcades, for vents of sweet air. *Visionaries* she'd said, and it made Justine think of ghosts. Two centuries later; the air's still slow. Man, she wants whooping great gusts of freshness to sting her clean. To wring her lungs inside out. She wants to stand on the highest hill and scatter herself, throw herself hard and trust to luck she lands somewhere soft.

She thinks of places she's been, places she's read about, and, all the while, she is walking away from home. Definitely not running because that makes folk think you have something to hide. Her leatherette bag creaks on her shoulder. The endless rain adds its own weight; everything monochrome, her feet sodden. All the world on her back. Not to mention that bloody itch. Hands in pockets, pressing her knuckles on the sore patch, pressing not scratching. *Pressing* not scratching, in little angry beats. Far enough now, surely.

It will be safe to stop here.

Justine takes her phone from her pocket. It's a shiny gizmo that has too many complex apps. She didny choose it. Carefully, she flips the back off, takes out the SIM card. There are very few numbers she'd like to keep, but to separate with them fully, at this moment, seems more dangerous. You must always leave an escape route. Every room you enter, every avenue you walk down: check the exit first.

Opposite the bus shelter, a white barrier lowers as a vehicle approaches the car park. A man in yellow saunters from his plastic box, tips slightly forward to the driver. He ticks something on a clipboard, wanders back to raise the barrier, let the car in. The sentry box has a logo with a flame, and *Sentinel Power* written beside it. It's on the back of the guy's jacket too, when he turns. All that power. See how wide it makes him swagger? Bet he plays at being a big man. Muttering into his lapel: *Yup, security code red the day. We're expecting a raid on wur pylons.*

As the car drives through the entrance, a bus comes bumping towards her, heading into town. Justine tosses her mobile beneath the wheels, sticks out her hand. Does not look back, not once, not even when the sense of being watched is so acute that the scales of her flesh rise. She gets on the bus, lays her profile against the coolness of window, avoiding the obvious smears. Her cheek makes the glass warm. In the panicked spill from listening to grabbing to running, does she feel safe yet? She concentrates: on her cold fingers, erratic heartbeat. On the skin on the nape of her neck. Feels electricity crawling, nothing more; sparking from the engine below her.

Her head, bobbing against the window, empties out; she pictures it opening like one of those speeded-up flower films where the petals unfold and spores fly everywhere. The long broad street with its charity shops and legal-advice centres draws away. Blurs. She remembers this street when she was wee. There was a fruiterer's and florist's; an old-fashioned watch-maker's staffed by two elderly brothers who lived silently amongst the ticks and chimes; an elegant ironmonger's where you could buy anything – and where they kept a talking parrot in a cage. Two butcher-shops as well, dressed in sawdust, and stinking of blood. She can recall the shock of black hook, pink flank. A whole dead tongue. Her mum's polyester skirt, her face, buried in it, and then she sees *his* face. Charlie Boy's. She *sees* it, twisted. Bouncing.

Feels the black hook sinking in.

He is running down the street behind the bus. He's pulled on trackie bottoms but his chest and feet are naked. Puddles splash up white nylon; his mouth contorts, he stumbles to clutch his foot. Instinctively, she ducks, hiding her head between her knees. *Oh God ohgodgodgod.* In a foetal curl, she waits for him to get her. But the bus trundles on. She hears a woman at the back of the bus scream.

'Fucksake! Has that nutter got a *gun*?'

'Where?' squeals her pal. 'Naw' – more calmly – 'just a big chib. Fuck! Look at him go! Prick thinks he can fight a bus.' They both giggle, pop gum. Justine can feel no impact from the blows, no sound of manic smashing. Still terrified, she raises her head a tiny bit, but they have moved further round the bend, and she can't see. From the driver's Perspex box, she hears a crackly beep, then the driver speaks, unhurriedly. Because this is Glasgow, and these things happen.

'Aye, Number 4 northbound earlyshift to Control. Just to

report, there's a total numpty wi' a baseball bat, beating crap out the Number 6 behind me. Suggest you get the polis . . .'

Justine cranes her neck. Skin pulsing.

The road behind is clear.

For twenty minutes, she stares at the road as it disappears under the bus. His feet will appear, his bleeding feet will be running, she will see them splash and—

Nothing. Her eye muscles ache. Stiff bones screaming. Eventually, they draw into the middle of the city. He was chasing a bus. He thinks she got on a bus.

Does he *know* that, though? There is no one beside her. She slumps in her seat, one delving hand reaching in to check. Still there. She eases a couple of notes out to prove she is not dreaming. A sepia queen's face uncrumples in her fist.

Fucking own you, Just. Body, thoughts, the fucking works. Understand?

He'll know. But he won't know where she's going, because even she doesn't. Blindly, Justine hoists up her bag, jumps off at George Square. The benign lions of the Cenotaph watch as she runs through the flower beds, the lions' stone paws folded so the claws don't show. Up the hill, towards the bus station. An ugly concrete square, ranks of double and single deckers all parked on the diagonal. She moves through sliding doors, into a foyer strewn with cans and chip papers. It must all be forward motion. Keep moving. Stop thinking. An old tramp dosses on one of the plastic benches. She weaves past, goes straight to the ticket counter, which is blessedly empty.

'Where to?' asks the man.

'Eh . . .' Her eyes won't focus, they're too dry.

'Where to?' he repeats, slowly. LOUDLY. Thinking she's a tourist, one of those happy explorers of history and life. It always

4

surprises Justine, that her city interests tourists. She grips the edge of the counter. There's a list of destinations on the wall above his shoulder. *Buchanan Street Bus Station – Gateway to the Highlands.*

'When's your next bus north?'

'Eh, Lochallach. Twelve minutes.'

'Nothing sooner?'

'Naw. It's Sunday, hen.'

'OK. A single.' Is Lochallach past Oban? She thinks they went to Oban, once, and it seemed to take for ever. She passes him the money. 'Long is it to get there?'

The man sighs, pointedly studies the timetable. 'About two and a half hours by the looks of it.'

Is that all? Well, she's bought it now. Once she gets there, she can travel further north. And further and further till she falls off the end.

She sits on a bench across from the flyblown Sleeping Beauty. They are all exposed in this glass-walled place. What if she's seen? A door gusts open. She shivers. Flicks up her hoodie. Two men in boiler suits are pasting up a poster. A parade of people, marching in one thick coil on a path the shape of Scotland. At the back, there's your Picts, your pagans, your Mary Queen of Scots (who, if the wee brass plaques in every Scottish castle are to be believed, really did travel the length of the nation). Beside her strides Mel Gibson as William Wallace, Bonnie Prince Charlie, a couple of beardie guys. Apart from tragic Mary, all the marchers are men. All plump and smug. Is that Rabbie Burns? The one with side-burns and a leery smile? Toting a telly comes John Logie Baird; then Alexander Graham Bell (with a mobile as a joke) then a whole wad of folk Justine doesn't recognise, then Dolly the sheep. In the foreground, a wee girl holds the Saltire aloft.

> *Vote for your History*
> *Vote for your Future*
> *Vote YES for Scottish Independence!*

An elegant, dark woman is reading the poster. She balances a toddler in one arm, wiping the tiny plaits of hair from her face as she stoops to speak to the little girl beside her. This referendum debate has been long, and strident. Tomorrow, the empty billboard next to the poster will no doubt be filled with other faces, insisting you:

> *Vote No for Unity*
> *Vote No to Separatism*
> *Vote No Thanks, we're Better Together*

Justine couldny care less. She puts one hand on her knee to stop it jittering. Beside her, another family: Mum outside having a quick fag, the children sitting on their suitcases, fighting each other for the most room. Dad is on the other end of the bench, her bench, reading the *Daily Record*, while the tramp snores on over the way. She watches him sleep. Lips cracked, parted and his eyelids dancing in some secret place. Beneath his chin, he clasps the neck of an old-fashioned brolly, placed like a sword across his chest. The skin round his nails is ragged and raw, filth in every crease, and he's dressed all in grey. Grey coat and baggy trousers, held up by the standard length of twine. His matted beard and hair, though, are startling orange. Crazy loops of individual orange, making him real. His shock of hair makes him unignorable, if there is such a word. She wonders how you can sleep so trustingly in a public place. Then she thinks, he probably has nothing left to steal.

Sitting down has made the itching better. She slides her hands into the waistband of her jeans, waits a second then, when nobody's looking, slides them deeper. She tries to shift the notes to stop them rubbing. Would the ticket-guy freak if he knew from whence those two crisp tenners came? Maybe he'd just breathe deeply. Let a quiver of saliva drip. A brace of police officers saunter in. Automatically, Justine rises. Hood right up, goes to the loo. Thirty pee just to pee. Inside the cubicle, she liberates sufficient cash to see her through the day. Six minutes till her bus. Man, her head is mince. She'd love a drink, but it's eight forty-six a.m. When she re-emerges, the cops have gone. Justine goes to the wee kiosk selling crisps and juice. Purchases Tropicana, two bags of salt and vinegar, and a puce-pink, cheapo mobile phone. She returns to her bench, but it's full now. The overflow stand in a loose, alert queue, poised to spring whenever the bus appears. No one has asked the tramp to budge up.

At last, the Lochallach bus pulls into the bay. Passengers alighting, the driver climbing from his cabin; Justine's breath is knuckle-tight, she doesn't even realise she's been holding it until the bus driver wanders off, leaving the little queue waiting. Then she feels sick, she isn't going to make it, Jesus, she's going to throw up right here on the concourse and they won't let her travel, they'll think she's drunk or on drugs and she *isn't*, she doesn't DO . . . She doesn't. Eventually, another driver comes and lets them on. Justine makes for the neutral middle, spreads and shapes her bag on the seat beside her until it's a bulging obstacle. She'll sleep alone and intact like the red-haired dosser, stretched diagonally, with her head on her bag. Behind her, kids call and bicker, but she's so tired she barely hears them. She closes her eyes. That way, she'll have no idea how she got there when she arrives. And neither will she know how to get back.

*

She must have slept about an hour, a dark empty sleep. When she wakes, brief panic, then a breath, then it's all brown heather and clouds of different grey, the bus climbing. To her left, the valley drops down, dipping to a gully. On the far side of the bus, the hills rise sheer to the air, rocks at every angle. It makes her dizzy. Bridged between Heaven and Hell, a foot-high barrier all that will save them from the fall. They chug a bit more, reach an open plateau. No trees, just a tiny loch like a cup of water left amongst the rocks. Justine narrows her eyes, so the colours blur in a tartan blanket.

'Excuse me.'

A black stick, a golden halo, closer, glowing orange. Wild orange curls and a face like peel. She sits up. It's the tramp from the bus station.

'Sorry. Would you mind if I sit here for a while? Those kids are doing my nut in.' He fingers the twine around his waist, examining the threads. Justine faffs with her bag, hoping he'll take the hint.

'Sorry. There's really nowhere else to sit.'

Justine grunts. The tramp sits down, slides his brolly between his legs. She waits for the whiff of pee to strike as his coat billows, is captured beneath his backside. But all he smells is loamy: a rounded rich smell of earth.

'So, where you off to?' His voice is mahogany. Consonants enunciated, only a trace of Glasgow glottal stop.

'Lochallach.'

'Me too. Well, a night in Lochallach, then Oban, then off to Mull.'

'Mm.'

'You been to Mull?'

'Nope.'

'Me neither. My dad was born there. I want to see if I can find the house.'

The tramp's eyebrows are dark behind the ginger furze.

'I know it's daft,' he continues, 'but he died last year. I want to get some heather for his grave. You know, from Mull.'

'Will it keep?'

'I've brought a wee pot with me. And some Miracle-Gro.'

Crackle go the notes. *Itch* goes her groin. *Crackle* goes the tramp's electric hair. Justine chews the inside of her lip. She doubts ripping a plant from its natural habitat and transporting it a hundred miles south to a Glasgow graveyard will work. Even if it does survive the journey, the heather will be in a bad way. In shock, probably, and needing the best of attention. And you wouldn't be digging very far down to replant it, would you? In a graveyard. Though, the soil's probably very well nourished. Dug regularly too.

'Was he buried or cremated?'

'I'm sorry?'

'Your dad. Was he buried or cremated?'

'Both. Well, cremated. Then they buried the ashes. I think. Why?'

'I was just thinking it might be easier to bring him to the heather, that's all.'

He sniffs a little, picks at the bamboo neck of his umbrella. The contraction is only sensed, not seen, but she knows he is drawing inwards. Justine has actually made a dosser recoil. The itching increases. She checks her watch. At home, *Murder She Wrote* would be starting – and he'd be looking for his first can of the day. Bastard never got up till lunchtime. Never. She wonders what woke him this morning. Not her, no way. She had been quieter than death. Three joints and virtually an entire bottle of Grouse had been consumed; she had glugged it out for him herself. Sat two hours on the edge of the filthy bath, waiting to bolt. Each time she flexed her elbows to push up, her stomach burned, and a little spit of urine escaped. As long as she stayed there, she could say she was at the toilet. Gentle rocking, dwindling to inertia. As dawn broke, she could see the open door slam shut – and that scared her even more. Without breath or sense or shoes she gathered what she had to, and got out. Askit was sleeping in the yard, barely raised his head. He's trained to keep people out, not in. She shoved her boots on, knelt to kiss the dog's ugly head. 'Bye, baby.' Half-thought about taking him too, but if he kicked off, she couldny control him. 'Love you.' A thump of his tail as she passed.

He would have woken to birdsong. A grey half-light of fag-stoured windows. He would have dreamt he heard a click perhaps? Or sensed some greater emptiness than was usual. How fast had it gone, that little winding mechanism in his brain, before he started looking? Not for her, but in the wardrobe, the drawers? That box under the loose floorboard under their aching bed.

'Sorry, folks,' the bus driver shouts. 'Road's closed up ahead. Looks like a rockfall. We'll need to go round in a bit of a circle.'

Fine by Justine. More time to be in limbo. She listens to the hum of engine and passengers, glancing up every now and then to check their progress. By mutual accord, the tramp and Justine have stopped talking. She sinks back to almost-doze.

They are driving down into a deep, long valley when she notices the first one.

Stones.

Hulking grey spears of stone, some in groups, some a single silhouette. Piles of smaller rocks studded in between, like gems in a chain, or foot soldiers in an army. Together, the stones form a thick rope of cairns and standing columns, marching along the basin of the glen. Beyond the valley, hills arch to sky: green and cloudy purple; to grey and milky-blue. The sun is low, heavy, and, just for a moment, a burn of orange flashes over the whole, sending shadows deep into the glen.

'Shit!'

She feels the bus lurch, slamming them forwards in their seats. A half-open ashtray, her forehead striking, the in-and-out lashing of a whip. Her neck springs back, is catapulted away. Another slam as movement stops. Shouting, the kids all screaming, folk yelling on the bus . . . she is on the bus so?

Justine is puzzled. It's raining. Her head dulls and shimmers, her head is opening out again but it feels nice and dizzy and it is raining. One by one, tiny droplets splash the floor, her boots. The splashes on the floor are pink.

'You OK? Here . . . look you've cut yourself.' The tramp's rough hand is holding her chin. He shoogles the wrist of his other hand so the sleeve falls back. He has a whitish shirt underneath, which he's using to wipe her blood. Showing her his knuckles as proof. His knuckles are red; the hairs on his knuckles are red. Somebody's red-headed son, once. She can't bear it. She shoves him away, batters down to the front of the bus.

'Can I get off? Please? I'm . . .'

'Whoah now, hen – gies a minute.' The driver starts to open the doors. 'Don't you go puking on my bus. And watch they bloody sheep!'

A rich brown boom follows. 'She's got a head injury!'

The driver releases her. She stumbles outside, thick-woolled sheep scattering, jostling her legs.

She recognises this place.

In the summer, hardy wildflowers will come. Straggly blooms of saxifrage and cowslip will push through moss and the tussocks of wiry grass, fleeting colour across the land; loping and long, across hills and glens that flow for ever beneath sharp sky. Five thousand years before, this pale sun would have struck off the same jags and curves that she is looking at now, buttering rocks that were old, seeping under crags that were ancient.

She wills the nausea away.

'Ho, you all right?' the driver calls.

'Yeah, yeah.'

She surveys the road, the sky, the land. About a mile away, on the hill, sits a little church, a row of houses facing. One hill erupts like a plook behind the church, all on its own in the middle of the plain. It's dotted with sheep. She squints at the different colours. No, it's people, bending and dipping.

'Can I just get off here, please? Stay off, I mean?'

'How? There's nothing here.' The driver follows her gaze. 'Ho, now wait: there's nae polis there. I mean, if you're looking to make a claim or something: that wisny my fault. They sheep are bloody kamikazes—'

'No. No. It's not—' Pressing her brow with the heel of her hand. A sticky lump is forming.

The driver climbs from his cabin. Lighting a fag.

'Look, hen. I could lose ma licence—'

'Honestly. I don't want to make a fuss. Can you just get me my bag, please?'

'Here, it's fine. I've got it.'

Somehow, the tramp has joined them. 'But you need to get that seen to. I think it's going to need stitches. And *you* need to get your first-aid kit replenished—' Umbrella jiggling on his arm, he's waving a white tin box at the driver; an exaggerated warding-off of his smoke.

'Here! Did you go in my cabin? That's a total liberty; that's authorised personnel only—'

'Excuse me!' yells someone on the bus. 'Can you all stop chuntering and get back on, please? I'm gonny miss my ferry.'

'I'm fine,' says Justine. Behind the two men, the strings of stone glitter. Behind the stones lies a bleached field of tree-bones. Acres of logging, then more stones and cairns. The skies closing.

'Trust me.' Deftly, the tramp applies a pad of lint to her forehead. 'I'm a doctor.'

'Aye,' says the driver. 'And I'm the Queen of Sheba.'

'No gauze, I'm afraid.'

'What is this place?'

'Kilmacarra Glen,' says the driver, breathing in his Silk Cut. He pats his sternum with his fist. Coughing it all up.

'Kil-ma-carra.' She tries the sound out.

''Scuse me . . . there.' The tramp stands back. 'All done.'

'Thank you.' She touches her hand to the pad. Soft and thick, like the inside of her head. 'Is there a tourist information place?'

'No really,' says the driver. 'There's a hotel, but I think it's

13

closed down. Or, you could try over by the church – there's a wee tearoom there. You could ask them.'

This will do. This place will do you.

Justine puts her bag on her shoulder, begins to follow the road.

'That you away then?' shouts the driver. 'D'you no want me to drop you off up the hill?'

'No. No thanks.'

'Here, wait. Take this.' The tramp comes after, is holding out his brolly.

'Och, no. It's yours.'

'Please. It looks like rain.'

The oiled silk glides like metal in her hand, the hooked handle warmer. It's a lovely thing.

'At least let me give you something for it.' Though how she's going to reach her stash of notes could be a problem.

'Absolutely not. Now, listen,' says the orange-doctor-tramp. 'If you feel at all sleepy, you must call a GP, right? Or NHS 24.'

'Yeah. Thanks. I'll be fine.' People on the bus are staring. She has to keep moving. 'You take care . . . ?'

'Frank. My name is Frank. You take care too, yes?'

'Cheers, Frank.'

'You sure you'll be all right?' says the driver. 'No that I'm accepting any liability or anything I mean, there's a' seatbelts fitted; it's up to—'

'I'm fine, I promise. I'm good.'

Which is a lie, of course. The money down her pants is testament to that.

Chapter Two

First thing you see of Kilmacarra is its dead. As you approach, there's a sweep in the road, then a clean rise beyond you, like half an egg. Squat on top, a small dour church, watching over the graveyard terraces that slope in tiers downhill. Sun-traps of a sort, these little flatnesses, facing east across the glen, positioned to see every arrival and departure. When the living go to worship in Kilmacarra, they can't ignore the dead. Even if they avert their eyes from the blunt gravestones and look upwards instead, there's the name of every dead soldier of the Great War, carved above the arched kirk gateway. That worries Michael. Such awareness of your own mortality. He'd much rather have grown flowers in his garden. Serves him right for living in a manse. He's thick with mortality – and morality. Thick and sick and tired. He thinks he might refuse to open his eyes.

Yesterday, Michael saw a ghost.

He has a pile of paperwork to read. A constituents' surgery to prepare for. A persuasive, upbeat speech to craft, and a sermon to inspire. And all he can think about is the Ghost. He'd seen it the day before too, in the bitter glint of a heron rising from the loch. Its empty beak was open, glistening, and it seemed as if all the world might fall into it. On the way back from visiting Ailsa Grey he was; well it was no wonder, because those are the times, the dark long times when sin sneaks in and bites you. You have to be on your guard. A grey afternoon spent praying with a grey, dissolving woman, who is tired, so tired and sore, getting deeper locked in herself, and you, praying with her, through the pain, and telling her how God loves her. That her illness is part of a plan. So it's no wonder at all, when you *are* wondering, when you're wondering about 'wonder', and you see another dimension in a simple bird.

No wonder at all.

But it's not an isolated incident. Four times now Michael's seen it since last summer. Kidding himself, the first time, that it was a trick of the light. His overworked, furious mind. And that seeing it was actually better than the perpetual plunging rush he fell into whenever he wasn't looking. It was a thing, a thing he deserved, perhaps. But frightening, all the same. Second time, he was drunk and lonely, and it was a graveyard and it was five a.m., so that's fine. Completely understandable. You can wake up from that one, and he did; he had many energies, bristling, rounded things into which he could pour his focus: his work, his constituents, his family; this momentum lasted several months. He became more settled. As well as work, he risked a hobby; fishing, which brought him to the third time, and the loch. That was horrific. Broad bright day, Michael's fishing rod swinging, a whoosh. He turned. Saw it smiling. Blatant. Bang. Bang. And then again yesterday. Twice in two days – that is not coincidence.

He's been smelling it too. Not sulphur – that would be ridiculous – but in the desolate clean grey that passes here for sky. Occasionally he'll see a hint of it in the standing stones, how they hunched and waited, and then he'd blink, and they'd be stones.

Yesterday, there was no duplicity. It was sitting in a tree; the Ghost, not Michael: a man of middle years, easing into thinning hair and with a nagging, deepening pain in his right knee that precluded any sports. Still daylight, and he was sitting in an oak tree, one with a parasitical birch growing right through the centre of its trunk. No amount of blinking would make this less so.

'Evening,' said the Ghost.

'Evening,' said Michael.

He – it? He was leather-coloured, small, with feathery tips to his ears. Huge, swivelling head and swivelling eyes. Could have been an owl, Michael supposed.

'That you been out fishing?'

'Yes.'

'Used to love fishing. Staring down into the water; seeing your own face glimmer. Helped me think better.'

'Yes.'

'You working on your speech or your sermon?'

'Both.'

'Think they'll listen?'

'Yes.'

'We'll see.' The Ghost had blinked, once, and flown away. All the leaves on the tree shook, and with them, a bird's nest, a clutch of blue eggs sclattering to the ground, and Michael trampling over them in his haste to get away. Damp trousers clinging, his heart doing an SOS.

It might have been an angel; God knows, he'd been praying for that at least. A guiding light. A torch would do him. Of course, Satan had been an angel. That had fully terrified him as a wee boy; that this beautiful, terrible creature was the product of good gone bad.

The gentle click of the manse door, smooth wood behind him. Shutting it all out. The manse was chilly. His wife was chilly. His nose was chilly. Michael ran a bath, took some whisky, then went to bed.

Today, when he woke, the Ghost was squatting on his head.

'Morning,' said the Ghost.

'Morning,' whispered Michael, going cold.

'Morning,' said his wife, slow with sleep and all the lovelier for it. 'You mind if I don't come to church?'

That's the first thing she said to him.

'But I'm . . .'

'I've got to do those edits.' Squeezing his hand.

'Oh. No, OK.' He'd known today was going to be difficult.

'And Ross needs picked up from Jason's house.' She'd let go of him then, rubbing her eyes as she woke to all the possibilities of a day that did not include Michael. 'And I've to take stuff over to Mhairi's—'

'All right! OK. That's fine.'

'And the house is filthy. That kitchen needs gutted – but where am I meant to find the time?'

'We'll get another cleaner. I promise.'

'Maybe one that cleans this time?' Hannah raised herself on one arm. He could see the line of her breast through her nightie.

'You've got to remember; there's less folk to choose from here.'

'Fewer.' She stuck her tongue out. Mumbled something about inbreeding. Only Hannah could find fault with how the inside rim of a toilet seat was wiped. What she really wanted was an au pair. A nice obliging girl who would do a bit of everything. The Ghost popped his head between them. Gave him a comedy-wink.

Michael tried to ignore him, it. The thing that wasn't there. 'You think Euan might—'

'He's in training? For the 10K? I told you last night. He's running over to Fraser's, staying for lunch, then running all the way back.'

'OK, OK. You said.' Turning over on his side.

'Anyway. It's probably better if we do our own thing today. Seeing as you're the enemy.' Hannah had tugged the duvet over her own back, leaving his spine exposed, but their bottoms touching.

She was probably right. Downstairs, he could hear the groan-and-gush of their kitchen tap, then a slam as the back door shut and his eldest son set out on his run. He envied Euan that steady pound, the freedom of filling yourself with sky. Michael missed jogging. Michael missed many things. He hoisted up his pyjama bottoms – the elastic had gone again – then had a little toe flex. Running might loosen things up, but Euan preferred to go alone now. He'd thought he might get the lad into fishing too, but that suggestion had been met with a snort. A good-natured one, certainly. But a definite no. Actually, the congregation reduced – possibly by a quarter – made him less sad than he thought it would. Lighter in fact, that there were fewer folk. Less? Fewer? Ach, but no, no. This one was going to be good! They wouldn't like it at first but . . . He wasn't even sure why some of them still went to church. Same reason Ross kept his cot-blanket at the foot of his bed?

At the end of the day, it was just words. Words that made folk happy.

The Ghost smiled at him. Licked his lips. No longer so bird-like, he wasn't human either. 'Breakfast?' he enquired, sliding from Michael's head and on to Hannah's breast.

'Mmm . . . ooh. That's nice.' Hannah stretched, but kept her eyes closed. As did Michael, so it was just the soft smell of her guiding him, that familiar flesh which was foreign now, and delicious and good for him and bad, bad . . . oh, but he loved it so. Even if it did make him feel lonely. And with a terrible tightness in his teeth.

Afterwards, he showered, got dressed. Put a big pan of water on to boil. Ate wholemeal toast and some hideous jam she'd made from hedges. The Ghost put a pale finger in the pot – it was definitely a finger this morning, not the wings, then plunged it, lasciviously, into his scarlet mouth.

'This is shit.'

'I know.'

'Nice arse on her, though.'

'Thank you. Eh . . . are you coming to church?'

The Ghost wrinkled his nose. 'What do you think?' He examined the jam pot, turning it and turning it with the clever tip of his tail. 'But on you go, have some fun. Knock yourself out.' He upended the jam pot into his mouth, gulping it down. It was all a bit *Tiger Who Came to Tea*. 'I'll just stay here with Helen.'

'Hannah. And will you hell, you dirty bastard.'

The Ghost grinned. 'That's better. Bit of fire in your belly. We like that.'

*

It is possibly the best sermon Michael has ever given, better even than the one he'd made as a probationer on Remembrance Sunday; the one where he'd almost cried himself (he'd had flourish in those days. What Hannah called chutzpah. The cascade of

20

red tissue petals he'd shaken from his cassock had been worth it, despite the Rev berating him for the mess).

Ten in Kilmacarra Church today – actual double figures – plus the Sunday School (five under-tens and an eye-rolling twelve year old). To weak protests, he'd trooped the lot of them up the hill to Mary's Well. No harm; they were of hardy stock, even the octogenarians. Turns out it was a rare hill for rolling eggs. Always has been, a panting Miss Campbell informed him.

'Every Easter your grandpa would bring us up here. At dawn.'

'Really?'

'To see if God had stopped the water.'

'Right.'

'Aye. They'd jam the spring with a big rock the night before, but us wee ones didna know that. We all joined in, clamouring for a shove – we'd a Sunday School of thirty then.'

'Did you? My.'

'Aye. Until Frances Gibson fell over the edge.' She nodded at where one side of the hill was shrouded in a thicket.

'You're joking? Kids: over this side, please. Now.'

'It wisna pagan, mind. It was to guarantee good crops.'

Michael had winced as a mashed-up yolk sailed through the air, commencing a brief but messy Sunday School food-fight.

'Ach, but this is fine, son. You're doing your best.'

Doing an Easter service: it's the furthest thing from what he wants. When they'd found out, though, that he was an actual, ordained minister. That he was old Reverend Archibald 'Baldie' Anderson's grandson, come back to live in the family manse . . . well. His card was marked. He'd not thought enough about reinvention when they moved here. He should have got his story straight.

He should have got a story.

Kilmacarra Kirk has no minister now, so the parishioners take it in turns. There are three churches in all, welded together in a spiritual wheel, which spins on a monthly basis. Although a member (how could he not be?) Michael has avoided giving most of the sermons for over a year, with a neat blend of work commitments and illness, of sporadic attendance at crucial 'choosing' times. But today? Easter Sunday? Friends to convince and support to consolidate? It had to be Michael. He'd even donned his dog-collar for the occasion. Ridiculous.

He traces his descent. It began so well. A son of a son of the manse, destined like his forebears to spread the word. A son of quiet-ticking clocks and dark rooms, of administrators and do-gooders, of pious, thunderous, certain-sure men and frustrated women. Of nice hats on Sunday, weak tea and stirring songs. Of starving black babies and monsters under the bed. Of wanting, more and more, to do. Things, not thoughts. Real, practical good.

This won't do. Michael has a busy day ahead of him. He is a busy man. Blowing on his hands; he just can't get a heat inside him.

Anyway. This morning had been grand. They'd rolled their eggs, then he'd marched them back down and into the church, bringing in smells of muck and moss, smirred cheeks and a high-wire sense of were we just outside? The full blue-grey sky they'd carried with them, and the purple hills, the cusp of where heaven meets earth.

'Every day, we're surrounded by wonder. The sky above, the land below. And all the wonders beyond that as well – the layers and glimpses of beyond. Sometimes, all it takes is to stand quietly – quietly, thank you, Gemma Jones – and drink it in. What better day than Easter Sunday to look at our world anew, at all the things it can offer us – and give thanks.' He noticed Myra's son in the congregation. 'And not to fear the worlds beyond either. Because God is with us, in everything.'

It felt good, to preach again. When it is like that, all true and open, it's wonderful. Michael imagines his words as leaves on the wind or twinkly dust, resting lightly, dissolving in people's ears, drifting and landing, perhaps as far as his son's running shoulders. Or in the dents on Hannah's brow. Her neck, the clavicle. The sweet dent between her breasts, and him, searching there not two hours ago, nuzzling, with the nipple in his mouth so round and full, how that would always be his escape from everything, just the pillowy blissful losing of himself, kneading and rising, and how, just as he was coming, it all shot back, like flying down the tunnel away from the light, and that he had wanted to bite down hard.

'Didna know I'd need my woolly bunnet and boots the day,' says Auld Angus, shuffling past him at the door. 'And what's the cooncil doing about a' these gay ministers?'

'Pardon?'

'On the telly. Gay folk. Getting married. I mean, they'd a guitar in here last month.'

'Angus, that's got nothing to do with—'

'No happy-clappy. No kissy-kissy. No needin' ma long-johns for church, right?'

But there is a ruddy vigour about Angus that pleases Michael. The man has not looked so healthy in months.

'Angus, you disappoint me. Here was me planning to start a tambourine band too.'

'Och, that was rare fun!' The Misses Campbell and Grey, bless them, are full of smiles. He doesn't mention the egg on Margaret

Campbell's hat. The Sunday School are on a chocolate high, from the mini-eggs he'd brought. Would have been nice for his own boys to be here. Folk expect it. Ross would have come, if he'd nagged him, or looked sad. Still, a good sermon. A good one.

When everyone has gone, Michael sits a while in the chancel. He flexes his gammy knee. Simple primrose walls, peeling slightly where the rain's come in. A carved wooden font, some old stone crosses at the back of the nave. It's a nice wee church. He feigns the contentment of a well-fed man; a wee bit oomph about himself again. Immediately, it melts to worry. Should he have stayed in the pulpit, reinforcing the convictions of the convinced?

No. He picks at a splinter on the altar table. No. He's been put on a different path.

So many paths, but then all things happen for a reason, don't they? Skittering like a numpty on ice skates, towards one bright certainty. A referendum looming – and there's him, been given the chance to be at the heart of it. Finally. Scottish Independence. Think on that, man. Be glad of the good things, of the very words, which had become so stale, and are now buzzing with lifeforce, and that he is alive to see it. It's been such a long-held dream. All through his teenage years, the 'nationalism' his father spouted was a dead word, the preserve of a few tweedy eccentrics, and, in the broadest, brutish sense, of young men with shaven heads – which wasn't the same thing at all, but you tarred yourself with that brush if you even tried to explain. But here, now, in Scotland in these early decades of a new century when the world is fluxing anyway, it feels like a brave word. It feels like you're opening up to something bigger, not barricading yourself in.

Michael has always found it difficult to articulate how proud he is of his country. You can explain the mountains and the heather fine; all that glorious spread; that's allowed. You can be ginger, mean and drunk, and wear a tartan bunnet. That's acceptable. But to be properly proud? To trust the fact of it? It saddens him when being pro-Scottish is seen as anti everything else. Being Scottish is no attack, no implicit insult to the status quo. It *is* the status quo. He is Scottish, that is fact. Why does saying he's a Scot make him part of an argument he never started? That his country, his language, history is made other breaks his heart. For three hundred years, the Scots have tholed this. Whining from their grubby teenage bedroom: it isny fair. And with every whinge and finger of blame, they collude in the Scottish cringe.

These last few years have been a miracle. (Aye, they've been a nightmare too, a horrible, terrible shattering, but that's personal – and it's mended now. It's done.) Michael's been in the dirty roots of nationalism so long, he'd forgot about the possibility of flowering. But the climate changed, the rain coming softer. A self-determined sun coaxing Scotland to grow tall. And for him to be amongst it, properly part of the drive and the decisions, when all he'd done before was collect subs for his local SNP branch. Oh, that has been a balm for his weary head. To say 'I am a politician.' It gives the snap to his spine the dog-collar once did. And it's a chance to do it right. To start again, if they'll all let him. His wife and his sons and his God and his Ghost. Independence. He wonders, occasionally, if it's he who is the ghost.

A good sermon, Michael? Really? From a man who is demented?

Christ (apologies, Lord), he has spent the best part of his professional life urging people to believe in things they cannot see, divining truths from unseen voices. And now one of them is answering back. The hairs rise on his neck. Soon, he'll have to go outside. What if it returns? When does this stop being sporadic and become permanent? He's safe with people. A shepherd with his spindly flock. Michael touches his nose. The normal bump and flare. But he feels like a veil has been stripped away, and he is seeing everything too clearly. Next will be the bones inside his face, the pumping heart, the liver purpling under the skin.

'Please Lord.'

He says it louder.

'Please Lord. Make it go away.'

This is not a reckoning, this ghost. Is it some form of transition, like a chrysalis? Michael raises his hand, checking for threads. There are none. He is a good man, he tells himself. Not mad. You do what you can.

What you can.

Oh the wind, up there. Would be fierce. And the swing of it, the concrete, the cables, the graceful arc. Did you look out and across? Down? Did you shut your eyes? Was your last conscious act unconscious?

Did you fly?

With a swoop he dives and it is spinning, his guts are spinning and his heart is in his mouth and up is down and in is out and—

'Christ!' Michael yells, in crystal air.

That word pirouettes. Takes a long time to settle.

When he comes out, the churchyard is empty. Except for the Ghost who is swinging from the keystone on the arch above the gate.

'Woo-hoo!' he screeches. 'You killed them, man!'

His upside-down belly (he has hooked his feathery tail round the arch and is suspended) reminds Michael of a crocodile-skin handbag his granny used to have. The Ghost birls round and round, then dismounts, flinging his arms behind him as he lands. 'Triple salko, that.' He is definitely larger, or rather, more in proportion. The furriness of his ears has gone, they are consolidated. Alert. 'Under-fifteens champion, vault and bars. Didny know that, did you?'

Michael swallows. 'No.' He struggles for something else to say, a thing that won't upset it, an opener to going 'It's not all bad then, eh?' and 'Why don't you go back and please, please, leave me alone.'

'You're awfully . . . upbeat, if you don't mind me saying?'

'Is that right, pal?' The Ghost's face – what there is of it – darkens. 'Shall we?' Offering the crook of his elbow. Michael can't bring himself to touch him. It. They begin to walk through the churchyard. There was a funeral last week, for old Molly Colquhoun. Still a nice display of lilies and laurel over-by.

'Am I going mad?'

'Not yet. Although,' the Ghost breathes on a flower, causing it to wilt, 'it's an interesting question. The very fact you're engaging with me would suggest that you are, wouldn't it?'

'I suppose.'

'But then, the very fact you're questioning this engagement would suggest you're not, eh?'

Michael can't answer him.

'I've met her!' The Ghost points at a gravestone. Then another. 'And her. And him. Smells a bit, that yin. Ooh, see those two. Witch trials, know? The way they go on about it. Wall-to-wall orgies.'

Michael thinks if he heads back to the church and barricades himself in; if someone rings for the doctor . . . A thin drift of ghostliness curls itself companionably round his arm. It feels of nothing. The sky slides a little to the left.

'It's a Sunday, pal. You'll not get the doctor on a Sunday. And those NHS 24 exorcisms arny up to much, believe me.'

Maybe by the stones. There's a chambered cairn, a hole really, but you can pull the lid right over—'

'Ho! Michael, man. You kidding? Going underground? I don't like to state the obvious, but it is kind of my natural habitat. According to the Goo-ood Boo-ook, that is.' The Ghost gives a finger to the sky. 'Cheers, Big Man,' he shouts. 'Your patter's pish, by the way.'

Michael tries very hard not to think, or do anything. He will just keep walking until this passes, the way you'd walk off an upset stomach or a bout of cramp. Inspiration could do this. Poets, artists, they all had breakdowns. It was the high of the sermon, he was the gatekeeper to other worlds. Our Father Who Art in Heaven, our father who art in heaven—

The Ghost sniffs, loudly. 'The communion of souls. I mean to say. Does that not sound a wee bit creepy to you? All those deid folk having a cheese and wine? Can you imagine the small talk? *Ooh, hi, Elsie, yeah. Well, not much really. Just the usual. Aye. Rotting. How about yirsel?*' Here, the Ghost verges on the slightly camp. Michael is sure he's swaying his hips.

'Ho, fuckface.'

A tongue, a hoarse voice rasping right inside his ear. 'I can be anything you want me to be.' But the Ghost is back standing by the gate.

'You know, I could show you anything,' he shouts. 'Anything at all. You want to see Hannah? What she's really thinking?'

'No.'

The Ghost returns to him, gliding. One of those step-ball-change things tap dancers do.

'Want a word with your old man?'

'What?'

'Would you like to converse with your dear departed father? How's about a bit of how's your faither?'

'You don't . . . ?'

'Is he down the stair an' all? Oooh.' The Ghost wiggles his fingers. 'Has the bogey-man got the wee daddy in his scary den? Christ. I was a funny guy. I was, you know. But, naw. If you put it like that, no. But I know a man who knows a man . . . You want to say ta-ta Dada? Say: I'm saaaw-reee—'

'That's enough!'

'OK then, what about your wee boys, eh? What about young Ross-me-lad? Did you know his wee soul's being crushed? Squashed out of him like a tight wee shite? Aye, you're good at that, aren't you? Crushing souls. Or ruined Euan? Running by day, wanking by night. All that frustration. Fucksake man. You've got sons, you bastard. Your own wee sons and you don't gie a fuck.' He thinks the Ghost is crying; his face is strained certainly, like he is pushing out its sharpness from primordial waters. Or something. It is more horrible to see than all the scales and feathers.

'Stop it!'

'But I thought you wanted enlightenment? So it all makes sense and you can say the right thing, always say the right thing?'

Michael runs back towards the church. Struggling with the door, the massive heavy stupid latch keeps passing through his fingers. The texture of the latch is changing; it is rougher, scaly. Comes away in his hand, it is waving at him, a hook ensnaring his anorak, dragging him gently from the door.

He is lying on damp grass. Above him, sad eyes, thick sky.

'Oh, come on, Michael. You know what I'm going to show you.'

The smell is unimaginable: it is guano droppings from St Kilda and the time he'd peed himself in school, it is the sodden carpet on which street children sleep, it is blind fury and spurts of blood, it is rotting breath, want, the sealing of a stone.

It is a boy on a bridge and a hand on a back.

Some dampness drops on him. Salt. Sour.

'Woopsy. You for the off, then? Hannah's pie will be getting all cold.' The Ghost makes a popping sound with his finger in his mouth. Another oyster of saliva, if that's what it is, falls on to Michael's lips.

'What? She's made a shepherd's pie. For lunch. But, hey. Tick-tock. You've missed lunch. You'll need to have it for your dinner.' With strange tenderness, he crouches, wipes the gobbet of saliva deeper into Michael. 'Duty calls, bud. See ya.'

And is gone.

Chapter Three

Closing over; a thick pewter sky. Justine climbs a stile which takes her on to a track at the far side of the field. She's in Kilmacarra Glen proper now. Boots stuck in runnels of mud. She could keep to the road of course, but she wants to be in this place: She wants to be at those stones. She wipes her hand across her nose. Her bag's hooked to the gate, where she draped it before she climbed over, so how come she feels the press of it? Damp pressure along her sinuses too. Rain or sweat; it's sticky. She wipes more vigorously. Snotter. Yup, she is, she's crying again. She unzips her jacket, unbuttons her cardi to let the heat out. Looks down at her breastbone, which bears the dull yellow bloom of recent bruising.

Bodies are strange, forgiving things. The crack she took to her forehead on the bus has gone from open-mouth aagh to pursed-tight and nippy already. But that's good; means it's healing. She retrieves her bag, follows the rutted track. Crinkle. Squelch. Sniff. Crushed grass. Earth. A freshness under it all. It's lovely here. Despite the damp, or maybe because of it. It is tender air, washing her. Frizzing up her hair and softening the edges. The breeze picks up, pushing hair and heathery sky in her face. The light comes in stripes, dull one minute then flashing shafts as the clouds shift.

Her forehead smarts. Part of the route goes through dense woods, the kind you can imagine being followed in. Hardly any noise here, except the trees, crackling and snapping when there's no one around. As the wood breaks into daylight, Justine can see two big brown eyes up ahead. She blinks. Observes curled and scary horns. The bearded mouth below it yawns, gives a cough. A Highland cow grins at her, goes back to the business of chewing. The path carries on, winding past a few single trees, then opens again, into the flat, bright landscape.

A sucking breath.

There you are.

The stones she saw from the bus. In glorious monochrome: one by one, the parade of rocks appears again; strewn like a giant has chucked marbles from his hand. She can see five or six cairns at least, with standing stones dotted all the way up the glen. Not a few wee groupings set artfully against the landscape; these *are* the landscape. They quiver infinitely, vertebrae on a spine. Justine shades her eyes, and the movement of her arm is like a gentle blow.

There is fringing, lace fringing. Apples. She is under the canopy of her pushchair, plump bare toes wriggling in front of her, and beyond: more toes, a tartan Thermos flask, red stones. Her mum's rings clink on the metal handle of the pram; she is crying, or was that later? Her father is present too. He has toes like hers, round and naked in open sandals. But hairy. They are there, distinct at the edge of her limited vision. The toes, some apples. A long line of marching stones.

This is what she remembers.

Justine pushes her hair from her eyes. Stares harder. It seems random, but each cairn, each cluster of standing stones, is in alignment with the one in front and behind. To her right, she can see a group of bigger standing stones, rising in spikes at the base of what she's christened Plook Hill. Up there. What were those bobbing folk doing? No sign of them now. She makes her way towards these big stones, sweeping nearer to the village. From this approach, the hill separates her from most of the houses. She's coming in the back way.

Up close, the stones by the hill are four, five times her height. Simple spears of rock, macho lines and columns, like they are flanking an avenue. Justine huddles by the largest two. They soar above her head, would make you dizzy if you stared up too long, like looking up a stairwell. She thinks about putting the brolly up now, before the deluge which is surely coming. As a compromise, she rests it, unfurled, on her neck. The air begins to curdle. Growl. If there's lightning, should she come out from behind the stones? It's dangerous with trees, she knows that much. Maybe go further up the hill? Where those folk were? A single yellow light clicks on in a Kilmacarra window. Or she could just go to the village, like any normal person would.

Justine watches clouds dance cheek to cheek. If someone had been with her, she could impress them. *Look – there's some cumulus nimbus. I'm smart, me. I have many skills. Did you know I can fit my whole fist inside my mouth?* But the valley is wide and bare. There's nowhere to hide. Rain patters. Panic pits. Here is actually very big. Open. Everywhere is eyes: sheep, hills, trees, drilling in like hungry worms. Worms. *Put you where the worms live, doll.* Justine sticks out her tongue. Nice clean drops. She counts them, slowly, until her belly settles. The rain slaps her face, faster, harder. Man, she hates when her jeans go claggy on her thighs. Makes her itchy; she doesn't like not being clean. She climbs a

33

little further up the hill. There's a flat stone there set against the hillside, like an altar, which rises slightly at one end. The stone is bedded with earth or rock underneath as well, but where it rises, it protrudes. Enough, perhaps, to shelter under. She crouches to get beneath its lip.

Which is a mouth. The overhanging stone is actually the rim of a lid; squared-off edges. She reaches up, feels along the top of it. Man-made smooth. Finds a handle. Stands. It's an iron staple, set into the flat stone. She sees there is a gap, the altar-top is actually an entrance; a piece of concrete made to look like stone, which slides on rusty runners. Justine hauls the handle, pushes it with her foot, then feet, until it gives. Insistent rain, stinging her skin where it's already sore. Inside is a hollow, maybe four foot by three, stretching backwards into the hill. Sufficient for a body to curl up and wait. Justine leaves the brolly outside, then clambers over the edge. She inches into the space, literally hunkers down. She is not a stranger to hiding in small spaces. As long as something solid's at her back, she's fine. Here, she has rock and earth and the soft press of her leather bag. A grass-framed window on the world, watching churning skies. There's a funny, sulphur smell close by. Crushed eggshells and half a hard-boiled egg yolk lie at the entrance to the hollow, level with her nose. Is it some country-bumpkin cult? Children of the Corn? Then it dawns: those folk were rolling Easter eggs. Huh. It's Easter, so it is.

Snickers, she thinks. If someone were to ever get her an egg, she'd like a peanutty Snickers one. She pulls the tramp's brolly closer across the grass, leans it upright at the entrance. She can use it as a windbreak. Could squat here all night.

There are layers of earth and rock all round her. Streaks of yellow clay, of glitter. A band of red, and seams of dark. This is lovely. This is the safest she's felt in ages. You could, you know. You could just give up and roll over, feel that weight of earth swallow you so that you and the money dissolve. It would be quick and clean. She'd like that.

Sun slices cloud, projecting Justine's shadow on the ground in front. She sees an outline, dressed in bulky coverings, something slim beside its shoulder, with a fierce fierce tip. The stones' shadow makes a pathway over grass. At the end of the glen, a rainbow spreads. Rainbows spook Justine. She'd seen a rainbow at night once; black and white and grey, the way animals see. The rain is pouring, coming under the stone lip, seeking her out. She burrows deeper, as far into the hollow, into the side of the hill, as she can go. Her jeans are filthy, soaking. Less daylight now; she can only see a strip of sky. But there are glimmers on the wall inside. Little chinks of quartz, fine drifts of mineral which move in spirals like firelight. Half-closing her eyes, letting the firm wall behind support her. She is in her own earthen recliner chair.

Until the wall behind her breaks.

Plunging backwards, only inches, yet it feels like miles. Her skull cracks, finding solid rock where the mud has slipped away, the mud she thought was firm and helpful. Fucksake. It all slips away, she can't help it. Justine bursts into tears. Her head aches back and front, and her neck where it's been jarred, and her breastbone and her spine. She reaches to cradle her battered head. A sharp edge scrapes her knuckles; she tugs away, sooks skin. Now her hand's bleeding too. What if the roof falls in? Justine struggles to turn round, to see what is behind.

Where the earth and twinkly quartz was is black mud and roots. And the edge of rock which tore her hand. It's a long, thin cave, stretching deep into the hill. The light's bad. All she can make out are some dull, broken pebbles, and the glint of wall at the sides. Shiny, like slate. A curving scratch gleams dully on the slate. She slides on to her stomach, puts her hands inside. Using her thumbs, Justine wipes away more of the mud and roots, twisting fibrous clumps until they break. Moving through the pebbles, pecking her head from side to side as she tries to squint in the gap. She just wants to . . . Not stop. Her perpetual downfall. Reaching in up to her elbow, one shoulder. All she can make out is the one curved, scratched line. It seems to continue upwards in a spiral, but it's hard to see. She can feel pitted grooves under her fingers. Feels it warm. Damp. There's a soft wssh behind; like breath moving. A rustle. Just a bird, settling on one of the standing stones.

Justine's not sure how long she hunches there. At least until the rain stops and the rainbow fades. Her belly rumbles. Man, she only wanted to keep dry. She rubs some of the earth off on her jeans. Using the umbrella as a kind of spade, she begins to push bits of rock and mud, so it covers up the hole she's made. She can hear the locals already. *Sheer vandalism.* Scooping and patting handfuls of disturbed earth to make it smooth. Her skint knuckles graze on something hard. Again. One of the quartz stones poking out. Blood and soil and stone; she'll need to give that cut a wash. Her mum used to take a scrubbing brush to gritty knees, whenever Justine fell. Which was often. Dettol and the hard brush she used to clean the stairs. Apparently it was for her own good. Justine's fingers close on the tiny cube, easing it from the soil. She tastes grit inside her mouth. A perfect square of ivory. Then she realises what it is, and drops it. Milk-white unmistakable. It's a human tooth. Man, she's seen enough of them knocked out to know a fucking tooth.

*

Justine stamps it into the soil, clambers from the hollow. She doesny want the blame for breaking stuff. Drags the lid across. It's nothing to do with her. She slithers back down to the bottom of the hill, away from all the stones. Walks the line of the burn round the base of the hill, and heads into the village. Keeping to the road would be infinitely more sensible, but creeping feels right. Her jeans stick uncomfortably to her legs. She climbs where the ground slopes up again towards the church. It's a small square building, surrounded by a wall and sloping gravestones. Justine's starving. The bus driver said there was a hotel . . . she can definitely smell bread. At last, she goes on to the street. It feels like her whole body is yawning. This dislocation of thought and purpose, the luminous possibilities of being free to do anything, means she's in thrall to doing nothing at all. Jumping on, then off, a bus: that is decision of the day. She's had her spontaneous combustion already.

A jumble of harled cottages faces the church: single, two-storey, all joined together. Next to the cottages is what appears to be the only shop, one of those tired places that sell milk and fishing tackle. Bread and cheese; she has an urge for bread and cheese. Sunday. It's shut.

The house that's joined to the shop has a YES sign in its window. A Saltire flies from a flagpole in the tiny garden three doors down. There's a Union Jack above the door of the trim cottage in between, red, white and blue bunting spilling over the fence. None of the public buildings – the church, the shop – are displaying their allegiances. Right next to the shop is a faded sign, pointing across the road and down a wee lane that she'd missed: Trinity Hotel. Justine squeezes herself past some bins and an empty gas canister, follows the lane down, round one dog-leg, before it comes to an abrupt dead end. A tatty pink-painted building, net curtains the colour of sand. Tri . . . y H . . . el.

Sunday. It's shut. But the view from here is immense. As the glen unrolls, Justine regards the standing stones for the third time. Imagine having this on your doorstep, every day. Her lungs can't cope. Single stones lurch in a field, clusters group in huddles. They're all over the place. A few cairns touch the village itself. The burn she'd been following meanders past the church, then disappears behind a garage where the bank slopes steeply. Kids have pushed crisp pokes through the wire fence at the edge of the burn. They flutter like weathered flags. In the distance, a massive, bright balloon bobs over the valley. A mini-Zeppelin. She hadn't noticed it from the valley floor.

'All right?'

Justine tenses, half-turns. A man, mid-twenties, with sandy eyes, sandy eyelashes, sandy hair, stands behind her. He has those Celtic freckles that refuse to sprinkle neatly on your nose, but spatter your eyelids and lips as well. 'Beautiful, eh? You all right? Look like you've been in the wars.'

She doesn't answer. His smile, which was open and inoffensive, sets awkwardly, until it fades and he looks away. He passes on. She returns to her view.

See guys that just think they can? That you're just there for them to talk to, like you're a convenience, not a person who might be tangled up in your own thoughts, might be busy and intact. *Cheer up, hen. Might never happen.*

Oh, it has, pal. It has.

Again, she gets a whiff of bread, or a smell-mirage brought on by starvation. The smell of baking is very strong. Is it coming from the church? Or the long white house next door? She

imagines a family inside, settling down to Sunday roast. The drifting scent leads her to a shed or an old barn, separated from the
white house by a lawn. But when you walk round the other side,
it dips to two storeys, and there's a big conservatory; not the tacky
white kind but twisted green oak, growing in easy catapult shapes
to cradle great handfuls of glass. Or it looks like that, anyway; it
looks as if it's growing cleanly out of the ground. She knows it
isn't. But when Alice stepped through the looking glass she
accepted her various stages of altered reality. It's no use struggling:
just go with the flow. While Alice had her *Drink Me*, Justine has
her *Take Me*, and she could have slipped the money in her bag but
the penance, the appropriateness of a thousand tiny paper cuts
slicing up her groin, ach, she can't remember if the bottle was in
Wonderland or behind the mirror but here she is. Trusting. One
door stands open, the curved-wood handle beckoning her in . . .

Oh man, the smell. A pile of fat scones sit on a countertop.
China plates spill with cakes – the lopsided, squidgy kind.

Take me.

She hears a woman's voice say, 'God, I know. But it's turning
out far more erotic than I meant.'

Justine's hand returns to her side. The conservatory houses a
café: five wooden tables carved in the same curvy chunks as the
oak frame. Wholemeal and earnest, all natural wood and hingy
things with feathers, beads, brown earthenware plates stacked on
the dresser. She picks up a menu. Pumpkin soup; mushroom
risotto; Stornaway black pudding and potato scone.

'And a bit worthy too, you know?' the woman goes on. 'I'd a
whole chunk about arranged marriages I just deleted. Any road, I
need to go and fetch Ross. I'll leave these with you. How many we
got coming?'

'About twenty.'

'Twenty? Is that all?'

The voice grows louder as a slight and golden woman gleams from behind the scenes. She is the kind of girl boys want to tuck under their arms and cherish. Justine hates her.

'Oh – Mhairi . . . ? Customer.' The golden woman smiles, with perfect teeth, snaps up the collar of her padded jacket to touch her golden earrings and shimmies past. Her perfume is divine.

There's movement from the open kitchen; a white shoulder, an arc of head.

'Sorry, we're closed.'

Justine walks to the counter separating café from the cooking. The chef is a broad, hirsute woman: plumes of grey wiry Brillo-hair, a few whiskers on her chin. Even her legs, bare and mottled beneath her bumphled skirts, have a healthy growth about them.

Her eyes flick over Justine's hair and face. 'Unless that's you early for the meeting?'

She's making some kind of savoury wheel filled with cheese and onion and sprinkled with chives. More smells coil from the range. The woman takes some loaf tins from the top oven. Bread comes out cracked and steaming, baked with poppy seeds and caraway.

'What meeting's that?'

'The windfarm. Did you no see our balloon?'

'Oh, yeah. I thought it was advertising. For your excellent-smelling bread.' Justine offers a crumpled tenner. 'Any chance of a wee taste? I'm absolutely starving.'

'Well . . . you can have that one.' The woman nods at a cart-wheel of flatbread. 'It's a bit burned at the edge. Och, put your money away. Unless you want to donate it to the cause, that is.'

'Sure.'

It's only a tenner. By Justine's calculations, she still has around a hundred of them. It is the lowest denomination they worked in. 'What cause?'

'The windfarm.'

'Oh. So you're supporting it? I thought folk usually protested . . .' She wipes her soiled hands on her jacket, chews the bread hot, without butter. Explosions of aniseed across her tongue, little fleeting bursts of happiness.

'Of course we're protesting. You daft? Did you not see how high that balloon is? That's as high as the turbines are going to be. Twenty bloody three of them.'

'God. That's awful. This is delicious, by the way.'

'Canny beat homemade bread.' The woman nods at her. 'What happened to your head?'

'Oh, nothing. Just a wee bump. You know, you should call this "artisan" – on the menu, I mean. The tourists'll lap that up.'

'The tourists? Oh aye, a daud of artisans'll have them flocking here. Did you not trip over them all on your way in?'

Justine stuffs more bread in her mouth. She watches the woman turn and flip her wrist, the bread falling on to a floured board.

'Is this place famous at all? I mean, would I have seen it on the telly?'

'Doubt it.'

'Hmm.' She chews a bit more. 'I definitely recognise it.'

'Well, we've been in a few calendars in our time. Oh, and there was a quick flypast on a Visit Scotland ad once. That's when I got the daft idea to open a café.'

'You don't do B and B, do you?'

'Nope.'

'Only I'm looking for somewhere to stay.'

'Tried the hotel?'

'The Trinity? It's shut.'

'No, not that one. The one when you come in the village. Big white one with "hotel" painted on it?'

'Is there? I must've walked right past it. I came up through the glen.'

The woman snorts. 'Story of our lives, that is. Everybody's so busy looking at all they bloody stones, they walk right past the village. Like we're invisible. Bloody *Brigadoon*. There's more to us than they stones, you know.' Justine must have pressed a button somewhere, because she's off. On and on about how ancient the glen was, how kings were crowned there, and folk lived in bannocks or crannogs or something. 'Nobody cares about all that, though. And if they stick they bloody turbines up, we'll no even get the stoners coming through.'

'Stoners?'

'Aye. My wee joke. But a lot of them are.' She screws her finger into the side of her head. 'Nae offence. If you are one, mind.'

'Eh, no.'

'Nothing wrong with hippies, I was one myself. But see all that bollocks about ley lines and convergences? Well, I'll tell you, if being stuck in a no-horse town with two mortgages and no decent men really was my destiny . . . I . . .'

She sneezes over the cooling bread. A wee swirl of dust or flour rises like Indian smoke. The woman looks crestfallen.

'Eh, thanks very much for the bread.' Justine shifts out of sneeze-range. 'Good luck with the meeting.'

Of course it would be full of nutters. Why had Justine assumed a small country village would be a place of refuge and anonymity?

Didn't everyone migrate to these places for the same thing? The retirees seeking the quiet life in a not-so-foreign land. The slow and failing businessman who knew a nice country pub was the answer. The suburban family wishing for only a muddy plot and organic carrots and then *JOCASTA WOULD SLEEP*.

The loner who is lonely.

You bring your shadow with you. The cold outside is amplified after the warmth of the café. Bracing. Justine returns to the churchyard, where the nutters are surely dead. An electricity van is parked outside. She recognises the red and yellow logo from this morning. Was that only this morning? Sentinel Power. Man, are they following her now? A narrow, pale man strips off his jumper inside the cabin. His T-shirt rises with it. She's trained not to look, but the play of ribs through skin plucks some visceral gut response, down by the money.

Fuck, she is messed up.

Imagine if Charlie Boy's hold extended from the scummy ring of miserable deviants who lapped at his balls, into proper organised crime. Imagine if he could infiltrate international companies, companies who could journey across the country, who could access a network of watchers who would track her down and pick her off. Or worse, bring her back to him.

But then he could. All it needed was a man with a van.

Justine begins to shiver. A deep and desperate blaze, beading through her pores, imprinting a net across her skin; she is a tiny, tiny fish, good with her hands which stink of work-dirt, nae bother to nae one just leave me leave me leave me. Her safe wee pleat is shaken out, and he'll catch her at the bottom. The fear burns through any residual goodness she might have retained.

She should have killed him.

The entrance to the churchyard is a stone arch which seems to double as a war memorial. Neat names carved above her head. She unlatches the gate. A mild pale air opens with it. You can feel the change again. Nothing fizzes, nothing screams. Just peaceful. Kilmacarra would be a good place to clear her head. It doesn't need to be for long, just till she decides what she's going to do. Disrespectful in her burgundy hair, she flits through tight-packed tombs. A lurid tourist, gawping. There's a bloody dog following her too now. A black and white collie. He seems friendly, but – after Askit – dogs make her wary: all those grinning teeth, like a crocodile. She hopes he won't crap round the graves. He's sniffing at the edge of Jemima White. Experiment. Died 1685. Aged 17. There's a smiling skull over her name.

The van drives off.

'Shoo. Shoo now. Away you go, stupid dug.' He limps off, looking hurt.

She examines the gravestone again. Keeps her head low until the van disappears. Experiment. Place or process? She feels that boom-boom pulse of exposure. Maybe it will never go away. She wonders if the church is open. Sunday; nothing much else is. The hooped handle of the door turns easily and she slips inside.

She looks for holy water, to see if it will bubble, but there is none. No crosses burst into flame, no chalices rise to strike her. But still. But still. Justine sits in one of the pews. A slight white bloom is spreading on the lower shelf, linking the holes where communion glasses go. The side of the pew is numbered. She glances wider. Every mouldy pew is embossed with a number. Her eyes seek out the number eleven. There it is, across the aisle. Legs Eleven. *All the way up to your thighs, eh?* In her pocket is a knife, a ittle pearl one. Useful. Not blunt. She slides one of the hymn books along the shelf, presses the knife into the soft wood before her. Barely breaking the surface, she carves out a J – shaky along the top, then a flourish as she comes back down. A baby-spider letter that no one will notice. She kisses her finger, traces it round the shape.

There's a greenish glass window behind the altar, leaded in small square mullions. At the top, the window splits in a kind of fanlight, three glass teardrops, outlined in stone. The design is echoed in the wooden pediment above a small door to the side – which you'd think would lead to the holy of holies but is probably where the minister hangs his coat, or does a pee. The pediment reminds her of a Girl Guides trefoil. As a kid she'd watch them march to church past the flats where she lived. Her and her mates would try to shoot them with spud guns, for the sheer joy of watching them bolt like gazelles when one got hit. The pediment is darker than the rest of the wood in the church. Each petal of the trefoil has a carving: the first is a humphy shape like a cartoon ghost or a hill, the middle one is carved with two of the same teardrop shapes, making a circle like yin and yang (except one shape dominates the other, curving bigger and higher over the top of it). The last petal has another grinning skull. They are clearly cheery folk in Kilmacarra. Apart from the stone crosses behind her and the silver font in front, there's no other ornamentation in the church: plain oak altar table, plain pulpit, stone floor.

She's shivering again. Justine clicks the knife into its sheath and goes back outside, which is actually less chilly than the church. Widdershins. Isn't that how you're meant to go round a graveyard? Opposite the motion of the sun. Justine has almost completed her circle when she sees him. A middle-aged man lying prostrate on the grass. He is a series of gently rolling peaks, his belly slightly higher than his toes, but lower than his profile. His eyes are staring at the sky, and he is very, very still. Black anorak, grey-black hair. Has she summoned up Death? She runs over, shakes him.

'Hey! Hey! Are you all right?'

'Leave me,' he moans, without looking. His face is glossy pink, as if he'd been dangling upside down.

'Right, sit up. C'mon. That grass is soaking.'

Unblinking, he gapes at the space above him. The guy must be on something; pished at the very least. She hoicks under his armpit, pulls him to sitting. His coat falls open, revealing a dog-collar.

'Shit. Hey, Rev . . . Father. Are you OK?'

'GET OFF ME! What are you doing? What do you want?'

Justine lets his arm drop. He wobbles a little, but stays in place.

'I'm just looking. How, what's your problem?'

The pink is getting purply. 'This is Church property.'

'Oh, and here's me thinking it was God's.'

He scowls. 'You've blood on your head . . .'

'What?' She pats her forehead. The pad's damp. Her fingers are rouged with blood. 'It's fine, I'm fine.'

'What do you want? There's nothing here to steal.'

Is that what he sees? An instant thief? Pour one cup boiling water, stir, then serve. Justine opens her mouth and her brain pours into it, quick as you like and bypassing any sense of planning.

'Excuse me? Steal what? You've a bloody cheek. I'm . . .' She scans the landscape behind him. 'Doing research. Looking for my father, if you must know.'

'Your father?'

'Yup. My dad. Frank. I think he might have come from here.'

Because that would give you a reason. People are safe if they have a reason. And questions; questions pad out time and build nests; they help folk help you to build your nest and she is not a shit-scared zombie, she is smart. Could read before she went to school. Justine is not crap. It is important she remembers this.

The minister wriggles, so his back is against a tombstone. 'Frank what?'

'Um . . .' Her eyes range the graveyard for inspiration. On one of the taller plinths, an angel weeps. Her marble heels are feathered, in her hand she holds a bow and quiver. Decades of moss and birdshit clag her breasts.

'Arrow. Frank Arrow.'

'No such name.'

'Aye there is.'

Why did she not say Moss?

'Not here there's not.'

The man is being unreasonable. Her father grows in stature. 'So you know everyone that ever lived or died here, do you? Frank. Big guy. Bright-red hair. This,' she wiggles the umbrella, 'was his actual brolly.'

'I see. Sorry. I didn't realise he was . . . passed. So you think he's buried here?'

She shrugs. 'I don't even know he's dead. Not for sure . . .'

Change the subject, doll. 'Are you all right, though? Seriously. No disrespect, but you look like utter shit.'

The minister creases like an ironing board, like she's kneed him in the balls. 'Are you—' he reaches wide, squeezes her ankle.

'Ouch! You fucking old pervert.'

He pulls his hand away. Covers his eyes. 'Oh God. Just get lost. Get lost before I call the police.'

'Maybe I should call the police,' she bluffs. 'It's not me lolling like an old drunk in the middle of a graveyard. Groping folk.'

'Get away from me! Do you hear?'

She retreats a little. Watches him shoogle the tombstone, testing it for sturdiness. He hauls himself to his feet. Arm trailing. His fist quails, in and out.

'Is there anyone I can get to help you?'

His laugh is mirthless. 'No.'

It's doubtful there are any cops within a ten-mile radius; she suspects Lochallach is the nearest station. Justine has a nose for these things. But given that he is a minister, with a hotline to truth and justice, and that she, Justine the unjust, would like nothing less than to provide her name, address and current location to the police, and given that he appears entirely unhinged – and we all know what that is capable of doing – she concedes.

'Are you sure you'll be all right?'

'Yes.' Then, briefly contrite. 'Yes. I will be fine.' A dry whisper. 'Thank you.'

Satisfied he isn't going to keel over again, Justine leaves the minister clutching at his grave. *Told you. All loonies here.* Out of the churchyard, past the Kilmacarra Hotel – ah, there it is. Looks all right: clean-white, wee glittery lights making the thickened window neuks all cosy. It's getting damp again – and dim. What they call gloaming; the light of day gone thin. She flicks up her hood. A gash of brighter light as a man emerges, wearing a kilt. A kilt. Of course he is. Black socks, green tartan kilt, black waistcoat, black Glengarry with a red rosette, and masses of thin grey hair. What do they drink here? He makes himself comfortable against the outside wall. Lights a cigarette. Should she say about the minister? The man nods at her. 'Ow doo', in broadest Yorkshire.

'Hi,' she replies. Keeps walking. She'll ask about a room later. If she decides to stay.

This floating feeling. Nobody knows her, or knows she is here. This place is negative space, and that minister none of her business. She has a sudden notion of a tent. Her and canvas and the stones and the sky. If she follows the burn, finds a knot of trees behind a hill and just lives wild. How good would that be? That collie is sniffing about again. In a garden this time, growling as Justine passes. 'Here boy, it's me.' She offers him her fingers. A wee boy comes from the house, stares at her. The dog snarls. She continues walking, the dog growling until she is far away from his house. His best buddy in the churchyard, now she's a threat. Defending his territory like the men above the gate. You'd think on a planet eight thousand miles wide there'd be room enough for everyone.

Oh for God's sake, just stop, Justine. Here is far enough.

But she walks further along the main – and only – road, her bag bumping on her shoulder. She's getting used to the weight: quite likes the solid reassurance of it pitching and settling. When she's dizzy from tiredness, she'll stop. There are no streetlamps beyond the houses; the grey light is turning black. Plenty of cats' eyes, though, running up the centre of the road. She'll go a little further yet, just to check the boundaries. She takes her old phone pouch from her jacket pocket. Rattling inside is the bus station pay-as-you-go. Untraceable. Very definitely pink. But it does have a dinky wee torch.

The high verges are fertile ground for weeds and wildflowers. People live outdoors all the time. Perhaps she could forage for her tea. Stay outside for ever. This sense of space expanding; she doesn't want to lose it. The road is empty; you can hear low traffic hum from far away, carried on the dulling air. But no one is coming to Kilmacarra. Where are the hordes of windfarm protesters? The crusties and the travellers, the greenies and the Druids? Poor hairy Mhairi has baked all that lovely bread. Justine keeps to the lower edges of the verge. Ahead is lighter. That must be west. She is moving away from the glen and up towards . . . Kinmore says a road sign. Will Kinmore be any different from Kilmacarra? No lights, no cars, no human noises. She flicks on her phone-torch. Glitters of quartz on the road catch bouncing light.

What exactly are you looking for, Justine?

A low serrated thrum, rumbling beneath her feet. She trips in the dark. This is stupid. She should go back, book a bed, get some dinner, some sleep. Tomorrow she can decide . . . she, Justine, can decide anything at all. The rumbling increases. She waits. Faint. Very faint like foil rippling, or wads of paper notes. A silvery whispering; the wind rising. And then a boy, emerging from the dusk in front of her: head down, thumping shiny feet in resolute lopes. An iPod wired to his ears. Justine moves in to let him past, he doesn't see her, then does. Is startled, stumbles out as the rumbling gets louder, Justine dipping, the boy going wide, away. Away?

Suddenly, a van punches past.

It's a mobile home, towing a wee car behind it – or she knows that after, or her logic says it while her eyes burst only with streaks of coloured light: a white metallic comet, then the swinging flash of the bright red car and a flapping flag and its residue of colour, glowing. And the whoosh and the whoosh and the whoosh. Her belly slackening. Then snapping back to hurt her.

The car misses her by an inch.

She stands a full two minutes. Flesh dancing, breathing in. Breathing out. Where is the boy? Was that a bang, just there, just then, just the two minutes ago, two seconds, ten hours, did she hear a screeching bang? Justine starts to chase the empty tarmac back towards Kilmacarra. To a bend in the road. Stripy chevrons banking the deep curve, white shining liquid in her phone-beam. She hadn't noticed, on the way out, how the white of the road sign is set to pulse when hit by light. No sign of a crash, no trace of boy, or motorhome. It must have skliffed a tree. What kind of a speed is that to drive on country roads? Hopefully the thing will have a great big dent in its side, at least. But where is he? The boy? She shines her phone in greater and greater circles.

Over by the grass, just before it falls into a gully; something dark and huddled. A bundle of clothes, half on the road. Bright colours: a purple sock, toe pointing at a training shoe further down the ditch. Justine drops bag, brolly, runs towards the heap; it, him, he must've been dragged along, it is only seconds since he passed, was running past all strong and solid on gleaming feet. With a whoosh, that fucking whoosh.

Keep running.

Only for an instant.

He is lying, one leg angled at a sharp obtuse. Pink bone pushing wrinkles through his thigh like puckers on rice pudding. His wee white face; he's just a kid.

'Ho! Hoi! Can you hear me?'

No movement. Then a gurgle, a tongue loll. A sliver of tongue comes away, where he must have bitten it.

'Ssh. Hey, it's fine. Don't try to talk, all right? I'll get help. You . . . I'll go—'

She tries to pull him off the tarmac completely; it's his uninjured leg that lies on the road, but still, he screams, not him exactly, but the cavity of his chest flares up, expels its outrage, and she can't move him any more. Her mobile is still in her hand. With stuttery fingers, she stabs three nines.

'Ambulance please.'

Bad line, a metallic voice. A woman. 'Yes, caller. You need an ambulance?'

'It's an accident. Just outside Kilmacarra. A boy's been knocked down really, really bad. His bone's out his leg—'

'Can I just take . . . few details. What's . . . name please?'

'Look, you need to get someone here now. Now, d'you understand? It's actually sticking out of his leg. He's unconscious—'

'Where exactly . . .' it drifts '. . . you are?'

'I don't know the name . . . we're on a bend in the road, just outside Kilmacarra. There's a sign for Kinmore and there's a massive big chevron on the bend that kind of flashes. Do you know where we are?'

'Kilmacarra? Heading east or west?'

'I don't know. There's a chevron, a bloody great chevron sign that glows in the dark.'

'A chevron. Yes.'

'He's by the road. Just at the big bend outside Kilmacarra. Tell them to go really slow when they see the chevron, right?'

'It might . . . helpful . . . flag . . . ambulance down. Do you . . . torch?'

'Yes . . . no. Look, what do I do?'

'It's important . . . keep his airways clear . . . he breathing?'

'Aye . . . well. He's gurgling.'

'OK. You . . . to check for obstructions. Can . . . finger in his mouth? Check . . . tongue—'

'How long will you be?'

'There'll be . . . soon as possible. Now, if . . . your name? Madam? Son?'

Justine hangs up. Raises the boy's head upon her lap. The hidden notes crack like dry leaves. 'Ssh now. It's all right. You hang on now. There's help coming. You hang on. Please.'

She tries to hook her finger in his mouth, she tries, but it's all blood and swollen. Cannot push herself inside that. Babbling at him, murmuring. Rocking him, rounded metal in her shoulder blades. Soft curls on her knees. Wet. Behind her eyelids is a pressing image. Curly waves. It was on the flag, the car's flag. Carefully, she inches her arm into her pocket. There's rubbish, sweetie papers, a hanky. An eyeliner. With the soft tip, Justine copies what she remembers. It is in her head, so it doesn't matter that it's dark. 'Dah.'

She bends her neck forward to the boy.

'Da-ah.' His eyes are crammed-tight shut, his whole face is crammed and twisted, all the wrong colours. Sulphur in her nostrils.

'Ssh. I know. It's fine. We'll get help. I promise.'

The ground is damp, she is maybe sitting in it. Sitting in this boy filtering from life, rising like mould on a wall, flooding over her legs, her shoulders. Already it is in her mouth. She can see the ivy growing, watches it creeping in the berry black. She has done this. If Justine Strang had stayed on the bus, this boy would have stayed on his verge. No, he would have reached the village by now, possibly his house. He'd be stepping into the shower and shouting to ask his mum what was for tea.

From a tangle of branches, a soft, whitish owl watches her. Blinks once, then flies off. The boy stirs, like he is settling for a nap.

'Hey! Hey you – don't go to sleep. Yes? Stay with me. Are you at school? What – first year? Second year? Bet you've got a girlfriend, eh?'

She holds him in her lap for ten, maybe fifteen minutes. The cold melting into nothing. All across the glen: silence. Softly, softly round them, whispering louder, until it rises up, growing strident and defined. Wailing. She has dragged him as far off the road as she could. Right by the chevron – they can't miss it.

'Look, I'm sorry. That's them coming now, OK?'

Gently, she puts the boy's head on the moss. There is a big branch skewed and broken behind the chevron, and she hauls this across the road. Curt stumps like blunt bone knuckles, all sticking up. They'll see that in their headlights, surely.

'I can't stay. You're going to be fine.'

She repositions the branch, so the angle is greater, the emphatic *Stop* of its twiggy arms more pronounced. Picks up her bag, retrieves the umbrella, then Justine starts to run. The bus stop isn't far. Get on the first one anywhere, or she can hitch, or she can . . . if she leaves a single trace, he'll find her. Fuck, she's already left a trace. Her lungs are tearing, but she still packs in more gulps than she needs, trying to force the tin taste from her mouth. Why didn't she stay on the bus? The road has stretched, has tricked her. It gets darker and further while her legs get shorter. Deep, insistent, the wailing screeches. Closer. Closer.

Is here.

As the ambulance lights appear, she hides herself into the undergrowth, letting it sweep past in trails of blue and red and white.

Chapter Four

Not a bad crowd, considering.

Hannah Anderson looks at the buzzing room. She counts thirty-one people in all, including her, her pal Mhairi and the man from the *Courier* Mhairi's bullied into coming. Granted, some will have come for the drama, the small-town theatre of it all, but some have come for honest debate. And, of course, the baking, which is being devoured in steady chomps, even as the first speaker takes the stage. *An air of distraction, as if he did not quite believe himself.* She slips her notebook back in her bag.

'When am I gonny get a swatch at that?' whispers Mhairi. 'I want to see the dirty bits.'

Hannah covers Ross's ears. 'There's no dirty bits.'

'Not what you said this afternoon.'

'Yeah, well. It's not yet fit for human consumption. Bit like your scones.'

There's a kerfuffle as an old man comes back from the toilet, and a row ripples to let him regain his seat. It's a roll-call of worthies: two bald farmers, a tight perm, set of blond dreads, grey short-back-and-sides (ex-military), grey bob, mousy-brown mess, another brown (chestnut; like a lovely horse), steel grey (cropped in at the nape, wavy on top). This is where Hannah lives. A town called serendipity. For the thousandth time, Hannah says it in her head. It's an elegant, sinuous word, which – like your horoscope – can be bent to many meanings. Hannah's a writer, one of those soft, beady creatures made of sponge and antennae. Before they'd even thought about moving to Kilmacarra, she'd been sketching the shape of her next book. She had this idea about stone circles, about the people who built them. Then the option of buying the manse came up – in a stone-strewn glen, thank you very much. The church was selling it on their website. Michael, casting round for a new charge, a . . . something. Saw his grandpa's old house, surplus to requirements. Saw himself the same. Saw the possibility of this place, the cleanness and the rightness of it.

He didn't want to do it any more, he'd said. *Preaching.* (Although that's exactly what he's doing tonight. She watches him lean his bum against the counter, clear his throat. The skin of his Adam's apple tightens. Lips soft. She's nervous for him; yet she wants him to fail.) Already made enquiries, he'd said. Friends in the party thought he'd be perfect. The local touch, the lad come hame. Hannah had heard him speak about Kilmacarra, though they'd never been. But if it made him happy? Then she could pretend the sacrifice was all her own, that she was doing it to 'save her marriage'. *It was perfect!* she told everyone. Fresh challenge for Michael; she'd get to live in a place she'd been trying to invent; country air; no crime; aren't you jealous? Too perfect to listen to Euan's protests and the too-quick chronology, and the whispering in her head. My God, it was all the answers.

'Ross,' she murmurs. 'Sit at peace.' She gives her youngest another chunk of scone.

Moving here, to Kilmacarra, gave enough oomph to the book idea to actually sell it: first to herself, then her hungry agent, her publisher. And – in a break of luck that has never ever before happened in the history of Hannah Jane Anderson – to an actual TV production company who have punted it on, provisionally, to actual TV. In a running motion of tumbling dominoes, the thing has raced off, with very little substance to sustain it. What was she thinking? How do you write a convincing cavewoman? *We've done teenage vampires to death, darling. We need something fresh. But still kind of . . . savage, yeah?*

The first speaker of the evening is her husband. His cheeks are scarlet. He has been weird all day. A thrill as the room falls silent. It's a layered silence, of coughs and chewing, of expectations and disbeliefs. Amuse us, says the crowd. You're talking shite, it echoes back on itself. The chairwoman smiles, Michael begins. A heckle right away.

'One, three, six, nine,
We don't want your wind tur-bines.'

A flash of camera clicking, as the *Courier* chap pivots to catch the culprits. The beast is stirring. Hannah's skin spangles; a revenant of that forgotten life of opinions and beliefs when she could wear her hair spiked and shout and feel and march. March for the miners, march against Nazis, sit down to stop traffic at Charing Cross. March with placards, with paper bags on heads (that was a genius CND protest; thousands of them lying 'dead' in George Square). Sometimes, you didn't know quite what the march was for, but it would be lunchtime and a *Socialist Worker* seller would shout 'Are yous coming on the march?' And the entirety of the Queen Margaret Union would rise from the refectory and take to the streets.

Her son wriggles on her knee.

'Why are they shouting at Daddy?'

'They're not, sweetie,' she whispers in his ear. 'They're singing.'

She doesn't intend to say anything tonight (translation: *Please, Hannah. You can't be seen to be political*). But her mouth has that cold, nervy dryness, running all the way to her throat. It tastes of outrage. *I don't want this. I am middle class, articulate. I believe in democracy, for Godsake. You cannot make me. You can't.*

She's always sensed she didn't care for windfarms; but had listened without dissent to Michael's careful justifications. Because he's always careful, isn't he? And this is not the time for further crackly edges to their life, not now when they are smoothing, buffing, my God you can almost see your face in the shine of them. But, last month, Hannah drove to Dumfries for a friend's poetry launch. She'd not been down for a couple of years, remembered the journey as a dull, long slope through practical farmland. Barely noticed the first one. Two, then three – ach they were just like big lamp-posts, really. Or pylons, or a wood, a forest, my God, a sea. All the way down the motorway: windfarms. The shock of them, teeming across the landscape. Arms akimbo, occupying, demanding. Fingers pointing, far as the eye can see.

You were profligate.

Like exclamation marks all across the hills. There was an ugly beauty about them, and a need, yes, a need. But not here, she thinks. Not in Kilmacarra.

'Why can't we put them in the sea?' someone calls.

Hide them there? She's heard that's why whales strand; their sonar addled. Great threshing turbines lurching through the watery darkness, to slice off fins and tails. Mince up baby dolphins.

But what to do, what to do? Her children need power, they will continue to need it, long after she is gone. The computer on which she writes needs power, and plastic and lethal metals that leak. Use a pen and paper. Paper munches trees; trees clear sheep; sheep clear people; people munch land. It is a horrible game, where nobody wins. Hannah just wants left alone. Here is nice, it's good. The thought of giant turbines, circling Kilmacarra. Panic. Noise. The flicker-flicker light and hum of no more peace. The *what if there is nothing you can do?* The fact of her husband, orchestrating it.

Kilmacarra Glen has been their home for fourteen months. Her love affair has developed slowly, the way the best ones do. Swirling in hints, but no cohesion to the thing, the way a story starts, so that you're afraid to reach for it at all. Then it keeps nudging at you, until it's obvious. Like this place. A broad, open valley swept by glaciers, studded with farms and rocks and secrets. Ancient cairns and standing stones marching in a row, making a linear cemetery miles across the great Moss. Some folk think the stones form a calendar. Others see war graves from prehistory. Beardie-weirdies (and possibly Mhairi) reckon they channel spiritual energies, like ley lines or cosmic telegraph poles. But no one knows. Hannah likes that. The stones are there, have been for five thousand years, and that's enough. Anyone who can't accept that, well, they have no poetry in their—

—*Don't you care about this place?*

—*Of course I care. That's why I'm doing it.*

Ross leans into her breasts. This is new Hannah. No more poems. Writing for young adults means more words, less deliberation. More money too, especially when you factor in the school visits and festivals. This book she's toiling with; they've commissioned an accompanying teachers' booklet – all tied up with the telly interest. *Mmm. Teenage Stone Age. Romance, violence, history, social issues – love it! Can you stick in a bit of super-natural too?*

She strokes the dimple on her baby's knee. Baby. He goes to school next year. The wee soul is bored. Euan said he'd be home in time to watch his wee brother, but there's no sign of him, and it's getting dark. At least Euan's out, though, not huffing in his room. Beside her, Mhairi fluffs up her bosom, folding her arms so her hands wedge under her armpits. They're a funny pair, her and Mhairi. In a village that is essentially one street, you've little choice over who or what you cleave to. But she thinks she'd be friends with Mhairi wherever they'd met. Both make something out of nothing: Hannah writes, Mhairi cooks – and was once an artist, though she keeps that quiet. First time they met, Hannah had found this wild, hairy woman round the side of the café, building a bonfire of thin boards and canvas. She'd picked one up. Hard-etched charcoal sketches, trees around a circle of grave-stones; thin and flat, curved on top.

'These are really good.'

'No, they arny.'

'Oh.' She'd put the paper down. Noticed another, then another, awaiting their conflagration. 'Where is this?'

'*Na màthraichean a'gal.*'

'What's that when it's at home?'

'You'll no have the Gaelic then?'

'Nope.'

'Weeping Women, I think. But most folk call it Crychapel Wood. Anyroad,' she'd flung another canvas on the fire. 'These . . .'re a loada shite.'

Full and prickly she is, like an overripe gooseberry. Look at her, scowling at Michael. *Raging, so I am.* Mhairi is always raging. There are times she can be magnificent. Hannah likes this about her friend, the way she sweeps you up in her convictions. Gives you a little buzz. Hannah Anderson, forty-four. Seeker of cheap thrills. She coughs on a bit of scone. At least she can still make herself laugh.

'You all right?' Mhairi whispers.

'Went down the wrong way.'

'You dissing ma scones again?'

Two press officers stand at the back of the room. They were distributing information leaflets when Hannah arrived – and doing lots of smiling. Still recently enough that it's not forgotten, the council PR unit was the subject of some unpleasantness involving social media and allegations of spying. Even in the remotest spots, Big Brother, it appears, is watching. The backlash to this was a suspension, some resignations (which provided the by-election backdoor to her and Michael moving here) – and lashings of transparency. This is a council with nothing to hide. An advert in the local paper. Free buses to ferry people from the remotest crofts. Public dissent is being welcomed, nay, encouraged. It is being bored into submission before her eyes.

The hecklers are fading as Michael explains the planning process in tedious detail. Hannah breathes on Ross's hair. The coppery whorls shiver. Ross fidgets some more. Did she really think being a local councillor's wife would be any different to being a minister's? They have multi-member wards here; it doesn't need to be Michael that's taking the lead. She thinks he may be doing it to test her.

I am a good wife.

Their MSP has sent careful apologies, despite Mhairi inviting him to attend. Good old SNP. We are all in this together! A concept that works, nicely, when you're down in the trenches. She remembers the last elections at Holyrood, Michael's thrill as the results came tumbling in, as the contours of the map of Scotland changed. A nationalist landslide. All that rhetoric, the unalloyed lust for freedom and justice that was gaining greater momentum as they rolled towards referendum. A vote for optimism. Change. Hannah even did a barbecue for the local branch. It was beginning to feel exciting. But power brings puffed-up men and disappointing choices. Not for a second had she thought the fuzzy green mantle they planned to wrap Scotia in would mean her glen being trashed. *You should have read the small print*, Michael quipped.

Yes. Same as when I married you.

But she hadn't said that. She didn't mean it.

This windfarm is one more thing for them to snipe about. Oh, they rarely fight, not any more. It's all careful sidesteps, tight smiles. Silences. Calm and bland as milk. Some days she wonders if Michael is simply in opposition to her. Her pals at uni teased her for going out with a Divinity student. But they didn't know. Under the quietness of him, how, when he did speak, she could see the words coming out, all lit and dancing, how they were so important to him, that he thought and weighed them first. How he dazzled her eighteen-year-old self with talk of sacrifice and glory. How his skin was slippery-slick. How he split the darkness in her, the blue-white veins of him, how her gold hair lay on his white shoulders, how she spoils the things she loves because she is greedy, greedy. Stupid. How he wore his white slash at his throat and you think these awful truths and folk ask you both for help, for ever asking you for help and who helps you?

Politics were always there, with Michael. It was one of those daft marches she met him on. Anti-apartheid, she thinks – something to do with oranges anyway. Politics and Faith: it was about sharing and giving and MAKING A DIFFERENCE. Who could not love that? And now Michael's politics have morphed from passion to profession: that was going to be their glue. She would be proud and supportive of her husband once more, they would be gleaming and good and full of promise. She owed him that. Over Ross's restless head, she fiddles with her bracelet. He's right. She should have read the small print. He doesn't know that, last time, she voted for another party.

Michael is getting frustrated. 'Can I just stress, this is only a pre-application consultation at this stage.'

'Aye, and we all know what consultation means. It's aw done and dusted, eh? What, is that you getting free electricity for life now, Michael? Eh? Getting your own wee pipeline straight into the manse?'

'Order now. Please!' The chair, who is the local primary headmistress, thunks her little gavel. 'Councillor Anderson. Please continue. Everyone'll have the chance to ask questions later.'

'Thank you, Brenda. As I was saying, a windfarm development has been in our local plan for quite some time now. All residents should have been aware of this – the plan is available on the internet, in libraries—'

'Aye – just you mind that we dinna get decent broadband here and you've shut all the libraries doon.'

'Angus, please. Will you let me finish? The Scottish Government has an ambitious renewals plan and this council has consistently been a favoured area for developers seeking to harness natural resources for energy.' Michael smooths his hands across his chest; an unconscious gesture that makes him vulnerable. Hannah's heart flares.

'We're very fortunate we've got Señor Escobar here tonight, from Sentinel Power, come to give us an idea of the kind of development we're talking about, the benefits it'll bring to the area. Now, can I just add, he doesn't need to be here, but – at the council's request – he's volunteered, because – and I quote . . .' He glances at the brochure he holds: '"It is vital that new projects promote community engagement in the planning process, and ensure that barriers to this engagement are minimised."' He regains his composure in the safety of these words, looks quite chuffed, as if he'd written them himself.

'It's high time we got some investment in this area,' says a voice at the front.

'Aye, and if there's jobs—'

'It's blackmail, is what it is. It's aye the wee folk get shafted. Folk wi nae voice, wee places wi nae clout—'

Angus Caulfield calls out again. 'Barriers to engagement? So where were the public notices in Gaelic then?'

'Och, Angus. That will come. Like I said, this is just a preliminary—'

'So how long will it take to go through?' asks a woman Hannah doesn't recognise.

'The planning application? On average, we – that is the council – aim for within nine months from receipt of application. In cases where there's no public inquiry, that is.'

Mhairi is on her feet. Ross sits upright, interested in this new development, in the pounce of air his Auntie Mhairi's made.

'Right,' she shouts. 'How do we get a public inquiry then?'

'Oh, come on, people. We're nowhere near that stage. Listen to what the man has to say, eh?'

The chair intervenes. 'Perhaps this might be a good time to hand over to Señor Escobar?'

A glossy, dark man unravels himself from somewhere down the front, takes an easy stride centre-stage. His teeth, hair, unstructured linen jacket and light suntan eclipse Michael's seabird grey. A flutter courses the room. Señor Escobar. *Escobar* – they roll it in their mouths like a new fruit. He perches next to the councillor. Mhairi sits. Her elbow is in Hannah's ribs.

'Oh. My. God. Where were they hiding him? Would you look at the arse on that? I'll never wipe thon worktop again.'

'Mummy. Auntie Mhairi said a bad word.'

'Ssh, son, I know. She's very rude.'

Escobar waits until the murmurs fade. There is a fine torque to his mouth. 'Ladies. Gentlemen. Than'you.'

'Laying it on wi a trowel,' whispers someone. 'All thon needs is a rose between his teeth.'

Hannah is determined not to listen. She will remain unrapt. At the end of the row in front of her, a brace of old women have the same idea. They maintain a steady witter as Escobar talks. One has a green felt hat on, the other a bubble perm. You can only catch one-way snatches of the conversation, because the woman with the hat speaks much louder than the other.

'Aye he does, a bit. The one with the wee moustache.'

'No, dear, it wasn't David Niven that was the angel.'

The hatless woman whispers her response. 'Swss . . . yishoor . . . psswss . . . mind?'

'No, Margaret – he was the bishop.'

The bubble perm moves her head and Hannah can see it's Margaret Campbell. Which means the one in the hat must be Effie Grey.

'Psshh, wshhw's awfy handsome . . . biglad . . . pstshww . . . so I would.'

'I know, Margaret, it's a sin. How's your veins?'

These two old ladies trundle round Kilmacarra together almost every day, walking the single street, purchasing their bread and their milk at the store. Why not? Far better to get out and about than wait for your four walls to smother you. Escobar nods and smiles at his audience. Holds court, holds gazes. Heat slides under Hannah's skin. She remembers this morning, Michael's teeth and tongue on her breast, her wanting to pull him in, deeper to her. Afraid he would break. Remembering that, after, as they lay there, her breast was still damp. Wondering what the dampness was, knowing how, at night sometimes, he still cries. How he thinks she cannot hear him.

She contemplates the crumbs on her plate.

'It is important to know that the turbines will be on the hilly moorland, not in the glen itself,' continues Escobar.

'But what about the noise? And the peat?'

'Aye, and you'll still see them—'

'Of course I appreciate how beautiful this place is – an' we would respect that, of course. But, according to your government, the glen is not of huge historical significance. Many of the stones have been removed, or damage by the agriculture—'

'But it's the whole of it,' says a man in the front row. 'What it symbolises.'

Escobar smiles. 'What does it symbolise? From what I

understand, very little people know this place, yes? No one really come to visit here, you have no industry, no tourism. Our development will bring jobs, we will build an eco-centre . . . is very good for you, no?'

'How many jobs?' demands Angus.

'Oh, many, many jobs. We will have the construction phase, of course, an' then there will be maintenance, supply, staffing of the visitor centre. Community-investment funds. Eco-awareness education. Perhaps we can offer you the specialised training . . .'

The natives are resting. This charming man is lisping them all to sleep. You can see the tilt of them, inwards, inwards. Literally coming closer to his way of thinking. Hannah knows she's doing it too, but it's such a pleasant toppling forwards. So . . . reasonable.

A blast of cold air as the door opens.

Hannah follows the other turning heads. It is Rory from the pub, charging in. Pale and floppy in his daft kilt. Realising he has caught everyone's attention, he wavers. Scans the room.

'Ho!' Mhairi raises her voice again. 'Not historically significant? What about Crychapel Wood then? And the cairn on Mary's Brae?'

Escobar looks puzzled. 'You mean your concrete bunker? Mm, it is a pity it was so . . . damaged by that funny little lid, no? And is empty, I believe?'

'Aye, well, there's plenty more stuff like that around here. Bound to be. Modern research'll be much more . . .' Soft gauzes of sweat are appearing on Mhairi's cheeks, her angry cleavage. Shit. She's going to say it; their secret. Not yet, Hannah wills her. Not here.

'Ever heard of the *Time Team*, pal? Well, we're getting a whole squad of archaeologists up here. Embarrass the lot of you. What d'you make of that, then?'

Michael catches Hannah's gaze. Escobar laughs. A pleasant, respectful laugh. Ross giggles and claps his hands, pleased something nice is happening. And the others laugh too. All except Rory, who clumbers and 'excuses me' until he reaches Michael. They consult in frantic whispers.

'Ho!' Mhairi calls. Hannah sees Michael move purposefully towards them. He's going to remonstrate with Mhairi, who is shouting, 'Did you just come here to take the piss, señor? I'm talking to you.' Her arm flies back, Hannah sees a scone soar through the air, make contact with the side of Escobar's face, butter-side down. Ross whoops, and slides from Hannah's lap, heading for the table with the cakes – *Ross!* – more shouts go up, the camera blazing, catching her and Mhairi and Michael, who is just standing there in front of her.

Her husband takes her hand. 'There's been an accident,' he says. 'You have to come.'

Chapter Five

Michael stares at the tea, the piece of toast. Listens to his wife talking in the hall.

'No, honestly. He's fine. He's conscious, he knows we're there.'

Pause.

'Yes. I do know. With his eyes. I told you; he can't speak yet. His tongue's in a terrible state – bit clean through one side.'

Pause.

'I know. God, I know. But they're dissolving ones, so . . . Yes. Yes, I know. And the nerves are intact, so . . . yeah. Yeah. Once the swelling goes down. Eh?'

Longer pause while mother-in-law decants more fears into his wife.

'No, they've got a kind of a cage over it. No. No, his leg. No, Mum, I told you – they can't put a plaster on it yet. He's going to need an operation.' A trembling sigh. 'Yes. I know they were really good trainers, Mum.'

More pitting and patting, until Hannah's tone becomes bright and final. 'Honestly, there's no need. I know. It's a long way. And you've the cats. Look, come and see him after the op, once we've got him home, yeah? Mmhm. Yup. Fine, Mum. Will do. OK then. Bye now. Bye-bye.'

Michael refills the kettle, switches it on. The thing has been on the boil for ever. He flattens his palms on the bevelled metal, keeping them there as the heat intensifies. But he can't get warm. His face, distorted in the silver, gazes out with one elongated eye. His wife, sharp and hysterical. His neighbours, stoic and offering lifts. Folk bringing platitudes and baked goods. His wee boy, pinned and skewered. His son is drained and broken and stitched and he is making tea again.

'Why is everything my fault?' Hannah kicks the door shut with her heel. 'Did he have his earphones in? Was he not wearing that luminous sash she sent? God Almighty.'

'Tea?'

'What?'

'Do you want some tea?'

'No. I don't want bloody tea. Did that policeman phone back?'

'No.'

'Christ, they must have got some witnesses by now. What about the person who phoned them?'

'No trace.'

'I bet it was them. I bet that was the fucking driver.'

'Hannah. Could you please stop swearing? You tell Euan not to—'

'Oh, piss off, Michael. Away and pray or something.'

Cupping the kettle as the whistle shrilled; his skin shriven. A sensation akin to pleasure. Then that raw rise of nausea, that shrilling in your gut. He is enjoying the pain. He should have been a Catholic. She is pacing, pacing. Ignoring his further offer of tea. 'Right, what's the time? I said we'd be back up by eleven. The consultant's coming at eleven, Michael. Michael – can you get a bloody move on?'

It's the stress, that's all. He wipes some crumbs off the work-top. Through the hatch – a handy thing, which Hannah wants boarded up – he can see their lounge. It's a peaceful room. High ceilings, plain cornicing and a rich smell of lilies. One vase on the coffee table, another in front of the mirrored mantel. Fluted glass, sparkling in filtered light. Hannah loves her lilies. She loves her manse too. That was her compensation. Not him. Ha. If he says these things out loud, will she laugh and call him Eeyore? Or tear off his head? Do things, Michael. *Do things*. Stop making tea.

The manse is a long white house, imposing beside grey neigh-bours. It sits to one side of the church, is grand with its square-paned windows and several chimneys, although the core of it would have been a blackhouse once, with folk living at one end and their beasts at the other. Grown and adapted for a large family and the needs of a thriving parish, it has become two floors, plus a Georgian extension, plus an attic, plus a basement at the back where the land dips down. The attic and two of the bedrooms lie slightly damp and empty. They live mostly in here – the deep, knocked-through drawing room – and the kitchen. Except, more and more, Michael has been going underground. His study is one of two rooms in the basement. You go down through the cupboard under the stairs. That's where he'd been skulking before the meet-ing last night. He thought Euan was in his bedroom. Michael was hiding in his dunny and Hannah was putting out cakes and Euan was probably in his room, or watching Ross or whatever, and he – distracted by his speech and the weird-shaped floaters at the corner of his eye – had gathered up his papers, put on his public face (he pictures a selection of them, arranged in mood order, and hanging like hats by the door), and left for the windfarm meeting.

No. Euan was lying with his mouth smashed and his leg snapped, ten minutes' walk from the house.

'Shit!' The kettle jumps; scalding water slaps his hand. Outside the window, the Ghost is watching. So here they are, in this room, he has a witness right here and the bloody thing is waving. Bold as brass. He's mouthing the same word over and over, which he combines with some scatological mime. *B-I-T-C-H*.

'Nice,' says Michael.

'What's nice? What in Christ's name is nice about our son lying in a hospital bed?'

'I said, you look nice.'

'Oh. Oh, don't be stupid, Michael. I look like shit. We've spent all night in corridors, sitting in chairs . . . ah . . . I can't . . .'

Quietly, she folds in on herself. Michael moves to kiss her, but she holds herself rigid, will not bend, will not yield. He kisses her brow instead.

'Hannah. It's going to be all right. He's conscious, he's breathing and his bones are young. They're going to fix him.'

'Do you promise?'

The fierce glare of her lights his heart. Glowering like a wee girl. His girl. Only her and his boys; that is all that matters. His boys. This, all this nonsense of mirages and duty and obligations, is toothpaste squeezed too far, too thin. He is all rolled up and jaggy at the ends, he is the toothpaste, the world is squeezing him, he was the tube. Michael is a tube. The Ghost presses his cheek against the glass. Watching. Michael concentrates on the flesh before him. It is smooth, slightly dry. It is warm.

'I promise.'

She sniffs. Jangles. He loves that she's all golden. Hoops and rings and pretty things.

'C'mon then. We'd better head. We'll get Ross on the way.'

Ross, who was deposited at a friend's house last night, has been demanding to see his big brother, has left a hundred plaintive messages on his mother's phone. They make it as far as the front door. Open it to see Miss Campbell bowling up the path. She carries a casserole before her. The Ghost has one finger down his throat, pretending he is puking.

'Oh for Christsake. Michael. I can't—'

'You go on,' Michael whispers to Hannah. 'You go in your car, get Ross, and I'll catch you up, yes?' He propels his wife to one side as he greets Miss Campbell at the other. Voice professionally sonorous, oh he hates this pantomime that is his life – 'Miss Campbell. Thank you for coming.'

'Oh. What a terrible, terrible thing. You poor souls. Oh, Mrs Anderson. Can I just tell you how—'

'Thank you. Sorry. Can't stop.' Hannah hurries to her car.

'My, that looks lovely. Thank you so much. We're actually just heading to the hospital now . . .'

'I told Effie you would be. I said, look Effie, that's them home the now. Probably for a wee wash and a catnap, I said. But they'll be heading off again, you watch. So I thought I'd better be quick. I mean, poor Mrs Anderson. She doesna look well, does she?'

'Can I take that from you?' Michael watches his wife drive away, him trapped between his own front door, a murky Irish stew and the Ghost, who has twirled inside the hallway and is standing, hands on hips.

'Oh God. You wonder what it's all about. I mean, he was such a good wee boy, wasn't he? You wonder, is there a reason—'

'Miss Campbell, I really have to go. We're meeting the doctor at Lochallach. Euan might need to go to Glasgow . . .'

'Och, of course you do. Of course you should be with them. I mean, I suppose you know all just the right things to say, don't you?'

'Pardon?'

'You're used to all these shenanigans. Bedside vigils; folk all upset. *Besides* themselves, I should imagine. I said to Effie, mind though, the cooncillor being a minister and all. He'll be a tower of strength. It's a test, most like—'

'Miss Campbell. It's my son. It's my son we're talking about. Not a test.'

Her delicate wee fingers cover her mouth. 'Oh.'

'Now, I'm sorry, but I have to go.'

'But what about your stew?'

He slams the front door shut, closing the Ghost inside. 'Just leave it on the step.'

'On the step?'

'Yes! On the step!' He jostles past her, Crimplene static cracking air. Can't stand to look at her soft old face oh Jesus. Jesus God. Why are you doing this to me? He stalls the engine. Too much gas. Takes it slower, again. Again. Once this bugger flooded, you could forget about going anywhere for the rest of the day. Why are you doing this?

'Now. Why should He get all the credit? Eh, Michael? Eh?' The Ghost, who's very small now, is a curled cat on his lap. Michael ignores him. When he was a wee boy, he saw faces in the fire. This is no different, no different, not one jot. He keeps his eyes on the road, he fixes on the road his boy was crushed on. When did he last speak to Euan, when was it not a row, or a query about what time he'd be back or the whereabouts of Hannah? The hot, wet,

75

unimagined weight presses on his groin my God my God why
hast thou forsaken . . . Medicine. He could go to the doctor and
get medicine. People will forgive him because of Euan. You are
allowed to be tranquillised if your son has multiple fractures.

No pills. Absolutely no pills.

At the bus stop, a girl yawns. He recognises her hair, a kind of
metallic red. It's her; the one who'd found him in the churchyard
yesterday, seen him flat on his back. He remembers her voice. Low
and gallus. The weight is suddenly gone. He checks his crotch. No
Ghost. No unnatural heat. No voice. A mellow glow wraps him as
he stops the car. Relief. He winds down the window.

'Hello.'

The girl frowns. He has no context now, no dog-collar or griev-
ing angels. Just a middle-aged man, patting his own groin.

'It's me. You um . . . you helped me yesterday. In the
churchyard.'

Her eyes widen. Green-flecked hazel. 'Oh. God, yeah. You.
How you doing?'

'Ah . . . not so good actually.'

She nods. 'You do look worse.'

'I'm on my way to the hospital.'

'Should you be driving then?'

'Oh, it's not me. It's my son.'

Another nod. More cautious, her eyes flitting away. Then,
laboriously, she raises her wrist, looks at her watch. He senses an
impatience in her, and he is impatient suddenly too. But he
doesn't want to leave.

'Bus late, is it?'

'Not sure.' She shakes her wrist. 'My watch keeps stopping.'

'I make it twenty past. You're fine. Where you off to?'

76

She shrugs.

He has to go. Hannah will be waiting. 'Did I tell you it was my son?'

'Yeah.'

'He got knocked down.'

Her body flinches, as if the word 'knock' has physically knocked her.

'Last night.'

'Shit. That's terrible.' She looks at him again. 'Is he all right?'

'He'll live.'

Her face is pale and thin, with tinges of lilac beneath the skin. Yesterday's blood has become a bruise, a wing of blue on her forehead. She wears the same black ankle boots with aggressive heels, caked in mud.

'Not be running again for a while, though. His leg's all smashed up. And his mouth. His mother's worried he's going to need dentures.'

That is not true, not once has Hannah even mentioned this. He doesn't need to lie, or make this a witty anecdote. A spoonful of humour to make it taste nice. The strangest sensation is on him; it is as if he's stepped in a bubble, and the world is continuing to thrash along outside, but muted. The warmth in his lap is only pleasant, the notion of scales and feathers daft. The Ghost – the feeling – has definitely gone. Twice now, this girl has thwarted the beast. Is she a sign, or a test? Michael's life has been a delicate scrabble across the cracks, all those twisty forks in the road, the strangers who might be angels, the monkeys on your back. He's been to university to study the paranormal, the divine. In theory, he knows all the hierarchies and the legions, and that only makes it worse. For this, they also expect you to be sane?

'I'm sorry about yesterday. When I shouted at you. Really sorry.'

'That's OK.' She is shivering. Skin so pale it is see-through. How could you yell at a wee scrap like that? You, Michael. You and your ugliness.

'How d'you get on with your dad?'

Her knife-edge chin juts at him. 'What?'

'You were looking for your dad. Frank? Maybe I could help?'

'Nah. You're all right.'

He follows her gaze, to the window of the store. A poster advertises the mobile cinema's latest showing. *Predator*.

'Are you coming back?' He has to go. But he can't leave her, shivering.

'What?'

'Wherever it is you're going – are you coming back?'

'Doubt it.'

'So where are you off to then?'

'I thought you were rushing to the hospital?'

'I am.'

Her white nose is glistening. She reaches for a hanky. Dabs it at her nose. 'I'm going to look for a job.' She falters, as if the hanky is somehow shocking. Fumbling in her pockets. A slow breath out.

'I need someone.'

The thickness of his desperation is mortifying: the sentence splatters round them, and he tries to wipe it up. 'A cleaner. Well, an au pair. We need a sort of assistant – my wife's in the middle of a book, the cleaner's just left. Euan's going to be in hospital for Godknows how long. And we've got a wee boy of four. Can you drive?'

'Do they let you loose in the Sunday School?'

'Pardon?'

'I'm a total randomer you just met at the bus stop.'

'No. No, that's not fair. In the churchyard . . . you helped me. You were kind.'

'Aye, and you were a total loony. Nae offence, pal, but I think it might all be a bit freaky.'

'Look – have you got a job already? You're cold. Have you got somewhere to stay?'

'No . . . Not yet.'

'Well, why don't you? Not that many jobs going round here. If you need work, we need help. Sounds like a plan to me.' *At least give her a hot meal.* 'Divine providence in fact! And we could . . . maybe we could go through parish records and stuff. You know. For your dad.'

'I don't think so. No.'

She hefts her bag higher. It's a large leather affair, looks like a Moroccan pouffe. Her eyes are firmly back on the road. Michael shrivels. Is stupid. 'Of course,' he says in a voice that sounds normal. 'Well, good luck anyway.'

'You too.' She lifts her voice above the engine and the grind of the wheels as they bite the road. 'Tell . . . I hope your son's all right.'

Michael drives a hundred yards before he has to stop the car. Or it is stopped, it bumps gently into something as, from nowhere, a lucky omen is crapped bountifully across his windscreen. He hears grunts, thinks possibly that he is making them. Rich white mucous streaked with black. A roar, bright sun. A piercing. He cannot see. Nothing he can do will ever change things. All the lost souls he gathers; it won't make any difference.

The heaviness of him. He does not look down, is rocking. He pretends the weight he carries is his baby son. A good weight. It is moments after Euan's birth, it is dark. Hannah has been taken for a bath: the afterpains are horrendous, so Michael is first to cradle him, not his wife. They sit one inside the other in an institutional chair, on a putty-pink vinyl seat. Euan wears a white sheet like a little spectre. The delivery room is unnaturally hot – Hannah's screams have condensed on to the windows. They are alone. Awe-struck, Michael breathes in his son. He unfurls created fingers, examines unused feet. The unfeasible head is bare, soft skull-shell has blossomed in his hand. He remembers crying; like it was he who had given birth. Somebody's son, who will become a man. Michael keeps his eyes screwed shut. He will always cradle his son.

'Hey. Are you OK?' A perfumed arm is in his window. Bright hair bends. Unstraps him. 'C'mon you.'

He is enfolded, his body held. Feet swung on to hardness.

'I don't think you should be driving in this state. You nearly hit that wall.'

Michael looks at the windscreen, to explain. It is clear.

Chapter Six

'My wife had an affair last year. I'm not coping too well.'

Justine has got the minister home to the manse, that white building behind the church. She took the keys when his hands wouldn't work, shoogled at the damp lock, switched on a lamp, placed him in a chair. His plumpness, she discovers, is in his face and the layers of jumpers – the rest of him is lean and brittle, she can feel sharp angles beneath his clothes. She takes off his coat, two cardigans, his shoes. No socks. They must have looked as if they were drunk, stoating up the road, arms over and under. No other bugger visible in the street. Maybe they were hiding, out of respect for their minister. *Did you see the state of that?* She'd thought of knocking on doors, but that would only prolong it. And he wasn't ill, exactly. Just pathetic.

She's missed one bus already – on top of being stranded here last night. After she'd phoned the ambulance, she'd run as far as the village, right up to the door of the hotel. But going in, signing a register – that would weave her into this place, to the crash that keeps repeating in her head. So she did what she aye does. She hid. The door to the hippy café place had been left unlocked. That must be how folk lived here. Deserved to have the place screwed. She didn't take anything, mind, apart from more of that bread. Man, it was good: warm and floury. Cushions on the chairs. Nothing to see, move along. Up early, early and out out out. Bloody freezing. Wandering. Shivering. And now she's missed the bus. Because of him. She cannot stay any longer, and this, this is the *dad*. Fucksake. But he looks so helpless. Like a bird that's just smashed into a window. He hasny said much, beyond that initial burst about his wife. He repeats it. Waits, hunched like she might hit him. Feet jostling, fingers in a circle, his thumbnail pinching at his index finger. What do you say, though? What do you say when a strange man tells you he's a cuckold? His eyes are raw. 'I'm sorry. I shouldn't have . . . you don't . . . Sorry. Ignore me.' A vague, imploring glance.

'Look. Can I get you some tea?'

'Please. You're very kind . . .'

He goes to stand, and her hand shoots out. To steady him, repel him, warn him of her comfort zone which is way beyond him? He keeps staring, though, at empty air. There's nothing there – paintings, a fireplace, some fancy flowers in a vase – but he scours the room like he is searching for some familiar shape. It's a beautiful room. Even without the fire lit, there's a faint smell of smoke, the piled abundance and implicit warmth of two neat baskets of logs. Green curtains edge casement windows and a view of more standing stones, smirred with the rain that's starting up. The dark clouds scudding compound the cosiness inside. Branches wave, the pool of crisp yellow from the lamp. On the back of the couch, a knitted blanket begs to be wrapped round Justine's shoulders. Her boots are discarded by the hearth. One of the antique fire irons is an actual toasting fork. She has never used a toasting fork.

'Please don't say about Hannah . . . my wife. She'll be home soon. Oh. No. The hospital—' Swithery and loose, gangling on bare feet. 'God. You phone her. Here.'

'Whit? No way, pal. She won't know who I am.'

'Please.' He offers an old Bakelite phone. 'I'm not up to . . . Just say I had a . . . fall or something.'

Reluctantly, Justine dials the number he gives her. The phone's not really old, there's a push-button square in the middle. But she likes the feel of the solid receiver in her hand, how it balances neatly on both sides, in the shape of a crooked bone. Straight to message. She lifts the phone from her face. 'No one there.'

'Better leave a message.'

'Jesus, you're one paranoid cleric, pal.'

'Please.'

Already, she doesn't like this woman. 'Hi. Don't worry, but your husband's had a wee accident. He's fine, but I've taken him back to the manse. Like I say, don't worry. There's no damage. And it wasn't his fault.' The beep cuts her out.

'Why did you say that?'

She isn't sure.

'Right. Tea? What d'you take?'

'Milk. One sugar.'

Oh, man. The kitchen? Green Aga: check. Rustic oak table: check. Some fancy coffee maker that is huge and silver: check. On the wall, a collage of photos frame the family who lives here. Cute babies; black and white back-to-backs of wee boys growing up. A puffball wedding; university gowns; old couple on a cruise ship; a line of grinning priests; light-drenched beaches, small slim woman with a wide-brimmed hat, who rocks her lime bikini. The collage hurts Justine's eyes: it's like staring at the sun. She smooths her fingers round the extra-large knob of a cupboard. It's plastic woodgrain. Oversized mugs with polka dots, or dainty floral teacups? Hmm. She goes for the big mugs. When she returns, the minister is stretched out on a wing chair, one hand over his eyes. Despite the podgy face, his belly falls taut, the way her breasts go when she's on her back. Outside, rain fingers the windows.

'Here you go. By the way, what's your—'

'Thank you . . . um?'

Almost in unison.

'I'm Michael.'

'Justine. It's French,' she apologises.

'Thank you, Justine.'

Man. She'd meant to give a made-up name. She's not remotely French either. That was her father's mum's fault, a mythical creature of whom she has no recollection. What an idiot: it is the cream Shaker units in the kitchen, it is the toasting fork, twinkling too hard. Making her smell crumpets. She has to leave. Immediately. She can hitch to Lochallach, get a bus further . . . north? East?

'Look . . . I really need to be heading . . .'

Which edge will she tumble off? But it's so warm in here. So clean.

From the middle of the rug, she inspects the full circumference of the room. Her feet don't leave the edges, are moving in a circle, the way a cat pads before it selects its spot. The guy has offered her a job. A proper job, not prefaced with hand or blow. How often does that happen?

'Your son. He's going to be fine?' Justine settles into the velvet couch, the one with the blanket.

'So they say. Eight weeks in plaster at least.'

'But everything's . . . you know. He's all working.'

Michael almost smiles at this. 'He's all working, thanks. Apart from his shattered leg, the concussion, a stitched-up tongue, the neck brace—'

'Sorry.'

'No. No, I'm sorry. I'm . . .' He agitates one hand, as if it's a duster and he is shaking off the dirt. 'God. Can I say something?'

'Fire away.'

Michael puts his mug on the floor. 'You look like the kind of girl . . . sorry, woman? You prefer woman, don't you?'

'Don't really care.'

Ah. This is it, the main event. *My wife doesn't understand me.* Silly cow. Why do they bother making excuses? It wasn't for her, it was never for her. It's done as a form of atonement. Her hand balls into a fist.

'What age are you? Twenty-one? Twenty-two?'

'Ish.'

'You look like the kind of woman who isn't shocked by anything.'

'You think?'

He's going to pull out a gimp mask. Or a knife. To come all this way and be smote by a man of God. Jes-*us*. Justine pulls the lovely blanket closer. Oh man! It's got wee silky fringes on the hem. She feels perfectly relaxed. This big woose isny going to hurt her. She knows this, absolutely. His eyes are lost, yes. But they're not enraged.

'I wasn't trying to . . . you know. In the churchyard. I was checking you were real.'

'Uh huh. Right.'

'I know.' He shakes his head. 'It's daft. But I've been having a bit of trouble . . . seeing things. Like when you have a migraine?

Visual disturbances, if you like. It's getting quite . . . well. But I can't say . . . I don't want to stop working. I need to keep working. There's so much to do; we're at a crucial time. And Hannah – I can't say to Hannah. I shouldn't have said anything about Hannah. Please don't . . . nobody knows that here.'

'Not my business, Rev.'

This velvet couch. It is the softest thing she has ever sat on. It is like a feathered nest. If you were mean, this gibbering man would be the perfect scam. She is embarrassed for him.

'I'm not actually a minister either.'

'Right. Just impersonate one, do you?'

'No, well, I am. I am ordained . . . still . . . but I don't have a parish any more. Not since we . . . we only moved here last year. I'm their councillor.'

'A counsellor?'

Man. And she thought she had problems?

'Local councillor. Elected member?'

She thinks of a dirty joke. Does not say it.

He gabbles on. 'I help out occasionally in the church, but only if they ask, but I don't really . . . it's not my job now. I mean, you can help folk in other ways, can't you? Real things that—' He rubs his hand across his chest, where his heart is. 'Oh, is it cold in here?'

'No.'

He nods. Lifts his mug. 'I didn't used to be . . .' Puts it down again. She watches it wobble on the carpet, then sink to one side, the dregs pooling on creamy wool. 'Do you believe everything has a purpose, Justine?'

She fucking hopes not. She sips at her tea, only it is too hot, so she pretends to drink while her breath echoes inside the mug and she thinks, how did he drink his that quick? and she can see a pale beige reflection of her eyes widening back at her, the heat from her trapped tea-breath making her cheeks blaze. Eventually, she puts the mug down. Eventually, she will have to respond. The man – Michael – has his hands clasped, his eyes open, fixed on her. His mouth flattens and flares; he is compressed, everything tight and small. Yet she is up in close to his garnet blood. Bones exposed. He has splayed himself open. Is it now? At what point does she mention his son? How she'd chucked him in the path of the sole vehicle on the road, and run away?

On a side table, a pile of thick pastel towels wait to be stowed. She can smell fresh-laundry sponginess, rising to meet the flower scent, the waxy wood. The rain beats harder. More than anything, Justine would love a hot shower. Her feet tuck themselves up on the couch, wee burrowing movements, searching for just the right spot. Toes poking through the holes in her socks.

'What happened to your boy? Does he remember?'

'Nope. Hit and run.'

'Shit.' She eases her toes deeper into the pile. Her long toenails catch like hooks. 'Does he . . . have they got who did it?'

A harsh laugh. 'No idea. No witnesses so far. And Euan can't remember a thing. Oh, but they were good enough to call an ambulance, before they disappeared.'

Justine arranges the blanket, so it rests across her shoulders. 'Seriously? That's . . . awful. I mean. I don't drive. I don't know what you'd do—'

The door opens, and the weave tears apart.

'Michael! What happened? Are you all right? I— oh.'

The woman in the doorway stops, her nails resting on the head of the little boy beside her. It is the jangly woman from the café.

The golden-yet-scarlet jangly woman. Justine has shagged plenty of married men, remorselessly. Justine is the very last one to judge but you can see it in an instant. Mrs Jangly is shining and busy, her painted nails match her painted lips, match her small son's knitted hat. Quick blue eyes sussing Justine, noting the unshod feet, the mismatched socks. Withering her husband. A man should expand in the presence of his wife.

'Hi there.' Justine stands, sticks out her hand. 'I'm Justine. It was me who called you at the hospital. How's your son doing?'

'He's doing fine, thank you. I'm sorry – who are you?'

She doesny even recognise her. If you run your words together, you can make them glide, and if you lift the inflection of them in a little flicky tail it makes you slightly posh. Some like it posh.

'I'm a friend of Myra's? At the church? It was so weird: Myra said I should pop in to say hello to you guys if I was up this way, and I was literally en route to the manse when Michael had his bump—'

'A bump?'

'He's fine, though, absolutely fine. It was just a skid. All this rain. But he banged his head, so I helped him home and we were talking, you know? And he told me all about your son, and here's me on a three-month sabbatical. So how bizarre is that, eh? I'm a nursery nurse, by the way.'

Genius, doll. Justine raises her eyebrows at the little boy. 'Hiya! You must be . . .'

'I am called Ross Michael Anderson. I am four.'

'Hey, Ross. Pleased to meet you.' Turns neatly to the wife again. 'So, Euan? How is he? Any updates?'

Tell me he's fine. Tell me I saved his life, really.

'Michael? What's going on? What did you do?' The woman scowls at Justine's forehead. 'Did you do that? Did you crash into her?'

Michael lugs his puzzlement from Justine, on to his wife. 'I didn't do anything. I skidded outside the store, that's all. Why would you think . . . I was just going too fast, to try and catch you up. How is he?'

'I told you. Fine. Still got concussion. They've managed to reset his leg, though, stitched him up. He's not going to need that operation.'

'Brilliant. So he can stay at Lochallach?'

'For now. Two weeks, they reckon. But he might need to have surgery on his jaw. Look. Can we talk about this later?' Pale-russet nails at her mouth. The wife sparkles like a trapped star. Silver charm bracelet, golden hoops, all *chinkle-tinkle*.

'But he's not dopey or anything? He still knows it's you?'

'Of course he does. Yes.' She is too impatient with him. 'OK – Janice, was it?'

'Justine.'

'Yeah. Well, thanks very much for getting my husband home in one piece. But please don't let us keep you. Everything's a bit chaotic . . .' She frowns. 'Sorry. Myra who? I don't know anyone called Myra.'

'Oh, not from this church, no—'

Justine stares directly at Michael. *Come on then. Make me purposeful, mate. Because I like this place. It's nice.*

Here is a fully furnished cocoon; a fortnight's breathing space to decide her future. As soon as the son comes home, though, she'll have to do a runner. Jesus. The thought of that poking, shattered bone. The desperate noise of air coming out. Staying here

89

means she'll know for definite he's getting better; that she didn't actually kill him. Oh yes. Rewind. That is the proper reason. She lets the virtue tingle, opening out her fingers till the webbed skin between them is taut. It will be like keeping watch. A GOOD thing to do. It will be the most conscientious thing Justine has ever done. Secreted here, she will be quiet and safe. And helpful. As long as she's careful – no mad spending sprees, no sex in grave-yards, no drunken brawls necessitating police action. If the minister-who-is-not-a-minister is mental enough – and he clearly is, very mental – to think Justine is in some way meant . . . well. He'll mend them. He did, in fact, ask for this.

Her teeth on dry lips. *Over to you, big boy.*

'No. From Clairmount, remember?' Michael's looking out the window again. Distracted, or concentrating on his lie? Justine can't tell. 'That church in Paisley. Myra ran the Brownies there, didn't she?'

Justine nods enthusiastically. 'That's right.'

'Isn't it good, though? That Justine's a nursery nurse? Sounds like the answer to—'

'Excuse us, Justine.' The wife sets her handbag on the side-board. Picks it up again. The air around her crackles. 'Michael? A minute?' Michael is dispatched to the hall. 'Ross, take your stuff off, eh? You can put cartoons on – quietly. Mummy'll be back in a wee minute.'

She shuts the door on them, even as the child nods, tongue out as he labours with Velcro straps on his shoes.

'Can I give you a wee help?' says Justine.

'No. I am putting my boots and hat in the hall.'

'That's a good boy.'

Ross swings the door open and the words whumph in.

'. . . nothing about her. Look at her bloody hair. And she's a massive bruise on her forehead . . .'

'. . . not exactly coming for a job interview . . . be . . . help . . .'

Ross trundles back into the lounge, neatly presses the door fast. He holds a black-bound notebook.

'You're a very tidy boy, aren't you?'

'Mhm. Also I am a good boy.'

'Oh, I can see that.' Justine pulls the blanket from the couch. 'Listen. Have you ever played at camping, Ross?'

He shakes his head. 'You're not allowed to—'

'Did I tell you I was magic? I can do magic things, so I am allowed. And I'm going to make us a magic carpet.' She drags two of the fat seat cushions on to the carpet. 'And a magic tent. I'm sure your mummy won't mind. Right. Can you put that blanket over the chair? See on the seat bit?'

He places the notebook on a side table, then crouches obediently. 'My mummy is called Hannah.'

Ross reminds her of her wee brother. Anything to do with hidey-holes, Chris loved. He had that same adult way of talking too, where everything is enunciated precisely, the new language you're learning so unfamiliar that you taste it slowly, offer it with care. Chris will be . . . She tries to calculate in her head. Six? Eight? It frightens her, so she stops thinking.

'Why don't you help me put the other end of the blanket on to the table. See if we tie it round the table leg?'

By the time Michael and his wife return to the lounge, Justine and Ross are in Samarkand. Billowy fabric conceals them, you can taste oranges and spice, the cushions are camel-humps and they are going faster and faster, diving now in blue-jewelled seas and—

'Hello?'

Under their woolly canvas, Ross stiffens.

'Right, King Rossino. I'll handle this.'

With a single sweep, they emerge. 'Ta dah! Did you know we were invisible?'

'Is that right? Well, you're also very red, both of you.' Michael smiles, and it makes him look different, boyish in a way.

'Daddy, I was flying underwater!'

'Were you, son? Can I try?'

Hannah remains impenetrable. 'Right. So. Justine. Bit hectic at the moment, with Euan and . . . Ross – pick up that blanket please.'

'Mummy—'

'Not now, Ross. I realise we'd be interrupting your holiday—'

'It's a sabbatical.'

'—but, it would be good, actually, if you could help out for a bit—'

'Mummy—'

'Ssh,' says Hannah. 'Two weeks, tops. You get bed, board and forty quid a week, yes?'

'Aye. Sure. Great.'

'Good. If I know you'll be here with Ross, I can be up at the hospital every day. And, when Euan gets home, an extra pair of hands will just be . . . We can make up a guest bed in the basement room. Of course, we'll need to see some references.'

This is the last place on earth Justine should stay. She has put their child in hospital. Which leaves more room for her. She will make it up to him. Them. She will be A GODSEND. For years after, they'll go 'Wasn't that Justine a *godsend*?' She imagines how comfy the bed will be, how big the bath. Roll-top most likely. The jangly woman has taste. She doubts it's mad Michael who chooses the flowers and plumps the cushions.

'Well, I don't have anything with me . . . but I can send for stuff. Last two employers, that kind of thing?'

'That would be fine. Thank you.' Hannah presents a set of neat straight teeth, perfectly bricked together.

'It would be so good if you can help us, Justine.' Michael shakes her hand. 'I'll write and thank Myra myself.'

Justine blinks at him; it isny coy as such, but he blinks back. Such a neat lie. They are an excellent double-act.

'Michael. Why don't you put Justine's um . . . boots away?'

'Sure.'

No wonder he's cracking up. He is apologetic to the point of submission. Justine could teach him secrets. Tell him how even the most craven of worms can turn. No one realises that, see. How they stitch you up. They think you're blind, that you feel no pain, so they run dull wires right through you, and pull you and pull you, tight until you burst. Yes. She and Michael could gang up against the snippy wife. They could be a team. Except teams are total lies. *C'mon doll, we're a team* means *do what I tell you and don't ask why*. By the looks of Michael, there are several million tense wires to unpick. Man. She canny stay that long. Then she sees him wink at Ross, pretend to do a salute. Ross giggles. He is a total cutie. Maybe she'll take him with her, when she goes.

'Here, I'll take them.' She holds her boots so the heels stick up. 'Sorry. I didn't want to get your carpet dirty.'

'No, it's fine—'

'Mummy.'

'What *is* it, Ross?'

Ross hands his mother the black notebook he's been clutching. 'Here is your story that came out. I was *telling* you. You did not zip up your bag.'

93

Michael takes it first. 'Hannah. Honestly? You were writing up at the hospital?'

'I told you, he was sleeping most of the time. At least I was bloody there.'

Hannah snatches the notebook from him. Goes to say something; clamps the words down, then exits the room. A fat vacuum of no-sound surges in her wake, holds itself tight as their separate glances meet. Solidify. There is a flurry of *wells*, like the beginning of a bad joke.

'Well,' says Michael, clearing his throat.

'Well,' says Justine. 'Will we finish our game?'

'Well,' says Ross. 'Am I allowed?'

Chapter Seven

He loves it. Pure fucking loves it with the wind-slap on his face and all those sour smells, kind of damp rotten earth when you wallop up the leaves. A wee slider of mud or shite and your boots slip through, spraying up all the crusty colours, how they're all slimy underneath. Fucking *loves* it. The dog tries to jump in too – or it would if Charlie Boy let it off the lead. Good as gold so it is since he kicked its cunt in – walks to heel and everything. But he keeps it tight. That feeling of it straining. He wraps the dog's chain hard round his knuckles and it's just him, his forearm with the veins up, his hands and sinews pumping, just the fucking force of him holding back this slevery big shite-monster with no neck and reams of teeth. Fuck. Folks' faces when you're walking by. Cunts never look you in the eye. Leather so it is, the lead. A leather strap with a big fuck-off chain – which is also an excellent chib, should the occasion call for it.

The dog's called Askit, like the medicine. Funny as fuck. He aye gets some prick trying to sook up to him, know? Usually once you've got out the car, maybe slipped off your shades and they can see it's you, it's Charlie Boy and not some cunt like daft Ally or the Teapot Twins with their squinty noses and skelly eyes. Fucksake. Nae luck, Mammy Teapot, to get two such identical plug-uglies. But, sometimes, people stare just when he's walking by, doing that pumpy kind of walk with his shoulders up and his hips all loose, kind of Liam Gallagher, only hard, know? You're not even wanting to talk to these plebs; you're all loose, the dog lead's round your wrist and some cunt'll whine: *Awright, big man? Whit's your dug calt?* Because they all know Charlie Boy. And he'll just give them a look, know? Just stop and give them the look, or sometimes he'll draw up a big grog, then plug it out so it lands at their feet. And he'll go, 'Askit.'

Not a glimmer of a smile. That is the joke, see, that's the joke that they don't fucking know it's a joke at all.

He loves it, man. Dog's got three collars. One for daytime, watching telly and that. It's blue. One for paying visits, which is black leather, same as the strap on its lead, with tiny wee cones of brass. Like a row of wee bullets. And one girly red one that's all padded inside *in case his neck gets sore*. He hasn't thrown it out. No yet. Still stinks of her, so it does.

'Fucking *ho*, you. Slow down.'

Dog's pulling again. He thinks it's seen a squirrel, or it's maybe got wind of a lady dug. Horny as hell, that dog. Humps anything – dogs, cats, cushions, legs. Not Charlie Boy's legs, but. He gives it a wee tug. It yelps. 'That right, pal? You'n me both. Both hump bitches, eh?'

He never talks to it if there's folk around. But it's nice to have someone to – More like a mirror to bounce your words off, because nae cunt gives you a straight answer anyroad, so you're as well talking to the fucking wall. Or the dog. They always had dogs when Charlie was a wean. His maw gave them all these Spic names, like Alberto and Perro (which means 'dog'. No imagination his *madre*). You think that was a brass neck, shouting for them in the park? Try being called Carlos in a housing scheme in Arden. Then she remarries and he becomes Carlos McGinty. Or 'Carol' as his new step-prick liked to say. Said it one too many times, but then they had a wee chat. Good as gold after. Since Charlie Boy kicked his cunt in.

Oh man. Fuck, he canny contain this fury. If he finds her . . . if he starts kicking, he won't be able to stop. No that it would bother him, crushing her fucking face beneath his boots. But it wouldny be enough. Nothing will be enough. He can't take this humiliation; they all know she's done a runner. Doesn't matter how many kneecaps he breaks, or pubs he torches, he's still the sad sack whose hoor cleared him out and ran away.

Justine. He cannot say her name.

'C'mere you!' He yanks the dog's neck away from a pile of crap. *Dear Green Place* my arse. Glasgow's over seventy parks, and they're all full of glass and shite. A jakey lies comatose, sprawled out on one of the benches. He *hates* jakies. Manky cunts. Two wee toerags kick a football through the empty flower beds, fouling the air with their language. Every second fucking word's a curse. You get lovely roses here in summer, but.

He broke a guy's nose last night; real beautiful job, because he did it from the inside. Rammed a corkscrew right up, one of they ones where the handles come out like wings. Aye, so it was more of a mangling, but the septum snapped, eventually. Boy'd already paid him all the money he owed, but so fuck? Charlie Boy shouldn't have to ask, not even the fucking once. Shouldn't have to ask for fuck-all. So he breaks and he terrorises and he shags his way through the whole fucking stable and it never goes away. It's not the money. He'd have given her all the money in the world.

You can aye find some cunt to give you more money. But he canny get another *her*. All that sleekit scarlet hair, how her skin tastes of cream and her wrists are that fine you could splinter them, easy. Why he thought she'd be a good earner.

Charlie Boy and Askit skirt past the boys. One of them goes to kick the ball; just for a sliver, time stops and he and Charlie are framed, floating, and the kid could strike the actual ball, and it would soar up, hang like a moon . . . and then smash into him; the boy is considering this very option as Charlie saunters past. He does not halt or hesitate. Does nothing other than continue to own the ground he walks on. The child deflates, swears something at his pal as he skliffs the ball across the park, in the opposite direction from where Charlie Boy walks.

He cannot get his hands to quit trembling. He has fucking bile, not blood, shooting up his arm. The dog squats for a shite, right in the middle of the rose-bed. He takes out his mobile. Holds it tighter and tighter till his jaw hurts. And he tries her number again.

Chapter Eight

Hot. Late. Damp breath. Too many layers, Justine has piled on every blanket, piles them up every night. Curtains tight so air is precious, the heat a breeding ground for dreams. Sleep naked. Cannot bear constriction on her joints. Been tied been tried been seen and done and push it off. The blankets fall. Cold-breath, draught-breast. Cold breast.

Her nipple is hard. Is aching.

Soft door slips. In the shadows. Do not move.

Unfamiliar bed. She knows unfamiliar beds. Lie still. Don't feel. Someone standing there. Is watching. She closes her eyes tighter. Turns over and waits till morning.

*

In Hannah's cream-tiled utility room, Justine folds the ironing. Dirty laundry; piles of the stuff: feels like all she's done since she got here. She has built two towers: one of whites and woollens, the other a wobbly mass of jeans and tops and sheets. Do folk iron sheets? She reckons Hannah does, so has given them all knife-edged folds. It even smells of flowers in here. Flowers and the seaside. Carefully, she balances Ross's socks on top of the second heap – she's balled them into pairs – and lifts it up. Through the kitchen, with the slatted, filtered sunlight, the big square quarry tiles on the floor. Upstairs to Ross's room, where she stows his ironing, straightens his bed so the cartoon face of the robot thing that's on it is no longer distorted. Into the echoing bathroom, with its fat pastel towels and the funny loo which has an overhead cistern like from school. But not the scratchy paper. Hannah doesny have an airing cupboard; she has an 'armoire'. *Just put them in the armoire, Justine.* Then pausing. Waiting for Justine to go: 'What's an armoire?' Before she made a tit of herself, started looking for a suit of armour or something, Michael said: 'It's the big wardrobe in the loo.'

She still has an hour and a half before it's time to collect Ross. He is in the afternoon nursery class, which gives Justine a wedge of time between one thirty and four that nobody's thought to fill. Hannah has kindly given her a list. Chores in the morning, making Ross's lunch, taking Ross to nursery, making dinner or clearing up at night; *we'll take this in turns* is written in helpful brackets, but with no indication of who's to do what when. Justine tries to do it all, keeping her head down and herself to herself. She senses that the more she makes herself indispensable, and the more she disappears to her room when not required, the longer she can eke this out. Poor Euan will come home soon. A week more, tops, she reckons, to root herself a little deeper in.

Hannah was at the hospital last night, is there again this morning, as if her presence alone will force him better. Such urgent mother-love. Is that normal? She reckons they're all a bit fucked-up in this house. Man, she's glad it's only a stopgap. What is it – three days now? This is a wee ledge; she's been climbing a mountain and now she's clinging to a ledge. Only till she gets her breath back. She'll count her money then too. At the moment, it lies in a baleful pile, stuffed in the back of her wardrobe. She swallows, rubs her neck. Ever since she did her mental, suicidal, do-or-die runner, there has been a falling dread which hides behind her, can be distracted with the muffle of this lovely place, but which bowfs out when she's not looking. Justine is so tired. But she'll feel better in a week; Christ, look at that pile she's hefted: already her limbs are stronger. She shoves a clump of hair from her eyes. Begins to stack the sheets in colour order, because the armoire has a kind of wire-netted front, and you can see the towels and linen on the shelves. If this was her house, she'd ditch the wardrobe, get a big power shower in instead. Maybe a corner bath in place of the stupid roll-top – which is not all it's cracked up to be. Massive big thing, which you can only half-fill with half-hot water, then you canny even relax because your back all freezes on the chilly enamel. Not comfy, regardless of how many of Hannah's bath salts you pour in.

She shifts the lilac sheets, so they sit between the aqua and the cream. Pretty. There is a jarring royal-blue set, which she hides at the back. These will be Euan's sheets; his room is white and blue, there is a Rangers scarf above his bed, posters of rap stars, heaps of smelly clothes she has been trying to sort. His room smells of boy. Probably pictures of girls beneath his bed, if she chose to pry there. She pats the bright-blue fabric so it's tucked under lilac. Every day, she asks how Euan's doing: one, because she wants to know and two, because, as soon as he comes home, he'll recognise her. There'll be a big stushie, the polis will be called and then . . . And then. Justine the scabby hoor will be infamous. A bad girl with her name in the papers, right next to the ads for fertiliser. Then he will track her down. A chill rinses her. Already,

Charlie Boy will be doing that. He will be sniffing air with his teeth exposed. Those blank eyes, shuttering. Beaten-leather jacket on. Laced-up boots and laced-up mouth. Fisted hands, lackey in tow. People to see. To hit. He'll know for definite by now that the money is gone. Can Askit track folk? He can certainly bite them. Justine doesn't flatter herself. It will be the theft that kills her, ultimately, not twisted 'love'.

She moves to the master bedroom. Purple velvet curtains, grey-mauve walls. First time she's done more than peek in here. It's like being inside a bruise. Checks out the bedside tables. On Michael's side – she susses this is Michael's side because there is a Bible and she honestly doesn't see Hannah reading a Bible, not even for practising being nice – so yes, there is a Bible, some medical book called *Germinal*, two pens, a box of hankies, some Rennies, two packs of Panadol and a nasal spray. She can see him scooshing and fussing and sniffing up all those potions before bed. Yup. Definitely Michael's side. But there is also a smell, coming up off the pillow, that is . . . she lowers her head, so her cheek lies where Michael's might. It smells of breath and moistness. And something acrid.

The other table has cherry lip salve, and fancy handcream in a dark-blue jar. Couple of notepads, a ton of books. She turns the top one to see the title. *The Testament of Gideon Mack*. Sounds religious. Maybe Hannah is a believer after all; how could you live with someone and not share their life's work? A bright image of Charlie Boy's bloodied fist appears and she immediately reconsiders. Beside the books is a black silk eye mask (or kinky sex aid? Nah. She doesny think so. In Justine's professional opinion, a big tin of antifreeze is what's needed here). Perfume, which she squirts idly as she browses. Gorgeous. Same lemony smell Hannah wore in the café. More books on the floor, beside pale-mauve slippers.

In her stocking soles (which are really socks, always socks, so why do folk say 'stocking soles'? But it's how she likes to operate. Slippers are for fannies. Bare feet are for idiots who don't care what they step in), Justine tries them on. *You shall go to the ball.* Nae chance. Even without her woolly socks, there's no way Justine is getting her size sixes into these.

Downstairs, the door bangs. She jumps from the bed, pat-patting the duvet, still a bum-shaped dip, plumps at it and kicks the slippers straight and shuffles the ironed T-shirts over the tell-tale unevenness.

'Hello?' Hannah calls.

'Up here,' shouts Justine. 'I'm just putting the ironing away.'

In the silvery mirror, her cheeks glow. She picks up a sweatshirt of Ross's that got tangled in the pile, hurries out as Hannah reaches the top of the stairs. She seems distracted.

'Hiya. How's it going?'

'Yeah. Fine.' A tight smile.

'Done the laundry. Just about to hoover downstairs.'

'Great. Good.' Hannah makes an exaggerated little sniff. 'You smell nice.' The smile is thinner.

'How's Euan?'

'Oh . . . the same. Quiet.'

'Did he sleep?'

'Not really? Pain's worse today.'

A quick slip of guilt. 'Wee soul.' Above Justine's head is a skylight of coloured glass. The centre is a yellow sun, then a rectangle of frosted white glass, etched with little stars. At certain times of day, she's seen the shadow of the stars, dancing on the stairs. The frosted glass is edged in thin rectangles of blue glass, with red squares where the blue lines intersect. Ross's sweatshirt is folded over her arm. If she shifts her elbow up, the grey marl takes on a yellow cast.

'Get some good writing done?' she says. 'At the hospital?'

Hannah scrutinises her. Justine smiles at the notebook in her hands.

'Yeah. A bit. Well . . . not really. My main character's in the middle of a dilemma. She's this Bronze Age girl: Maraq, who's pregnant—'

Justine tunes out. Some chis about cavemen. Bound to be a bestseller. The coloured light jiggles on her arm.

'. . . it's a bit of a trauchle, to be honest.'

'Then why are you doing it?'

'Sorry?'

'If you're no enjoying it, and you're finding it hard, why are you writing it?'

Hannah frowns at her. 'Because I'm being paid to. I mean . . . all work is hard, isn't it. If it's good?'

'I guess.' She has an urge to stick out her tongue, to catch the star-shadow and swallow it. Work that is dire and vile and squelchy; how would shimmery Hannah quantify that?

'. . . need inspiration. Like filling up your creative well . . .'

Oh, shut up, doll. This house was nice and peaceful without you.

'. . . and we've got the archaeologists arriving today. So that's all good. No word, I take it?'

'What?'

Would a star taste of silver or gold? Or ice? 'From archaeologists? No.'

'No. From the police. Anyone.'

'No.' Justine moves past her. ''Scuse me.'

'Did the people from the John Muir Trust call?'

'The what?'

'About the windfarm. You have noticed that giant balloon floating above the village? Massive turbines that high, all round Kilmacarra?'

'Oh yeah. Mhairi mentioned it.'

'But they haven't phoned?'

'No one's phoned.'

'Right. See if they do, just take a message.' Hannah's long nails tap against the door jamb. 'Don't let on to Michael, right? Oh, and don't forget the duvet covers. Did you do them?'

'Not yet.' She lays the sweatshirt on Ross's bed. Moves to the door. 'Sorry, Hannah. Can I get . . .'

'And the police definitely haven't phoned either?'

'Nope.'

She heads back downstairs. Click-clack, click-clack. Hannah following. What was the point in her coming up? The woman is hovering. Not passing, not quite in the road. Justine is not sure if she's supposed to speak, or bustle silently in the background. Up till now, they've not really been alone together. Ross was their wee buffer, but nursery started back yesterday. Bizarrely, the Easter holidays have already been. Before Easter. Justine gropes for conversation, safe phrases that will ingratiate her – but not involve much input.

'Your house is really nice, Hannah.'

'Thanks.'

'It's a funny place but, isn't it?'

'Pardon?'

'Kilmacarra, I mean.'

'I'm not following you?'

Aye you bloody are.

'All those stones and that. Having them right outside your door; it's a bit creepy, no?'

'No.'

'Mm.' She tries again. 'Did folk live there, then? Was that their houses?'

She hears a *pfuh* or a sneer; there is unpleasantness, certainly, in the noise Hannah makes. Then: '*No.*'

The colours from the skylight skip across Justine's toes. They've arrived at the foot of the stairs. Her hand rests on the wooden acorn at the banister's end. Banister's End. There was a book in Hannah's bedroom called Something's End.

'No,' Hannah says again. 'They're more like monuments.' She puts her notebook on the hallstand. 'Folk didn't live here. They'd move about, I think, but come back here at special times.'

'Like church at Christmas?'

'They didn't have Christmas then.'

'I know that. I mean, coming home. Going to places you always went to, because your family did.'

'Yeah.' Hannah considers this, her pretty mouth turning. 'That's quite a good way of putting it. The glen's definitely been a gathering place at one time. Lots of different people have passed through here.'

'Yeah. Mhairi told me all that too. Crannogs and kings. You should write a leaflet.'

'What?'

'Well, I was just thinking.' An idea is growing itself, and is emerging, and is fully formed. When she prods it, Justine revels in her complicated brain, how it rises to the occasion and frequently reminds her: she is not thick. 'The archaeologists and that – what you were just saying. When you were going on about the windfarm—'

'I'm not "going on" about anything—'

'Yeah, but if you wrote it all up for a wee booklet, you know, stuff about the stones, walks round the glen, all that kind of history stuff, you could maybe sell it.'

Hannah flicks her golden hair. 'I write books, Justine. Not booklets.'

The wood under her fingers feels hard, but when you press down with the ragged edges of your nails, there is a soft, pleasing give to it. Justine is making the petal-shapes of her ideas with her nails. And not imagining it is Hannah's face.

'So,' she changes tack, 'why don't you like this windfarm, then?'

'What? It's not just me – loads of us are against it.'

'But why?'

'Because . . . well, they're ugly. And inefficient. They industrialise the countryside . . .'

'But Michael's for it?'

'Michael's for toeing the party line.'

'Even though the folk that live here don't want it?'

'Some do.'

'Like Michael?'

Hannah makes that same curt noise. 'Michael will do whatever he can to make the best of all possible worlds. He is "open and receptive to all points of view" – it says so on his campaign leaflet. I think it's a Church of Scotland thing: you must never give a definitive opinion on anything.'

'Except God.'

Hannah stares, as if she's just noticed her for the first time. Her mouth gives a sad, wry ripple. 'Indeed.'

'So how come he's not a minister any more?'

'Sorry.' Hannah wipes her finger over the dado rail in the hall. 'Sorry, Justine, but this is really filthy. Did you not think to dust here?'

See those long nails? You could just rip them out her fingers. Poke her in the eyes with her own painted nails.

'Well, there's been quite a lot *to* dust. I will get round to it, don't worry.'

She can hear her heartbeat in her ears. It's so quiet when Hannah stops yakking. She can hear Hannah's breathing too. Their eyes lock, point-to-point, until Justine breaks the awkward post-stairs stance. She will finish off in the lounge, be busy and useful. Will she fuck as like dust the *day*-do.

'Just going to make a quick coffee,' says Hannah at her back. 'You want one?'

'Eh . . . sure.'

Yet again, the woman wrongfoots her. And follows her. They both end up in the lounge, where Justine has the Hoover plugged in already. Proof, thank God, of her intentions.

'Oh great. You got the fire to light.'

'Aye. It was a bit of a struggle. I think the kindling's damp.'

'Mm. We don't usually light it till the evening.'

'Oh. Sorry.'

'No, it's fine. No worries.' Hannah runs her finger along the mantelpiece.

'I've still to dust there too.'

'Yes.'

She slides her foot on to the Hoover. But the notion's niggling at her, it's taking on a life of its own and she's buggered if this woman's going to ignore her.

'But you could, though.'

'Could what?'

'I was just thinking: if you did really want to stop that wind-farm, would that not help? If you could show folk about the real place? There's all the stones, and there's that cave—' she bites down on her lip. 'I mean, there must be all sorts of hidden stuff. For tourists and that.' Disconcerting this; talking over your shoulder to the disembodied mistress of the house. All she can hear are bracelets jangling. 'You could even get a website.'

'A website?'

She's heard Hannah use the same sing-song tone with Ross. 'So,' says Hannah. 'Your references? How we doing with them?'

It appears Justine's idea is dismissed. The front door opens; Hannah floats off to the hall. Justine gives up on the Hoover. It can wait till madam leaves. She hears Michael's voice. 'So. That's those archaeologists arrived.'

Hears Hannah snip, 'Euan's just the same, thanks for asking.'

'I know. I went in to see him on the way to my meeting, Hannah. Do you want to tell me what's going on? Why? Why would you do this?'

'And why would you assume I had any involvement?'

Justine is not remotely interested in their fights. Is this fighting? Michael is pained, and Hannah pecks. She'd heard them last night too, after Ross was in bed, and she'd snuck to her basement room – *But you're welcome to join the family in the evening, Justine. If you like.*

Footsteps outside her bedroom. Finally. She'd been bracing herself for 'the chat', expecting Michael for the last two days. Had been preparing a cover story, embellishing it, all the coloured patches, a full service history one careful lady owner. So easy, too, to invite the opening, for Michael to go: *You never told me you were a nursery nurse*, and for her to embroider something fanciful, explain 'Myra' as a desperate hook flung out to *help* you, *Michael. I could see she wasn't happy* . . .

But no. It had been Hannah, not Michael – and it was not for her, either. Hannah was outside Michael's study (where he must have been all the time, and she'd never even heard him come down), Hannah saying she wanted to get the man from John Muir to speak to the planning committee, and Michael going *you know I can't*. Justine thought it was a man called John Muir, but clearly not. 'Please don't do this, Hannah.' And Hannah swearing, 'Oh for Christsake, Michael.' Flouncing off. Sounds like she's doing the same thing now.

'Still. As long as it helps your writing,' Michael is saying, quietly.

'It's my job. It's my bloody job.'

'Oh we know that.'

'And you still haven't sorted those bloody posters.'

The voices stop. A door slams loudly.

It is nothing to do with her.

Chapter Nine

Hannah Anderson is hiding by a standing stone. No, she's leaning on it, that's all. In the same way she has not been hiding in her room until Michael and Justine left the kitchen. Without being shown, Justine has located all the crockery, she knows which cereal Ross likes best, and is a demon with the Hoover. Hannah opens her phone, texts Euan. *How sore r u now? Tell them if u need more med. C u soon, sweetie xx.* He'll not like the kisses, but tough.

Justine Arrow. What kind of a name is that? *Ooh, just write a wee booklet instead of a book.* From a woman with a certificate in wiping bums and making macaroni pictures. If she even has qualifications. The girl left a bright-red bra on the clothes horse this morning, and Hannah's Crème de Mer's been sampled too: a swirling gouge in it that is far too greedy for her. (36 double D, that bra. It was hung label-side out.) Of course she's used to her home being full of strangers. Years of being a minister's wife does that. *Bring me your hungry* . . . But there's a feeling of collusion about this one; a joke or a secret she's not in on. The way Michael had a go at her; Justine must have heard. Twice now, he's done that. Michael does not shout. He knows nothing about catharsis.

Knife in, and – twist. Ah. That's better. Haven't felt guilty for . . . ooh, fifteen minutes?

She fingers her notebook. Why is getting some archaeologists up here so bad? Or writing in the hospital for that matter? Sitting, staring at her half-sleeping boy, she has to do something. With one hand, she strokes Euan's cold arm. With the other, she writes. Why is that unmotherly? Whatever she does, it seems to be wrong. Michael's still going on that she didn't take Ross to hospital on Monday; that she'd not got him till she was on her way home. *But why Hannah? After we'd agreed?* She wants to roar at the sky. Ross is only little; not an irritant, not at all – she hates how Michael looks at her when she tries to explain. That it can sometimes be too much. She just couldn't cope with Ross in tears and his brother semi-conscious, and all the nurses and the doctor talking at her. Not on her own. She'd a feeling, too, that Michael would fail to appear. St Michael of the perpetual predictability has become anything but. He looms, then quivers, recoils, then ravishes. (Fair enough, she's not complaining about that last one. But where is his head? Where is her Michael?)

And then, in the midst of it all, she comes home to find he's adopted Justine bloody Arrow. Jesus. Wouldn't anyone weep?

Of course, Hannah can take the credit for her entire broken family. *Look on my works ye mighty* . . . Crumbling man; tight-buttoned baby; wilfully speeding son who neglects to wear reflective stripes. It's all your own work. You must be so proud.

No.

And was it worth it, Hannah?

No.

But did you come alive? When your lover loved you on those dull afternoons?

She'd felt less dead, put it that way. Oh, that sounds so glib, and it's not. She's not. She was sleepwalking on to razor blades.

Gil was an English teacher. Hannah had being doing a series of poetry sessions at an arts centre in Glasgow. He'd waited at the end of one of her workshops, invited her to talk to his Higher class at school. 'I'm sure we can manage some Live Lit funding too. Your poems are so insightful. I think they'll really speak to the kids.'

Yes. Pass the sick-bucket.

Gil was dark and defined. Ross was two years old, and still a surprise. Gil's face was angular, unknown, he wore fitted floral shirts. Hannah had been a wife for fifteen years. A minister's wife. Such a rubbish gig. You never possess your husband fully. He has claims on him far more important than you. He is a respected community leader, a beacon, an example. You are his sensibly-clad helpmeet: an infinite supply of patience and sacrificial smiles. You don't mind the groups and endless meetings. The Sudanese family who sleep in your lounge for six weeks. The cakes you bake badly for the fundraising for causes that are good. Your children's needs being superseded by the needs of everyone else. You must be quietly human, never contravene nor contradict. He is . . . whisper it . . . *holy*. Your home is not your own, it is open house and you, too, must be always open.

She'd grown faded. Poured herself into nice clothes and 2-D poems until she was ripe for the picking. Obvious. Gil spent his day doing interpretations; Hannah was no mystery to be described. She was a latter-day Madame Bovary. In her sad defence, she stumbled into infidelity. Gil was younger, not much, but enough that it added gloss, made it improbable, in the beginning, that this was anything other than harmless flirting. Tender partings, a hand too long on top of another. The listening *to her*. Gil was a consummate listener. They had talked about books (again;

textbook), their lives, their pasts, their presents, their aspirations, before arriving at desires. If you plotted it out, you'd see the story arc: narrative tension building, the dramatic spikes, the twist leading to inevitable denouement. The End.

She never did get paid for that first session.

Michael was told by a friend, a concerned parishioner who was for ever snuffling round the edges of their lives. Hannah can't remember her name, only that she had badly dyed yellow hair that sprung from the crown in a series of stripes: darkest, darkish, light. That is the only distinctive feature Hannah can remember (thus proving how dark her soul is). Maybe she was bloody Myra? No. It wasn't that. Agnes? Angie? She was an art teacher at the school, Gil's school, no, of course Hannah hadn't known that, but there you go. It is a bald, unyielding fact, as is the evening when Hannah left Gil's car for hers, both parked up in the staff car park and Mrs Stripy-Head had been shaking out her paintbrushes or dust sheets, oh but she could have *said*. She could have shown herself, declared her hand and threatened the worst. That would have been all it took. Right there, in that instant, Hannah would have stopped. She would have humiliated herself, sunk grass-reddened knees to the asphalt playground and prayed for mercy, discretion, a modicum of kindness, let he who is without sin . . . Oh God, anything to keep from hurting Michael. She would have punched Gil's lights out as proof, ridden naked through the town.

But no. The serpent slid away, straight to Michael's ear. Whispering secrets, which he brought home with him. Presented at Hannah's feet. Hannah can't stop remembering his face; how it seemed to darken and die in front of her. Seeing what she had broken there made her sick. To have wounded him so publicly.

And for such a . . . for nothing, really. Some ridiculous head-rush to validate she was still extant. She would have been as well getting a new haircut – or a tattoo. Either thing would have provided the same transitory high, and neither would have crucified their marriage. Beside Michael, Gil was ridiculous. Deep down, Hannah suspects that's why she chose him. But this only magnified the sin, to the point she could – can – no longer look at Michael, is constantly furious with him, when in reality she is furious with herself.

Moving away was a condition of repair. She would have done anything then, to make it better. They were talking properly at that point, when they weren't crying. Unified almost. Both shamed: the way they held their heads outdoors, the looks they flinched from, then ignored. They were raw, they were oozing honesty. And when he'd said – unbidden – that he no longer wanted to be a parish minister, she'd seized his hands and kissed them.

She thought they'd be all right.

Kilmacarra is their fresh start. Everything fresh: the air, job, people, them. The purposeful silence. A brittling. Michael's new, hopeful career bleeding into the patterns of the old. Now he's invited another cuckoo to their nest. Justine. A watchful, burgundy cuckoo, with the exact same violent shade of hair that Hannah used to have. Does he even remember that? Justine who? From where? There's still no sign of references.

You can tell she's a nursery nurse, though; she has that firm, solid way of managing them all. A glue of sorts. Food on the table, Ross washed and dressed. Ross giggling at some puppet she's made from socks. And she keeps asking after Euan, as if she's genuinely concerned. What must she think of the Michael and Hannah roadshow? More like Punch and Judy. Hannah's face feels hot. The archaeologists were Mhairi's idea, not hers. Six months ago, when rumours of the windfarm started filtering in. OK. As soon as Hannah had read the committee reports and told her, in a worried what-do-you-make-of-that way; when she should have talked to Michael. She cannot bear this. He was her best friend.

She checks her mobile. No reply. Hopefully Euan's sleeping. It's worse when she isn't with him. Then you're free to imagine: that he's shouting for you; they've forgotten to feed him; he's died in the night and nobody said. But his dad will be going shortly – unless the lovely Justine is distracting him. From here, Hannah can see the bonnet of Michael's car. So he's not left yet. Euan loves his dad, and vice versa; not that either would admit it. They are both fine examples of Scottish maledom: emotion is for jessies (and football) only. But she shouldn't have screeched about the posters; it was only last night he offered to do them. After telling her to get stuffed about the environment people, mind. Michael had waited a while, then come up to the kitchen to find her.

'Why don't you go to bed?'

'I will when I've finished these.'

Very gently, he'd pushed away the reward posters, taken the pen from her hand and replaced it with a glass of water. 'I'll do them tomorrow.'

'What if we don't find them?' she'd said. 'What if we never get the person that did this?'

'Does it matter, though?'

'Yes! The bastards left him lying there. Don't you see that?'

He didn't answer, only held her.

*

She cannot believe there are no witnesses to her son's accident. Or culprits caught. Who phoned the ambulance? Why did they not stay with her boy? Because they are the ones that hit him. Had to be had to be had to be. She presses her face into the standing stone. It is cool and smooth. It is fine. It's fine. Euan is alive; he's safe. But the bastards left him lying by the road. Michael copes by giving. He always has. If he's tired, he'll offer someone else his bed. Hungry? Have his chips. If Michael is busy, then he's needed. If he's needed, then he needs Hannah less.

She slides off the boulder she's been sitting on, brushes her backside. From the shadow of the standing stone, she retrieves a shopping bag, one of those thick plasticky 'green' bags-for-life (that are probably not green at all). In it are three audio books and a flask of butternut-squash soup. Ailsa's house is next to the old Trinity Hotel, tucked down a wee vennel like it's a secret. From her bedroom, though, she has a fine view of the glen. Ailsa's son answers when she chaps the door. He looks exhausted.

She smiles, wanly, lifts up the bag like it's an apologetic shrug. 'How's things, Terry?'

'Not so bad. How's your boy doing?'

'Och, he's fine. Bones mend . . . Can I go up?'

'Best not,' he says. 'We didna have a good night.' He nods at the bag. 'Is that stuff for Mum? She canna really eat cakes now.'

'It's soup.'

'Ah.'

'And I brought a couple of CDs. Book CDs. I know how she loves her reading.'

Ailsa had invited her to join the local book group, the week they moved in. She was a long, thin woman with beautiful cheekbones. Wore her grey hair in a spill down her back. Hannah had recently shorn it, to make it easier to wash.

'Cheers.' He takes the bag, but doesn't move from behind the door.

'Are you sure you wouldn't like me to sit with her a while? Give you a wee break?'

He shakes his head.

'It's no bother.'

Terry's eyes glisten. 'No. I'd rather not. I don't know—' He begins to cry.

'Ssh.' Hannah takes his hand. 'I understand. You want it to be you two, eh? Look, will you tell her I called round?'

'I will, I will. Thanks.' The door shuts gently, the glimpse of room within narrowing, narrowing. Gone. She looks up at the bedroom window, gives a wee wave just in case. Sometimes, Terry props her up on pillows, so she can see their flat, wide sky.

A white sun hangs there, behind the grey. It isn't too cold. Hannah's head is tight, she craves big spaces. She will walk to Crychapel Wood, where the sky is huge and open. There's always an ache about the place, as if the land has gone to sleep. She'll walk and walk until it comes right. The steady, meditative pace will focus her on her story, which is now two chapters behind schedule. (Hannah likes to write in word-counted chunks.) En route, she can see where the archaeologists have set up camp. She comes back round the side of the old hotel, shields her eyes to look up the brae. Mhairi reckoned they'd focus on Mary's Well, but the hillside is clear.

Crychapel's on the far side of Kilmacarra village, near the primary school. It's playtime; wee bodies skip and twirl in front of the low grey stone, two pointed dormers sentinel over their charges. A line of solar panels gleam between the dormers. She sees a boy grab a smaller one under his arm, gripping his head. It's that Johnny Green again. He signals to his friend to kick the younger kid's bum, tapping really, but enough to make the wee one cry.

'Hey!' shouts Hannah. 'Leave him alone!'

All three children turn and run.

'I'll tell your teacher!' she calls. Johnny stops, sticks two fingers up at her. Lovely. Ross will be going there next year. She walks on, trying not to think about it. From the moment they go to school, you kid yourself it's fine, healthy even, that the cord's being clipped. They are gaining independence; it's what you made them for. But the first time Euan toddled home going 'The teacher says we've to do it this way', it hurt. Then, the playing with friends-you-do-not-know, the stabilisers off so they can pedal further, faster. The *Just out!* replies to *Going where?* The slamming doors and silent shrugging. The distance. You imagine every sort of harm and desolation, whenever they are ten minutes late, or not where they say they are. For a heart-flinch, you feel the fear, and you push it down like sick. Because your job is to look after them.

Euan is going to be fine. She needs to stop mithering. Lose herself in the book. Or chuck it altogether. If she said, the TV folk would probably shift the deadline. It's only provisional, nothing has been promised. But what if this is her one big chance and someone else comes along with a better, similar story? And she doesn't want to let folk down.

The track past the school is empty. Crychapel Wood sits on the far side. It's an odd name, for there is no chapel, and very little wood. Only a scatter of trees, enclosing the circle of stones. These are not the majestic pillars of Stonehenge, mind. They are humps, no more than waist height above the ground. In the middle, it's all filled in with pebbles and cobbles. Right up until last century the locals called this Crychapel Hill. A wee hill – that's all they thought it was. When the peat was scraped off after the war, Mhairi said they found the remains of a cairn, then discovered the humps of the stone circle sticking through.

'Why would they pile stones on top of their circle?'

'Put it out of action? Seal it up? Either that or preserving the power.'

Hannah had laughed at her. 'What "power"?'

Mhairi hadn't answered. 'Anyway. Look at this.' She pretended she was indifferent to the place, but she wasn't. It had been infectious. Mhairi leapt like a skittish kid, pointing and oohing. *Look! See there? And what d'you make of that?* The northernmost stone has a spiral carved on it. Mhairi said that was to do with sun worship. It isn't even a circle any more – the stones on the east side are long gone, taken by builders and farmers. One must have broken while being shaped into a millstone, abandoned, half-carved where it lies today. Hannah had pushed her finger into the millstone's hole, tight and weighted like the inside of a bowling ball. If she goes there now, closes her eyes, that feeling will come back. She will be where life slows and stops, and fine filaments of light are your fingers and the ground, where there is a silent slotting into place of everything, and you are totally alone. There was no birdsong that day, just a hard blue sky and the sound of beetles crawling.

Something jags her. A twig's caught in her hair. It keeps lancing her fingers as she tries to untangle it, jagging and jagging until it tears away. Strands of yellow hair remain on the broken branch. Holly. Bad luck to cut holly. Keeps the witches away – they used to reroute roads rather than chop down holly. Hannah sucks a drop of blood from her thumb. She takes out her notebook. Writes *Witch*. Then writes *Cailleach*, which is the same in Gaelic. A wee blood-smudge covers part of the word.

As she nears the stile into Crychapel Wood, she sees two white vans parked there, by the dyke. Those bloody electricity people. If they even think they're going to put turbines near Crychapel . . . Men's voices float from inside the trees. 'Careful now.' A shout. 'Don't butcher it, John. Slower.'

'Yes, slow it right down. Peg out this section first, like I showed you.'

Four men are crouched inside the circle, sorting through rocks. One is using a pick to ransack a corner of the rubble. *Chop-and-crack, chop-and-crack*. The stones shudder, grey puffs of dust bursting into air.

'Hey!' yells Hannah, scrambling over the wall. 'You can't dig there.' The men stand. They all hold metal in their hands, honed edges glinting. 'Leave it alone!'

She's right at the opening of the circle when a fallen branch snares her ankle. Her pens, notebook spilling from her hand as she trips, falls on one knee.

One of the men comes towards her. 'Are you all right, dear?'

'I'm fine.' Stiffly, Hannah gets to her feet. Her hands sting, her knee smarts. But the embarrassment is worse.

'Here.' The man gives her the pencils he's retrieved from the grass. He's about her height, has ruddy cheeks and gravy-coloured hair that sits in waves. His hands are calloused, cuffed with bright yellow. There is a sheen of healthy sweat about him. She looks towards the others, still watching but pretending to be back at their work.

'Thank you,' she mumbles, brushing herself down.

The man holds out his hand. 'I'm Tom Wilson. Professor. Pleased to meet you Miss . . . ?'

'Mrs. Mrs Anderson. I'm the local councillor's wife.' It sounds absurd, like she is bartering for status. Her grazed fingers shake his.

'Did we give you a fright?'

'No. It's just, I saw you bashing at the stones . . .'

'I'm sorry. But I promise, we're not damaging anything. We're being very careful. Look.' The professor gestures to the circle, strolls from the perimeter towards the centre. Hannah follows, wobbling on to the cobbles which clunk and rattle like hoofbeats under her.

'You're not with the electricity people, are you?'

'We're a dig. An archaeological dig.'

'Here? I thought you'd be working up at Mary's Well?'

'Yes, we intend to. But we wanted to spread over two sites; make it worth our while.'

'But there's nothing here, surely? They dug it all up after the war.'

'They certainly cleared it in the twenties, exposed the cairn and so forth. But that was primarily for fuel – and agriculture. As far as we know, there's not been any significant archaeology done on the actual site itself.' The professor kicks at the carpet of pebbles. 'Under the cairn stones, I mean. We're very interested in what lies beneath these little beauties. We're just removing a section at the moment, if you'd like to see?'

Hannah would. But in private. She doesn't want these people here. 'I don't think you should. What if it . . .' She circles her foot, rubbing where it throbs. 'I don't know. It just seems like

isturbing it to me. We're trying to keep this whole glen as it is,
ot destroy it even more.'

'Oh, everything we move will be numbered and labelled, I
romise.'

'No, I don't mean that. It's just, this is a special place. I think
ou should leave it alone.'

'But how much more special would it be if we knew more
bout it? Who knows what else is buried under here? Aren't you
urious?' Tom Wilson smiles. Properly, showing large, ivory
eeth.

'Hoi, Tom!' A man waves his trowel at them.

'Excuse me a minute. Won't be a tick.'

'I'm a writer, you see,' she calls. 'I'm writing about this place.'
t comes out desperate and childish.

'Tom. Come and see this, will you!' The shouting is more
nsistent.

'A writer?' says the professor. 'Well. How can you resist?'

They hurry over to the group, the archaeologists all babbling at
once.

'It's a cist of some sort.'

'No, it looks too small.'

Tom Wilson surveys the chink of paler stone that shines under
the cobbles.

'Well, smooth it away. Carefully. Graeme, are you noting this
down? Take your time. I want the location sketched exactly.'

The man has cleared the cobbles carefully to one side. Now he
begins to ease the earth away with the tiniest of trowels and
brushes. The stillness sinks a shade deeper. Nobody speaks as they
stand in a ring, watching him unwrap the corner of what is a slab.
Scrape. It becomes a box. Scratch. Scrape. Clink. Scrape. Becomes

a stone shoebox without a lid. *Uneasy thrill* . . . Treasure, secrets . .
Hannah reaches for her notebook.

'What is it?' she asks. 'You said a cist?'

Swallowing and focusing. A little bile comes into her mouth.
Burn of bile – she writes that down too.

'Hmm. Yes. Oh, this is exciting.'

'What's a cist?'

The professor is distracted. 'Hm? A container, a chest. OK.
No, Graeme. Wait. Another photo please.'

'A container for what?'

But she knows, really. This is perfect.

'Remains, most likely.'

The shadow of an owl swoops over them. Hannah sees the
glint of one massive yellow eye, feels almost like a god.

Chapter Ten

'There you go, Michael. I thought you might be hungry.'

There is a strange woman in Michael's house. An emollient. It is nice how they can run on wheels around her. She sets down a plate of soup, and a sandwich cut in triangles. Things are being done, useful things. She untangles and sorts. His jaw is becoming unclenched. It's the most pleasant feeling.

She puts down his plate. 'I'm away to get Ross.' Slips off. It's late afternoon. He ate his fill at the council buffet anyway, but doesn't like to say. Michael flexes his fingers, feels the blood. There has been no Ghost whatsoever since Justine came. He feels . . . well, he feels good again. In control. All the same, he swallows a couple of Panadol. Better to avoid the headaches before they start. Come on, come on. He wriggles his fingers harder, waits for the energy to flow.

Some meat stews in a pot. Smells good. He inhales the woody fragrance of thyme, and thinks of the cedar fireplace in his office at the council, which still gives off the scent of fresh-cut wood, even though it must be a hundred years old. Big chunky pillars, with an age-spotted mirror above. He loves it there, with his flock wallpaper and his big desk. A cosy nook in which to carry out the business of the day. It makes his meetings feel important, and his

meet-ees grateful. It's even comfier than his office here at home.
Like a sanctum.

Not today, mind. Donald John McCall summoned him for a
'chat'. When the Leader of the Council calls, you jump. Councillor
McCall's fireplace is enormous: a huge and ostentatious stone
mantel. It is post-modern Gothic, the tourist brochure said. Yes,
tourists come to the council chambers sometimes, when they do
Doors Open Day. Take in the cabinets, the fancy stairs, the florid
portraits.

'Have a seat, son.'

Donald John was at school with his dad, has been instrumental
in finding this niche for Michael, so he tells himself 'son' is a sign
of affection.

'This whole windfarm fandango is growing arms and legs, eh?'

'Mm.'

'Renewables, renewables, Michael. That's oor mantra, eh?
All anyone bangs on about now. Schools, houses, roads: you
get laughed out the park if you put them before the great god
Wind.'

'I know. I'm sorry. But the other night, I had to leave—'

'Aye, your boy. All sorted, is he?'

'Well . . .'

'Scotland's fastest-growing energy source, wind.'

'Yes.'

'Still no fast enough. Can I remind you that the government –
our government, mind – has a target of one hundred per cent
renewables by 2020? Even if that means foresting every hill, moor
and sea with the whirly buggers . . .'

'I know. I understand.'

'Good lad.'

For an SNP-led local authority to fail to push through an SNP-approved flagship key-plank policy, green-revolution future-deal windpowered whatever-they-call-it, is political suicide. If the independence referendum succeeds, but this windfarm fails, well, it's a no-brainer. The ship will sail without him. There will be no place in Free Scotia for a promising start who stutters to a stop.

The referendum is only months away. He cannot thole that there's the promise of something he's wanted all his life so close, and that it might come to pass, and that he could miss it. Michael has done everything correctly. He has leafleted and campaigned. He has orated, counselled, schmoozed, borne witness. His party are top-dogs, after so many hungry years. They are the breath of change. Folk aye say they like change: they are frequently daft enough to vote for it. But he's learning that, when push comes to shove and the promise of the bright new world you were elected on becomes hard fact and brass tacks, they all revert. Nimbies and naysayers, the lot of them.

Now his own wife seeks to thwart him. Humiliation. It wakes him at night, like trees tapping on the windows, like the nagging sense of things not done, of things undone, of wrong, of wrong . . . Michael clutches his spoon. He is calm. He is sitting in his kitchen. Concentrate, Michael. You have sensible problems. You have an unwell son who needs you to be strong. You have matters of state with which to deal. A referendum looming. Scottish Independence. Important, real things. Any time his confidence wavers, he simply turns on the news. Looks at how the government in Westminster is destroying all semblance of social-ism, is crushing anyone and anything that is fragile and speaks of care, not profit, any structure or safety net – no matter how essential – that does not offer value to a rapacious world, and thinks: *you do not speak for me.*

He checks the kitchen clock. No rest for the wicked. But it's good, busy. He's been chasing his tail all day: trees damaging field drains; a neighbour dispute over night-time chainsaws has finally been sorted; he's had a meeting with a lady who wants to open a therapeutic nature and nudist holiday camp (he thinks there may be licensing issues with that one). Michael checks the clock again. Its movements are jerky, automatic and he is taking nothing in, he sees a flash of red, sees a ribbon of blood, it's just a jug, a bit of red glass, sees a blue, blue wing outside. He steadies his breathing. Quick bite of his sandwich. Busy, busy, busy. He wants to snare Euan's doctor before visiting starts. And he'll need to arrange a meeting with these damned archaeologists. Damage limitation. He stands up to get more bread. Sees Ross scampering up the path, waving at him. Michael raises his soup spoon in reply. Those wee stout legs do a mini-haka, then the door opens. Ross launches himself at Michael's knees.

'Daddy! Daddy! I made a bunny face!' Pink tongue poking through a yellow-crayoned mask.

'Woah! That's brilliant, Rossie. Really good. Hello, Justine.'

'Hiya.' Justine leans over the range, stirs the pot. 'Ross, would you like a bit of cake?'

'Ooh-ooh.' He stomps and skips.

'I thought you were a bunny, wee man, not a monkey?' In one fluid move, Justine sorts plate, knife, cake and child. 'Come and give your daddy peace.'

'Are you going to do that brown colour in your head now?'

'Mmhm.'

'Can I help?'

'Nope. Come on now, monkey.'

Quietly, she closes the door on him. Michael sits, stretches out his legs. To eat a meal in peace. This is bliss. Where is Hannah anyway? Upstairs? Out? No matter what she says, he's positive she had something to do with those archaeologists. There's a wee slide to her eyes, a levelling of her mouth when – he chews the dry bread. When she lies. Och, maybe he approached the whole thing wrong. Un-politically. He needs to practise being like Donald John, where every hiccup is an opportunity to convert, cajole, bad-mouth, reinvent, restore. But not confront. *Catch mair bees with honey, son.*

This archaeology thing's been niggling him. If he's honest, a tiny bit of him is sad that he didn't think of it first. He knows Hannah's struggling with her book. Heard her say so to Mhairi. *I don't know who these people are.*

Years ago, when she'd been stuck with a poem, he'd taken her to Tantallon Castle. The poem had been about the sea – any sea, really – but she'd written it in Glasgow. It's not working. It's too . . . passionless. So, this one Saturday he'd got them in the car: Hannah, Euan – who was just a wee tot – and driven east to Tantallon. A majestic ruin, the castle sat clifftop-square to the raging sea. Oh, Michael didn't have words the way Hannah did, but he'd seen spume that day, and silver fishtails and a deep dark pulsing power that rocked and shimmered under the water. By afternoon, the poem was written. As they were driving home, she'd said, 'That filled me up', and leaned over to kiss the side of his face. He'd been going to say something crass like *Oh, I'll do that later, if you don't mind*, because they'd joked like that, in those days. But Euan had been there, and anyway, he'd known exactly what she meant. It's why he prayed.

Michael doesn't know any writers, other than his wife. Occasionally, when they are in Glasgow or Edinburgh, she'll drag him to a book launch or literary event, so he meets the odd one there. Odd being the operative word. But he doesn't know any of these folk, so he can't compare them with Hannah. Do all writers work the same way? For a woman who lives by her imagination, Hannah frequently needs to touch things, smell them, see them. He'd caught her in front of a mirror once, with her hand clasped up at her mouth, as if she was going to punch herself.

Longing, she'd smiled. *I'm trying to see what longing looks like.*

Perhaps the dig could be a good thing. Donald John said nothing about stopping it – and Michael doesn't think he can. It won't interfere with the windfarm; the men are up at Crychapel, which is nowhere near the planned site. In fact, he'll tell Hannah that he doesn't mind. That it's all good. Indeed, it shows transparency on the council's part. He'll arrange a meeting as a surprise, and take her too. Present it as a gift. If digging trenches in Crychapel Wood and hoicking up old bits of pot can make Hannah write well and be happy, if Michael can show he's relaxed . . . Digging up the past will be a good thing. It will be a big bomb of distraction, and he can get on with representing the people's interests. Even if the people rarely know what those are.

Michael set out, twenty years since, to be a good minister. To give the people what was good for them. In that, he failed. Is he going to fail again? He's only following orders. Folk understand that, surely? And it is for the greater good. How can people not see that? How can't she? Without renewables, the world will dry up. No oil, no gas. No heat. No oxygen. His head aches. The clock in the hall chimes quarter to five. Is it that late? The kitchen clock assures him that it is. Visiting's at seven. Dammit. He said he'd do those posters.

Hannah's written several drafts on foolscap, but they're all a bit angry. 'Find the car that hit our son.' That kind of thing. He's worried folk will turn away. People need to care about what's happened to Euan, so they'll help. He puts his bowl and plate in the dishwasher (unsure if the kitchen is now Justine's domain or if Hannah's rules still apply. Michael Anderson: *New man*). There's some cardboard in his study. If he does the posters now, he can go over his transport committee papers at the hospital. Michael pauses on the stair. OK. This is the point the Ghost should appear: 'Reading your papers at hospital, eh? Like Hannah and her writing, eh? But yours is proper work, eh, Michael? Eh?'

He listens hard, but there is only the happy hum of the boiler and bursts of xylophonic chase music from the cartoons Ross is watching in the lounge. Cheered by this good news, he treads the narrow stairs down to the basement. His study is panelled and dim; is perfect for containing all your thoughts. He can climb inside himself here, like he's walking inside his brain. A middle-aged explorer, poking murky corners, disturbing the occasional cloud of birds. So far, the Ghost has not visited him here either. Justine's room faces his study. Outside her door, he hesitates. It is not quite shut, he can see her towelling her hair. It's one of the turquoise towels Hannah keeps for guests. Should he say . . . He blinks. Her back is naked. Shaped like a violin. Oh.

Oh.

Why did she come here?

He could just ask her, he could just say what is your game or who *is* Myra but it has been calm, so calm in the manse and the nice food, his shirts are clean and when he goes too deep it hurts. For the present, he will skate lightly on the surface of his life. Ask no questions, tell no lies. Justine is beautiful. It makes him happy just to look at her. Not with desire. No. She is a hungry soul, with capable blue-white shoulders. If there's any point the Ghost will rise up, it will be . . . NOW! Whispering temptations in his ear. He steels himself. Feels a well of peace. The Ghost has gone. It was a blip brought on by overwork, that's all.

He watches Justine rummage in her wardrobe. Reaching far into the back, mouth moving like she's counting. He turns away, to give her privacy. Gathers up the transport file from his desk. Gets out the cardboard, slams a few drawers. Returns to the little hallway that separates them, waits a moment, then chaps the door.

'Justine?'

'Yes?'

'Would you mind giving me a hand with some posters? Hannah asked me, but I'm a bit pushed for time . . .'

'Sure. Be up in a minute.'

'Great. We'll do them in the kitchen, eh?'

He goes up, fills the kettle. Feels light and high. The coloured china on the dresser gleams, the sky outside is polished from the rain. His son will – is – getting better. He is a fortunate man. His wife is beautiful. He should relax.

Justine's hair looks darker when it's wet. He switches on the kettle. 'Tea?'

'Sure.'

The house is very still. Ross's cartoons are muted. Michael goes through, opens the door to the lounge. 'All right in there?'

Ross nods, eyes glued to the screen. He keeps the door open. Justine has poured the water on to the tea bags. 'You take sugar, don't you?' Spoon poised already above the cup.

'Please. One. I thought we could use a photo,' he says.

'Sorry? Of what?'

'Euan.'

She blanches. It touches him she's so upset for his son.

'Why?'

'To try and get some witnesses?'

'For what?'

'For the accident? We're making posters about Euan's accident.' He lays out the coloured card. Justine's in the middle of drinking her tea, and it shoots out her nose as she coughs.

'Sorry! Here!' He hands her a piece of kitchen roll. 'You all right?'

She's dabbing her lips. 'Shit. I think I got some on this.' There's a sheaf of papers on the dresser. 'Is that Hannah's book?'

'Is it? I don't know why she's left it up there.'

'*Fool Circle*. By Hannah Anderson.' She turns a page. ' "First step on foreign soil . . ." '

'Better just . . . don't mess up the pages.'

'OK, padre!' She raises her hands, palms up. 'Calm down. I wasny hurting it.'

'No. It's just . . .' Michael copies her gesture. 'It's fine. She doesn't like folk looking at her work.'

'Why? Is that no the point of being a writer?'

'I don't know. Anyway. I thought we could use a picture from here maybe.' He goes to the collage of photos Hannah made. Two decades of his life sparkle and take a bow. 'What do you think?'

Justine fixes on the one photo that has no people in it.

'What's that?' She points at an army of red stones. It is like a thousand Kilmacarras: crops of standing stones that are dotted in sheaves, on every bit of land. A million red spines. You couldn't even begin to count them.

'That's Carnac. In France. We went there on holiday a couple of years ago.'

When Hannah was in the midst of her affair and he did not know.

He peels the picture from the board. 'I think Carnac gave her the idea for the book, actually.' It had been a brilliant holiday, full of wine and sex and laughing. 'So. What about this one?' He chooses a recent school photo, in which Euan is almost smiling.

'Sorry. I thought we were doing stuff for the council?'

'No. For Euan.'

'Are you sure posters are a good idea?' says Justine. 'Should you not just leave it to the police?'

'Hmm. Not that we've even heard from them today.'

'Well, they're probably . . .' she shrugs. 'Busy.'

'Yeah, but it can't do any harm, though, can it? To ask for help.'

'I don't know . . .'

'Please?'

They work quietly, efficiently, reworking the words, choosing the best photo of Euan, going down to the basement to scan it in. Tricky thing the scanner, but between them, they manage. It is a printer-scanner-copier, too many buttons. He keeps it to the side of his desk, half-hidden by an old lectern, a splendid gilded eagle that Hannah picked up for him in a saleroom. Justine seems unimpressed by his study. She fingers the Bible on the lectern, a fat, tissue-papered tome, leather-tooled. He doesn't use that one much. Too delicate. But he likes to breathe the smell of it when he works.

'This where the magic happens?'

'Sorry?'

'All your God stuff. This where you cook it up?'

'I work here, yes. There.' Michael shows her the scanned-in photo. 'Can you put the heading above that, see how it looks? But I told you, I don't preach any more. Oh! That reminds me. Did you want me to dig out the parish records? I think they're stored in the wee vestry in the church. I've got the key in my desk.'

'Nah, you're all right.'

'You sure? It's no trouble. I'm the official keyholder anyway, because we live so close. No one would mind if you had a rummage.'

'I said no.' Justine clears a little space on his desk. 'Ta.' A column of pocket-sized booklets fall over. Several *Your Scotland Your Futures* spatter to the floor.

'Man. You into this pish?'

'Would you like one?'

'Nuh. No way.'

He retrieves the booklets, not sure why she's getting angry with him. 'I'm an SNP councillor, so yes, I am "into it". Definitely. Yes.'

Once upon a time, his religion fed a hunger that was social as well as spiritual, dosing the populace with schools and structure and morals. Country folk like Auld Angus, thousands of them, washed up in teeming city sprawls as industry took hold and the clearances began again. Those wee, quiet, douce folk who were looking for a haven, his kirk gave them magic lanterns and bold missionaries. His kirk was once a sweeping vehicle of change, a pseudo parliament even, in the absence of a real one. Order and community, promises and rules. *In loco parentis*, in God we trust. It gave folk hope for tomorrow. He's not sure it does that any more. But this does. He runs his thumb over the cover of a booklet. He knows this does. He has faith.

He's too tired to launch a mini campaign in his basement though, and it usually causes friction anyway. Despite the painkillers, a band is beginning to tighten across Michael's skull. He fiddles for ages, arranging another photo on the scanner, one of Euan in his running gear in case it'll look more appealing. Eventually, Justine breaks the silence. 'So what d'you do, exactly? What's a councillor?'

He's shocked that a young woman in her twenties doesn't know. He always is. 'Well, you know in the local elections—'

'No.'

'I get voted for by local people, then I work on their behalf at the council. I'm their voice, if you like.'

'Aye, but what do you do?'

How to explain? Does he start with the concept of democracy, or should he boil it down to the basics: *I make sure the holes get filled in the roads.* Pulpit and hustings – that's how his father raised him, so he finds it hard – no he finds it unforgivable actually – that people don't care enough to even understand the how and the why of who keeps their lights on and their streets clean, who builds the schools for their kids and stocks their libraries with books. 'I help run the community, I suppose. We ask the people what they want, then we try to make it happen.'

'Right. So the people wanted this windfarm then?'

'It's complicated.'

Michael continues scanning; his son face-down on the printer.

The headache hovers. This evening, he'll tread softly with Euan. Hannah is too strident – *but you must remember* something. *Try. Try really hard.* Michael will go easy. *Imagine you're on a country road.* Or maybe he won't mention it at all. The boy will remember what he wants to. When it's time.

'Good money, though, eh?'

'Pardon?'

'Council pays more than the church, does it?'

'Slightly.'

'So how come you chucked being a minister then?' Justine is picking her teeth with her thumbnail. 'If it's no the money.'

'Well . . . I still am. On paper. But,' he takes the printed poster from the tray, 'I suppose I felt I was being called in another way. No, that first photo was better, wasn't it? Can you just finish off that heading? Bit darker maybe?'

' "Called"?'

'Mm. You know. That God was pushing me in a different direction. That I could help people in a more . . . practical way.'

'Scamming expenses instead of talking shite?'

He switches off the scanner. 'Do you have a faith, Justine?'

'Nope.' She concentrates on the letters she is writing, going over and over them until they are bold. 'Aye, well I do. Faith in me. That I'll survive. Like a fucking cockroach.'

Her hand continues tracing the letters, he can see the pen nib split the paper. It will go through to his desk. It's antique oak; another Hannah find. 'Here.' He puts his hand over hers, to stop it. 'I think that's probably enough.'

She pulls away. There is a cut there, a scab he hasn't noticed on the back of her hand. The edge breaks, there is blood, blood coming on his skin, from her.

Her hand goes up to her mouth.

'Sorry, padre. I'm not feeling too great. Think I'll have a wee lie-down.'

She leaves him in his study, arranging the faces of his son in a neat pile.

Chapter Eleven

A thousand paper cuts.

Sing yo ho, boys.

Spinning circles and whoosh and scattered headlights. Askit's tongue on her wounds. Leathered man with orange bunnet in a cave, warm cave. Apples, bright and round. She is warm and there is singing.

Let her go, boys.

Hannah is singing Ross a lullaby.

Justine is outside Ross's door. Not dreaming. A slit of light lets her see; see his plugged-in panda light which glows a pale orb around their heads. Mother and child. His sleepy fingers stroke Hannah's hair, twining it across his lips. One fist falls on empty air, and she holds him, his neck protected in the crook of her arm.

Hannah's eye flits. Ross coughs, and is hefted closer to her breast. A tiny moan as he snuggles in. Folds of linen, it will smell of the washing powder Justine used.

Sssh. Sail her homewards.

Justine shuffles back from the light. Finds the stairs which takes her down in slow and silent steps towards the kitchen. She is starving.

*

Justine shoves hair from her eyes. The dye has made it thicker; it feels like a curtain, not her hair. Through steamy windows, she sees the police car door close. The thistled crown above 'Semper Vigilo'. Always watchful. Sleekit bastards.

'OK. Thanks then, officer.' Michael's head bobs at the open front door. He's thinning slightly at the back. 'Yes. No. That's very good of you, really. Give my best to your inspector, won't you?'

She glances at Hannah, who gives a watery smile. 'D'you want more tea?'

'No. Ta.'

Ross tugs her skirt. 'I would like more juice-tea please. Jus-tee.'

'Oh would you? Here.' She pours him another orange juice.

'Joos-tee,' he repeats, giggling. He does a wee dance in front of his mum, who doesn't respond.

'Yeah, yeah. Justi: I get it. Now scram and get your teeth brushed.'

Justine picks up the last of the ironing from the floor. Her wrists feel weak. Man, when those cops came into the kitchen, her first instinct had been to chuck the iron at them, then barrel it out the window. *They will* know. *Check you out. Match you up. Find the money in your room.* Each word rising in steam from her iron. She made herself stay very still, nice and mechanical, barely looking up as she lifted and smoothed and folded. It worked. Camouflage is when you are so much a part of the furniture that they don't even ask your name, and assume you've always been there. Thank Christ she's damped her hair down. Goodbye Burgundy Fizz. She found a dusty packet of mid-brown dye in the store. Combined with the burgundy, her hair is now a nasty shade of nothing. There's no need to be so scarlet here. But, fuck – she needs to ditch that phone.

Michael returns to the kitchen. 'OK. Here's what we're going to do.'

'Michael, I don't want to talk about it. And while we're at it, yes, I did use your bloody photocopier. All right?'

'Hannah. You need to calm down, all right? It doesn't matter. Now, will you listen to what I'm saying?'

Justine goes down to stow the ironing basket in the utility room. Not her business. She has never experienced a *ménage à trois* before; well, she has, but not lived one. It's the most odd sensation. You can take their knickers from the laundry, fold them neatly into piles, but you canny say, '*Ho*. You two need your heads bashed together.' She's like a cobweb round them, a silent, sticky shadow – there, but transparent. How servants must have felt in the olden days. Justine is skilled at not getting involved. Click your brain into neutral and you just get on with it. Watch the fallout from a distance, or focus on the ceiling. They've been sniping all morning, long before the police arrived. Apparently the scanner downstairs has 'haemorrhaged' a cartridge of coloured ink. Michael is insistent that, while he supports Hannah's right to campaign, he doesn't want council equipment used for any protests. They do actually talk like that: 'I support your right'; 'I respect what you're saying'; 'This is not about protest, it's about history.' Such dainty, dainty two-steps. Poor Hannah.

Poor Hannah. Would you listen to her? Having lived with them a few days, though, it's fair to say Michael is a bit of a creeping Jesus. Nice guy; kind, nice guy – but in need of a massive jolt of electricity. He is no advertisement for the joys of the Lord. Rather, he is a gentle sheep: bemused, obliging, scrawny under all that wool, and with a resigned, benevolent stare that makes you furious. He has a face you want to slap. He is fucking with her head.

Michael is refusing to acknowledge their shared lie, and it's driving her mad. He hums and smiles and potters round her, *pass the potatoes please*, writes in his study, stares at his hands. Lets the days roll, content to let it drift. Man, he is not normal. There they were, doing the posters. Perfect opportunity: working side-by-side, a careful selection, peeling photos she didny want to look at off the wall, laying them on the coloured card. They were properly alone for a good stretch of time, and she waited, waited for him to *say*, or bitch about Hannah, his eyesight, his fainting fits – whatever the hell is wrong with him. But it is like none of it has happened. Michael makes her more nervous than Hannah does.

She moves from the utility room to her bedroom. Bone-white windowsill (that is the actual colour, she's seen the tin, some fancy heritage paint at forty quid a pop. It's possible Hannah leaves the stickers on deliberately). From her window, she can see two tree trunks, the roots of a standing stone, and the bottom half of a shed. Ross has asked if they can build a den in there. *Then we can hide*. When she asks from what? he simply shakes his head. Oh, man. Justine needs out of this fraught house. She could be in a posh hotel; a Caribbean cruise. What's the point of having hundreds of pounds stashed away if you canny enjoy it? She's yet to count her money, could've easily laid it out in nice fat slabs, totted it up with glee. But she hasn't. She extracts cash from the rear of the wardrobe like honey from a hive. Head tilted sideways, blind hand grasping. The stupid pink phone sits on her bedside table. She checks that it is off, then stuffs it inside its pouch. They've got her number. Shit. What if the polis had come down here? Found the phone; Christ – found the money? Or if Hannah finds it? A casual sweep inside her wardrobe would harvest you . . . she delves, pulls out a big wad of—

Fifty-pound notes. She sits on the edge of her bed. Fifty-pound notes. They spring out in her hand, the creases of them like little grins. Fifty-pound notes. She thought they were tenners. There were tenners, look, here is a fold of tenners, and another. And . . . no more. One after one, she pulls out the wodges of cash and they are all fifties now. Fifty *pounds* each sheet; she cannot believe it, the smug face of Sir Walter Scott, master tartan-story-weaver, smirking at her, each one is fifty: FIFTY, and here, this is one sole, lonely handful, only ten will make five hundred and she is holding crumples and crumples of them, and there are bundles more behind her jumpers.

Jesus God.

The world feels benign when you have money in your knickers. When that money is stolen, and becomes terrifyingly multiplied, it turns malevolent. If she was frightened of Charlie Boy before, now she is . . . She slams it all back in the wardrobe, vacates her room. She wants to crawl into that cave under the hill. How much has she stolen? Oh Christ. Oh Christ. She sits for a while in the utility room, until the smell of bleach gets too much.

Only Hannah in the kitchen when she comes back up. Justine shakes her hair free of her collar. 'All right?'

You can tell Hannah's been crying. But there's a happy blur to her eyes. 'I'm fine. Thanks.'

'Good.' The telly's off in the lounge. 'Where's Ross?'

'Getting ready. Michael's taking him to the hospital.'

'Oh, right. Good. We were going to do finger-painting actually.'

Hannah shrugs. 'I guess the lure of Burger King was too much for him.' She opens her ever-present notebook. There's a cling-film-wrapped sandwich on the table beside her.

'OK, ladies, that's us away.' Michael claps gloved hands together, every inch the smart businessman in his tweedy coat. He suits it far better than his dog-collar.

Suddenly, Hannah rises from her chair and seizes Michael's face in both hands, kissing him hard. They break apart when Ross bounces in. 'Eugh.' Hannah ruffles his hair, then Michael's. The man is grinning like a loon. 'I'll drop Ross at nursery, Justine.'

'Great. OK.'

'Ross, where's your hat?' says Hannah.

'I posted it.'

Justine opens the back door. Busies herself at the coal bunker. Nobody ever closes it right, coal everywhere, muck trailing in. She kicks the hard black scatter into place with her feet. Secures the little hatch at the front. Forgets she has no boots on. The sky is white and high, there's a bend to the trees. A good day for drying, but she has nothing left to dry. Washing machine's empty. Dishes done. Justine is floundering for something constructive to do and not get in their road and not think of the money. Can he trace it? Say if she spends it all, would he know? No. She is affording him too much credit. Charlie Boy is a doer, not a thinker. His network comprises muscles, genitals and eyes, not brain. Scrunching and scrunching her fists, till her fingernails bite her palms. She'll start on dinner.

In the kitchen, she takes out the meat. They eat too much meat, even if it is organic. Hannah's still there, but contained now; drawn in on herself and frowning at her manuscript. Man, you need a barometer to chart these people's moods. Thank God, *she* is an uncomplicated soul. She boils the kettle. Onions, carrots, stock cube. Justine will never tire of having a pantry. She has plans to rearrange it, so all the dry goods are at the bottom, herbs and spices grouped alphabetically. At the table, Hannah scribbles, coughs occasionally. Lets her work for ten, fifteen minutes, until the smell of hotpot drifts from the stove. Then her nose recoils. 'Is that the lamb?'

'Yes. Is that all right? There was tons of it in the fridge.'

'I was keeping it for tomorrow.'

'Oh. Sorry.'

'It's just – Michael's got a community council meeting in Longbridge tonight. He won't be home for dinner. Can go on till all hours sometimes.'

'Right. Nobody said. Well, it could keep till tomorrow.'

'Mm.' Hannah puts her pen down. 'Thanks for doing those posters by the way. Michael said you put them out.'

'What?'

'Judging by Constables Haud It and Daud It, we'll need all the help we can get.'

'Hannah, I didn't put any posters anywhere.' She moves the pot off the heat. 'I thought Michael had.'

He'd chapped her door last night, when he'd got home. Asked through the wood if she was feeling better, and when she said yes, went: 'Good. I didn't upset you, did I?'

'Nope.'

'Good. Eh, d'you know where Hannah is at all?'

'At Mhairi's maybe? They were both here earlier.'

'Oh. OK. Is she all right? I've barely seen her all day.'

'I think so.'

She's your wife.

'Um . . .' he'd said. 'We'll need to get those posters out soon. I forgot to take them with me.'

'Mm.'

Mm is not a promise; it's just a noise.

Hannah looks as if she might greet again. 'I thought they were done.'

Man. Get a grip, doll. That pearly nose. Soft kissy-lips. She *is* like one of those smooth china things, eyes fluttering as she tilts her head down.

'Hey, don't cry. I'll do it. Don't worry. Where d'you want them to go?'

'I hadn't . . . I thought they were up. That's another day wasted. He told me—'

'Look, my fault, OK? I must have misunderstood.'

'Sorry.' Hannah lays her chin on the table. 'Michael says I've to write, but I'm knackered. Ross didn't sleep well. He's such a good wee sleeper normally. I think Euan being in hospital is really upsetting him.'

'Yeah . . .' Justine flicks through the papers on the dresser, searching for the coloured card. 'There. There you go. We did five. Is that all right?'

She gives one to Hannah. 'We made them a wee bit different. Thought it would look better with a photo on the front.'

ATTENTION! ACCIDENT! REWARD!

Then the slightly fuzzy school photo of Euan below. A tawny, open-looking boy. His unformed face stares hopefully into the future, waiting for the world to come and meet him. It reaches into her, and pulls.

'Oh.' Hannah, too, seems unnerved at the sight of her son. As if the poster is nothing to do with him. 'I don't . . . It's not really what I . . .'

'I know. But Michael thought it would be more eye-catching this way. Less words. I mean, I'd be more likely to look at a picture first than a bunch of words.'

'Yes. I'm sure you would.' Hannah turns it over and over, although there is nothing on the back. 'Where did you get this?'

'The photo? From here – up on the kitchen wall.'

Hannah's almost gone. Eyes shiny; you can see wee bubbles ready to spill.

'He looks like his dad, doesn't he?'

'Mm.' There is a sigh. 'Yeah . . . you're right, actually. No. That's great. The posters are great. Thanks. Well done you.'

'Cheers.'

With the heel of an ink-stained hand, Hannah rubs her eyes. A smear streaks her hairline. 'Right. I think I'll go do some research.' She brightens. 'See what the professor's found today. Michael made me a sandwich, isn't that sweet?' Off she wanders, into the hall.

'Bye then. I'll just put these anywhere, will I?' Justine rolls the posters into a tube. 'How about the bin?' There's a wee fluffy hair bauble lying on the dresser, which she pings round the tube to keep them tight. Then she pokes her hotpot. It's going claggy.

'They've started the dig at Crychapel, did I tell you?' Hannah returns. She's donned pink trainers and her white Puffa jacket. 'They unearthed a burial cist, right under the cobbles. Right when I was there!'

'What's Crychapel?'

'Oh, it's this place: you go through this kind of tree tunnel, you don't even know what's coming, then it spreads out – it's like going into a keyhole, you know? You go down the wee thin bit then into the circle. That's what Crychapel is. A stone circle. Women turned to stone.'

'You're joking?'

She wrinkles her nose. 'Duh. It's an old legend. For dancing with the Devil or something. You should see Mhairi's pictures.'

'She's got pictures?'

'Paintings.' She stresses the first syllable, as if SPEAKING TO THE CRIMINALLY INSANE. 'By the way: did you manage to get those references yet?'

There is always that with Hannah, always the small withdrawal and reassertion of rank.

'They're in the post.'

'Hm.' She touches the notebook, then the pile of typed sheets that lie beside the posters. 'Been having a wee read at my manuscript?'

'What? No.'

'I didn't mean to leave it lying about.'

Oh lady, you don't half talk some bollocks. You put it there, angled outwards, just like you angled Michael's chin in your hands to kiss him. Leaving Justine with nowhere to look at all. She scratches the back of her neck. Hannah's lips are slightly parted. Expectant. *What?* What is Justine supposed to do now?

'Would you like to read it?'

'Oh. Yeah, sure. Maybe later?'

'Sorry.' Hannah rubs her pale-pink trainer on the top of her other foot. Along with the white jacket, she's wearing her sugar-pink trackie bottoms (*Delicates wash, OK, Justine? It's Juicy Couture*). A coy flamingo, bathed in rose-light from the red glass bowl which sits on top of the fridge, and is placed, artfully, to catch the light.

'I don't usually show my stuff till it's done. Work in progress and all that.'

'Jesus.' Under her breath. 'Right. That's me away to do the loos.'

'And you will do those posters?'

'I'll do them! I'll do them in a wee while. I need to . . .' Justine gestures at the mop '. . . crack on.'

Hannah takes the fluffy bauble off the posters, twists it twice round her hair to make a rough ponytail. The carefully packaged roll springs open. 'I'd better get going too.' Beneath the pink, her skin looks dusty. Is she too frail to wield those big heavy posters all by herself? It's a menial task, of course, therefore it falls under Justine's remit.

'Hannah,' says Justine. 'You've a dirty mark on your forehead.'

After Hannah's gone, and the house is hers and she has sat awhile at the kitchen table, Justine gathers up her stuff. She does not want to do this. Outside the manse, she pulls in her stomach, stares at the landscape which spreads wantonly before her. She is trying to feel it, really get whatever it is you're meant to feel when confronted by 'your country'. But it remains just stones and bright sky, and the shush of sparkling trees. Nice to look at, aye, but how come it makes folk crazy? Michael and his skirly pipes and 'freedom', Hannah with her stories. Now the woman's into old bones as well. Thinks these archaeologists are going to rescue Kilmacarra. From what? Justine screws up her eyes, trying to picture turbines on the hill. Bit of a whishy sound – not much different to the trees probably – a few eerie white arms going round and round. So what? Will they no be just one more creepy protrusion coming out the glen?

There's a thud at her feet as something falls. The bloody posters. She snatches at them, spears the roll deeper into her pocket. She could just say she lost them, or that she did put them up, but someone must've taken them down. Or she forgot? Aye, right. To refuse to distribute them would look even more suspicious. Like when Michael suggested using Euan's photo and she wanted to shout *please no*. She must show willing. Not that she's staying. She can't. But, oh man, she'd like to. Settle in that big house, sit at the oak table. Wear Juicy Couture and clack around the place. Nah. Not the pink pants, though. Forget that bit.

Ooh – you want to read my fabby book? Well, you can't, so fuck you.

No. Fuck you.

Justine has no idea if Hannah keeps a back-up copy of her manuscript – which is still splayed on the dresser – but she is very tempted to stuff the whole wad of rubbish in the stove. *Oh Justine. You managed to get the fire lit. Well done you.* The actual thought of it warms her, like a hard red coal. When she leaves, that may be her parting gift. Aye, and when is it you're leaving now, Justine? Now that you know the expensive, expansive magnitude of your death sentence? He will. Charlie Boy will kill her for this, and he will do it slowly. She narrows her eyes, lets the light slide past as she watches the drift of the air balloon.

Turbines this high!!

They're tearing it up! Killing them off!

They're closing it down! The ice is melting . . . melting!

Folk who get upset about crap must have no real problems to worry about. That's why they expend their energies on worthy campaigns. Justine does not get all the angst. Same with this independence bollocks. Who cares? Two years of noise and soapbox ranting already. It's like you're finding something to worry about. When is it going stop? (Well, after the referendum, obviously; only it won't, because then there'll be the post-mortems and the promises, the agonies and ecstasies.) Who cares? What normal folk care about is: have you got enough food to eat, are you safe? Can you afford a new telly, and can you get the bastards next door to turn theirs down? Justine is proud to say she's never voted in her life. Bastards never listen to you anyway.

'The bastards!' she yells, a sudden rush of energy sending her running, faster and faster round the stony silence, arms thrust out like wings.

'Feel better?' A sarky voice from behind.

'Yes, thank you.'

'You decided to hang about then? No Ross with you the day?' Mhairi is flapping out a tablecloth at the door of the café.

'Up at the hospital.'

'Where you off to?'

Justine thrusts her hands in the pockets of her borrowed coat. 'Just a walk. I'm putting up some posters for Hannah. How?'

'Is that no Michael's jacket you've got on?'

'Aye. I'm wearing Hannah's knickers too.'

'Funny wumman.'

'Amn't I just?'

'Gies a poster for the café, then. In fact; wait there. You can do me a favour.' Mhairi nips inside, emerges with a clutch of folded papers. 'Gonny put these out too?'

It's a leaflet. 'Crannogs and Kings' is printed on the front, in shades of green and blue.

'Good, eh?'

Justine is speechless.

'Hannah's idea. Rattled them out last night. I did the photies and sketches; Hannah wrote up the words. Just like that, off the cuff.'

She is aware of pulsing in her inner ear. Nipping the bridge of her nose with finger and thumb.

'Right wee cottage industry, aren't we? I don't know why we didny do something like this ages ago.'

The back of her eyeballs prickle. Justine flips the leaflet over. Reads the last paragraph out loud: ' "Soon, all this wonder may be despoiled by the coming of a massive windfarm. Please add your voice at www.noturbinesintheglen." For *fucksake*.'

'I know! You can just buy websites off the internet. It's mental. I'm gonny do one for the café too.'

'Mhairi, this was my idea.'

'Eh, I don't think so.'

'It fucking was—'

'Ho! Language! You talk like that in your nursery?'

She feels her cheeks go hot. Squeezing off the throbbing. Moving her feet, but they are going all wrong, squinty.

'Right, Miss Potty Mouth. You can put these in the shop and the hotel. I've left some in the café, and I'll take a load to Lochallach. I have business there,' Mhairi mutters darkly. She divides the pile she's holding, thrusts one half on to Justine. 'I'm shutting up early. Oh, for God's sake. What's the matter? You look like someone's stole your scone.'

Justine shakes her head. This jacket is far too big for her; it must look stupid. Her spike-heeled boots are sinking into damp grass. She stabs them deeper. A pop of mud.

'Why you even bothering about this shite?'

'It's not shite.'

'I mean, who cares? It's not even your hills, nobody fucking owns them; they don't do anything. So what if there's some stupid windmills on them?'

'I care.' Mhairi buttons her coat across her massive bosom. 'You're right: nobody owns them, so how come a bunch of outsiders can come and change the place we live in, and make money off of us. Us, no them. It's our community – and naebody asked us.'

'Nobody ever asks you anything. Christ, what planet d'you live on?'

'Same one as you, you cheeky – oh, hello Miss Campbell.'

'Oh, hello there. It's yourself.' A spindly old dear waves her walking stick at them. She totters, returns the stick to the ground. Rests her hands on the top. A sweet, pink face, lemon-coloured raincoat. 'That you shutting up?'

'Aye. I'm away to catch the ten to.'

'Off shopping, is it?'

'Aye. No Effie the day?'

'Ach, it's her veins again.' The old lady beams at them, her wee nose snuffling. 'Thought I heard shouting ben the café?'

'No, no, we're all closed up.'

'Oh.' She sucks her teeth. She is the perfect pocket-granny. Give her a shawl and a Werther's Original and you're away. 'Who's this then? You the lassie fae the manse? Lovely to meet you. I'm Margaret.' Behind her specs, milky eyes blink. 'Was your hair not more . . . funny, before?'

Justine is being assessed through net curtains. *Would you look at the state o' that.*

'Suits you better, mind. No so harsh, eh?'

'Yeah. Change of scene, change of colour. I'm Justine.'

'Justine. And who are your people, dear?'

'Oh, I'm not from round here—'

Mhairi is quick as quick. 'I thought your dad was, though? That's what Hannah telt me. Somebody Arrow?'

'Arrow? That's a gie funny name. Don't think I know any Arrows round here.'

'Miss Campbell's lived here all her life, haven't you?'

'I'm no deaf, dear. You don't need to bawl. Aye,' she says proudly. 'Eighty-seven glorious years—'

'Afternoon, ladies.' A guy in a yellow jacket passes them up on the road.

'Traitor!' shouts Mhairi.

He stops. Opens the jacket in an apologetic flash. His fluorescent bib says Sentinel. 'It's only temporary. I have to go where the money is, Miss Cowan.'

'You selling Cardrummond off to them an all?'

'I'd never sell it. You know that, Miss Cowan. Why I need to go where the money is.'

'Oh, so man mind thyself, is it? You'll just exploit the res—'

He puts his hand up to shade his eyes. Wiry trunk, pale forearm where the yellow slips back. His muscles move in complicated ripples, elbow rough. Freckled. 'Miss Campbell, you're looking lovely so you are. New coat, is it?'

'Och, Duncan. I've had this old thing for years. Ma spring coat, so it is.'

'Well, it's very nice. Hello again.' He addresses this to Justine.

'Hello.' Has no clue who he is.

'Enjoying the Killie nightlife?'

'What?'

He grins, continues up the road.

'Daft big sod,' says Mhairi, smiling.

'Och, thon Duncan's a lovely lad.' There's a wistful hunger pressed on Miss Campbell's face. She keeps looking, even after he's gone. 'It's a sin, up there on that farm on his own.'

Justine begins to ease herself from the huddle, a careful unhurried motion that is barely walking is infinitesimal is almost—

In a neat pincer movement, Miss Campbell seizes her arm. 'Arrow, did you say?' Some grip on her. 'What was your daddy's first name?'

'Och, it's fine. I'm not sure that he was from here exactly . . . it was maybe further north.' Justine shuffles the leaflets Mhairi's given her. 'I should—'

'But what was his name, dear?'

'Frank.'

'Frank Arrow, eh? No . . . never heard o' thon. There was a Frank Simons over at Polnoon. But Arrow? Tell you what, dear. When I get home I'll check through all my daddy's records—'

'There's really no need—'

'Miss Campbell's dad was the Session Clerk here.'

'Aye. 1895 to 1950. It's no bother. No bother at all. Kept records of everything; his own records mind, over and above thon churchy ones: births, deaths, censures—'

'Censures?'

'Oh aye. Goes way back, beyond his time. All the juicy details too. Fornications, adultery,' she hides her mouth behind a dainty, liver-spotted hand, 'there's even one for *bestiality*.'

'Oh my God!'

'I know! Can you imagine? Thon big, smelly cows . . .'

Gently, Mhairi touches her arm. 'Margaret hen, I need to away and get my bus.'

'Oh, what am I like? Well, I'll have a wee look for you anyroad, dear. See if there's any Arrows listed. You'll pop in and see me maybe? I'm the wee cottage at the end of the row, the pink one.'

'That's very kind. But please don't go to any bother.'

'Och, it keeps me off the telly, dear.'

'Aye, and the bestiality!' calls Mhairi as she heads up the road for her bus.

Chapter Twelve

From where, Hannah? She rests her pen on her lip and wonders why – really why – she's picked these people, this place to write about. What makes the grit settle? And why is it working now? Because she likes the view? Because it's new; it's handy? Because some trace memory leeches up and calls her; starts the story spinning?

If she understood, it would not work. And if it were voices outside her own, it would be deafening. How would she filter the cacophony she'd be hearing now, because she'd know how the Duke of Cumberland's men chased a straggle of Jacobites all the way to Furrow. Burned them alive. She'd know how wee Johnny's mum lives on Diet Coke and anti-depressants, how the miles of sky here frighten her indoors; she'd know that Edward Keppie at number seven's great-great-granny was a speywife, and that Duncan at Cardrummond can trace his ancestors back to the Covenanters, to a seventeen-year-old girl they drowned in the loch; how Iron Age settlers dropped mirrors there – in that same loch – as votives. How Margaret Campbell's daddy was terrified they'd steal the parish records, how he hid his paranoia far better than the tremors left by nerve gas and the rats; how the imprinted blood from her son still lingers on the roadway; how Effie's brother and Margaret's lover lives on in the lintel of the churchyard; how the sheep droppings covered every inch of the cleared-out croft; how Auld Angus sees Mhairi as a fine bit of flesh, and would roger her senseless if his prostate wasna killing him. How her husband grieves.

How her husband grieves.

Hannah studies her notebook.

The ceremony was that night. When the sun slipped and the animals stirred, men lit fires and brands. Maraq's wrists were seized and she was dragged, roughly, through a ring of stone. Threading in and out of the pillars, damp stumps of miserable proportions. Had these people never seen the greatness they could build? The women spun her round and round, in the centre beside the fires, light sweeping pink-gold circles, she was the fire, she was burning, giddy, round and round, flung into a solid chest.

Him.

Her wrists released. Bound onto his. Led to a shelter of long rocks and branches. The moon was the colour of fish here. They went inside.

A flood of words, all come from nowhere, everywhere, and she has pinned them down. It's the dig, the cist, the excitement, making everything come alive. And Michael seems like Michael again. Taking charge after Hannah had her wee flip with the police. He was right about the writing too, calming her. Thank God for this unbuttoning of him. Maybe, finally, they are moving forwards.

'Ross and I will visit Euan,' he'd said. 'We'll get some burgers. Have a boys' lunch.'

'Euan can't eat.'

'Well, we'll have milkshakes. With straws.'

Her fretting didn't faze him. And this is the glorious novelty that stops her fretting. It feels like they are running in tandem again. They'd even managed to laugh at the picture in the paper:

Kilmacarra Bun Fight

The photo from the windfarm meeting. Mhairi's face was a scarlet howl, surrounded by fizzy hair. Michael's mouth, open to speak, looked like a seal about to catch the airborne scone. Bound to win awards.

'Go on. You take the morning to write, yes?' Michael insisted. 'Euan is absolutely fine, they've reset the leg, his tongue's healing. He'll be coming home soon. I'll take Ross, Justine's got the housework under control. You go, walk, think about your book. Please. You need some fresh air.'

She forgot he did that; he made these little pockets of kindness for her.

Fresh. Why does that feel so dangerous? That's what the police said: they were looking at fresh lines of enquiry in relation to the vehicle that crushed her son. Which really means they haven't a clue. Now that Euan is stable, her panic has turned to anger. Christ, she lives in a one-horse town, there were loads of people in the village on Sunday – all the folk at the meeting for a start. Surely someone saw something. But that is the problem, apparently. Everyone was at the meeting. Except, that is, the person who phoned.

'So was it a man or a woman?' she'd asked. 'Local?'

'Hard to say. Fast, low-pitched. Probably a woman. Probably.

Or a kiddie. A woman or a boy. That's what the operator thought at first. But not a man.'

'A kid? So, not the driver?'

'Aye. No. Well, we can't say. One of Euan's pals maybe?' The policeman had looked hopefully at his colleague. Justine, who was ironing, had stopped, the steam phhting damply up.

'Did you get the number, though? From the call?'

'Oh aye. It's a mobile, mind.'

'That's brilliant!'

'Pay-as-you-go. No registered, I'm afraid.'

'Well, have you tried calling it?' asked Hannah.

'Och aye, of course they'll've . . . we'll. Aye, that will definitely have been done, Mrs Anderson.'

'Well can you check? Or give me the bloody number—'

'Oh, we couldna do that. Data protection. But I will check. You have my word. It's no actually us now; the main investigation's been passed to Traffic.'

'Can he no tell you anything himself?' the colleague asked Hannah. He had oily black hair, too long for his cap. It stuck out at the sides.

'He can't speak?'

'I know. But could you try writing? Drawing?'

'We tried all that, Roddy,' said the other policeman. 'But he couldna really remember. No the now. So, we'll interview his pals, eh? A fresh line of enquiry.' The cop nodded, entirely satisfied with this new development he'd decided on, then his baldy brow had risen like the sun. 'Maybe you could offer a reward . . . ?'

'For Christsake—' And then the ironing basket tumbled over. Or Hannah kicked it, perhaps. Tripped on it, certainly. Who was to say, who is ever to bloody say if a thing is accidental or not? How do you know it yourself, in your head, even at the very second it happens? It's only what you tell yourself after that decides. People use that as a defence for murder. *Were you angry?* Yes! *Were you furious; clouded with rage?* Yes! *Did you mean to do it?* I don't know. *Did you crash into a kid, phone for help, then drive away?*

After the police left, assuring Michael there was *no harm done*, and they *quite understood*, they sat her in the kitchen. Michael rubbing her shoulders, Ross curling on her knee. Justine had dished out sugary tea, and seemed, at one point, to be crying with her. Michael insisted she take a break, get outside. Even packed her up a sandwich. She doesn't deserve it; it's she should be fussing him.

She fouters with the clasp of her notebook. Sometimes it's easier to love the thought of Michael than it is to look him in the face. The notebook's black cover is muddy from the dig; it's packed with notes and sketches. When she gets the words right, it makes her feel fixed in purpose. The site at Crychapel's been transformed. She looks up. Already, almost half of the cobbled cairn is bald: just raw skinned earth, with two deep trenches cut parallel to one another. Smaller holes have been drilled like little wells, and tarpaulin strung everywhere. The air is full of copious, fusty smells, which Hannah has been sniffing, and labelling, like wine. 'Dry earth and dust'. 'Maggoty tumblings'. 'A dark, forbidding decay'. When she looks at what she's written, it's mostly phrases like this. It's mostly poetry.

It doesn't matter. She's enjoying this dig so much, the sweat and muck of the work, how layers of life are being peeled away.

So long as she goes where she's told, the guys are happy for her to wield a trowel. One has even offered her a shot of his mattock, but she's not sure if that's a euphemism. So far, they have recovered: an old plough blade; a beaker, some flints, three clay pipes; a tiny shard of slate – and some interesting 'traces' in the unearthed cist. Professor Tom believes they're cremated remains. Hannah's on first-name terms with him already; he's quite a funny man, though he doesn't realise this. They know not to disturb her when she's writing. And she knows not to walk across till summoned either. She sees Tom striding over, wiping his hands on his backside. 'Well. Very exciting! Very. I'd say we have evidence of several interments.'

'Yeah?' She stands up. 'So, are the standing stones grave markers then?'

'No, no, that's what's so interesting. They're nothing to do with the graves at all. The actual stone circles appear to have been built hundreds of years before any burials. We think a couple of the stones date back to at least 3000 BC. The burials begin around five hundred years later.'

That's not good. The story thread Hannah has been embroidering won't work if that were true. She has her heroine building the circle, and the grave needs to be . . . She chews the top of her pen, briefly. Then decides: *Meh*. Occasionally, her kids possess better vocabulary than she does.

'But you think more than one grave?'

'Definitely. We've got traces of the cremation in the cist you found—'

She dimples. They both know she had nothing to do with finding it.

'—plus signs of two or three cremations from much later on.

Judging by the topographic survey, I think we may also have another cist under there as well. We'll start on that area after lunch. But, as I say; when the cists and urns were placed here, I'm sure the circles were sites of great significance already.'

'You're saying circles? Plural?'

'Yes! We had anecdotal evidence there may have been a north and a south circle, but it was never recorded. But . . . walk this way . . .'

The professor steers her to where one of his colleagues stands deep in thought. They have a singular pose, these archaeologists, that says: *This is not me in a dwam. No, I am pondering some great mystery.* Back straight, hip tilted. Arms optional – either lightly folded, or one-in-pocket while other-cradles-chin. They all do it. A bit like quivering meerkats; it was the signal to gather round. Although this poor chap, Bobby, looks as if he's been voguing it for quite some time. All the other meerkats have drifted to the pub. He perks up when he sees them coming. 'Behold!'

A hole. Just a wee hole in the ground, but deep.

'See?' says the professor. 'Wooden sockets. This north circle was made of timber – that's why they couldn't find it before!'

'Yeah.' Bobby joins in. Pretending to be casual, but speeding, speeding his delivery as the excitement gets too much. 'We've found a few stones too, which suggest they started replacing the timbers, but the circle was never completed. It seems they covered it over with cobbles and started on the other one. Then, of course, the peat came . . . climatic change, you know. So, it kind of disappeared?'

Hannah goes back towards the south circle. Only a few yards separate the two. Levers and rollers: hundreds of hands pushing and

163

pulling until they got the stones into place. They'd drum in time to the movements, keeping the rhythm going, singing with the wind. Line them up with older cairns, with the sun and the stars, with shadow, with the moon. Calculating where the light would bleed beneath. She can feel the beat of the rhyme, there's a shape it's making, a long, rolling drumming. Pocking the stone with pits and grooves, in patterns like ringed cups. Then they would feast: shellfish, milk and curds. Mashing barley in clay bowls for the children, masticating it for the babies. Origin of the first kiss: mother-chewed food passed to hungry gums. She opens her notebook again. Scribbles: 'land healing itself from human intrusion'.

The professor, with Bobby at his heels, follows. 'Looking at it, we think this older north one was built to align with the sun.'

'At midday on the winter solstice,' agrees Bobby.

'Well, that's the theory . . . We'll have to wait till December to find out.'

'And this one?' Hannah stands on the edge of the stone circle.

'Again, we're not sure. This isn't really our area of expertise. I have a colleague who specialises in megalithic astronomy. We'll need to run a series of surveys. But I suspect these circles may, at least at some point, have worked in tandem. Possibly both lunar and solar observations.'

'Yes,' says Bobby. 'Potentially the entire landscape is being used here. It's very exciting. If you look at these preliminary sketches I've made,' he thrusts his clipboard at Hannah, 'the north-east direction of the Crychapel Wood circles most likely orientates to the rising major standstill midwinter full moon. But the long axis of the southern circle is towards the Nether Meikle stones – and the setting of the southern major standstill moon.' The clipboard droops. 'Obviously.'

'So, wait.' She's been puzzling what Tom said, not Bobby. 'The cist we uncovered isn't in the circle at all?'

'No. It's possible that the interior of the circle was still sacred at the time of burial. Too sacrosanct to disturb.'

'Like a church? And this was the graveyard?'

'I suppose so. It appears they built the cist just outside the circle, topped it with this slab – what we call a kerb – and then built a flat cairn on top. Whether the cairn was part of the burial ceremony, or something built years later, for some other purpose, we're not sure. Anyway, over time, the cobbles that seem to have been placed inside the circle have joined up with these outer cairns. All a big jumble, really.'

'But why all the cobbles? I don't understand.'

The professor is animated, sharing his knowledge generously. 'Well, around 1700 BC, we think smaller river cobbles were used to fill the gaps between the standing stones, to stop people getting access to the interior. Sealing it off, if you like.'

'Mhairi said that too!'

'Who's Mhairi? Is she an archaeologist?'

'No. She runs the café next to the church.'

'I see.' The professor glances, briefly, at Bobby.

'It was her that contacted the uni.'

'Splendid. Well done that lady. Well, it looks like an outer bank's been added at some stage. Here, see how there's been another spiral carved higher up on the northernmost stone. I think that's because the earlier spiral was hidden by this bank. Then, something changed too about the nature of this space. Burials started happening inside the circle – the cremations we've discovered. They were covered with cairns as well. Haven't managed to date them yet, but they're definitely later than this cist. Then, what with agricultural improvements and so on over the last few hundred years, I reckon fieldstones have been dumped here too. Hence our lovely guddle.'

Hannah kneels down, smoothing her hand along the worn edge of the cist. Trying to imagine it. Dark and drumming. Flames and chants, the body curled.

'How d'you know there was an actual burial?'

The professor rubs muck from his specs. 'We don't, yet. Let's just see what cist number two reveals. GPS indications are that it's considerably bigger than the one we've already excavated.'

'So there's still more to be found here, you think?'

'Gosh yes. Oodles, I imagine. Unfortunately, we don't have that much time. Another week at the most, then it's back to Glasgow for me, I'm afraid. And we've yet to make a start on Mary's Well.'

'Unless we get an extension,' pipes Bobby. 'I don't mind camping if it means—'

'Yes, but I have the Balearic dig to arrange. Plus, there's all this hoo-hah with the electricity company now. I don't want to be some pawn—'

'What hoo-hah?' says Hannah.

'Apparently we don't actually have the correct permissions. Historic Scotland are fine with us being here but . . . ah.' He rubs his specs again. 'What do you know about all this windfarm nonsense?'

'I know there's a proposal in, for further up the hills. But we're fighting it. They can't build something like that here.'

'You'd be surprised. I've seen motorways constructed over Roman villas. Had to scrabble for what we could get – literally gouging up hunks of mosaic before it disappeared. All very undignified.' He replaces his specs. 'Very little stands in the way of progress nowadays. And it seems your Sentinel Power folk are very prescient. Over a year ago, they bought up several tracts of land in Kilmacarra – including the access road past the primary school, various fields and pockets of moorland – and a large chunk of these woods, I'm afraid. Part of some solar-power scheme for the school.'

'You're joking. Bought from who?'

'Local landowners, the council—'

'The council? So they were doing deals with Sentinel over a year ago?'

'"Doing deals" might be a little harsh, but it's fair to say some, um, collaborative groundwork's been done. Oh, don't worry. I'm sure it'll all get sorted.'

'This is unbelievable. How can Sentinel have bought up half the glen without anyone noticing?'

'Well, I'm not clear on the specifics: the local-authority bods are being a little difficult.'

'Not Graeme,' says Bobby stoutly.

'No, but then he is one of us – Graeme's the council archaeologist. Anyway, there's all sorts of issues over rights of access, particularly if we want to extend the area.'

'You're here now. Can you not just dig out the rest of the circle, at least?'

'But we've never had permission for that. You must understand, dear: the conditions for excavations are very specific. Every time we swing a pick, we inflict some damage on the land. Our work is about conservation: each action is a careful balance between discovery and destruction.'

He has slipped into lecture mode. Over to the east the blue hills roll like waves. The stones sit as they have done for five thousand years, turning mauve as the tree-shadows move. Squat, not soaring. Squat and graceful, quietly in their place.

'In the meantime, we'll continue to do what we can,' says Tom. 'I'll certainly lobby hard for a continuance. We'd need to attract more funding of course . . .'

'But we think these could be amongst the most sophisticated astronomically significant alignments in Scotland.' Bobby hugs his clipboard. The small, nervous bursts he speaks in seem to exhaust him.

'It could,' smiles Tom. 'Although how many people that will set the heather on fire for, I'm not exactly sure. Without unfettered access to the whole area, we can't do a definitive survey anyway.'

'But what can Sentinel do? Block access to the site? There's no trespass law in Scotland—'

'Hannah, Hannah.' The professor zips up his anorak. The wind is getting up, you can see the tarpaulins fill like sails. 'Rich, determined companies – and individuals for that matter – have a remarkable way of bending the rules to fit them. And I do not wish to get embroiled in some political contretemps. It's not what I envisaged when I took this job on.'

'Professor, I promise you. There won't be any trouble. I'll speak to my husband. We've got a petition going, a website, we're lodging an appeal – but you must keep working. Anything you find here that can help prove Kilmacarra's historical significance—'

'Will become the property of the Crown. Not Kilmacarra, I'm afraid.'

'Yes, but with your influence and expertise . . .'

'I'm just a jobbing archaeologist. We all live hand to mouth, certainly as regards funding and approvals. I can't afford to fall out with anyone.'

'I'm not asking you to fall out. Please.'

He clips his shiny poppers shut. 'Let's just ca' canny for now, as my old grannie would say. Now. Who's for the pub?'

Chapter Thirteen

There's a dribble of milkshake on Euan's chin. The traces curl in a pink apostrophe round his lack of stubble. Michael worries about that. For all his fitness and running, Euan is a late developer. No muscles to speak of, skin as smooth as his wee brother's, his voice still—

'Oh Rossie, don't put the Burger King crown on Euan's head. He doesn't like it.'

'But he is King Euan.'

'No. See! Ah.'

'Naargh!' Euan thumps at his brother, who starts crying.

'Well, it serves you right, Ross. I told you to leave him alone.'

'You are a grumpy . . . jobby!' snivels Ross. 'I hate you.'

Euan gives his brother the finger. Michael smacks half-heartedly at this offending hand.

'That's enough, Euan. He's only little.'

Ross scrambles to the far end of the bed, well away from the frame round his brother's leg – he's been warned, twice, then kicked at, once, by Euan's good leg. He curls up, one thumb sneaking into his mouth. Michael begins to say something, then turns the telly louder instead. 'Oh, look. *Transformers* is on!'

Ross whimpers. Euan rolls his eyes. Closes them.

Euan's voice not breaking: it seems trivial, but it's not. Michael dreads that he'll be like him; at the coo's tail, when all your pals swell and boom, and you're still the class runt. Then, finally, it comes. Your shaky roar into manhood; that disconcerting inability to modulate this stranger inside, a deep, unexpected voice that can slide from bass to treble at any moment, leaving you stranded and squeaky – but feeling ten feet tall. For now, though, Michael would settle for any voice at all. There is a distinct lack of clarity regarding the injury to Euan's tongue. One doctor says it's healing nicely, the other – a young woman – keeps checking the stitches, tutting, and then applying more antiseptic gunk which makes Euan retch. They squeeze it through the metal gridding that holds his teeth and jaws in place. Michael's hand hovers over his son's brow. A bevelled plane of skin, with all that brain inside. The beautiful, frowning flutes. What does his boy think, in there? A long time ago, Michael would have known every thought and question; it would have been taken out and shared with Daddy. Omniscient Daddy, whose approval was all. He doesn't disturb him. Wee soul seems flat today, spaced-out, almost. Michael said as much to the nurse. Did they not look at their patients, beyond locating the correct orifice to be plugged or drained?

'Is he all right, though? He seems very listless. And hot.'

The nurse patted Euan's cheek. 'He's just fed-up, aren't you, gorgeous? Much rather be out chasing the girls than stuck in here, eh? Although, that hasn't stopped him trying, eh? I saw your fan-club.'

Under his wirework, Euan blushed.

'Anyway, you'll be getting home soon, won't you? So your entourage'll just have to visit you there.'

'What entourage is this?' Michael felt himself grinning; suddenly elated that his boy might have some secret life.

'Oh, patient confidentiality. I couldn't possibly say.' Winking at Euan as she left.

'That lady smelled funny,' pipes Ross from the foot of the bed. 'She smelled like sore fingers.'

Michael moves his chair forward, so he can kiss his baby's soft, sweet head. His wee surprise. The harbinger of . . . well. A beginning and an end, Michael supposes. He kisses him again. 'She does actually. She smells of what Mummy puts on to make it better.'

'And Justine,' says Ross.

'And Justine. She's nice, isn't she?'

Ross burrows deeper into his nest. 'Mm-hm.'

'Mmngh!' Euan bangs his notepad on the bedclothes. WHO IS JUSTIN?

'Justine. She's . . .'

What is she exactly? The new au pair? Michael's guardian angel? A consummate con artiste? She could be, judging by the way she has picked up his deceit and run with it, outstripping even the deceiver. Michael has been both impressed and unnerved. She is breathtakingly gallus. Still not a word from her, no explanation. Not even when they were making the posters, when they had all that time together, acres of time for her just to clear her throat and go: 'Michael. About this "Myra . . ."' She had left him no option . . . This cannot go on, it feels weird to acknowledge her outside of the house. Then he remembers the calm in his home, in his head, and he has to keep reminding himself it had been his idea; he'd to force her, almost, to come home with him.

He had to crash the bloody car . . . Then he thinks: that could be part of the con too. She could have made it happen, she could have dazzled him with a carefully positioned handbag mirror, aimed right at the sun so the light bounced off his windscreen before she moved in for the kill. It could all be one big set-up.

And then he remembers it hadn't been sunny.

She is a poor soul, that is all. But they mustn't take advantage. Who knows what the girl is looking for? He's no longer sure it's her father; she seems uninterested in anything except cleaning their house and feeding them. She went very quiet at breakfast, though, when Hannah kissed him. Did they shock her? It shocked him. He was standing up, gobbling Weetabix or something, and Hannah just claimed his lips with hers. That familiar, beautiful lurch, the pierce, the taste that bitter taste, his eyes screwed shut, desperately chasing the rush. Through his coat he could feel her breast. Both surprised. Hannah ruffling his hair, like he was a trophy, and laughing.

'I'll make your sandwiches,' was all he could think of to say. And Justine had left the room.

His hands are hurting. His closed-off wife kissed him, full-lipped and spontaneous, and he's frightened about the next move. He's holding his hands too tight, so that the purple bulbs of his knuckles swell, the veins inside thick with blood, contracting like they're going to give birth and his head is pulsing with visions of those plastic eggs the kids like; filled with jelly-aliens about to hatch. Should he pin her arms and take her again? Take his particular blend of rage and lust and blow it all away? She seemed to like it, before. Now, that was confrontation. But it wasn't him. Hannah casts a delicate light around her; her fine, tense frame is too fragile. It's treasure, not spoils. It gave him his boys. He looks round at his sons, sees clean white bone, pink brain, and dark. The whisper. Stop thinking.

'DAH-GH?' The notepad flaps.

'Sorry, son. Justine's a lady who's staying with us for a while. Babysitting for Ross mostly.'

'I am NOT a baby.'

'EH-U-AGH.'

'No am NOT!'

Michael stretches his hands; a hiatus of numbness, then the trapped blood, bursting. His head pounds. Still no Ghost since Justine came. Not in the garden, not in the churchyard; not even here, and Lochallach is a good eight miles away from Kilmacarra. The milkshake quivers on Euan's chin. 'Here, son. You've a wee bit . . .'

He's wiping off the dribble as Hannah comes in. Euan yowls at the sound of the door opening, shoves the napkin away.

'Ssh. It's all right, son. It's only your mum.'

'Sweetie. What's up? Michael, I told you not to get him excited—'

'Hey,' he says. 'How's it going?'

His wife ignores him, is fussing over Euan's covers, his face.

'Ross. Get down off that bed. I've told you before—'

'Hannah, he's fine. I told him he could sit there.'

'And I told him he couldn't.'

'Heu-ggh.' Euan is nodding.

'What? What is it, pet?'

He nods again, pats the bed. Ross inches his way up, nearer to his big brother's shoulder. Euan reaches over his head, turns up the volume with the remote control.

'See? They've been getting on fine.' Michael smiles with it, so what he says is not triumphal or smug, but his fingers are throbbing again, and his heart. Always his heart; it could hold its own breath now, and did so about a hundred times a day.

'Everything OK?'

Hannah pulls out a chair. 'Mm.'

'How was your writing?'

'Fine.'

'Hannah,' he lowers his voice. 'What is it? What's up?'

'What's up? For Godsake, Michael, do you think I'm stupid? Do you think I wouldn't find out? You talk so much shit. "We'll listen to both sides of the argument" my arse.'

'I don't know what you're on about.'

'I don't "go on" about stuff. Why do folk keep saying that?'

Euan is watching them.

'Will we go outside?'

'Will you keep your voice down?'

'Hannah—'

She pushes closer, so the words snap against his ear. 'I've just found out the council sold a whole tranche of land to Sentinel last year. All round Crychapel Wood.'

'You're joking.'

'Don't say you didn't know that.'

'But I didn't, I promise. How do you know? Was it Mhairi?'

'No, it wasn't Mhairi. It was the guy in charge of the archaeology dig.'

'When were you speaking to him?'

'Today. There, the now.'

'Why?'

'Michael, I've been going there every day.'

He picks at a hangnail on his thumb. 'Even though I asked you not to?'

'No you didn't.'

How young are they, these archaeologists, these new men in town? Do they have big muscles, are they better looking than me? *Ask her*. He forgets he was going to suggest this very thing. He remembers underhandness, though. And betrayal. He and Hannah stick grimly to the conceit that this wide fresh air, the lumpen stones, the dreary people are constituents of a wonderful move. Inspirational! they say, brightly and regularly. And there was that initial rush of enthusiasm where Hannah gripped stoically to her keyboard, and wrote, wrote, wrote. But then she stopped, looked up and took her bearings, and the fear shrilled through Michael's veins again. He is hiding her like Rapunzel in a tower; they both know that, pretend otherwise.

'Fine. Good.' He looks up. 'I was going to set up a meeting for you anyway. With the archaeologists.'

'You were?'

'Yeah. I thought it might help with the book. Look, I swear I didn't know anything about this land. Let me speak to Donald John, OK? I'm sure it won't be true; they'd have to declare an interest or . . .'

He doesn't really know the protocols. But for now, his wife is nodding at him, and there's the semblance of a smile. A thank you. There is a soft kiss. Michael's chest swells. Absurd.

'So, it's good then? The dig?'

It's like a light flicks on, and she is shining from inside. He recalls that glow, how it would set him on fire, and he's to turn away. 'Oh, it's incredible. You wouldn't believe it. They found a stone chest! Right in front of me. They actually uncovered it when I was there.'

'Today?'

'No. Before.'

'Why didn't you tell me?'

The brightness wavers. Turns. 'So. How is my boy?'

'I am good, Mummy.'

'Oh, I know you are.' She pats Ross's hair. 'I meant Euan. How's your big brother?'

Euan grunts.

'He is making funny noises. Like Buddy.'

Buddy is a local collie who has an amazing repertoire of grunts and moans, quite separate from his barking. Michael takes Hannah's arm, to bring her attention back to him. Whispering. 'I think he's awful hot. And a wee bit woozy? See what you think.'

Her gold hair against his cheek. Her, nodding, the scent of her coming up.

'Hey, mister. Ho!' She walks between Euan and the telly, arms on hips. 'Look at me when I'm talking to you. How you doing?' With confident, easy energy, she stoops to stroke her son. 'You a wee bit hot today?'

'Ngh.'

'You sure? You drinking plenty?'

'Mgh.' He jouks his chin, trying to see the screen. In addition to the wiring on his teeth, he wears a neck collar, his jaw set on top of the padded cotton like he's trying to peer over a wall. It makes every movement large and stiff. Hannah continues to keep the back of her hand on his forehead. Michael waits for her assessment, a slight, stupid chill running through him. Ever since Euan was born, Michael would fumble, would tentatively sort, wipe, lift or lay, before Hannah swept in to do it right. Women moan, but they must relish it. They must do. Why else would they lay claim, with absolute authority, to every aspect of family life?

Michael frequently can't even get the shopping right; he waits with bated breath to see if the eggs he purchased are pronounced correct. He'd once, in a crazy haze of bravery, bought a set of kitchen knives – the kind that come in a wee wooden block – because he'd noticed the old ones were blunt. Dear God, you could have ridden the outrage like a wave. *But why? How much were they? From where?*

From across the bed, Hannah nods. 'Bit hot,' she mouths. She comes back to sit on the chair beside Michael. 'Need to get you a bed-bath, young man.'

'Nnng-yae.'

'Yes, way.'

Euan fires the TV volume even louder. Ross has returned to the foot of the bed, where he is lassoing his bare foot with his sock.

'Do you want to head now?' she says to Michael. 'I'll stay with him for a bit.'

The muscle in his jaw starts twitching.

'So, this stone-chest thing. Are you going to use that in the book?'

'Definitely. It held human remains, the professor said. I mean, you know how I said before, that it was coming out too worthy?'

'Hmm.' No, he thinks sadly. You must have said that to someone else.

'Well, with this whole school thing, each chapter having a topic for discussion, and classwork and blah?'

'Mmm.'

'Every sentence just about, when I was writing, I was thinking . . . ooh what topic can we take from this? Teenage pregnancy, displaced peoples, blah blah. Then I went the other way, focusing too much on the emotions and it all went a bit . . . I'm forgetting about the story, you know? Just letting it come as it comes. I can worry about themes and stuff afterwards.'

'Yes.'

Her left knee is jiggling, she is excited. It is almost touching his, there, there, it did touch, is touching.

'But when I saw the cist—'

'Kissed?' He freezes.

'It's what they call the stone-box thingy. Right off, I had this idea. At first, I thought she might lose her . . .' Hannah glances at her boys. 'I thought someone might die.'

Euan shifts on his pillows. He lifts his hand to rub at his collar, and the opaque cord of his drip shivers all the way back to the plastic bag. It swings on its hook. Michael should be used to it by now. Writers are vampires. There's a tinny clink as the hook rattles off its T-bar. He stares at the quietly plopping liquid. Saline and sugar. Milkshakes are all very well, but it is this that is feeding his boy.

'Here, son. D'you want another wee drink?'

Euan shakes his head. His eyes half-shut. Glazed.

'But then I thought: how about a murder?' continues Hannah. 'I think I'm going to make her kill someone.'

'Is that not a bit extreme? For kids, I mean.'

'We're talking teenagers here. You've no idea the sort of stuff kids read nowadays, Michael. Not everyone goes to Bible Class when they're sixteen.' She nudges him. It's a soft nudge, encouraging him to nudge back. 'Come on. You and Ross go up the road. You could maybe give old Donald John a bell, eh? Ask him about the land deal.'

'I'll need to think how I'm going to approach it.'

'Fair enough. But you will ask, though?'

'I promise.'

'When?'

'Soon.' There is no point in telling her about their run-in today. Which Donald John would call 'motivational agenda-setting'.

'Do you not want to get up the road anyway? Check on Justine?'

Hannah wants to write, he knows she does. Knows that hunger, radiating in the unstill leg. The pitch of her voice, her too-wide eyes. And she wants rid of him.

'Why would I want to check on Justine?'

She shrugs. 'I don't know. We still haven't got any references for her. D'you think you could chase them up? Or get me a phone number even, and I'll call Myra myself.'

'OK, OK. I'll do it. D'you not trust me?'

Trusst.

'Yeah. Of course. But I mean . . . she's wandering about our house unsupervised. I think she's been using my perfume . . .'

He bursts out laughing. 'Oh Hannah.'

'You're hardly there. How would you know anyway?'

'Look. Do you want her to go?' He calls her bluff. 'I'm sure we could manage . . .'

'Och . . . just on you guys go home, eh? Let me sit with Euan a while.' Hannah looks slyly at Ross. 'I could bring chips in for tea . . .'

'But we had chips already today. With our Burger King.'

'Oh Jesus. Well, I don't know then.' She reaches for her eldest son's hand. 'Stop and get a bloody cabbage if you want. I was only saying.'

'We'll have the casserole,' says Michael. 'The one Miss Campbell brought. I froze it.'

'No but Justi made us hotchpotch, Mummy. Remember?'

He hears her mutter 'Oh for Godsake' as she takes Euan's hand.

And there's the light, extinguished. Shut your eyes. *Ssh*. Shut your hand over Ross's wriggling toes, as you tug him, get his shoes on, and your head splits with the downward movement. Shut out this pounding in your head, the anger, the dizziness. Kiss your eldest boy goodbye, shut the door.

The Ghost slides his fingers along the hairs of Michael's neck. He sees new, red light round the glowing buttons of the lift. Dabbles through the light, pressing buttons like his life depends on it. He is going to visit Ailsa; he's asked one of the nurses about getting her in here for respite, and he's a community council meeting to prepare for and he needs to go to Furrow to see a man about a roof.

'Do you trusst her? There? Now? When she tells you nothing?'

'I thought you'd gone,' he whispers.

Ross frowns. 'No. I am here, Daddy.' Squeezing his fingers. 'Silly.' The lift comes, they get in.

'Hurts, doesn't it?'

Michael can see nothing save the frenzied glow. Red light, a squeezing hand. The voice in his ear, inside it.

'Doesn't it? Eh? I'm asking you a question.'

'I don't know.'

They travel downwards. No one speaking. The red glow abates, melts to a fanciful haze. Michael is compressing his throat. With his fist? It might be, or perhaps he's only swallowing, but his other hand is firm in Ross's. They get to the bottom. Doors open. Out.

'Daddy. Are you all right?'

'I'm fine, son.' Michael crouches, grips Ross by the shoulders. 'Listen, son. Your daddy's feeling a wee bit funny, but I'm going to be absolutely fine, OK?'

Chubby fingers patting his face. 'I know.'

Michael seizes the fingers, draws them to his mouth, so he can cover them with kisses, scratchy kisses – has he shaved today? It feels like blade-cuts, all across his lips.

'It's the silence that hurts, isn't it?' says the voice in his ear.

'Please.'

'We creep up to the silence. Fill it with our neuroses, our demands. Our pointless explanations,' the tongue tickles, although Michael is nowhere near a face; he is all inside his booming head. 'You left your wife in a vacuum. Didn't you? Your wife and your weans. All the things I haven't got.'

'Daddy! You are hurting.' He can hear Ross, distant.

With an effort that is bigger, far bigger than he is, Michael throws off the pain, which is looping round his neck. It feels like a cat's tongue, all rough and urgent. This insubstantial air. With an even greater effort, he opens his eyes. Laughs. There is nothing there.

There is Ross's hand in his. 'Daddy?'

'It's fine, pet. Daddy's fine. Let's go get those chips. We'll get some for Justine too, yeah?'

'Aah,' says the voice, as, head unsteady, Michael strides towards his car. 'J-ust. Rhymes with lust. Just in case, just in time? Just? Not. Fair.'

'But it's not teatime. Dad. I need to go to nursery now.'

Michael straps Ross in to his car seat. 'You do not exist.' Hissed from the side of his mouth. Ross stares frantically ahead. His fingers are tight and troubled.

The Ghost unrolls like smoke, passes into a shape of air, or fumes from the hospital incinerator. 'They burn babies in there, you know.'

Michael opens the driver's door. He can't choose which of the wavery seatbelts to grab. 'I am begging you. Please. Leave me alone.'

'No can do.' The Ghost touches him lightly on his head. 'I didny ask for this either, chief.' He melts in the smoke, is waving now, from the top of the roof.

'Bye now. Bah-byee.'

Michael starts the engine, and a CD of Disney tunes comes on.

Chapter Fourteen

'Go through a leafy tunnel,' the 'Crannogs and Kings' leaflet tells Justine. The words are exactly right. A tree-tunnel. Oaks and rhodies and cellophane sky, flashing diamonds of light. As she moves forwards, the intermittent sun catches shadow, and leftover threads of raindrops. Everything's polished and crackling: the gloss of evergreen, the buds, the lulling sun. It glistens, almost, and she has this sensation of standing on a moving pavement, where she is still and it's all around which glides and flickers, moving on and catching her up, in continuous fluid lines. She is rushing in an artery. And then, she's out of the trees, returned to the real world, where no time has passed at all and it is an ordinary afternoon.

She can see scattered tools, a discarded pencil. Soft footprints leading out. The archaeologists must be in the pub, because if Mhairi's closed the café, there's nowhere else to go in downtown Kilmacarra. Unless they're in that wee tent?

'Hello?'

No reply. Justine's nose is bothering her. She has always taken a cist to be a kind of warty growth. Her temper's bothering her and all. She is vivid with anger, actually. That Hannah is a bitch. All: *Website? Ooh. Leaflets?* Toss of golden locks. *Och, that's daft, you silly girl.*

Total bitch. Simpering and greeting, fucking playing her – one of Charlie's favourite phrases. *Think you can fucking play me, ya prick?* Usually at the moment before he lashes out. She takes off her shoes and socks. Man, it's cold. Justine has never been inside a stone circle before, but it feels as if you should go barefoot. What if Hannah had been going to say about the leaflets? She could have forgot; all that hassle with the polis could have made her forget. Maybe she'll remember, and thank Justine this evening. Maybe she should be flattered Hannah's adopted her idea. Aye, and maybe Charlie Boy's wishing she'd taken even more of his hard-grafted cash, because *she's worth it*.

She stuffs her socks inside her boots. Right. This is what all the fuss is about. This is Crychapel. She wonders what will happen. Will she billow up like Hairy Mhairi, as all the power of Mother Earth flows into her veins, just at the moment her feet step on hallowed grass? Filling her up so she'll never be weak again, but able to rise at will and smite her enemies and touch the sky? Hannah has a picture in her lounge, a vast, ethereal female called the *May Queen*, whose body is all loops and swoops. Justine imagines she too is wearing a diaphanous gown. Her toe hovers at the edge of the cobblestones. She has always wanted to touch the sky. When she was a kid, she'd sit on the swings at the top of the park near her house. They'd built them right on the brow of a hill, so the sweep of your swinging could take you out over nothingness. She'd drive her legs higher and faster, flexing her toes to points as her back buckled in its eagerness to impel. But it was the swing up, up and away, the anticipation of falling forward and then taking off that thrilled her most. One day, she vowed, she would let go. Course, she always crapped it.

The cobbles look smooth, except where the guys have been digging. She wants to get the full bhoona. She's not going in naked or anything; just the bare feet. It says in the leaflet there's a spiral on the northern stone: 'a common talisman to symbolise and invoke light'. One step, two step. Justine stretches out her arms, tightrope-wide. Personally speaking – and if any bastard had bothered to ask her – she thinks there are too many words in Hannah's leaflet. Wordy ones. She takes the cobbles like stepping stones, enjoying the spread of her skin on their solid curves.

A wobble. She steadies herself, takes it slower, searching her way round the perimeter of the circle. No idea which way's north. She squints at the lemony sun, stopping every so often to see if she feels any different. Nope. Not a single tingle. Every standing stone has scrapes under lichen, pit-marks, dents. How would you know . . . then she finds it. A single, sunshine whorl, not in the centre of the stone at all. It is like a child's finger-drawing of a Catherine wheel. Justine pictures a compass in her head: if that's the spiral, this must be north. You have north at the top, you spell WE underneath – so, that side will be – east. If there was a side there. That must be where farmers took the stones. Enclosures, run-rigs – see, she remembers all that from school. She was good at history – and English. And French, mais oui. She excelled at that just to piss off her mum. School was all right. It was the bit after that was unpleasant.

At first, it was simple jealousy. For years, her mum and she had bimbled happily along, with an array of interspersions. That's what she'd called them. Uncle Tim had morphed to Uncle Bill, who stayed longer and later, but was really quite nice. Uncle Bill had made Mum cry, and had become Uncle George, who was a builder that smelled of sweat. He had moved his toothbrush in, and his dog. Parked up his manky van. Kept funny hours, so was often home before Mum was, in that precious white space between end-of-school and tea. He'd have Sky Sports on instead of *Tracy Beaker, cause I bloody pay the bills. Make us a cup of coffee, hen.* Mum got pregnant when Justine was twelve. George did a runner, then came back when Christopher was a toddler. His business hadn't been doing so good. *My. You're a big girl getting. You're never fifteen! Come and sit here. Say hello.* Within six months, she'd left home for good.

The irony is, she left to stop anything bad happening.

She feels bad for that old lady, Margaret, searching for Frank Arrow. Justine doesny know what her father is called, apart from 'that French cunt'. When pressed, her mum would say, *Aye and he wisny even that. Only on his mum's side. How you got your stupid name.*

—But what was his *name*, Mum?

—*Away and play under a bus.*

She's walked round the circle twice now, skirting the dug-up bits. Still no *zap*. The fault probably rests with her. Dodgy wiring. She envies people who have faith, folk like Michael who get a headrush from singing hymns. Even seeing ghosts – she'd always liked the idea of being sensitive to 'the other'. It would appear, however, that Justine is a grubby creature of earth, damped down to all but survival. Which is a shame, but there you go. Not her fucking fault.

'Excuse me.'

Justine hops to a halt.

'Are these yours?' It's the guy from earlier, with the freckly arms. Only he's shed the yellow jacket, is wearing a suit. And he's holding her boots.

'They might be.' Trying to hide her bare feet one behind the other. They are filthy, and a wee bit blue with cold.

'Here you go.'

'Cheers.'

'Doing a bit of t'ai chi? Get the ground beneath your feet, eh?'

'Mm.'

His tie is brightest violet, but loosened so that the ensuing V of neck is perfectly framed. Behind him, the sky lowers and broods; to the left, the hills rise in deeper blues and green-grey. In front of him, Justine feels like a total tube.

'I wasny really . . .'

'I know.' He almost laughs at her. 'You better watch you don't get turned to stone.' The violet tie does nothing for his pale spattered skin, or his faintly ginger hair. He sees her looking, flicks the tie. 'Got a job interview.'

'Yeah? I thought you worked for the electricity folk?'

'I do, but it's only temporary. And part-time. Though I do get the use of the company car.' He holds out his hand. 'I'm Duncan, by the way.'

'Justine.'

Her hands are full of shoe, so he shakes her pinkie. 'Hi, Justine. I saw you the other day, at the graveyard. Miss Campbell tells me you were looking for your dad?'

She remembers the long, tight torso stripping off in the Sentinel van. Appraises him more carefully. But he still reminds her of David Lamont at school, a violent, ruddy boy with orange curls. David, Trevor and Darren, who would squeeze your bum or nascent tits in the free-dinners queue, every bloody day.

'So, what's the job?'

'Car sales at Lochallach.' He grimaces.

'No really your thing?'

'Nup. Far rather be up at the farm. But it's a job. And they might give me an actual car.'

'Let me get this right. You work on a farm and for Sentinel. And a garage? Christ, you're one greedy bugger.'

'I am that.' He smiles, a sleepy, assessing smile. 'What is it you do, Justine?'

'Au pair at the moment. For the Andersons. But I'm a nursery nurse too. And I sing sometimes, in a band. Back in Glasgow.'

'Yeah? What's it called?'

Oh fuck, fuck, it's called it's called – 'Crazy Cows,' she blurts.

Now he is laughing, openly. 'Is that right? And what kind of stuff d'you sing?'

'Och, anything really. Rock, folk, pop. Whatever folk want really. Good money in it too.'

Why does she say these things? Now he's going to ask where she plays, or to sing him a song and she canny even bloody sing.

'Justine Arrow and the Crazy Cows.' Duncan nods. 'You sound more like a Country and Western band.'

'Oh, yeah, we do a wee bit of that too.'

She's pleased, and troubled, that he knows her pretendy name. How does it happen, that information transmits here in a lightning-rod flash? Where do these people gossip, when there's nowhere to go?

'Think you might sing in the pub one night?'

'Who knows?'

They are face to face. He's a good foot taller than her, and Justine's five six in her bare feet, and she feels quite petite, which is nice, because beside dainty Hannah she is perpetually a lumbering ogre. Ogre-ess? They watch each other. His eyes are proper grey. She thought grey eyes were a myth.

'Well, if you'll excuse me, I need to fly. Oh. Good luck with the interview.'

'Cheers.' He has a smile that splits and redefines his face. You would buy a used car from this man. 'So, is that a date, then?'

'What?'

'You. Singing in the pub. Will I tell Rory?'

'Oh, aye. We'll see. I don't think you guys could afford my prices.'

She plunges her arms out; one boot at either end. Then she flees the circle, keeps running, does not look back at his bemused face; keeps going until she is on the track past the primary school, cheeks slapping, cold wind in her teeth, and her, bouncing in air then smashing on rough dirt with the jaggy burrs and the sharp-teethed stones and her feet in ribbons. Doubles over, laughing. Lets the sounds ring out of her. Running is going on the swings for adults; you still get that breathless flight. The laughter makes her light; she feels like she is levitating. She's not run that way since she was a child, is amazed at the longness of her limbs, how they piston in powerful juts. There's something pleasing in the swell inside her too, that it works still and isny crushed beyond reach. Not that Justine's in the market. For anything. Not any more. Not ever ever ever.

Right. Work.

Euan loved running. Another press of guilt. Man. Justine should go to see him. She should've done that first. Even if she stood at the doorway; Christ, she's eyeballed Duncan twice already and she didny recognise him, and the boy's eyes were shut almost the whole time apart from when they bumped and passed and she needs to, she just should, that's all. If he saw her, and he didn't know her . . . Could she just stay? Not for ever, obviously. The wee pink phone in her pocket is like a beacon, or a grenade. Bin it? Bury it? Smash it first, with a big rock, then burn it in the fire – no, the Aga, man. That thing is totally roasting, would melt plastic no bother. Sorted. Get these done first, then back to the ranch for some torching. She shakes out one of the posters, which are now bent in the shape of her arse. Stuffs her raw feet back in her boots. Fuckknows where her socks have gone. Takes a tub of pins from her jacket pocket. Mhairi's got one poster up in the café already. She'll put another in the shop, two in the hotel, and the rest on random trees or lamp-posts. Duh. She's not brought any Sellotape. No lamp-posts, then. And they can go fuck themselves about the crannog leaflets. She is not distributing them. Her crannog leaflets. A breeze licks the edge of the poster she's holding. She can't not put them up. One small release of pressure in her thumb, and the paper will catch on air, will fly away. Hannah will simply make more.

She will visit Euan, before she goes. Justine draws her eyes over the glen and the distant hills, the scattered farms, the street and the jumbly houses. People live in them, every one of them; they open their door and walk inside. Put the telly on or fill the kettle. Go *ah* as they settle in chairs. Do they know how lucky they are, when they draw the curtains, switch on their lamps?

There's a tree near to the churchyard, a gnarly fat one. She clamps the heads of two drawing pins inside her lips, goes over and flattens the poster against the tree trunk. As she reaches to insert the first pin, there's a sprinkled warmth across one foot. A black and white dog is peeing on the top of her boot.

'Piss off! Get away!'

She kicks out her leg, not at the dog exactly, more of a combined warding-off and drying action all in one. The dog continues to pee, his happy face panting as he does so. It's the same collie she's seen here before.

'Don't you bloody kick him!'

On the verge beside the road, a boy straddles a bike, a rusted contraption too small even for his slight frame. The disparity is compounded by his trousers, which stop just above his ankles. No socks. No jacket. Ferret-face poking from a sweatshirt hood. An embryonic ned, who wouldny last five minutes in Glasgow.

'Is that your dog?'

His scowl intensifies. 'That your face?'

When she doesn't respond, he gives her the finger.

'You're a right wee charmer, eh?' Justine smooths her hand over the poster, pressing down before she sticks in the final pin. 'And, for your information, I didn't kick him. Did I, Mr Dog?' The dog wags his tail, has a final, proud sniff round the tree. 'You're a very rude wee boy, by the way. Your dug's much nicer than you. Even when he *is* peeing on my foot.' She stands back a little, to check the poster is straight. Beneath the strident heading, there is the photo, then this:

Road accident last Sunday evening, approx. 6 p.m.

Please help us find out what happened to our son. Euan, who is fourteen, was out running last Sunday, when he was struck by an unknown vehicle. He was found unconscious at the flashing chevron on the bend as you leave Kilmacarra, heading towards Kinmore. If you saw or heard anything, or are the person who called the ambulance, PLEASE phone or call in at the manse, or call Lochallach police. Any information will be gratefully received. Please note, a reward is offered. With grateful thanks for all your support at this difficult time.

Councillor & Mrs Anderson, Kilmacarra Manse

'You gonny phone them, then?' The boy is still there, finger hovering at the crust inside his nose.

'Why would I do that?'

'Cause I seen you. In my garden. You seen me an' all. That's how you were walking up that road. That exact same time cause I know cause *Antiques Roadshow* was comin' on the telly.'

'You're talking a load of shite, wee man.'

'It was you what phoned the polis, wasn't it?'

Her heart slips. '*No.*'

The boy regards the poster. 'Says there's a reward. What if I tell them it was you? Does that mean I'd get the reward? Will you get the jail?'

'The only person getting the jail'll be you, if you start annoying folk with stupid stories.'

'You think I'm a daftie, don't you?'

'No.'

'Aye you do. I'm gonny phone them—'

'And say what? That you saw me walking up a road? Big wows.'

'And I seen you running back.'

Her shoulder blades tighten. 'Don't talk crap. Why would I be running?'

'You tell me.'

Wee shit. She wants to punch him. She forces herself to walk away, but he comes after, on his clattery bike.

'Ma brakes don't work.'

'So? What d'you want me to do about it?'

'Maybe if I get a reward I can get a new bike.'

'Oh, for fucksake – Look, so what if I was there? Not that I bloody was. It was a *car* that hit him, not me.'

'Aye, but see if you seen the car, you could tell them what it looked like. So how come you don't just get the reward?'

He does a wheelie as she ignores him. 'Euan Anderson's all right, you know. He's got a cracking bike. Gies me shots on it sometimes. I wouldny mind a bike like his.'

Wee bastard is swinging a lasso round her neck. In the absence of any vehicle being traced, the police will keep looking for the caller. Imagine coming forward now, going: *Actually, it was me. All the time! Surprise!* She can picture Hannah's face, how it will ripple, then crack as she turns to rip her head off. Fuck, she should just leave Kilmacarra this minute. Grab her bag and run. Where? There's no bus for two hours – and she knows this for a fact, she's learned the timetable off by heart. Justine lets cold air flow through her nose. Holds it in the soft part of her throat. Go where? From the churchyard, a battered angel stares. On Justine's thigh, the tattooed numbers prickle. She's not ready.

She has to harness this prying avarice before she gets hog-tied. It's just a wee, stupid kid. Think. Think. What would *he* do? She sees the long curve of Charlie Boy's tongue as he wets his roll-up. Always a smoke before a decision, although the decision will already have been made. He is an expert in misdirection. A torture that is quiet and slow. Often, there's a sexual charge in the anticipation; she'll see him growing hard – or would sense it if she was pinioned on his knee. On his throne, surrounded with acquisitions as he

194

passed judgment or directed fates. Oh yes. That made him very hard indeed.

Justine grips the boy's handlebars, so he's forced to put his foot down. 'Do you do deals?'

'What?'

'Well, you're right. You're no a daftie. In fact, I'd say you were a very clever boy. So. Supposing I had seen something. But, for personal reasons, I didny want to get involved. How would it be if I told you what I saw, and you pretend it's you.'

'Me what?'

'That phoned the ambulance.'

'I'm no a fucking lassie!'

'I know, I know. But I heard the police say it could be a boy or a girl. They don't know. I mean, it's not as if . . . well, your voice isn't . . . you know.'

'Naw?'

'What's your name?'

'Johnny.'

'And what age are you, Johnny?'

'Ten.'

'Ten, eh? Wow. Think of the money, Johnny. You tell them what you saw, say you were . . . och, I don't know . . . scared or something, so you ran away. That way, you get the reward, and I get left alone.' She scrutinises his skinny face. '*Do* you get scared of anything?'

He shrugs. 'Naw.' But his eyes have a firmer gleam to them. 'So? What would I tell them?'

'Ah-ah. First, do we have a deal? You keep the money and you keep me out?'

'Aye.'

'OK. You tell them that a big white motorhome whizzed past, right? Heading in towards Kilmacarra. You know what I mean? Like a caravan, only you drive it?'

'*Aye*. Course I know.'

'Good. Now, listen. On the back of it was a wee red car. They were towing it, right? I don't know what kind, but they were towing it, so I couldn't see any number plate for the motorhome. You. You couldny see any number plate, right?'

'Right.'

'I never saw what happened, but I think maybe the car's clipped him? So the driver might not even know. But: this is very important, Johnny. Are you listening?'

'*Yes*.'

'On the back of the car was a wee flag-thing. It was like three wee swirls with a dot in the middle. Look.' She opens her phone pouch, takes out the scrumpled wrapper. She hasn't looked at it since that night. 'See? I drew it down.'

'So you *were* gonny tell them?'

'I . . . I don't know what I was going to do. Maybe, when I left here. Here – you take it. Practise drawing it out yourself so . . . you know. Make it look like you did it, yeah?'

Solemnly, he takes the paper, folds it in two.

'Much d'you think the reward is?'

'Haven't a clue. In fact, here.' She gives him her phone, killing two troublesome birds in tandem. 'You'll need this too. That's what I phoned them on.'

'It's *pink*.'

'I know. I'm sorry. Look, take the wee pouch thing too. It's black.'

'Aye, but I still wouldny have a pink—'

'And here, here.' A wedge of tenners – forty, fifty quid? She's started so she'll finish. Pressing the money into his hand, which slips with surprising rapidity, both the notes and the phone pouch, into his sweatshirt pocket. The phone itself is still in his other hand. He traces it up and down the line of his thin, freckled mouth. 'I suppose . . . now I've got all the evi-dunce an that . . . I could still tell them it was you. And still get the reward.'

'Right, you wee shite.' Justine grabs the cords of his hoodie, drawing him closer so his legs are flailing, and the bike keels over. The collie begins to bark, a snarling circle of cower, but no pounce.

'You know what? See the reason I don't want to let anyone know I'm here? Cause a very bad man is after me. Very, very bad – you understand? And if he knows I'm here, he'll find me and *get* me. But, you know what?'

Johnny whimpers, but doesn't speak. She loosens her grip, slightly. 'See, when he knows you've just taken some of his money? He'll come and get you first. You with me? He'll come and take a Stanley blade to your bits and leave you to bleed to death. How d'you like that then, *Johnny*?'

The wee boy starts to cry.

Roughly, she brushes at his collar, as if she'd been making some motherly adjustment to his clothes. 'OK now. Come on. I didny mean to scare you. But this isn't a game, Johnny, this is serious. And you started it, you know?'

He sniffs. Nods.

'So. Do we have our deal? Or will we just pretend this was all a bad dream? Because, let's be honest. Who the fuck's going to believe you?'

Chapter Fifteen

Michael's car is almost at Kilmacarra. Or Furrow, he could head on to Furrow after all because that's even further and it's over the river and evil things can't cross water, can they? But it's not evil, his Ghost. He is not. Oh God, just away, just anywhere that is away, and he feels the car is running liquid and he's swinging round a bend and there's a tractor in the middle, Malcolm Greig, you'd know him anywhere by his oily perma-tammy and the greasy hair that hangs beneath and he sees the whites of Malcolm's eyes as he skirts and screeches past. Only just missing; a man could kill a person on a road like this, driving like this, could crash a car or knock a cyclist. Or a kid. If you are insane. He is *not* insane.

Michael slows down until he's barely doing twenty. Feels the tight purse of his breath come out, lips vibrating, a faint harmonica-buzz. Is it his conscience come alive? That little spark of celestial fire?

Fucking pug-ugly conscience then, pal, eh? What like *is your heid inside?*

See, now that was a definite conscious exchange: no visions (apart from this painful fuzziness round his right eye), no real voice. Michael just made that up, the way Ross talks with his

Transformers, or like he did with Action Men when he was wee. Maybe his consciousness is his conscience. The simple fact of being aware, like the wee voice that reminds you to put the bins out or post that letter? So, what happens to all the bits he ignores? There must be a sump of oil inside him, all the undigested debris he's sluiced through in his life. The source of his evil demon.

His Ghost is not evil. No one is evil. No, a person must be mad to be evil; you must explain away evil with synapses and psychosis. Yet revere the notion of goodness. Of God.

Please Lord. Please.

At last, he can see the half-egg rise of Kilmacarra, can see his house, the church, which makes him speed again. He makes himself speak out loud. 'You all right, Rossie boy?'

Ross doesn't answer.

'Ross.'

He is sharp, too sharp. 'Daddy asked you a question.'

'No. My tummy is feeling sick.'

'Well. We'll soon be home.'

'But I have to go to nursery. Miss Thomas will be waiting.'

Michael cannot face the thought of Miss Thomas, wittering about the Easter Eggstravaganza and how Michael's to explain the mystery of the resurrection. The kids are four years old for Godsake.

'You don't have to go to nursery. Not if you're not well. Here. D'you want a play on Daddy's phone?' He pokes the contraband through the gap in the seats. Hannah will freak.

'You mean like how Euan is not well?'

'Yes . . . no. Not like that.'

As they drive towards home, he sees Justine, scluffing along the pavement on the other side. He sees her, and feels a pop of pleasure, the way you do when the sun comes out. Scruffy leather bag swinging; her shoulders hunched up to her ears. It's not that cold, yet she's wearing a Barbour jacket. His Barbour jacket. And she's pinned her hair back, the way Hannah does, so it drapes her spine in a single snake. Justine's hair is dense and heavy-textured. Well, he doesn't know that, it's not as if he's touched it, but you would definitely not call it 'flyaway'. Whenever he goes the messages, it's always 'flyaway' shampoo Hannah asks for. He looks closer. The colour's changed too. Shame. He liked that colour.

'Look, Ross. Who's that?' Winding down the windows.

'Justi!' he squeals. 'Justi. It is me! Ross Anderson.'

Michael thinks for a second that she's not going to stop, she must be going out, not in; she's already past where you'd cross the road for the manse. But she does stop, eventually: Ross shouts her into submission. Slowly, she takes her bag from her shoulder. Shakes off her stoop and pokes her tongue out at his son. Her eyes are rimmed bright pink.

'Hello, guys. What you up to? How come you're not at nursery, Ross Anderson?'

'Because my daddy drived me too fast and my tummy is sore.'

'Don't be silly, Ross.' Michael leans his elbow on the open window. He is being jaunty. 'Where are you off to then? Look as if you're going hiking.'

'What? Oh. Yeah. I borrowed your jacket. Hope that's OK?'

'Of course it is.' It is not unpleasant, the thought of her inside his clothes. Oh, that's amazing. His heart has calmed right down.

'You all right, Michael? You look a bit . . .'

'My daddy is not well.'

'Are you—?'

'I'm fine. Now. I mean, I was feeling . . .'

The bare spring light. The blue moving over her lidded, sore eyes. Her uneven mouth.

Tell the truth.

He looks at the pavement. 'Justine. It happened again. That . . . thing.'

'The seeing-things thing?'

'Ssh. We'll talk later, OK? Ross,' he says brightly, 'do you want to go to nursery, then?'

There's a little *cheep*. Ross has discovered the Angry Birds app on Michael's phone. 'No. I am too late and it will make Miss Thomas sad. And you said I was not well so it will be a fib anyway.'

'Smart kid,' says Justine.

'Can we give you a lift somewhere?'

'No. Ta. I'm just . . . I thought I'd go for a walk.'

There is a flicker in Justine's demeanour, a blink that goes from casual to luminous pain as she glances at Ross and he knows.

'Are you leaving us?'

'No.' Scornful, swinging up her bag. 'I told you. I'm just off for a walk.' He thinks he sees their toasting fork poking out the top of her bag. That's ridiculous. Only his imagination. A gold-glinting devil-fork.

'Please, Justine. Please don't go. I'm begging you.'

'*Fucksake,*' she hisses, and Ross gasps.

'Justi. You are not allowed to say that word. My mummy hit Euan with my Lego when he said that word.'

'Ross, I know. I'm really sorry.'

'Can we talk about this? Will you get in the car and talk? Or we can go to the house. Hannah's out.'

'I know.' She's clutching her bag across her belly.

'What is a fucksake?'

Michael sees old Miss Campbell emerging from the village shop. Instantly, she spots them, bears down as fast as her wrinkly stockings will allow. She'd been to his surgery last week, to complain about Johnny Green. 'Needs a good hiding, so he does.' And he'd promised he'd see what he could do. And he hasn't. He's not a policeman, for Godsake, he's a councillor. If he speaks to the school, then the Social Work might get involved again. Johnny's poor mum needs time.

'Can we not have this conversation out in the street, please?' He opens the passenger door. 'Justine. Will you just get in the car?'

'Ha! You said "just" to Justine. That is funny, Daddy. You are a funny daddy.'

'I know. Thank you. Justine. Please.'

Wordlessly, she complies. He releases the handbrake, rolls off as Miss Campbell reaches them. He pretends he doesn't hear her chapping on the window.

'Where we going?'

'Furrow. To see a man about a ceilidh.'

'Right.'

Justine rests her head, closes her eyes. With her hair tied back, the skin pulls bluntly across her cheekbones. Not angular, though; there is a flatness, there's no glimmer left on her. She is dull. Up close, Justine looks as tired as him.

'It's for a party fundraiser. But the hall roof's leaking, so I need to get it fixed. By next Friday.'

'Right.'

She's still beautiful, though. Ah. The hair. Michael knows, now it is gone, why he liked it: Hannah had the same kind of metallic red hair when they met. He recalls the brilliant flash of her as she sailed into lectures. Arts and Divinity occasionally overlapped, in murky, fluid options like Philosophy when you were encouraged to open out your mind. Well, he'd like it shut now please. Tight, if anyone is listening.

He drives out the village. Green earth around him. Bright sky above. The bubbling inside him has subsided. Five minutes talking to a girl who doesn't care; that's all it takes. It is inconceivable, when it's gone, that the Ghost has ever been here; it's like those mornings you wake bitten by your dreams, you feel the marks, but can't remember what made them. Or vomiting. Yes, seeing the Ghost is like being sick: an uncontrollable surge that leaves you weakened and ashamed. He cannot let Justine go. She is his talisman, he's sure of it.

'What's up?' he asks.

'Whit?' It is a leave-me-be drawl.

'Did something happen? Has . . .' He hesitates, then is disloyal. 'Has Hannah upset you? She can be a bit of a nippy sweetie, but she's a good person. Honestly.'

'Yeah? Even though she fu—'

'Justine!'

Her eyes snap open. 'Sorry. God, I'm sorry. Hey, Ross. What ya doin'?'

'I am doing Bad Birds.'

'No. You are doing *Angry* Birds.'

'But if you are angry it is bad.'

Justine twists in her seat to face him. 'No. Not always. Sometimes if you're *not* angry it's bad.'

In the mirror, Michael sees Ross frown.

'What Justine means is, you can be angry if something's unfair. But not to hit,' he says quickly. 'Angry hitting is always bad. Oh look, Ross. Tell Justine where that is.' He points at a bigger version of the lone hill behind the manse. This one bursts from the wide-open moor they are travelling over. The Great Moss. Or the Big Bog, as Euan calls it.

Ross sighs, barely glances up from Angry Birds. 'It is a king's hill called Dumbledore.'

'No. Dun*add*.'

He, Hannah and the kids had climbed Dunadd last spring. They were still exploring, still tentative and delicate in their new surroundings. The boys were quite disappointed. Michael had filled them with stories about this mighty hill where the first kings of Scotland had been crowned. How its summit, rising central from the face of the valley, saw warring Picts and Gaels united, their king anointed from a font hewn in the rock. But the hill looks more like a blister. A double-headed blister in the middle of a field, with a couple of houses hinging off its base. Not very impressive. Hannah had urged them on. *You wait till we get to the top, you'll see.* Not that she'd been up it before, either. They'd left their bikes at the start of the footpath, puffed their way up. It was indeed higher than it looked. The moss covering was springy, and they'd pretended they were walking on the moon, bouncing deathly slow. On the summit, Michael showed the boys what a good view the settlers would have of anyone entering the valley. *That's why it was so important.* It wasn't as high as the surrounding backdrop of mountains, but it was placed in the middle of the valley, so people could see all round. Enemy or friend – they'd know who was coming. *It's called strategic positioning. Do you know that word, boys? Stra-tee-gic.*

They had all solemnly, one by one, placed their feet in the carved-rock footprint, just as Michael and his dad, and ancient kings had done. Euan was nonplussed. *It's not that big. Thought you said a giant made it?* Hannah's throat went tight, scrawny with the effort of making them all have a nice day out, and he'd handed Euan a placatory Twix. *This is where your nation began, son.* Michael had learned almost no Scottish history at school. He was keen his sons' education would be different. Euan had begun some hybrid Scottish Studies course at school, but it was like damage limitation. Generations, growing up without a basic knowledge of how their nation came to be. What kind of country suppresses the teaching of its past?

'Is it a volcano?' Justine's asking him. 'It looks like the hill behind us.'

'Think so.' He's surprised she'd notice. 'They reckon they might've both been islands once, when all this was water. It's an ancient hillfort. Capital of Dalriada. You've heard of Dalriada?'

'Is that the place where Scotland lost all its money? I thought that was abroad.'

'No, that was Darien.'

'There is a boy in my group called Darren. He smells of pee-pee.'

'Ross! That's not nice.'

'Darren is not nice. He has bogies up his nose.'

'You know, I'd a boy called Darren—'

'Enough. Right. C'mon. We need to get a move on, or the roofer mannie will have given up on me.'

They pass hills of blue and skies like water, pass water like stone and long purple fields. 'Potatoes,' says Michael knowledgeably. Well, they could be. Do potatoes grow in spring? In the back, Ross has given up on Angry Birds and fallen asleep. Michael drops down a gear, takes in the vast panorama of open land. He notices

Justine's holding a booklet. Can make out the word: 'Crannogs'.
'What's that?'

'Leaflet.'

'Can I see?'

She sighs, opens it up in an exaggerated motion. He recognises Hannah's style, is surprised she's found the time to write it. Then he sees the web address, and returns Justine's sigh.

'That you been drafted into the cause too?'

Justine shrugs. 'Just do what I'm telt, me.'

There is a pause, then she says, 'Hannah's a very definite person, isn't she?'

'How do you mean?' He knows exactly what she means.

'Knows what she thinks about everything. Good/bad. Pish/perfect. You know?'

'Mmm.'

He thinks about when Hannah seems happiest with him, and it's when he challenges and argues back. It's when he's brave enough not to be careful; it liberates them somehow.

'Why do women like bad men?'

'What?'

'Nothing. Sorry. Nothing.'

They drive in silence until they get to Furrow, and the corrugated shed and awkward brick building that was church and hall combined. Bill Teague's flat-top van is about to drive away, and Michael jumps out to catch him. The hole in the roof isn't big, but he knows from experience that, if he leaves it, more tiles will come away. There's not enough in the funds (party or council – who own this sorry site) to pay Bill. They do a deal for cash, which Michael will pay himself. He wishes it was the olden days, when priests could offer indulgences for money. They haggle; Bill wins. They shake, he waves Bill off, gets back into the driver's seat.

'That you done?' says Justine.

'I am. You all right?'

'I'm fine. It's really lovely here, isn't it?'

'Yeah.'

She presses her head into the seatback, a slight arch in her back like a cat. 'But lonely?'

'Yup. It can be very lonely.'

'Still,' she says, switching on the radio. 'We've always got Myra.'

On the way home, Ross begins to snore.

'We should wake him. His mum will crack up.'

'Why?' says Justine.

'Because he won't sleep at night. He's not been sleeping well.'

'But he's tired now. And he seemed a bit upset. I think he's worried about you.'

'Why? What did he say?'

'Nothing. Maybe he's worried you're not very well. You're not, are you? I mean, you look like death warmed up.'

'Cheers.'

'Well, you do. All pale and clammy.'

Michael drives on through the slim channel she's made. It's another vacuum to be filled; she's waiting for an explanation. A politeness at least. But it's a relief to be quiet beside her. He carries on driving and not talking, although what he really wants is to fold into her lap. Time is flashing past as the standing stones come into view, grow big, diminish. More stones appear, grey and bowed against the centuries of wind. They will be home in less than ten.

'You don't want to talk about it?' she asks.

'No.'

'Fair enough.'

That's wrong. She needs to prise it out of him, or coax it like a little bird. Why does nobody know that what Michael wants most in the world is to be looked after?

He sees Justine check her watch.

'Fine,' he says. 'I'll tell you. If you tell me why you were leaving.'

'*Were*?' she says.

'If you were really going to go, you wouldn't have come with us in the car.'

'You think? You practically dragged me in.'

'Please?'

She sighs. 'I did something stu— look, I just need to get out of here.'

'*Is* it Hannah? I can talk to her.'

'Why would you think it's Hannah?'

'Well . . . She's not always as friendly as she could be.'

'Put yourself in her position. Some strange lassie gets the run of her house – and I bet I'm not the first one, am I?'

'I don't pick up women, if that's what you mean.'

'No, but I know your type. So busy trying to save the world—' she stops. 'Do-gooders can be right selfish bastards, actually.'

'I think you're being unfair.'

'That right? Well, I know a social worker that got me two black eyes and a broken nose.'

'He gave you what?' His knuckles are white across the steering wheel.

'No. *He* didny. But if he'd left well alone, I wouldn't of bloody got them.'

'But he was trying to help you, yes?'

'I don't see why some people aye think they know what's best. When they have absolutely no idea of what's going on. Or how some folk really live.' She folds her arms. 'Do you have a single clue, Michael? Of the shit that happens to some folk, for no reason at all? Not cause they're bad and they deserve it, not cause—'

'I think there can be reasons. We just might not understand them.'

'What? Like you were a real bastard in a previous life? Or God's just having a pisser of a day?' Justine sniffs. 'I don't know how you believe all that shite. How's a whole bunch of weans getting shot up on a bus fair? What's the reason for that, smartarse?'

He shrugs. 'Free will? Man's inhumanity to man? I don't know. Faith doesn't have a reason. It's trust, I suppose. You trust that there is a reason, you just don't know what it is. But you trust that God knows. God knows the secrets of your heart. You don't know his. That's what I believe.'

'What a load of fanny.'

'Is it about her stupid face cream?'

'What?' She unfolds her arms. 'Christ, *no*. It's not about Hannah. I just . . . it's time I was moving on. You've clearly got a lot of stuff going on, you and Hannah, and I'm only in the way.'

'Justine, we really need you.'

'No you don't. I'm not a bloody barrier for yous to hide behind. What you need to do is sit down and talk to your wife. Properly talk to her. Tell *her* what it is you're cracking up about, not me.'

'I can't.'

Justine snorts. 'So how come you stay with her then? If you canny even talk to her. After she fucked another guy?'

209

The barbed fricative of the *fuck* makes him flinch; he checks Ross is still asleep.

'Because she's sorry. And I'm not cracking up.'

'Is she? Sorry?'

'She said she was.'

'So, if someone says they're sorry that makes it OK? Whatever it was they did?'

'Yes. It's called forgiveness.' He sounds whiny. He hates when he is whiny.

'Fuck off. That's called bullshit.'

'Honestly, it's not. It works . . . if you let it.' The inside of his lungs hurt. 'It has to.'

'Where does all the rage go then?'

'You let it out. You don't hold on to it.'

'Bollocks. You must still be raging inside. Maybe that's why you "see stuff", eh? All that anger's got to seep out somewhere.'

He glances in the mirror again. Ross sleeps on, his wee fists up at his face.

'Who hurt you, Justine?' He says it partly as a distraction but mostly because he worries for her.

'Fuck *off*. Tell me what you see.'

'What happened to you? What did you do before you came here?'

They are approaching the manse. An angel in the graveyard catches a shaft of clear gold light; the quiver on her back is trembling.

'Man up, padre. Fucking tell me.'

'A ghost. I have a ghost.'

'Oh man. Classic.' Adopts a nasal whine. '*I see dead people.* What: white sheet? Chains? The works?'

Even his traumas are pathetic. A van emblazoned with Sentinel Power cuts in in front of them. It is going far too fast for the twisting road. Michael brakes, toots his horn as the driver raises his hand. He is shocked to see Justine raise her hand and wave, not shocked at her hand, but at the way she pouts her lips. An almost-kiss of air.

'You know him?'

'Aye. He's one of my regulars.'

She clasps her hands in her lap. Presses them over the place where, later, he will learn she is tattooed with her stable number. She swallows and chews her lip and fidgets with her fingers. They're pulling into the driveway of the manse before she speaks again.

'You asked me what I did before I came here. I was a prostitute, Michael. A great big, dirty hoor.'

Chapter Sixteen

Day Five in the *Big Brother* house. There is a claustrophobia about Hannah's home; the manse is a brew of strange energies. Ross is demanding more and more stories; he's very clingy, and Hannah's run out of books to read him. She can't face another round of Dr Seuss. You *write me a story, Mummy*. But her brain is fried: it's full of stone cists and bones and Euan. His temperature's still too high. Justine's in some almighty huff too, ate last night's dinner in her room. Will speak when spoken to, and that is all. Good. Perfect, in fact, because she's still doing the housework. Hannah thought at first she was pissed off with her, because of those daft history leaflets; was ready with a sharp *you're being very childish, Justine, you can't copyright ideas* (which of course, you can, but Hannah wrote all the damn words, *and* she'd bought Justine a big box of chocolates which she'll not be getting now if that's her attitude). But the girl's also strange with Michael; they won't look at one another.

Hannah feels uneasy. She doesn't know why. It's the same slithery chill that's been nagging her since yesterday morning; it's to do with the police coming; no, after, when she was crying and Justine was – did she pat her? No, not that. It was the tea. It was when Justine made the sugary tea and she passed a mug to

Michael. It was automatic. With no words. Have they fought? A violent ugly thought comes to her, which she dismisses. Michael wouldn't. And then she remembers how he held her by the wrists, pushed her legs apart with his knee and fucked her like a man possessed.

'I'm sorry?' says the doctor.

She collects herself. Smiles her winning smile. 'I'm sure you've considered all this already, but I wondered about getting a dental specialist in? If his jaw doesn't set right—'

'His jaw is healing well, Mrs Anderson. I can assure you, he's getting the best of care.' He pats Euan's hand. 'Aren't you, young man?'

She nods. 'And what about his memory? D'you think he'll remember what happened soon? We need to find who did this.'

'I'm sure the police are doing their best. Let's just focus on getting Euan fit for going home.'

The doctor stands. Are they allowed to sit on patients' beds? It's hard to grab them, as they bustle past, nose firmly in a clipboard, two nurses at their heels. But they're just men, underneath the dressing-up. She's managed to corner this one for a whole five minutes.

'When do you think that will be?'

'Soon, Mrs Anderson. End of next week, if he keeps doing as well as he is? Just need to get that temperature down a little more. Get some home-care support organised as well.'

She smiles her appreciation. Will they need Justine more or less once Euan is home? She's not sure she wants her teenage boy bedbathed by a girl with a bright-red bra. The doctor leaves. On the bed, Euan sighs and flumphs.

'You want a wee sleep, pet? Should I go too?'

'Mngh.' He shuts his eyes.

'All right. Now are you sure there's nothing else I can get you?'

Another sigh.

'Fine. You have a rest. I'll see you later. Tonight? Your dad's meant to be coming but I can—'

'Nng.'

'OK, sweetie. Tomorrow then. First thing. D'you want me to bring some school books in? You don't want to fall be—'

'*NGHO.*'

Hannah takes her vending-machine coffee. 'Bye then. Love yooo.' He's so like his dad: he'll talk if he wants to, but the more you force, the less you'll get. When she and Michael were first married, she'd tried every trick she possessed: airy blethering; pouting; dancing in front of him; long and hearty sighs. *But what do you want to 'chat' about?* he'd say. *I dunno. Everything.* Poor bemused Michael, who talked all day for a living. She even yanked up her jumper once and yelled *Newsflash!* That did get a response, mind. A very good one. But she wouldn't let it go. *Why don't you want to talk to me?* she'd say, day after day. And he'd reply: *Why don't you want to be quiet with me?*

—*Do you love me? Just say that.*

—*Oh Hannah. More than the world.*

—*But* why *do you love me?*

He would kiss each one of her fingers. *You make me look forward to tomorrow.*

Something turns inside her; a wash of contentment rushes out of nowhere, like something healing. Her bracelets jangle as she unlocks the car. Euan will be home next week. They'll have a party. She'll invite that wee Julie girl, definitely. Hannah's not sure how many friends he's made since moving here, but Julie appears to be a constant. The list at the front of her brain scrolls down. The police have agreed to do door-to-doors round the village. Tick. Posters flapping everywhere. Tick. No phone calls yet, but it's progression. Mhairi is organising a petition for the windfarm, the leaflets are out, website built. Tick. Her five hundred words are written for the day. Tick. Hannah trills stiff fingers. She could be conducting an orchestra, or moving a jigsaw back into place. Artists are meant to be chaotic, but she likes her life ordered. She keeps telling herself that. Lower down the list: Justine's references. No tick. Telling Mhairi about Sentinel buying that land: that's one to be saved for later, with a glass of wine. They'll hear the sonic boom in Glasgow. She cannot believe the cheek of Sentinel. Their avarice. Their, well, their canny acumen. Sly bastards. But Michael says he'll sort it, and she believes him. She has to believe him. It's going to be fine.

She's not ready to go home, though. Hannah wants to go back to the dig. Justine knows to get Ross from nursery; she can have a few more hours at Crychapel, do another five hundred words, easy. This evening, they will eat Miss Campbell's defrosted stew, Hannah will have a few beers to accelerate the writing, continue this glorious roll she's on, and then she'll climb aboard the good ship Michael. They have many months to make up for. Perverse as it may be, having a young female stranger under their roof is making Hannah amorous. Hysterical? She has an insistent need to mark her territory anyway.

She takes a tentative sip of her coffee; no, it's still too hot. It's definitely not healthy, this urge to show off in front of Justine. Lots of clever-scented sprayings: *These are my words, my book. My kitchen. This is* my *husband. Look, I'll snog him in front of you.* She wonders if she and Michael become better people, though, in front of an audience. Like when you put on lippy to go to the pub. You are still essentially you, the same old you who would be sitting in front of the telly, drinking the same old drinks. But in a public space, you are by necessity transformed. You can't be in your jammies, can't be picking your toes and staring glumly at the wall. Let loose, you must sparkle.

There's a spreading stain on Hannah's T-shirt. Coffee dribbles. One more thing for the wash: which she's delighted to say is being done very nicely, and without any colour-run mishaps. Although she looks like she could smell dirty, Justine is very clean.

Hannah Anderson, *wash your mouth out*. But it's true: it's nothing specific she could insist be rectified; merely a hint of wetness at her lip, of blue, unspecific shadows. And Justine wears clothes for a body she doesn't have: shapeless, when she's clearly not. Hannah likes her sheets being ironed, her dinners made. She does not like her wee boy being in love. *Justi says – Justi, can you read – Justi, can you make macanonie?* Apparently it tastes better with no lumps.

Ach, that's not fair. Justine's a funny wee thing. Sweet in her own way. Does that sound patronising? Good. She needs to feel superior. The girl is simply a bruised fruit. Another soul for Michael to save. Hannah opens the car window, tips the scalding coffee out.

Chapter Seventeen

A smell of dry tobacco. The box of cigars is flanked by a bigger box, same pale wood, open at the front and tucked with straw. Inside it rests a bottle of golden brandy, which Señor Escobar pats as he leaves.

'Enjoy.'

The man has barely left the room before Donald John McCall speaks.

'Slimy codfish, that one. Wouldna let Kitty in five feet of thon.' Donald John keeps his home life separate from his work. Even in the expense-scamming days when everyone's wife was also their secretary, he eschewed Kitty's involvement in his sphere. She wouldn't understand it, he told Michael. He's a different man at work, see. Prouder, louder. He reveals parts of himself here he'd never do with Kitty. Despite being his boss, Donald John seems to enjoy these brief confessionals with Michael, who's never sure if it's because he sees him as a priest or a protégé.

My own Mary Maaahg-daah-lene.' The Ghost is humming to the tune of 'Lily Marlene'. Michael's only half-aware of the conversation DJ's having; the pain in his head is intense. If he grinds his teeth, he can reach a state of not grace, but detachment. Putting his fingers in his ears doesn't work; the Ghost is wormed inside. Justine's revelation has shocked him, utterly. It plays constantly on a loop. Her protective charms shattered; he wants her out of his house, away from his child. It's a knee-jerk, heathen response; it's the antithesis of what the Lord would do.

'What *would* Jesus do?' The Ghost is currently reclined across the Leader's huge mantelpiece. A shadow is anyway, a sore dark fuzziness he thinks might be scratching itself. Or masturbating, but he doesn't like to look. Loud-buzzing hymns are his incantation; that and hiding in the church. The Ghost still doesn't come there.

'You see the way Liz dribbled when she gave him his coffee?' says Donald John. 'Fair give you the boak. Still. Very nice brandy the man brought with him. Very nice.'

Donald John is a pragmatic operator. He believes it's rude to refuse gifts, yet tells Michael never to compromise himself. 'Thon wee fund for the playground refurbishment's no to be sniffed at either.' He pops the cigars in his desk drawer. 'Did you want something else, Michael?'

How to approach this? *Focus*, Michael. Focus. He's been putting it off, hoping there'd be a natural drift in their discourse with Escobar, a mention of land sales, an assumption or assurance that all is in order. But nothing was said. 'I wanted to talk to you about the land deal. With Sentinel.'

Donald John blinks. 'What land deal would that be?'

'The one where they got to buy the access areas round Crychapel Wood. From us.'

'Did they now?'

'I believe so.'

'Tell me, Michael. Did your daddy ever tell you it was wise to
put your own house in order, afore you start elsewhere?'

'I'm sorry?'

'Have you see this by any chance?'

His boss hands him a copy of the *Courier*. The photo with him
and the flying scone is there, but it's the letters page he's pointing at.

Sir,

   With regard to the council's claim that wind power is clean and
safe, can we point out that the construction of Kilmacarra Windfarm will cause colossal ecological damage due to the proposed
excavation of the ancient peat bog, and release huge amounts of
CO_2 into the bargain.

Michael cracks the pages of the newspaper straight.

Furthermore, there is the building of access roads; the carbon-
intensive cement used in the foundations to stabilise the structures;
the ugly ancillary support buildings, not to mention the mining
and smelting of huge amounts of metal to build the actual turbines.
Then there are the health risks posed by noise: to animals and
humans alike, the danger to birds, in particular our precious
eagles, the destruction and industrialisation of our wild landscape
and the knock-on effect to tourism . . .

The list goes on and on. And on. As do the appended names,
which are only a representative sample of the two thousand signatures amassed on a petition, which, according to the letter writer,
is winging its way to Donald John's office. It's Mhairi, of course,
that's written it. The name after Mhairi's is Hannah's.

'Were you aware your wife was going to publicly embarrass the council? No to mention yourself, son.'

The weight of Michael's heart, his head, feel like they're collapsing inwards.

'And that bloody Mhairi too. Ach, see that woman? Why can she never be content?' Donald John rummages through papers on his desk. 'There arna two thousand people in Kilmacarra Glen, so how the hell's she worked that one? Traded tray bakes for bloody signatures? Did you know they've applied for funding to start a damned museum too?'

'No. I—'

He has nothing left to say.

Donald John picks up a binder. 'There's this an' all. From our own damned archaeologist. I mean, they're clearly told, these lads, tae follow a simple rule of thumb. It's damn well written out for them. "*Is the proposed development such that it would affect our understanding and appreciation of the site?*" And the fecking answer when there's new investment, new jobs *and* a big tick in the manifesto box is always, always no!' His boss thumps the report with a pudgy forefinger. 'Thon reads like he's in cahoots with Mhairi and your missus. All "significant interest" and "encouraging stratigraphy". "Maintaining an integrity of the sacred landscape", for Christ's sake.'

Donald John loosens his collar further. He always wears his shirts like that; it gives him a hurried slickness, as if he was that jam-packed with energy and busyness he'd not had the time to dress right. He also shakes your hand too firmly, is permanently glancing over your shoulder when he speaks and is best friends with the local MSP. Michael reckons Donald John has been promised a punty-up come the next elections; the council is his stepping stone to greater things. But, if old DJ cannot deliver a shiny new windfarm with the minimum of fuss, then—

'Yous are fucked,' says the Ghost, as he hops to the open window. 'It's a pigeon, Michael. What is wrong with your eyes? It is a fat blue pigeon and there is no shadow on the fireplace and your withered brain is . . . Hannah lies to you. All the time, she lies to you.'

'*Plus* the environment folk have started bleating about rare ragwort. Which sounds like a bloody disease. Michael! Michael – are you listening to me? Do you even *gie* a shit? See, when we selected you—'

'I think it's a flower?'

'Is that right?' The Leader slows. Stares right through him. It is horrible. 'OK, Michael. How you gonny handle this one?'

'Me? I thought you would want to—'

There is a crash as the door slams open and all the wee geegaws on Donald John's desk jump.

'You little shit!' The prow of Mhairi's kaftan precedes her, all of her other folds and flounces tumbling in behind. Liz is at her back, trying to push through the entrance too, but the bulk of Mhairi is such that it's proving impossible. 'Councillor McCall – I'm so sorry. I told her—'

'And I telt you. I'm no interested in talking to the monkey. So you away back to your typing and—'

'Well, if I'm a monkey, you're a bloody whale—'

'Mhairi! Elizabeth! That is quite enough. You are in the Council Chambers.'

She isn't wearing a bra. The Ghost is no longer visible, but Michael can hear him in his head. 'I can see her *nipples*. Look at the sweet round teats of her, dancing at us.'

Nowadays, folk call Mhairi shapeless, but there is so *much* shape to her, creamy sweaty billows of the stuff. Look at those calves: great barrels of flesh, planted like an insult in the room. As a wee boy, up visiting his grandpa, Michael observed grown men gasping as Mhairi Cowan sashayed past. Curvy, yes, but gorgeous with it. If he remembers right, she and Donald John were a bit of an item too.

'I apologise, councillor,' says Liz. Then, 'Shall I call security?' comes, in a sly wee voice. At once, poor Mhairi becomes the joke, drooping and flushed, the dignity of her mouth belying the fear of ridicule in her eyes.

Fat heifer ejected from council headquarters. Took four men to heave her out, witnesses say.

'No, no, it's fine,' says Donald John. 'I always have time for Miss Cowan. Away in, Mhairi. What can I do for you?'

'Hello, Mhairi.'

Mhairi ignores Michael so completely it's like a slap. She dumps the two carrier bags she's lugging on the floor, fluffs her hair out. Stray strands of wire float up through the light, then drift down to land on the desk, the carpet. Liz tuts as volubly as is possible, before slamming the door.

'You know fine well what you can do for me.' She unwinds first a purple scarf, then a turquoise one. Michael watches, fascinated, as her neck reveals itself. There are three chubby folds of skin where her throat used to be. 'That bloody test turbine – it's going up already.'

'Yes? And?'

'And we were told it wouldny be sunk till next week. We were planning a big march and everything.'

'Mhairi – that was only ever a provisional timetable . . .'

'Provisional, my arse. You're sneaking it up on purpose.'

'You can hardly "sneak up" a two-hundred-foot pole now, can you? Anyway, it's no up to me. The council disna have daily tête-à-têtes with Señor Escobar, you know. Once we've given the go-ahead—'

'Of course! It was his idea, wasn't it? Only cause you're too bloody thick to—'

'Now. Which is it to be, Mhairi? I'm either a criminal master-mind out tae hoodwink you, or a daft sap that lets Spanish boys shit all over me. Which is it?'

'Don't play your politics wi' me, Donald John. *Politics*? Without me you'd never even of heard of politics. "Whi – whi – whit's the SNP?"' she whines. 'I *took* you to your first meeting. You remember?'

'Do you no want a seat, Mhairi?'

'*No*. All the times we talked about independence, and how it would work. Never once did you say: "I know. Let's free our land, then sell it on to someone else."'

He lifts his chin to her, but stays in his leather chair. 'It's no about "freedom". You're showing your age now, pet. Like we keep saying, we'll be the best of friends with our neighbours and we'll—'

'Och aye, that's right. "*Dinna be feart, Scotland! Independence equals the status quo. You'll no even notice it's here!*" That's your lot's new slogan, isn't it? We're keeping the monarchy now, and the pound. *And* the nuclear weapons . . .'

'Oh for Godsake, woman. You canna be a revolutionary all your life.'

'How? How no?'

The bounce of her putters out. The way she crumples makes

Michael angry, annoyed at how she wobbles, at the meaty lips of flesh around her eyes.

'You're being ridiculous. We're not "selling" the land, you bloody know fine well we're not. It's no as if it's *going* anywhere. It's a natural resource . . . we're exploiting a natural resource.'

'Aye, well. You'd know all about exploiting, wouldn't you, Donald John?' Mhairi gathers up her scarves and shopping bags, which she proceeds to shake out over his desk. Sheets and sheets of paper pour on his head, his lap, slide from shiny wood and shinier trousers on to his shoes.

'There's my latest petition.'

'Good for you.'

'Fuck off, DJ. I'll tell you something, you smug old bastard. You are going to be sorry you ever started this.'

'Mhairi—' Michael gets up. He's trampling on the petition.

'Oh, piss off, Michael Anderson. You're as bad as him.'

There's another battering for the door as Mhairi sweeps out in flurries the colour of kingfishers. Patchouli oil and that slight, sweet smell he's noticed fat folk can have will linger on for several minutes. Michael's sense of despair, though, will remain throughout the afternoon, following him all the way back to the manse.

Chapter Eighteen

Justine needs a drink. She wants rinsed with spirits. Hannah has been out all day. Michael has just arrived home. Being alone with him is awful. *Hello, I'm Justine, and I'm your friendly neighbourhood hoor.*

Why? Why does she always break and damage and be so bloody thrawn? *You're fulla shite and spite*, her mum would scream. And Justine would smash a vase, or spit on the carpet, daring her mother to love her.

What does Michael think of her now? Does he view her differently as she navigates his home? Is the sway of her hips alluring or repulsive? Does he see her face and imagine her cunt, spread and glistening because she is a receptacle for sex? Or does he see a pitiful wretch, rejoice that he gave her shelter? Man, it was his fucking fault, making her say it, him pushing and pushing. *I can help you.* Let me explain your life for you, because I talk all posh with fucking bools in ma mouth and you don't, ergo my brain is so much bigger. Christ, you just want to slap the fuckers when they go like that.

Her bag's packed. One more night with Ross. One more night in her big soft bed. She'll soak in their massive bathtub, use up all their hot water, every last glob of Hannah's bath oil. Be on the

first bus out tomorrow. To fuck-knows where. To do fuck-know
what. What is the point of you, Justine? Gripping the edge of the
marble worktop. *You are a nothing person.*

That is what Charlie Boy told her. Not at first, Christ, no.
Initially, she was cream of the crop, the wee darlin' who got to sit
on his knee, like a cat or a court-jester. She was his girlfriend, not
a working girl at all. She despised the other women who clustered
round him; jaded, track-marked, spent. Sad cases, the lot of them.
The men in his gang both scared and thrilled her, each with that
tang of unhinged menace. It hung about them, a testosterone
miasma. Being that close to the action kept you on your toes.
Imagine a family, of sorts. A gangster and his moll. His herd of
cows, his labouring, thuggish children. Smash. Imagine being
told you have to earn your keep. Imagine saying no, and the
breaking thump of an arm before you are held down, tattooed.
Claimed.

Charlie Boy likes things neat and numbered.

Knuckles crackle, gripping metal. Smooth metal, warm sun.
Her body. Cold.

When it is over, you are ripped and small. You recall, years ago,
being jack-knifed over the bath, so a stepfather could smack your
bottom and you wonder: Is that why he did it? Then you are sick.
Not physically – although it's a common response, it is a purga-
tive after all – but in your soul. You think of the times you sat on
your uncles' knees, you think when that nice teacher leaned over
and brushed against your shoulder, you think of your friend's dad
tickling you and you are.

You blame your breasts, you blame the smell of you that rises like
unwashed, like you are a bleeding wound. All you want is to shutter

yourself, lay planks across your heart and cunt to stop them weeping. You want so much to say you fought it, with every violated particle of your skin you railed and kicked and bit and beat. You despise the weakness that capitulated. The strength that wasn't your own. You are no longer an autonomous capsule. You are shameful. Despicable. You are a quaking heaving bloody filthy mass.

Who *did* you think you were?

You want that hour, that day, your life to begin again. You want the paths you chose to come with warning signs, a shepherd. You want your mum.

You pretend you have a choice. When there is a currency to it, conversely, that gives context. It's a tin can round the sordid contents, protecting you; you pretend it does; you are empowered and you have a choice and you are contributing and this is business, money in the slit-slot and you do it because he loves you. He does, he really loves you, and if you loved him you'd do it. It's only sex not love and so you do, again, you do and you turn your face into the wall, but you are *choosing*. Reimbursed.

It's why all the money she stole will never be enough. Tomorrow. She'll leave Kilmacarra tomorrow. And then she will start again.

'Oh.' Michael stands, framed in the kitchen doorway. 'I thought you were— You all right?'

'Yup.'

'I just . . . d'you mind if I stick the kettle on?'

'It's your house.' She steps away from the sink, so he can get in to the tap. 'By the way, a woman called *Sha* phoned for you? She sounded pissed.'

'No. She's not. She's not well. Her name's Ailsa.'

'Whatever.'

Christ, this is awful. 'Look, Michael, I'm sorry I took the pish out of you. And I'm *so* sorry I told you . . . fuck, I'm going to go, all right?'

'No.' The kettle batters down.

'Is that not Alessi? Man, don't break it. Hannah'll freak.'

'Please don't go.' There are beads of sweat on his brow. She thinks he might puke.

'OK. Cool your jets, padre.' Blank relief that he's not repulsed by her. That she is needed, still. She goes all brisk. 'Here, is your head hurting again?'

'No. I'm fine. It's nothing.'

He shakes himself, and she's not sure if it's a tremor or deliberate. You can chart the flow as it shivers from neck to shoulder to trunk. Then his body settles. His eyes don't. 'Michael. I think you should take a couple of Panadol, eh? For your head?'

'Mm.'

Winding the tea towel round her fingers. 'Michael. Did you tell Hannah? What I said?'

'*No.* Did you?'

'Of course not.'

'Justi. What's for dinner?' Ross charges into the kitchen. 'Hi, Daddy! Can I have a sleepover with John-boy please?'

She wheechs him up, so he is flying in her arms.

'What would you like, gorgeous boy?'

He's giggling and shrieking, so she blows a raspberry under his chin, the most delicious tender place where he is tickly, she knows he's tickly here, *and* under the side of his ribs, and in the crook of his elbow; the scent of him is apples and baby flesh and love. Pure love.

'I . . . want . . . fishy fin . . . gers!'

'Who's John-boy?' says Michael.

'Johnny. Can Johnny and Buddy and me have a sleepover? He wants to be Euan's friend but I would like him too. Please? He is a big boy.'

'Right, down you get now. Let Justine make you your tea.'

'But can he?'

Justine sets Ross back on the ground. 'I don't think he's a very nice boy, Rossie.'

'Yes he is. He's my friend.'

'Is he not a bit big for you?'

'No.' His face puckers. 'I am a big boy too, cause Euan has left me alone anyway and there are no more boys here except Johnny and Buddy.'

'Euan hasn't left you, silly. He'll be home soon.'

'No. *You* are silly, Daddy.'

'Mm. I probably am.' Michael nods. He shuffles out, kettle forgotten.

Later, in her basement room, after Ross is fed and bathed and bedded, Justine opens her wardrobe. Carefully, she lays her jumpers back on the shelf, shakes out her two cardigans and a single T-shirt dress, puts them on their hangers. The base, the bulk of her bag is carpeted with fifty-pound notes. What the fuck is she going to do with all this money? Tomorrow is too big a deal to think about right now. One hour at a time, one chunk of a day; if she slices it up in sections then she won't be overwhelmed. Feed her body, unknot her mind.

Forty quid should do it. Enough to get a glow on. No danger of her slipping up or saying the wrong thing: she is an expert at holding her drink. She drinks the way animals sleep: one eye always open. Jesus, Johnny? That awful, snotty kid she scared the shit out of. She doesny want him anywhere near Ross. But she can't stop thinking about him. Who picks wee Johnny up from school? Who tucks him in at night? Probably can't sleep at all, because of the nightmares she's given him. Man, she panicked. Is an idiot.

For one clean week in Kilmacarra, Justine has tried to live like she is nice, but the self-loathing is shoving up, filling her with cement. You'll do anything to survive. You will cheat, lie, trample small children. You like to think you're good, but humanity, in her experience, is pretty base. A man asked her once what she thought the definition of 'good' was. She couldny answer at the time (her mouth was full), but she's thought about it a lot. She thinks it's to behave like someone is filming you, when you know you're on your own.

Oh man. Justine needs cauterising alcohol, and a nice long chat. If that freckly farmer-guy's around.

Chapter Nineteen

Charlie Boy checks his watch. It's a fuck-off Rolex, a real one, none of your green-wrist crap. He minds the cunt he took it off. Took his wedding ring and all. One nice slice and a permanent reminder. *Ho! Cunt!* You may live up in the Mearns in a big white house with four cars in the sweeping drive. You may wear cashmere coats and run a *legitimate* business which has paid for your weans' private schooling and your new wife and her new tits. You may have mere cash-flow problems that you think a slap on the back and a twenty-year-old malt can fix. Do not mess with Charlie Boy.

Six thirty. One more visit to make and then it's phone time. The grip on his ribcage returns, that moment when the thump-thump press becomes the thump-thump migraine and the tears start rising with the futility of the repetition. Only he canny stop.

Canny stop calling Justine's phone. He knows how her mind works – well, no bastard knows how her mind works, but, aye. She's done daft things before, got a wee bit spirit up and kidded on she'd balls on her. Then she'd crap herself. Coorie in all soft and greeting till he was fucking liquid with the power. And he never hurted her that much. He was good to her. Fucking good. He *liked* that she stood up to him. Aye. To a point, until it's just pure cheek and far too close and then . . . Aye. Fuck. You have to take control, man. Have to fucking *show* them. So they know. And he knows her, the insides of her, the soft black bits that smell of blood. He knows she'll be thinking he's got an army out, scouring the countryside for her, pulling in every favour from every cunt who's ever owed him anything. But how can he? He canny humiliate himself with this loss bleeding out his pores. Folk smell that on him, and he's dead. So he rations the phone calls to once a day. Seven o'clock. Phone time.

He takes a wee dauner through Kelvingrove Park, Askit straining to burst at the ducklings, with the rim of algae round the edges of the pond and a lassie jogging by. Every time Charlie Boy phones Justine's number and gets the message, it gets worse. Back to square fucking one. The scab's ripped open, pus and blood and guts out. That her voice is out there. Is not breathing into her phone.

A grog comes up in his throat. He bullets it to the ground. Fuck: is that all he's made of? Snotter and shite? Quarter to seven. He's at the other side of the park now, near the scabby tenements as opposed to the swanky terraces behind him. Forty-four, forty-six . . . A nice round fifty. He chaps the peeling door. A minute. Chaps again, with the heel of his boot. It's good to take your turn on the shop floor. Keeps you connected, know?

The door shunts open. A *WELCOME* mat appears. There's a baby crying in the background, and a careworn lassie who is haunted by the ghost of her prettiness. She pulls her dressing gown tighter.

'Please,' she whispers. 'I promised. I'll have the money by the end of the week.'

He shrugs. 'Hear you said that last week too, doll.' He disny mind her name. They call her the merry widow. Charlie Boy comes inside. The wean cries louder, and Askit barks. He yanks the fucker's lead. 'Shut it!' The lassie's eyes are mental.

'Please. I'm begging you.'

He does a nice wee sigh. 'Listen, doll. I'm a reasonable man.' Sits himself in the armchair. There is one mock-leather armchair and a couch. It's a comfortable chair. Two clear tears run either side of the lassie's nose.

'You've absolutely nae money in the house?'

She sobs, hair in hands and hands in mouth. Charlie tuts, as if he is sad. Charlie unbuckles his belt.

The alarm on his Rolex beeps. He lays his hands on the lassie's head. 'Hold that thought, doll.' Charlie's not superstitious, but seven is his lucky number and it's like your lottery tickets, know? The one time you don't get your numbers is the one time your numbers come in. With his left thumb, he dials Justine's number. With the right, he pushes the lassie's neck down. Askit is panting. His dug's a fucking pervert. The second before the recorded message kicks in, the hope, the fury; it's like a fucking boil bursting, know? All this pus pure rushing out; he disny know what he's saying fucking bitch fucking bitch; even imagines it's ringing, ringing in his ears, fucking sobbing in his lap, the cow, all fucking cows, and there will be the silence after, the dead silence he cannot bear.

Only this time, someone answers.

Chapter Twenty

Hannah takes a swig of water. She's knackered, they all are. Some are garrulous. Some are very quiet. The police have just left Crychapel Wood. A TV crew's come up from Glasgow, but they've not been allowed in till now, and there is much grumbling about not making the teatime news. There's a clutch of local stringers, some snappers, and a man from Talk FM. Professor Tom is waxing lyrical about Druids and Celts, says fourth century BC a lot, and – *of course we can't be sure* – but you can see how he is loving it, all this attention when his day is normally knee-deep in mud.

The men have uncovered a second grave. It is a stone-walled square, the size of a hearth rug.

One night, when they'd had too much wine, Mhairi showed Hannah the only painting she'd kept (stashed in her kitchen pantry). Two foot wide, it was a mass of splodgy purple and green, with the Crychapel standing stones looming from mist. It had been painted as if from underground, with tangled roots framing the scene. On closer inspection, you saw they were fingers. Bone-white and grasping, clutching at the stones or dragging them down, Hannah couldn't be sure. The whole curve of stones lurched like drunken teeth in an open mouth. *My wacky-baccy phase*, said Mhairi.

There is bone-white grasping now; real and brittle, spread in the dust below her. Hannah looks into exposed earth, to where the newfound bodies lie. Two of them. Dusty, crusted like barnacles, curled side by side. The mother skeleton is curved round the little one, like she's shielding it, or trying to hold it back inside her belly. There is the fine dot-dot-dash of ribs and spines, there is a haunch or shin. There are porous dips and open fingers like an iris flower. Ochre in parts; in others translucent. Neither body has a skull.

There are more interviews, more flashes. The police return, same two cops who should be looking for Euan's . . . attackers? Yes. What else would you call the driver? A woman with white paper slippers crinkles past; the fiscal has already been, and a doctor. People come and go in a single, taped-off route, inspecting. Erecting. There's a palpable vibration in the air. Clusters form and reform, Tom at the centre of it all, orating on how the head was sacred: a vessel for the immortal soul.

'They believed the heads of the dead could intercede for the living.'

'Like ghosts?' asks a reporter.

'No. More in terms of animism. Everything. They thought all natural forces had spiritual power.'

'Like Buddhists?'

'No—'

'But where are the heads?' asks another. 'Did they eat them?' 'Was it sacrifice?' says a third, then there's a long-winded explanation of how, till medieval times, folk would exhume skulls; put them in confessionals or on top of towers, to keep watch on the living.

'Some churches have niches in the doorframe,' smiles Tom with his tombstone teeth. 'Just to keep human skulls.'

She listens to them chatter, these archaeologists that were content to scrape for fragments, and she thinks about her children. Eventually, there is an adjournment to the Kilmacarra Hotel. Hannah declines. She said she'd wait for the guard to come. Imagine. They are employing a guard, until the bodies can be transported. For now, they're swathed in tent.

After the circus packs up for the pub, she sits on the ground, leaning against the spiral stone. Stares at the trees, the scrubby grass, the rough, muddy cuts the men have made. Stares so long, the edges blur. It grows colder, duller. As the light fades, the colours switch off: green and brown become tissues of grey. In twilight, the glittering stones come into their own. Even the piled-up cobbles shine. Glimmering quartzes everywhere, like fireflies. There are no streetlamps round Crychapel, nothing to mediate the encroaching dark. The sky glows in front of her, dust-red, gold, violet. Soon, the stars will come out. She and Michael used to love it, lying on the roof of their car. They'd drive out to the dams at the back of Glasgow, and try to count the stars.

That's how much I love you.

Out of the car, dark glade. That crick in your neck. Breathtaking. All those infinities, a billion million trillion swirls of stars, stretching in boundless reams. *There's your proof!* He'd laugh. *And there! And there!* Yelling it into the silence. Deep, deep longing as her nails dig into the ground. Moss under her fingers, stones ridging her palms. *Can you feel it?* She used to sit here and be happy, and all the time, she was sitting on top of bones. Would you curl round your babies to protect them? Of course you would. The tarpaulins flit like ghosts. Still kneading the fibrous earth. The ground beneath, so dark. It cleaves. Fingers in with the worms. Like a kid in the sand, full weight of earth that presses down. Deeper. Kneading.

All the soft powdered loam. Pushing her fingers in the stones.

Chapter Twenty-one

The Kilmacarra Hotel is dark and smoky – not cigarettes, they've been pushed to the extremities of every pub in Scotland. No, it's peat burning, giving off its damp-earth warmth. Justine recognises the smell from the manse. There's a rottenness about it she likes, how it borders on dirty. Three men are playing darts, another tugs the puggie machine, its cherries whirring wildly past the mark. A group of mud-streaked men, who must be the archaeologists, are whooping and laughing at the two corner tables they've commandeered. There seems to be an awful lot of them. Two old ladies sip sherry by the fire, the curves of their dainty glasses catching flame. One is Miss Campbell. Shit. No more interrogations on Clan Arrow. Please. Justine kind-of smiles, then turns to the bar, where a naked, tanned elbow rests. The elbow crooks out from a short-sleeved shirt, which is wholly inappropriate for the time of year. Behind the bar, the kilt-wearing Yorkshireman whose name is Roger but Michael says you must call Rory, fiddles with his sporran as he watches Sky Sports.

'Pint, please,' says Justine, pushing into the huddle of the bar. 'And a . . .' she scans the gantry, '. . . *Grouse*.'

''Ow do. You the lass staying wi' councillor?'

'Stella's fine, ta. Yup.' She looks around for Duncan, sees he's in with the crowd of archaeologists. He lifts his pint in greeting.

The unclad elbow moves along the bar. There is a delicious draught of air; she is drawn to follow the retracting elbow, honing in slightly on the space he has left. The bar counter has a beery moistness about it. She's not had a drink in five days, hasny even missed it, but now there is a tingle in her mouth, there is the loose, wild feel of unfurling. There is the sound of the man in the short-sleeved shirt's breathing.

'A pint?' Rory adjusts his sporran, so it's centred exactly below his little paunch. 'Furra lady?'

'Tell you what,' she says, allowing herself one brief and furtive glance up. Black-haired. Flashy. The man at the bar stares directly at the screen. Which is also perfect. A player, just like her. Sand-coloured Duncan is entirely forgotten, kindling at most. Justine is best when she's a bitch. 'Make it two.'

'Two pints or two whiskies, love?'

'Two of everything. And one for yourself.'

'Cheers, love. I'll 'ave a Coors Light.'

If she is quiet and still, they will have respite from saying anything at all. There will be nothing implicit in this. Just two people having a drink. She passes him the pint. He smiles, and takes it. Justine luxuriates into the silence, their silence, which is coated, protected from the dartboard whoops and jeers, from the two old ladies' yipping, the football commentator's rambling on and on. They sip. A fleck of foam rests on his upper lip. His nose is fractionally crooked, which she likes. A lot. He is significantly taller than she is, his eyebrows just the right side of thick, are possibly groomed in some way, but she doesn't want to know this, so she focuses on the unadulterated stubble on his neck, the strong and random hairs that populate his upper chest. He's just one button short of showing off. She downs her pint. The alcohol fizzes. Makes her reckless. She is regarding a menu, nothing more.

'By 'eck – they's playing crap the night, your boys.'

Rory is standing, arms folded, head swaying in fake-dismay at the telly.

'Yes.' Her man answers, but doesn't engage. From this, she deduces he is polite and businesslike. Good. How they are standing now, him behind her. A crackling, live unit.

'You like foo'ball?' He speaks very quietly. Man, he's foreign! French or Spanish maybe. Yuss! She likes them dark and hard.

'No.'

'Huh.'

He touches his hand on the base of her spine, and she presses, lightly, against it.

'What team's playing?' she says.

'Barca.'

'That where you're from? Italy?'

'It is not Italy. It is *Cataluña*.'

'Where?'

He sighs. His thumb stops rubbing.

'What you call Spain.'

'Oh.' She stares intently at the telly. Considers saying *si*, then segues into '*So* . . . why're you here? Long way from home, eh?'

'Ro-ree. Two more, please. An' two doubles.'

They both watch the football, him slightly overlapping behind her. Pressing. His thumb starts up again, rotating like a tiny toothbrush. It begins to chafe a little, but she is scared to move in case it stops. She wishes they hadn't begun talking, it's too familiar,

239

this façade of pleasantries which is futile. She simply wants a no-strings fuck.

'Ah, Spain. You work for the electricity company?'

'I do. I am the boss.'

She does not imagine the little dunt he gives her. It is a definite thrust to the dent above her buttocks. *Oh, man. Do not become a fanny, pal.*

'Hi there.' Duncan is beside her. He smells like fresh grass. 'Evening Mr Escobar. Enjoying your night off?'

Escobar grunts into his glass.

'Justine, I'm really sorry, but I'm not going to get to hear you sing.'

'What? I'm not bloody—'

He laughs. 'I *knew* you were feart.'

'I'm nae feart of nae one.'

'Is that right? Well, I'll take your word for it. But I need to head right now. Got a wee job on.'

'Another one?' she says. 'How did the—'

He shakes his head, eyes on to Escobar. Rory, she notices, has moved from their line of vision. She hears him say: ''Ere. We don't want none.' An aggressive edge to it.

Duncan interjects. 'Rory, it's all right. He's fine, pal.'

Her Spanish man pushes a second beer at her, breathes inside her ear: 'We can drink these in my room, you know.'

'Oh, can we?'

They have gone beyond subtle; she can sense the old biddies staring at them. Or someone is. Very cleanly, they are stripping the side of her face; she can see a cheek, a cloud of ginger furze moving in.

'Ach, it *is* you.'

A pale hand reaches in, splitting their circle of two. She recognises the grimy nails, how utterly ingrained they are.

'Jesus! Frank?'

Brown teeth beam. How is this possible, that the tramp from the bus has found her, here? A thick slab of, it might be terror, but she calms it right down, dousing it with common sense. This is where he left her. Justine forgets, for a minute, that the ginger dosser is not part of Buchanan Bus Station's furniture, that he's a real-live moving entity, was on the bus that brought her here. That he must have a life, and that this will simply be a coincidence.

'How's the head?' says Frank.

'All better, ta. Frank, this is Duncan and—'

She doesn't know.

'Baldomero,' her dark man says.

Justine snorts into her pint. In her head, she will call him Miguel.

'So what brings you here?'

Kilted Rory is hovering, clearly unhappy. She smiles airily to show him it's all right. *I can vouch for this orange dosser. He will not run amok and steal your meths.*

'Actually,' says Frank, 'I was looking for you.'

There's a blow to her belly, *thud jab-jab-smash*. It is true. Charlie Boy has been tracking her with tramps. Justine calculates how fast old Frank can run, reckons he will be carrying a knife at the very least. The tramp reaches into a tattered poly bag. The concrete inside her does its job, keeps her fixed and rigid in her spot while her head is screaming *Run*. He tugs out a piece of newspaper. 'Yeah. If you were still here, that is. Thought someone might be interested, anyway. For the museum.'

'What?' Relief becomes derision. He is merely an old nuisance.

'I saw this when I was up in Mull. About the windfarm?'

It's a front-page photo of Michael catching a bun.

'Says you're starting a museum up.'

'Are we?'

'Says so in here. Some woman called Mhairi says there's going to be a Kilmacarra visitor centre, with history walks and artefacts.'

'Lemme see that. Please.'

Baldo . . . *ugh* . . . Baldomero takes the paper. Soft Spanish murmur, a shake of his head. 'This is rubb*ish*. Who is saying this?'

'I told you. This Mhairi-woman.' Frank removes more newspaper from his bag. 'I'm glad you stayed,' he smiles. 'It's a nice place here.'

'It is,' agrees Duncan. 'Can I get you a drink, pal?'

'Ooh, I'll take a wee lemonade, if you don't mind. Anyway. Seen as I was coming back down the road, I thought, if you were still here, you might like this. Sorry, dear. I don't even know your name.'

'This is Justine,' says Duncan.

'Excuse me, please.' Baldomero is addressing Justine. 'This Mary? Is she the fat woman who has the café? She will not be providing a visitor centre – we have a contractor.'

'That's right,' says Frank. 'It says she owns the café. I tried there, but it was shut. But d'you think'd like this?' There's a sprig of heather stuck on his lapel. The tiny bells of it tremble as he rummages. 'I'm not a fan of windfarms, myself. Bit like a virus, to my mind. See if your wee museum—'

'Frank. I don't know anything about a museum.'

'Ta dah.' He unwraps a framed tapestry. It's an old sampler

faded roses round the edge, joined by swirly stems. Justine reads the embroidered letters:

> East, West
> Home is best
> North, South
> Here is the mouth
> The light of day
> And dark of night
> Where all points meet
> And all is right.

'Very nice.' She tries to hand it back.

'I know,' says Frank. 'You think I'm loo-loo. Away with the fairies.'

'No, not at all.'

'Who is Lulu?' says Baldomero. 'Is she with Mary? How do you know this man?'

Och, it's no use. She cannot shag a man called Baldomero.

'What does it mean?' says Duncan, handing Frank his drink.

'Cheers. I don't know exactly. Home is where the heart is? Found it in a junkshop on Tobermory.' Frank is digging in copious coat pockets, bringing pieces of string, a hanky, a crumpled bus ticket into the light. 'Ah.' He unpicks a lolly stick from a five-pound note. 'Here you go.' He offers it to Duncan.

'Away. Don't be daft, man. Put your money away.'

'Thanks, son. That's very kind of you.' Frank takes a long draught of his lemonade. 'Aye, I always have a wee nosey in junkshops. Amazing what you can pick up. That's where I got my brolly.'

243

'Oh, God. Yes! Your umbrella,' says Justine. 'It's up at the manse. I need to give you that back.'

'Did it keep you dry then?'

'It did.'

'Aye, it's a good brolly that.'

'Can I see that tapestry a minute?' asks Duncan.

'Sure.' Frank passes Duncan the frame. Justine is aware of Baldomero grabbing for it too. Deftly, Frank sweeps the frame away. 'Ho! Excuse me. My pal here asked to see it, no you.' He hams up the Glaswegian, but Justine is struck by how authoritative he is. For a moment, she can imagine him respected and cool, directing some kind of crisis. Or operating. Yes, she sees him as a surgeon, palm out, scalpel in, crisply cutting, until one terrible day . . .

Aye. If he ever was a doctor. It seems unlikely. But then, look at her. Could people tell her story at a cursory glance? Man, she hoped not.

'See the wee letters all round the edge? In amongst the roses?' says Frank. '*Jemima W is my name; And Scotland is my nation; Kilmacarra is my dwelling place; And Christ is my salvation.*'

'There's a date too. 1678.'

'It's not much, I know.' Frank takes another glug. 'But it is old. And it's part of the history of this place, eh? Some wee lassie from here took a lot of time and care to stitch this. So if it helps for your museum – and your windfarm campaign . . .'

'There is no campaign!'

Baldomero is being loud and beery. Justine's worried about Rory, who's rolling down his shirtsleeves with a purposefulness that suggests he's not about to clear glasses.

'Aye there is,' she says.

Baldomero grips her wrist. 'When you say campaign, what is it that you mean? Are there many peoples?'

'*I* don't know.' She pulls away. 'I don't know about any of this. Look at one of their leaflets, go on their website. I just came in here for a quiet drink.'

She hears Rory go: 'All right, mate. Enough. This in't a doss-house.' Hears Duncan say something too, though it's hard to make him out, with Baldomero nipping at her ear. Man, talk about a space invader. 'They have a *website*? Leaflets? How I do get their leaflets?'

'You can get one at reception. Christ, Mhairi's got them every-where: here, the shop . . . There. Look. There's a bunch of them on the windowsill.'

Baldomero goes to get a leaflet. '*Merda*. This is *bad*. I was told this digging is to prove there is no archaeology left. Not to promote . . .' He stops reading. 'Are you with this campaign also?'

'Oh, aye. I'm a regular honeytrap, me.' There is a beer-bubble filling her throat. Deliberately, she makes a burp. In the second it takes to round, then dispel, Baldomero's fate is sealed. Like wait-ing too long for a complicated meal, Justine has lost her appetite.

There is a whoop, a catcall as the TV changes and the news channel comes on. Familiar hills roll, the stunted stones of Crychapel appear as the table of archaeologists and hingers-on cheer and *shush* in equal measure. The whip-slim, tanned presenter on the telly smiles. 'Archaeologists are tonight pondering an amazing discovery—'

'*Ooh. Pond*-ering,' go the archaeologists.

Baldomero mutters a word that sounds like *puta*, wheechs out a wafer-thin phone. Justine hears the door close. Turns to look for Frank, and Duncan, but they've gone.

Chapter Twenty-two

Evening. A carefully crafted vintage kitchen. A man, humming a tune. From the outside, he must look happy; this middle-aged man with his hands in suds, zithering 'Rock of Ages' through his teeth, a glass of Sauvignon perched on the windowsill. Michael rinses the last of the dishes, carefully avoiding the naked haunch that is straddling the draining board.

'You missed a bit. Oh, Michael. You really need to get a grip.'

He clangs two pots together.

'*Ooh*. Get you, grumpy.'

The humming grows more demented. *Rawk On* trills above it. He takes two Anadin, another slug of wine. For his whole life, Michael has clung to his rock. Whether it's from fear of what lurks elsewhere, whether it is the frozen-on grasp of dizzy heights or true volition that *in God we trust*, he can't be sure. All he was sure of was his wee rock, and the fact of his persistent fingers. It's a strange, quiet rock, Michael's faith. Over the years, when he's thought about letting go, when he's tried to shrug it off and walk away – it's been there all along. Spread under him, the full shadowy girth of all his world. Some folk have washed by his rock, others clambered over when he waved. But it's been carrying him all that time. And it's always been easy, really, to reach down, seize

246

your wife's hand in yours and keep going. No matter what. No matter that you cannot—

No matter.

He thinks of his last sermon in Kilmacarra Church, of the lift he got from the people. The love in that vaulted room. He is desperate for love now, searching and scrabbling like those men at Crychapel Wood.

'I love ya, baby.' The Ghost kisses the top of his head.

Michael holds his hand to the light. Solid flesh. Wiggles his fingers. Apart from the transparent webs that link them, they are solid. Solid. Doubt lets the chaos in; it eats away the certainty. He takes a long breath, swilling it like the wine.

He should call Ailsa. And go see Johnny's mum. He promised he'd keep an eye on her. Husband shot in Afghanistan, so the poor lass comes home to hide. It's not his problem, he's not a minister any more, but his friend was their chaplain and he promised and it's not fair, life's not fair and he has to work and go to the hospital and speak and eat and pee. But he wishes he didn't. Each day has become a steady panic. As well as the Ghost, Michael can now see bones. Inside the ground.

It happened just there, when he was coming home. As he often does – *you mean when you want to avoid Hannah* – he took a wander through the graveyard. Felt a gentle rippling, like a person turning in bed. As is natural in these circumstances, an elbow or a buttock will rise and dip, settle into a more comfortable position. And it did. They did. First Michael saw a humerus, then a grinning pelvic bone. Quick, impatient ripplings, making it plain that Michael's footfall was disturbing them. He does press particularly hard when he walks now because the Ghost has decided he likes to ride on the base of his skull. Whispering, whispering. A tinnitus of whispering. Michael has forgotten how his own weight feels. All he can do is hum, and ride the pain. He is aware they are building to a crescendo. Very soon, this; all this air and walls and fleshy casings will snap, and he expects to fall through the ground into some netherworld from which he will never escape. It will be like falling off a bridge.

The doorbell chimes. He waits a minute, then remembers no one but he and Ross are in the house. Hannah never came home for dinner. He doesn't want to see anyone, but what if it's the police? It might be the posters, jogging someone's memory. Michael dries his hands, puts on his here-to-help face, goes to open the door.

It's not.

'Are you the minister?'

'Oh.'

A faded man is outside, faded except for the bright-red hair that burns in the electric lamplight. Michael's used to all sorts: junkies, thieves, lonely widows.

'I'm sorry to bother you.'

Stars clink past his eyes as the Ghost flurries himself. He is mostly human now, but still with the swallow-tail. Michael ignores him.

'I was looking for the manse.'

That the manse is a beacon in the darkness is good. *I was a stranger and you took me in.*

'This is the manse. And you are?'

'I'm Frank.'

'Come in, Frank. Sorry, I thought you might be the police.' He shuts out the night, leads the man into his glowing hall. 'What can I do for you?'

'You expecting the police?' The man frowns, a frown so kindly, so solicitous that Michael would like to hug him. 'I'm sorry. Should I come back later?'

'No, no. It's fine. Our son was—' Michael goes to say 'knocked down', he's pushing his tongue behind his teeth make the 'nn', the Ghost is screaming: 'Fucking *squashed*, pal. Like a manky hedgehog. Here! This yin eats hedgehogs. Rolls them up in mud and bakes them whole.'

'Knocked down.' It comes out shrill. *Down, down, deeper and –* 'Shut up!' Michael whips from side to side, clattering into the hallstand. A black silk brolly which isn't his slides through the oak spars.

'Here. You need a wee seat?' The tramp, Frank, helps him over to the flip-top pew they keep their boots in. One arm is cradling his waist, easing him down to the hard surface.

'I'm very sorry to hear about your boy.' He sits beside him. The Ghost moves his leg out the way. Tightens his grip round Michael's neck.

'Is he badly hurt?'

'He's all right,' he says quietly.

'Listen, reverend, you don't look so good. I'll not keep you.'

Michael shakes his head. The Ghost's bloody tail keeps whipping, deliberate as an angry cat, past his face.

'*Language*, Michael,' admonishes the Ghost. 'You'll make the Big Man cry.'

That might be nice. Drown out other noises.

'Yes. But I can scream louder than the wind. It was the wind that carried me down, remember?'

'It's fine,' he tells Frank. 'Our son . . . since the accident, we're at the hospital all the time. It's been quite a week. I'm a bit tired, that's all.'

'Well, like I say, I'll not keep you. I'm just after my brolly, if you don't mind.'

'Pardon?'

'My umbrella.' Frank points at the black umbrella skewed on the carpet. 'That's it there. I lent it to Justine.'

'You know Justine?'

'Met her on the bus up from Glasgow. Nice girl.'

'Yes.'

'He wants to fuh-uck her, he wants to fuck her. You want to fuh-uck her—' The Ghost jiggles on Michael's back. Hoof-tap jigging – singing. It is like wearing a dancing, malodorous bear. The hall clock does its wee half-chime.

'Quarter past,' says Frank. 'Look, I better be heading for my bus.'

'Oh, there's no bus tonight.'

'There is if you know a friendly coach operator. There's aye space on a pensioners' bus tour – someone falling ill or . . . Anyway. I'll just take my brolly, if you don't mind, and be off.'

Michael stands to show Frank out. Cracks his spine straight. The Ghost shakes, but is not stirred. '*Fuckwit*,' he hisses.

'It's OK. I'll see myself out.'

'I'm fine, really. Here. Your umbrella.'

'Thanks.' Frank runs his hand along the fabric. 'It's a lovely silk, this.' He doesn't speak like a tramp should.

'I should have . . . Sorry. Would you like some tea?'

'No thanks. Need to be off. Hitch the bus to Oban, tramp till dawn, then have a wee kip. Folk tend to leave you alone more in the day.'

'Can I make you a sandwich, then? For the journey?'

'No. Honestly, I'm sorted.'

A poor man and a prostitute. *Could be a leper an' all. Looks it.*

'Ssh. Frank. Is it urgent, where you're dashing off to? Would you like somewhere to stay tonight?'

'Oh for fucksake.' The Ghost slithers from Michael's back. 'I'm off. Can't take any more of this puke-fest. You canny have him here; he's *honking*. Hannah will freak. Smells worse than me.'

'No. Thank you.' The tramp has his hand on the doorknob. 'You mind if I ask you a question?'

'Mm.' Michael counts in his head the number of seconds it will take before the Ghost speaks again. Ten, maybe twelve?

'Do you see as well as hear?'

'Pardon?'

'I don't mean to intrude. But you're not well – you know that, right?'

'I told you. I'm tired. We're under a lot of stress at the moment.'

'Oh, sure, sure. I realise that. Is it only the one voice you're hearing, or a bunch of them?'

The air breaks. Is this it? For all Michael knows, the tramp is another visitation. He must be cautious. 'I don't know what you mean.'

'Ah. See, most people would frown and go: *One, of course. I can hear you.* But you, my friend, are immediately defensive, which speaks volumes.' Frank pats Michael's arm. 'It's called an auditory hallucination. Doesn't mean you're going mad. Honestly. About fifteen per cent of folk experience hallucinations at some time. Do you have visual disturbances too?'

'What?'

'Do your voices manifest as visions?'

Michael holds on to the hallstand. The messenger is confusing him. Perhaps this is intentional. He must just rest for a wee bit. Lie down on the couch until his mind is clear. His fingers are sticky. The hallstand is living wood, and there's all bloody sap pouring from the nail holes.

'Please. Will you just go.' He can see crucified hands in the nail holes.

'I promise you. Talking about it helps. There are all sorts of talking therapies. And drugs, if you need them.'

'What I need is for you to go away.'

The pinioned hands cup in pleading, catching their own dripping blood.

'You should also have a physical, in case there's some—'

'Will you leave me alone!' Yelling it, at this poor, kind man.

'You'll have to let someone help you. Trust me, you can't just block it out.'

'Justine. Justine is helping me. She'll be here any minute.'

'Eh, I hate to tell you, but Justine's getting dry-humped in the pub, even as we speak. I wouldn't expect to see her back tonight.'

'Rubbish. Justine doesn't know anyone here.'

'Well. She knows you. And me. And she definitely knows the guy that's groping her.'

'You're lying.'

'Why would I do that? Look, I promise you. If you do see visions, it's no different from dreams. Or when you get an idea, or a tune in your head and you don't know where it came from. You never planned to think about it, and now you have, you can't get rid of it. Honestly. It's no different from that.' Frank touches Michael's forehead. 'Trust me. The mind always wants to heal itself. You'll find a way.'

Ssssh.

The tramp's voice is growing fainter. 'Have you tried talking back to them? Sometimes you can make them positive. Make them guide you. But you've got to make yourself stronger than them. If you run away, they just chase you.'

'Just leave me alone,' he shouts, thinking that Hannah will find him. Hannah will hear and come and rescue him; that's all he wants. That's all he's ever wanted, and his neediness makes him weak. Repulsive. He sees this in Hannah's eyes, in her stiff turns, the subtle recoil. In vain, Michael waits for his wife to come, but he doesn't even know where she is.

'Right, right. I'm going. But you have to calm down, eh? Have a think about what I said.' Frank lumbers into the twilight, shoulders flat. 'You shouldn't be on your own.'

'Just. Go. Away.'

The tramp does not look back.

'Daddy?'

A wee voice drifts from up the stairs. Michael pauses, then hurries into the kitchen. Closes the door, and puts off all the lights.

Chapter Twenty-three

'How you doing, Mrs Anderson?'

The guard they've sent to Crychapel is Duncan Grey, a young farmer who'll turn his hand to anything. He lives up on the ridge, in a family farm that runs to sheep and ruin: every month, a little more tumbles down. Hannah feels sorry for his constant enthusiasm, because she's sure it's feigned. He looks a bit dishevelled, hair sweated to his brow.

'I'm fine. You all right? You look like you've been running.'

'Och, no, it's fine. Just a wee bit hot in the pub. How's Euan?'

'He's doing well, thanks.'

'Good stuff. So. This it?' He peeks inside the tent, shakes his head. 'That's horrible.'

'It is, isn't it? Everyone's jumping round like they've found a treasure trove. They've been *dusting* them with pastry brushes.'

She won't look at the skeletons again. Epiphanies should be glorious, but hers has come with a thud. Sitting here, spiral stone imprinting on her spine. Thinking. Thinking why it is that you push out children, or put your name on books. Why you might get a whole stone circle devoted to you. It's so folk don't forget. But they do, and all your stories go with it. No matter how much digging and assembling and surmising happens now, no one will know how these two souls died. How they felt, or who went first.

'Nae wonder the women were weeping.' Duncan tips his head at the stones. '*Na màthraichean a'gal.*'

She likes how the Gaelic sounds in his mouth; the thickness of it, and the music.

'Away you go up the road, Mrs Anderson. I'll sit with them now.'

He's a brave lad. It's growing dark, but they're only bones. There's nothing in them.

'*Oof.*' She scrambles up. 'Think my backside's gone to sleep. There's some coffee in that flask if you want some.'

'Cheers.'

'Night then.'

'Night, Mrs Anderson. Safe home.'

She's not sure she wants to write her book any more, because it worries her, the words flowing up her hand as she was sitting there. To her greedy writer's belly, which is filled with rank unmentionables, the graves, the grim tableau of headless mother and child are food. And it's frightening and exciting all at once. As she starts the car, the clock on the dashboard glows green. God. That late? Should Michael not be worried about where she is? She checks her mobile. No messages. But then, she didn't call him either.

Unsettled air about her as she drives. She can feel the molecules she disturbs, feel them form behind her. Hannah clicks her jaw back and forth; it's always her neck where she carries tension. She parks on their cinder path. Very quietly, she makes her way into the manse. This is her home, and Justine is the guest, but there is something furtive in Justine's sclutterings, like a little mouse inside their walls. It makes Hannah uneasy. It smacks of ownership, as if their house is Justine's; a space through which she can pass without permissions or explanation. She wants to see Michael on his own, so she can tell him about the bodies and he can hold her. And she wants to have Ross to herself. She checks her watch. Eight thirty. Shit. Did someone give Ross his tea? Carefully, she creeps upstairs to check. Yes, her baby is there, asleep. Hannah's heart aches. He's so pretty. Her selfish, splintered heart. She sits on the edge of Ross's Transformers duvet, wipes some pink stickiness from his mouth. Fair hair fanned across the pillow, one arm thrown behind his head. He's always slept like that, from the moment he was born. On his back, fists balled. Until recently, he'd sleep through Armageddon. Unlike Euan, who would thrash and scream and feed-vomit-feed, Ross would acquiesce to bedtime. Whatever way you laid him in his cot, he would swivel into place, flat out and neat. As if he had read all the leaflets about putting baby on their back. *Look Mummy. I am being a good boy.* Yes you are, baby. She leans in for a kiss, absorbing the soft warmth that's part her, part Michael. There is evidence of baked beans on his chin too, so that's good. *Thank you, Michael.* You don't let our children starve. He and Ross and Justine will have had a quiet kitchen tea. If she goes downstairs, Hannah will probably find a half-tin of beans covered with clingfilm and some cold cooked meat set aside for her. She should go, sit. Ask her husband how his day's been. Share a glass of wine. Hopefully Justine's out, or in her room.

Hannah returns downstairs, stands for a minute in her muted hallway. Light pools from the lounge, forms a triangular slice across the hallway's wooden floor. But there are voices coming, definitely, from the kitchen. Which is in darkness. One is agitated, the other soothes.

'But don't you see?'

'I have no good energies, padre.'

'You do, you do.' Is that Michael? 'You don't judge me.'

'Ssh. You'll wake Ross.'

Through a chink in the door, Hannah observes her husband. He is on the floor, with his head on Justine's breast. His hands are hungry, kneading at her. It is the rooting of a newborn about to suckle. His eyes are closed, otherwise he would see her. Justine is mostly shadow, although there is a steady flash of skin as her hand moves over Michael's hair.

Hannah feels her bones crack. A fissure splits from her heels to her skull, finding all the little weaknesses, and shattering them. Her skin keeps it all in place. Her mother's clock in the hall ticks on. She continues to watch her husband and this woman as they stroke. Both fully clad, but there is a nakedness about them. A desperate yearning which is killing her.

Justine speaks. 'Just tell her. Why not?'

'I'm frightened. What if it's *me*?'

'Well, there you go. If that's true, it's coming from you. Which means *you* can control it.' Her fingers linger on Michael's brow. Caressing, pointed nails. 'Unless . . .'

'What?' he whispers.

'Is it because of her, d'you think? Fucking with your head?'

'Who?'

'Hannah. Have you really, truly forgiven her?'

And then Hannah's skin falls away, and she is flayed. Alone. She bangs her arm against the door. The door strikes the tiled wall, stutters back.

'What the *fuck* is going on?' Words rolling low from her belly, scattering like buckshot into the darkened kitchen. The pair of them flinch.

'Hannah!'

'I let you stay in my house, look after my child, and you try to fuck my husband?'

Justine jumps to her feet. Her hands are up and open, her scratchy nails all pink, that's *Hannah*'s nail polish. *Hannah*'s husband.

'*Jesus*. I am not fucking your husband. *Man*. He's just upset. Do you have any idea what he's going through?'

'Get away. Get away from him.' A thing, a creature grabs at Justine's face; it's Hannah; isn't that strange, she thinks, full of the need to scratch off flesh, her nails want to rip out Justine's hair; it's not a cliché at all. Justine is yelling: 'Don't blame me. It's not been Michael that's doing the fucking, is it? It's *you*.'

Hannah cannot breathe. She holds herself tight, hands cupping elbows, and she is rocking, rocking. 'What have you been telling her?'

'The truth.' Michael's arms are over his head; his own human shield. 'I had to tell someone the truth.'

Justine moves behind him, soothing like they are the couple and Hannah is the assault. With chill clarity, she realises this is true. And that it's too late to care.

'Then what's the point? What is the point of moving here and smoothing it all over and pretending we still have a marriage?'

'Because I love you.'

'And you show you love me by sleeping with someone else?'

He unwraps his arms from his head. 'You did.'

There will always be that, wedging in between them. Her body is singing wires; she has to get out.

'Where are you going?' says Justine. 'You're in no state to drive. Look, why don't we all get some sleep and talk about this in the morning. Hannah, I swear to you—'

Hannah addresses her husband. 'You are supposed to be the dependable one. If you can't even be that, what is the point?'

'You don't have a bloody clue. I try, and I try, and you keep on. Shafting. Me. It's like you enjoy it.'

'What do I enjoy? Christ, you don't even speak to me, you never talk about *anything*, then when you do you talk in riddles. I am *not* a bloody sermon.'

'The protests, the snide remarks. That letter in the paper? Do you even care—'

'Ach, Christ. Stop your bloody *whining*. It's always hand-wringing and whimpering with you; I cannot stand it.'

'Hannah. You need to stop shouting at him. Trust me—'

'What did you say?'

The girl shakes her head. She is thin and wiry, and packed, packed, packed with sparkling energy. She is a force-field round Hannah's husband.

'Get out, Justine. Get out my bloody house.'

'No! For God's sake. Where can she go at this time? Hannah, baby. Be reasonable.'

A stupid, happy song is spinning round her head, about not calling me baby and cars and going far. If Justine won't leave, Hannah will. She will go and see her son. There is a chair there, he is in a single room. And in the morning she will feed him breakfast, help him wash and she will think about an ending for this story. There's no space inside her brain to think. She considers waking Ross, but he will be sound till eight and regular as clockwork, and there will be the explaining, and the tears. She cannot deal with that. There's no need to disturb her baby; she will get him in the morning.

'Hannah. *Please.*' Michael is all touching her and sobbing; it is a dribbling grope, she can actually feel his saliva, that is all there is and snot and prising-off fingers and GETTING OUT. She runs for the car, Michael hobbling after. *Go then!* Screaming *If you go, you are never coming back!* and Justine has disappeared; shame that, because in all the excitement she could have run her down but there it is, a missed opportunity probably for the best oh—

Michael, my love. How could you?

The car is clean and cool. It will drive her straight on sleek, empty roads to the hospital . . . no, it's too late, they won't let her in; to her mother then . . . no, too far, and she wants peace not lectures. Mhairi. She will go to Mhairi's house where it perches, apart from the village, by the Nether Meikle stones. To Mhairi, who will care and has a warm empty room and would have made an excellent mother, she is a bad mother to leave her boys, but if Ross is sleeping and he has not slept . . . Did the car that crushed her son glide like this? Did the driver have no real consciousness of what they were doing? Did the road have an unedged fineness about it, where the corners bled away to nothing and you could be skimming earth or air? Hannah parks by the side door of Mhairi's cottage, presses her forehead on the lintel. Then she pushes her finger into the bell, keeps ringing and ringing until a light comes on.

Chapter Twenty-four

In the kitchen of the manse, the Radio 1 DJ witters to himself in a plastic accent. A crow caws outside. Lorraine is on the telly in the lounge, saying *Really?* and *Och, wee soul.* The walls are thick, the ceiling cracked. A spider's web trails from the starry skylight.

'Want down now, Justi.'

Justine lets Ross slide, his feet connecting with the bench-thing in the hall they keep their junk in. She turns so she's facing him, then lifts him to the floor. 'There you go, wee man. I think Caribou needs a drink.' She has tried everything to keep him amused at home, but they are both stir-crazy.

Ross is a weary old man in pyjamas. 'I don't want to play at horses any more.'

'OK.' She gives him a hug. 'You go on up and get dressed, and I'll be up in a minute, yeah?'

'Is Mummy coming today?'

'Not today, baby.'

His face falls.

'We'll see her soon, I promise. Will we have pancakes for breakfast?'

He stops, partway up the stairs, and rubs his eye. 'If you want.'

Enough. They are not in purdah. Michael is slowly losing it.

He hasn't shaved for days, and jumps when she or Ross enter the room. She has a sense he's continuing a conversation, and that she has interrupted it. Friday night keeps spooling in her mind, it's like the heartbeat start of *Casualty*: spikes of drama then a dip, drama, then a dip: Frank, running into the pub to fetch her. Michael in the kitchen, on the floor, Hannah coming, a storm of shouting. Hannah going for the (literal) jugular; Michael sobbing like a girl. Her heart, breaking for him.

Now he just irritates – and frightens – her.

Michael is being pathetic. He is refusing to let Hannah see her son. Bolted the storm doors when Hannah came back, wouldn't let her in. When she phoned the house from outside, again and again, he made Justine answer. (And that was only after Hannah threatened the answer machine with the police.) He has flipped from woose to belligerent fuckwit. To crazy, if you ask Justine.

At first, all she could hear was a muffled swallowing sound on the end of the line.

'Is Ross there?'

'Hannah.' She glanced at Michael. 'He can't talk right now.'

'Why? What's wrong?'

'Nothing. Look, d'you want to speak to Michael?'

Michael's rabbit-eyes, skittering. When Justine held out the phone, he shook his hands, wild semaphore signals of *No*.

'I want my son.'

'I know.'

A broken sob. 'Where is he?'

'He's upstairs. Playing Angry Birds. Fuck, I'll go and get him.'

'No you bloody won't,' said Michael, grabbing the phone off

her. 'You left us,' he shouted into the receiver. 'I told him. You left us.' Slamming it down.

'Michael! You can't do that!'

'I just did.'

Immediately, it rang again. Justine got there first. 'Hannah, I'm *sorry.*'

'You tell that bastard he'd better get himself a good lawyer.' She was crying.

'Hannah, please, please believe me. There is nothing going on between us.'

Some breathing. A gulped: 'Just put Michael on.'

'He won't speak to you. Michael is . . . he's really hurting, Hannah—'

'No I'm not! Best thing ever. I should have chucked you out ages ago!' He yelled, seizing the phone from her – *you do that again, and you're fired. Understand?* – and a bawling match ensued, ending only when Michael marched out to hide in his study. He's been doing a lot of that.

'Hannah?' She'd picked up the discarded phone. 'You still there? Wait and I'll go and get Ross.'

'Just bring him outside. Now!'

'I can't. Michael . . .' She checked behind her. 'He'll chuck me out too. What if I get Ross to the window, though? So he can see you?'

'*No.* No.' A little sliding descent. 'Don't upset him. Oh Christ.' She could hear muffled panting.

'You OK?'

'I don't want him to see me . . . like this. How is he?'

'He's doing all right. How are you?'

'Never mind me.' Justine could make out clicking. She moved quietly into the hall, then the lounge. Looking out the window

263

for Hannah's car. Saw the top of Hannah's head, resting on the dashboard.

'Hannah? You all right?'

'D'you think Ross heard that?'

'Doubt it. You know what he's like when he's lost in Angry Birds.'

'I don't, actually. I didn't know he played it.'

'Yeah – not much. Don't worry; I said I'd do potato prints with him later.'

'Did you?' Her voice becomes clipped again. 'Look, just tell Michael I want Ross brought to Mhairi's house tomorrow. When he's calmed down.'

'OK, Hannah. No problem.'

'And I'd prefer if you weren't present.'

'Of course.'

'And tell him I'll be sending Mhairi over to fetch some clothes.'

'Clothes. Yes. Do you want me to look out some stuff for Ross too?'

'Yes. Thank you.'

'There's just one problem. What if Michael doesny calm down?'

'He will; God, it's me's the injured party here, not him.'

Justine wanted to scream: *Credit me with some taste. I do* not *go for middle-aged crazies.* Well, no unless they pay well. Instead, she sighed. Repeat, repeat, repeat. 'I am *not* having an affair with your husband. Not interested, haven't kissed him, nothing. He's delusional—'

'Delusional? I know what I bloody saw.'

'Fuck, Hannah. *Him*, Michael. The guy is a mess. He's having some kind of breakdown. Fuck knows. You *must* have noticed. He needs help. That's all I was doing. Helping. I know you don't believe me, but I swear on Ross's life.'

A long, slow drift to icy cold. 'Don't ever swear on my son's life again', before the click of termination.

Justine has tried talking, and begging. Shouting. Michael is resolute. That woman will not set foot in this house. He has refused to take Ross to Mhairi's (though he did kindly lob a heap of Hannah's clothes into the garden for her). They've spent the weekend hunkering indoors; Justine's not allowed to take Ross to nursery today, in case Hannah grabs him en route. She recognises all the signs of being a wounded animal, but she canny forgive what he's doing to Ross. What he and Hannah are both doing.

Stupid prick's off on a 'fact-finding' mission this morning. Suited and booted. Buzzing with newfound energy, all the alert, jingly supremacy that a snort of liberation can bring. Aye, well if it's anything like cocaine, the high will soon wear off. Then she can look forward to increased paranoia and even more irritability. Deep joy. When she asks, though, he claims he's never felt better. 'You were right, Justine.'

'Was I?'

'No headaches, no noises. All good!'

For now, she will humour him. If he starts his 'I see ghosts' shite again, she's phoning a doctor.

'What is it you're "fact-finding" about?'

Blowing out his cheeks. 'The Great God Wind.'

A car from Sentinel collected him, driven by a handsome man. Baldo-bloody-mero; she saw his saturnine features. Though it might be Michael's demon, come to take him away ha. Ha. It's as well Michael's not driving, though, because she doesn't think he's fit. At least they have two hours of peace, before he's home.

She goes into the kitchen for some water. If it wasn't for Ross, she'd have done a runner. Can only imagine the rumours zipping round the village, a fiery ring of *did you hear about . . . ? Shouting and bawling so they were; I heard she caught them in bed; Dirty wee cow . . . och, hello dear. What can I get you? Just the milk and the papers, is it? How are things? How's wee Ross?*

The truth? Since his mum went, Ross has been crying in the night; soft keening which coils all the way down to her basement. Justine waits for Michael to go, but he never does. So she's started sleeping in with him. Doubtless Hannah would not approve, but she's not here and Michael doesn't appear to care or notice. When Justine's wee brother got scared, she'd calm him by swaddling. If he *couldn't* move, then he would accede like a trapped bird, would close his eyes, find his sister's shoulder and, finally, sleep. Ross is too big to swaddle, but she can cuddle him. He knows his mummy and daddy are being silly billies and that they've had a fight – Hannah might not approve of that either, but tough. Kids are not stupid. When Justine has children, she'll tell them everything. Together, round a scrubbed-pine table, they will reach democratic decisions and eat delicious meals. Her children will not forage for two-year-old Supernoodles. At night, she thinks these things and she holds Ross tight, so the warmth of him seeps in her fucked-up innards. 'I love you, Justi.' He says it factually, with uncomplicated grace, and his chubby hand pats her cheek.

Four pancakes later, she and Ross are dressed, brushed, ready for adventure. If Michael's allowed out of this madhouse, so are they. What's the worst he can do?

'Rossie. Where's your other shoe?'

He shrugs. 'I posted it.'

'See you?' She opens the lid of the hall bench, retrieves his shoe. 'I keep telling you: this is *not* a postbox. And you are not Postman Pat, underrstaand?' She kids on she's going to chase him, but he doesny crack a light. Just stands there, waiting for her to put his shoe on.

Justine feels every eye on them as they walk the length of Kilmacarra main street – although there's nobody about. She clutches Ross's hand tight, wants to protect him. Does not want more bad thoughts in his brain. But, like his daddy, he barely speaks. Man, they are *not* in purdah. Breenge right in, that's what she needs to do. Take no prisoners; apologise for fuck-all. If you hang about like a timid dog, folk kick you. March up like you own the place, like you are blessing them with your presence, and they think they're the lucky ones. For years, she has used this trick professionally. Why she never thought of using it for herself was odd. *Odd.* Hello. My name's Justine, and I'm *odd*.

They've nearly made it to the swings when Miss Campbell and her pal intercept. They're coming out the store, chattering, but they have their octogenarian wits about them, and snap off the babble sharpish. Turn their permed heads as one. 'Oh, Justine!' Miss Campbell's voice carries with remarkable clarity. 'Glad I caught you.'

Ross, like a good boy, stands patiently. 'Hello, Mrs Bramble.'

'Hello, Ross, my wee darling. Justine, I'm no having any joy with Frank Arrow, I'm afraid—'

'That's OK. Don't worry about it. Come on, Rossie.'

'No, but I've asked ma pal Grizzel to speak to her grandson. He works for the cooncil, in the registrars'—'

'Please don't worry about it. It's fine.'

'Well, why don't you drop round for a wee cup of tea? To-morrow maybe?'

'I don't—' Shrugging and shifting. Scanning the horizon for escape.

The other lady smiles at her. 'And how's young Euan doing? Any news of when he's home?'

'Don't know,' she calls, pulling Ross away. 'Soon. Very soon.'

She takes Ross to the play park. He won't play.

'Will I push you on the swings?'

'No thank you.'

'The chute?'

'No.'

'Do you want to get an ice lolly?'

'No.'

'Can you tell me anything you'd like to do? Anything at all? Will we go to the dig? You know, where the men are finding buried treasure.'

'Am not allowed to.'

'Says who?'

'My daddy says.'

Probably for the reason Justine thought of taking him: Hannah might be there. It's not right, this keeping them apart. If she could engineer a meeting, accidentally. Then it wouldn't be her fault. Give Hannah back her son, and be done with this whole place.

She's getting desperate. 'Will we go and see if Johnny's in?'

'He will be at school.'

'Oh, yeah. I forgot.' Good. She's relieved. Though that's another mess she needs to deal with. Wee Johnny Green appears to be a typical man: all mouth and nae trousers. There's been no sudden police activity; she assumes he's never phoned them. There's a shifting, hard veneer of suspicion round Johnny that she recognises in herself. People like them don't go to the polis. At least, not directly – and how else would he get the reward? Her description of Euan's accident, the vehicle, isn't much, it's hardly needed now he's on the mend, but it's the right thing to do. She will tell the police herself. After she's fucked-off from here. It's better than nothing. Justine will rewrite this episode as a noble vigil. She has not been cowering in Kilmacarra. She was waiting till the time was right. She looks at forlorn Ross, how he stands: a compact press of dejection. Where she'll go is another matter. She has money, a passport, her health. And she is feeling better. A bit. Almost brave. Cooried up here, it's hard to imagine people like Charlie Boy exist. Hard to imagine the world outside the glen. It's a big, brooding comfortable scoop that's kept her safe. Like a hug, a proper hug just for holding, nothing else.

She would, she thinks. She will. But she canny leave Ross with Michael.

They risk going to Mhairi's café. A cold serving of scone-and-jam for Justine, much petting for Ross, who squirms politely as Mhairi kisses him.

'You know your mammy loves you, don't you, son?'

'Mmhm.'

'If you need anything at all, you just come to me in the café, you hear?'

'Yes, thank you.' He sooks up his Coke, continues staring at the standing stones outside. When Mhairi goes to the kitchen, he whispers: 'Why has Auntie Mhairi got a beard?'

When they've finished, Justine takes their dishes over.

'Doing me out of a job?'

'Mhairi. Where's Hannah?'

'That's none of your business.' A wet dishcloth is slapped on the counter.

'Man, I didn't *do* anything. I swear to Christ; she's got it completely arse for elbow. I mean, c'mon. Me and Michael Anderson? Guy's a joke.'

'I know.' She scooshes some Dettox. 'That's what I told her.'

'Really? And what did she say?'

'Not a lot.'

'Is she around just now?'

'Nope.' She works in vigorous circles, scouring wide, then rubbing hard on all the awkward bits.

'Can you give her a message please?'

'Nope.'

'Can you please tell her I'm sorry.'

'Four days. Four days that lassie's been without her wean—'

'Mhairi. Please. Is she at yours?'

'Christ. You want a wee gloat? You want to dance on her bloody grave?'

'I can bring him to her. Ross.'

Mhairi stops scrubbing. 'She's no there.'

'Where is she?'

'Away to—' she reconsiders. 'Is a' this just bullshit? Are you spying on her? For him?'

'*No.*'

'Aye, well, she disny need your help, thanks very much.'

'What d'you mean?'

'You'll see.'

'Just tell her. Please? Any time Michael goes out. I can bring Ross.'

Ross is drawing through spilled cola with his straw; round, sweeping spirals. Justine feels a sharp pain; maybe it's how his wee shoulders are hunched, or it's a future vision of him at school, head over desk, laboriously controlling his pencil.

'Right, come on you. Let's go.'

He wriggles down from his seat. 'Bye-bye, Auntie Mhairi.'

'Bye, pet.'

They go outside. A tractor rumbles by, trailing a blast of ripening grass. Both take a deep breath in.

'Aaah,' says Justine.

Ross copies her. 'Aaah.' She sticks out her tongue at him.

'Do you know Cal Drumming?'

'Is he a big boy?'

He giggles. The sugar in the cola's pepped him up. 'Cardrumming! Where Duncan has all wee baa lambs? Oh, it is nice there, Justi. You can see all yellow flowers. Can we go up there?'

'Where?'

He points to a farm, up on the ridge of the glen. She can just make out white blobs, truffling through yellow grass.

'Duncan? That farmer with the freckly face?'

'Mm.'

'It's a bit far, pet.'

'It is my anything else, though. You said I could do anything else. *Please.*'

It's something to do; she is curious. And Ross is smiling anxiously at her. It'll be an hour at least till Michael returns home. Mind, they could do it quicker if they drove. Of course Justine can drive – Michael's such a sap; he actually makes it easy to lie to him. The countless times a pished Charlie Boy needed picking up or dropping off? Man, driving was one of her essential talents. They return to the manse, where she helps herself to Michael's car keys.

'Don't tell Daddy we pinched his car, OK? Or I'll make you walk the plank.'

The road up to Cardrummond is a strew of haphazard cobbles, stepping stones almost, and much steeper than it appears. Would be slippy in the mud, but it hasn't rained for days. Windy, though, up here. Exposed. Michael's Volvo only makes it three-quarters of the way up, before she has the burning sense in her belly that the car is rearing backwards, will stutter and buck them off. She parks on the verge, in the inshot of a metal gate, and they continue on foot. Each stunted tree, each bug is examined as they go, her pockets becoming laden with 'interesting things' (mostly pebbles), which Ross insists he might need.

'For what?' she asks.

'For *stuff*.'

'Ooh, c'mere you.' She grabs him. 'Monkey Boy.'

'I am Monkeee Boy!'

This is her favourite spot, that scoop of ear and neck and shoulder. She blows a raspberry on the rubbery folds of flesh as Ross squirms to get away, sets him down again. 'Right, enough. C'mon, Monkey Boy. We have a mission, remember? We have to climb all the way up this mountain.'

'Mm.' He pouts. 'But I am tired now, Justi.'

'Ooh, wee boosie-face.'

'Will you carry me?'

'No way!' A flurry of pebbles splash and crack, kicked loose by her scabby trainers. The echo bounces down the track. It gives the impression other footsteps are behind them. Justine's toes feel damp. Brand new: eighty-five quid Hannah said these shoes cost her, and they're falling apart already.

'Just*ee*. Carry me.'

'No! You said you wanted to come. You need to be a big boy. Big giant steps, come on. Raah-rr, raah-rr!'

Ross stops dead. 'That is not a gianter's noise. Gianters say "Fee fi fo".'

'So they do. My apologies. Now fee-fi-fo your little butt up this hill.'

'Raah!' Head down, chubby legs stomping. A definite frown of his mother about him. It's Hannah's face when she's concentrating.

'Are we nearly there yet?'

'Yes, honey. Two more minutes.'

'Promise?'

'I promise.'

'Justi, I need a one more rest.'

'All right, wee man. Seen it's you.'

They stop for another minute, Justine peching. She hears the crack of breathing trees. Birch and oak. A few rowans. Her arms ache, thigh muscles throbbing. *Och, it'll be fine*, she'd thought when she saw the farm from the distance. *It's just a wee hill.*

'Wee hill, my arse.'

'You are not allowed to say that word. It is *my bottom*.'

'See when you go to school, you'll need to stop being such a smart-bottom, young man.'

Ross frowns, looks at his bum.

'Right, c'mon.' She slaps her thigh. 'Nearly there.'

'You *said* that already.'

'I *know*.'

*

Cardrummond Farm is big and crumbling; looks more like a country manor. Definitely bigger than the manse, but patched and boarded. What might have been a pretty pond is filled with slurry; there are sacks and tyres and junk all round the place. They find Duncan in the yard. He's hosing something disgusting off his boots.

'All right?' she says.

'Hello you.' He lets the hose slide to the ground, where it spurts and writhes. Inside the house, a dog barks. 'Thought I heard a car down there.'

'Hope you don't mind. We've come to ask a favour.'

'Dun-*can*. Please can I pat the lambs?'

Hands on knees, hunkering down to talk. His canvas trousers are damp. 'Hiya, Rossie. How are you? Wow – you're getting big.'

'I am fine, thank you. Please can I pat the lambs, please?'

'Well, there's a couple in the byre there, but they're a wee bit scared the now. Why don't you and Justine come back next week, when they're a wee bit bigger, eh?'

'Aw.'

'It's just, they only want their mummies just now. But I prom-ise you. Next week. And you can feed one.'

'Oh-*kay*.' He scuffs the dirt with his trainers.

'Tell you what. There's a new puppy in the house. Bess had babies, and I kept one. You want to see him? His name's Fly.'

'Yes! Yes!'

'Come on then.'

Duncan halts in the doorway. 'Sorry. Is that OK?'

'Sure.'

A vast bird wheels, and with it, a funnel of green, sharp wind. It whistles to Justine through skies vague with distance.

There you are.

'You coming?'

'Yeah . . . Man. It's beautiful here, isn't it?'

There you are, say the hills. *There you are*, say the stones. *There you are*, says the dirt, and the roots in the dirt and the dampness through the roots, the rooted stone, the trees, this great crease of land that runs the spine of Scotland. She senses him at the back of her, in the fold of air between them.

'It is.'

There you are.

They say it to everyone, of course. And no one. They say it to themselves, have said it all the time Justine has not been here, and will say it all the time and times after she's gone. Whispering in their long ridges and peninsulas, their parallel, fish-gill sea lochs, their pleated Caledonian earth. Maybe her dad did come from here. Maybe that is what she remembers, and it's not an imagined, fanciful yearning.

Maybe he did.

Maybe she's as bad as all those fifth-generation emigrants, who twist themselves purple to sense connections. Maybe that's why this wasted landscape drips with a melancholy that is more than history and rain. It's an entirely different view to that from the manse. From the long hill Cardrummond clings to, she can see an abandoned steading – no more than a gable end, arched in surprise at what's left of its world. Wisps rising from the distant loch. Water peaking, collapsing. Black moving beneath waves in shoals of prehistoric beasties. Why not? Loch Ness has got Nessie. Why can't Kilmacarra have a Kraken, or a Kirsty? You can just make out Crychapel Wood, with two vans and a big white tent.

And something else she'd never seen before. Fine dark markings radiating from where the archaeologists' tent is, like veins on a leaf. Running shadows under the grass. She can see them too, over at the hill behind the manse, where another tent's been pitched, and by the other cairns, needle-faint, feeding like tributaries into one thicker line that runs through the glen. Like the lifeline on your palm.

'What's that? Those lines?'

Duncan leans in over her shoulder. She feels her breast rise; it is the swift gasp of air she's taken in. Their hands almost touch. Their curving hips do.

'Where?'

'See all those wee lines in the earth?'

'Changes in peat, I suppose. Or lines of rock maybe, under the soil? Could just be the way the light hits. You get all sorts of weather up here.'

They go inside. The door opens into a spacious hall, damp patches festooning the ceiling. Flock wallpaper peels below a dado. This was once a fine house.

'How's Ross's brother doing?' Duncan shows her into the kitchen. Warmed by an enormous, rattling stove, it's clean and freshly painted, though the cabinets are worn. Pine table. Three chairs. Battered oak sideboard. An empty clothes pulley overhead.

'Good, I think.'

'Still no word about the hit and run?'

'No. Not that I know of.'

'Shocking. Bloody shocking they could leave a wee kid like that—'

An unexpected tightness, the pull of tears welling. 'They

phoned, though. Someone phoned an ambulance.' She flares her nostrils, because that tricks you into sneezing. 'They don't really tell me much. But he's getting better. Far as I know he'll be home soon.'

And I will not be here.

'Home where, though?' Duncan pulls out one of the chairs. 'Have a seat. I hear it's World War Three at the manse.'

'Jesus! I haven't done anything wrong. It's not true.'

'What's not true?' He seems genuinely puzzled.

'Whatever you've heard. Whatever folk are saying about me.'

'Ach, it never is round here. Trust me.'

He makes them both tea, while Ross gets filthy with the dogs.

'Ross! Get that out your mouth. That's the doggie's chew, not yours. Now, sit up.'

'Cheers,' says Duncan, raising his mug. 'I've got your tapestry thing, by the way. Well, I say got. It's at the pub still, but I got Rory to put it in the store room.'

'Oh, yeah. I'd forgotten about that thing. But thanks.'

'Justi, I am hungry. A hungry, hungry hippo. Can we get crisps?'

'I've no crisps, wee guy. But I could do you a cheese and ham sandwich?'

'Cheesy ham! Cheesy ham!'

'We don't really have time,' she says, stretching out her calf muscles. She wants to take her trainers off, so her toes can splay on the cool flagstone floor.

'Flying visit, is it?' Duncan grins. 'I can be very quick.'

They have two rounds of bread each.

'You bake this yourself?'

'Oh aye. Man of many talents, me.'

She takes another sandwich. They are laid on a carved wooden platter, which Ross keeps spinning like a wheel.

'Don't do that, Rossie. You'll break it.'

'But look at the whirlies, Justi! They are like Johnny's!'

'Just stop playing with it. It's not a toy.'

'Ach, he'll not break that. It's indestructible. My great-granda's brother sent it back from the war. We've his medal somewhere too.'

'Yeah? What for?'

'Dying mostly, I think. Brittany or Normandy, somewhere like that.'

'I'm sorry.'

'Och, I never knew him. Though according to my Aunt Effie, I look just like him. Poor sod, eh? Peely-wally skin and freckles.'

'Another proud ginger, you mean?'

'Excuse me—' pointing at his fringe. 'I'll have you know this is authentic Celtic colouring.'

'I like the whirlies, Duncan. Can I have it please?'

'Ross! Don't be cheeky.'

'I asked it nicely, Justi. And Johnny would like it for his secret.'

'Yeah, but you can't just ask for things—'

'Yes you can, Rossie boy. Does no harm at all to ask for things. But I can't give you the plate, sunshine, cause it was my uncle's. However—' Duncan gets up. 'Give me two ticks . . . I think . . .' He rifles in a drawer. 'Would this do?' Gives Ross a postcard. 'My auntie sent me it when she went to see his grave. See. It's got the same whirly picture on it.'

'Oh, no, Duncan. Don't be daft. You keep it.'

'Thank you, Duncy-boy! I like you.' Ross jumps down from his chair.

'You mind the puppy doesn't eat that now,' says Duncan, as Ross disappears under the table. 'It's fine,' he says to Justine. 'It's just junk.'

Sitting there, his legs spread comfortably wide, his hooded eyes bright, she is struck by how nice it is. Not to flinch when he gets up or moves his cup, or wonder which voice he's speaking to. There's a poster on the side of his fridge, held in place with magnets. It's preprinted with 'Today's Specials', but in the space below, someone's written in black felt pen:

We're the Yes! Campaign too.
Yes for Keeping the UK United
Meeting every Friday, upstairs. (After Poker Night).
   Volunteer knitters required.
See Rory for details.

'Knitting?' she says.

Duncan glances behind him. 'Ah. Don't ask. It's Rory's idea. Rory in the pub? He wants everyone to make a Better Together blanket. You know, each square representing the Union: red pillar boxes—'

'When they're privatising the post office?'

'The NHS.'

'When they're privatising the hospitals— ow.'

He chucks a heel of bread at her. 'European funding for farmers.'

'When the UK's campaigning to leave—'

'Yeah, yeah. That's why I said it, daftie. I take it you're your master's voice then?'

'Don't. Don't say that. They're nothing to do with me. I just live there.'

She falls quiet. Sips her tea. When did she become a sponge, absorbing and excreting the arguments at the manse? The silence widens. *My name is Justine Strang. And I really don't give a shit.* She imagines standing on the limits of Cardrummond's glorious view, bawling it across the glen.

'Anyway,' Duncan reaches down to feed the dogs – or possibly Ross – another crust. 'They're just things. Wee things. D'you no think it's about more than that? It feels like they're cutting our arms and legs off. Security, economy, currency, the army, the BBC—'

'Och, we'll still get *Dr Who*, you know.'

'Just being British. No one's got the right to take that off me. That's what boys like my Uncle Alec are lying dead in France for.' Back of his fingers, dusting imaginary crumbs from the table. 'I don't want Scotland to shrink away to nothing. I'd much rather be part of a family, you know?'

'You not think it's good, but? To be alive at the start of something new. When history's cresting?' Another thing she's heard Michael say. But finds that she likes the sound, the sense of it. It mimics how her belly felt when she looked out over the glen.

'You think?' says Duncan. 'A lot of folk are scared of change.'

She sees herself, crouched on the rim of the bath. The thickening dread of moving. The greater, rising terror of inertia. A slop of tea splashes on her lap.

'Can it not be all change?'

'What?'

The spilled tea burns a circle on Justine's thigh. It heats the piece of skin on which her number is tattooed. Own Brand Hoors. Charlie's little joke. For as long as you are breathing, there has to be the chance to start again, to do it better. She presses down the sick tastes, the shivering. 'Life,' she says. 'Otherwise we're done. We're stuck.'

'You OK?'

She gives him a big, sexy smile, which is a default, yes. Which she could change, yes. But it is a useful bright, deflective thing, mostly. 'Can I ask you something?'

'Fire away.'

'Do you work for Sentinel because you think the windfarm's a good idea, or because you need the money?'

'Ach, I do it for love, obviously.' Duncan gestures at the tatty cupboards. 'What would I want with money? Fix the roof? Maybe I like knowing if it's raining without going outside?'

'No moral dilemma then?'

'About what?'

'Oh, I don't know. Anything? What gets your morals going?'

'Ah, now that would be telling.'

'Ross, don't.' A shoe is kicked, skites across the floor. Then bare, wiggling toes. He must get that urge from her.

'I amn't doing it.'

'I can see you under there. Take your sock off the doggie's ears.'

'But he likes it.'

'No he doesn't. You want to go home right now?'

A wee sad voice. 'No.'

'Well then. Behave.'

'Kids,' says Duncan. 'Knacker you, don't they?'

'You got any?'

'Nope. Well, two actually. Billy and Nanny. They're in with the lambs.'

She puts her hands behind her, twisting her fingers through the spindles of her chair. 'You live up here alone?'

'Yup.'

'Who do you talk to?'

'Ah, well, I've no pals at all, you see.'

'No, I didn't mean that. Sorry. I don't . . . there's not really folk I speak to. About stuff. You know?'

His heavy-lidded eyes drill through her. 'Yup.'

'I've got a bit of a dilemma.'

'There's this guy you love—'

'*No.*'

'Girl?'

'That turn you on, does it?'

'Might do.'

'More than goats?'

'Ooh. You are one nasty lassie.'

She half-laughs. 'Gonny listen?'

'I'm listening.'

'What would you do if—'

'You can't find the loo . . .'

'Who said that?' says Duncan.

A strangled chortle from beneath them. 'Meee!'

'Je-*sus.*' Justine leans back in her chair. 'Never work with children or animals.'

'Sorry. That was his fault, that time. What were you going to say?'

'Doesn't matter.'

'No, come on. Tell me.'

'Right. This is just a hypothetical, OK?'

Michael has his work, his status. The Andersons will still keep living here long after Justine has fled the scene. Normally, the joy of flight is that you don't care what you leave behind; that is the point of the moonlit flit: you shit, get up, go. But she's already made them gossip-fodder, Michael and Hannah. And she knows the cruelty of being labelled wrong.

'A hypothetical?' says Duncan. 'Will that hurt?'

'You're really funny, you know that?'

'I aim to please.'

She lowers her voice. 'See, in theory, if you thought a person was sick, but they thought they were fine. What would you do?'

'Talk to them about it.'

'And if they wouldn't talk?'

'Leave them be.' He chucks a piece of cheese in his mouth. 'Or risk getting your head bitten off.'

'But what if they could be at risk? Or other folk could?'

Good work, Justine. *At risk* is a phrase social workers frequently use. It is suitably vague, and threatening, and comes wrapped in connotations of superior knowledge, that they know you better than you know yourself. Aye, like that's possible.

'Mm. That's different.'

When Duncan eats, the muscle in his jaw goes taut. She follows its rope-line down his throat. He swallows neatly, takes another bite. He has a compact way of moving, expending just enough energy for the task. If Justine is *odd*, she would describe him as sensible. Not in a I'm-Michael-and-I-have-a-favourite-jumper way (*though I'm really a bag of crazy*). It's about warmth and solidity. A big brick wall? She is aware that she is staring. Flustered. She chews the last of her sandwich.

'Talk to someone else, then?' he says. 'Someone they might listen to?'

'Tried that.'

'Just-eeh! I am a doggie too.'

'Good for you.'

Ross has climbed fully in the dog basket. 'I am called Spot.'

'Good for you.'

'Spotty Botty.'

Duncan stacks their mugs on to the wooden platter. 'At the risk of sounding like a tool, my Aunt Effie always says: "Do the thing you'll regret not doing."'

'What?'

He leans in to get her plate. 'Effie's answer to everything. I think it means go with your gut.' Moving closer as he says this. 'Finished?'

In his basket, the pup sticks up his leg, begins to lick his balls. Ross gasps in admiration. 'Can I lick myself as well for cleaning too?'

'*No*,' they say in unison.

Chapter Twenty-five

Michael fits his key in the lock.

Unfit.

He's been in the church. Which doesn't work.

Unfit mother.

No hiding place from the rage. *Unreliable, unloving.* From the painful noises and faces and the absence of his wife. Hannah not being part of Michael is like a missing limb.

Unadulterated, adulteroussshe's a lying HOOR!

Seems that's your speciality, Michael.

She's gone. Hannah has finally gone. You had a lovely dance, skin flitting and your eyes in hers and it was there again, you saw her eyes pour delicately into yours, you felt it flood your limbs and you were sure.

And now she's gone. She hates you. And you hate her.

They all hate you.

Christ you're a moany bastard. He slams his hand against his head. For a moment, the singular pain is dissipated, becomes a burst of sharp droplets. Then regroups.

That fact-finding mission was an ambush. Escobar and Donald John had cornered him. Quick, pointless tour of an established Sentinel windfarm over at Cordyke, much mud on his trousers,

Ghost gibbering at a hundred miles an hour, then off to Donald John's lair. As the membranes of his life shift and blur, Michael has no option but to go with the flow; and try not to speak out loud.

Donald John to Michael: *Come in, Michael. How's yourself?*

Ghost to Michael: *Can you hear him, Michelangelo? What he's saying about us?*

Ghost to Michael, in a very convincing approximation of Donald John's lilt: *Looks like shit, thon. Well, you would if your wife'd left you. Gaunt, cadaverish streak of pish. Scare the voters, so he will. On appearance alone, the man is a liability. No tae mention his marital mess.*

Donald John to Michael: *Take a seat, son.*

Donald John to Escobar: *How was your site visit?*

Escobar to Donald John: *Interesting.*

Donald John to Michael: *How can I put this?*

Ghost to Donald John: *Eh . . . bluntly is probably best.*

Donald John to Michael: *Cards-on-table time. Michael, I thought you'd be a shoo-in. Bobby Binns dying was a disaster; our majority, as you know, is slim. Folk telt me I needed a safe pair of hands. Instead, I go for a newbie.*

Ghost to Michael: *Thought he could mould this soft flesh into the man he needed for the job.* Like a PUPPET on a striiiiiiiing.

Pause here for the shrilling to make Michael jerk, and for Michael jerking to make Donald John and Escobar uncomfortable.

Donald John to Michael: *I kent you were a minister. A fine orator. Knew your faither and your grandpa, for God's sake. Keen as Colman's mustard, so you were, all talk of 'making a difference' and 'being at the sharp end of society'. Upstanding background, pedigree, the works. Now there's rumours you're pumping the nanny.*

Michael to Donald John: *That's not true.*

Donald John to Michael (steepling his fingers): *What's going on? We're losing lots of public support for this windfarm scheme – no damned thanks tae being on the evening news.*

Escobar to the world: *Phhu.*

Donald John to Michael: *We're at the stage we need big thinking, positive dynamics, aye? I canna have one of my lead councillors embroiled in some love-tug scandal triangle.*

Ghost to Michael: *See what he did there? You're just a big tongue-twister, DJ. A big tongue-tease.*

Michael to Donald John: *It's not like that, I promise.*

Ghost to Michael: *Aye, but you would, wouldn't you? You'd do her in a fucking minute.*

Donald John to Michael: *It never is, son. But your wife is out the house now, aye?*

Michael to Donald John: *Yes.*

Donald John to Michael: *Uh-huh. So, Michael. Plans?*

Michael to everyone: *Eh?*

Donald John to Michael: *What are your plans then? This a wee hiccup? You and the good lady effecting a reconciliation?*

Ghost to everyone: *No way, José. Not fucking again. No fucking way. When she knows him so little? When she thinks my Michelangelo's a cheating bastirt comme elle, elle what's that smell—*

Michael to Donald John: *SShNo.*

Donald John to Michael: *Then I'd like you to talk tae ma cousin. Fergus is a top-notch lawyer. Very discreet an' a'. Because we need to get this sorted, son. Quick and clean.*

'Michael?' says Justine. 'Is that you?'

He goes downstairs. Michael would love to sleep, just turn his out-of-control brain off, just for a tiny second. Justine follows him, down into his study. She's holding the cordless phone, the one that looks like an old-fashioned dial-up. You think it'll be heavy when you pick it up, but it's lightweight. Another expensive piece of crap. '*Michael.*' Her hand's over the mouthpiece. 'That's the man from Yes Scotland on again. And are you remembering that lady Ailsa? Her son's phoned twice now. He sounded pretty desperate.'

'I'm not here.'

'What will I say?'

'Tell them I'll phone them back. Has Hannah phoned?'

Her pointy chin quivers. 'Oh for Godsake.' Door slam.

'Would you look at that, Michael. Those peachy buttocks in Boden cords, chewing away at themselves. Winking at you, so they are. See how they're just that wee bit too tight, too short. So the juice of her's spilling out. They're Hannah's trousers, by the way.'

Michael sits at his desk. An important man.

'*Hannah-nah-nah.* Bitch took your balls. Now she wants your boys?' The Ghost gives his ear a playful lick. 'If they are your boys.'

Justine doesn't know her father. He wonders how that feels, to look at every man you see, thinking *they could be my dad*. Not knowing your lineage, not knowing all the weight of expectation and generations to be proud of. Pretty much any man could be your dad. That tramp was called Frank, maybe he was her dad. Maybe it was him right enough, why not? At least he was a decent man. Is Michael old enough to be her dad? Is Michael Ross's dad? Oh Hannah. To make the shrilling quiet, to make her laugh, make her love him again. He would have done anything, just anything to salve the raw stump of their marriage.

He is going to lose his job soon. That's what Donald John was hinting. He will have no wife, no role, no money and no sons. Michael turns on the radio. Brand new, but it's made like a vintage wireless. The final strains of 'Summertime' ooze from the speakers. Those were the weeks the Ghost first visited him, in the summer; up high in the summer-red sun glaring, punching hot and the noise of the music doesn't drown him out; it's as if all the noises simply converge and amplify to match the pitch he chooses, until turning a sheet of paper is like opening a bag of crisps.

— *These are private companies.*

He recognises that voice; it's switched from the song to a discussion. It's Mhairi Cowan.

— *They're not doing it for the good of Scotland's future. It's about money. Profit and money; and none of it will come to us.*

He fumbles with the dial, knocks the radio to the carpet. Justine returns. He sees her grit her teeth. Pick up the radio. Open up her face to him in a calm and efficient smile. 'OK. He says to tell you that they'll lobby for the windfarm, if you'll come and speak at their meeting. And, while I've got you, you've also had a call from the Rural Workers Collective. They say if the windfarm doesn't go ahead, they'll come out in support of the No campaign. Seen as you'll be reneging on a whole bunch of jobs.'

'But what about the dig?'

'What about it?'

The Ghost is standing behind her, rubbing his tummy like he's famished. He is almost entirely formed, and recognisable. Michael refuses, every second he is awake, to recognise him. He gets up, moves out of the line of sight.

'I *know* what everyone's saying. I've had my ear bent about it all morning. But after Crychapel was on the telly, this windfarm is becoming really contentious. I've had folk from all over Scotland saying we should protect the area.'

'But what do *you* think, Michael?'

The Ghost nods enthusiastically, sticks his thumbs up. 'What do YOU think?'

'I don't know.'

They both sigh at him.

'Well,' says Justine. Forbye his best efforts to quench it, there's a perkiness about her. Ponytail high on her head, cheeks pink. As if she'd been outside. 'You're the politician. Why don't you put it to the vote?'

'Eh?'

'Do something dramatic. Let the people decide. Local folk. Put it to the vote, everyone that lives here, everyone that's affected by the windfarm. Not the planning committee. The people. Let them decide.'

'But you can't . . . that's not the way it works.'

'Why not?'

'It's just not.'

'Well, that's just stupid.'

'Stupid,' simpers the Ghost.

'But then no one could blame you, could they?' Justine persists. 'If you tell them the facts. Let them decide, instead of forcing them into it. Takes the pressure off everyone.'

'But I can't . . . I don't have the authority.'

'How not? You *are* the authority. Literally. Are you not meant to represent the people? What the fuck's the point of droning on about "independence" if you never give folk any power? Set up a big for-and-against discussion, let them decide, then you come out the good guy no matter what. Massive brownie points.'

'Hear that, Michael-doodle-do? You'll be the *good* guy.'

'Will you bloody shut your face!' he yells, then claws the noise back into his mouth.

'Well, fuck you, sunshine.'

'Justine, I'm sorry.' He takes her by the arm. 'Not you. I didn't mean to shout. I'm sorry.'

'Right. Whatever.' Turning to go. 'So will I tell him you'll be there? Tomorrow night.'

'Where?'

'At the frigging *Yes* meeting.'

'No. I can't . . .'

People are laughing at him. Escobar, God, *Escobar* even commiserated. *Is not your fault. I think women like your nanny, they are what you call a prick-tease,* sí? He can't stand on a platform, in front of folk.

'He says the Leader told him that would be fine.'

'Here we go follow the Leader,' sings the Ghost.

'Will you go to the hospital and see Euan then?'

'Me?'

'Tomorrow night's my turn. I can't ask Hannah, can I?'

They all know, of course. Even at the hospital, after Hannah came in, and they started yelling at each other. The humiliation of being asked to leave, of the doctor saying they could only visit one at a time from now on. A rota being devised. *For the sake of the patient.*

'Michael, I can't go. *Man.* He doesny even know me.'

'Well, what will I do then?'

'Oh, for fucksake. Grow a—' Justine glowers at him. 'Just grow up, will you? Talk to Hannah, see a fucking shrink, I don't know. You need to be a man.'

'I *was* being a man when I wouldn't let her back in – and *that* was wrong too.' The wall is looming at him, towering over the stupid golden lectern, bashing into his forehead. 'Christ Almighty! What do you all want me to do?'

'Michael! Fucksake. Here.' He feels Justine, squeezing at his nose, the bridge of it.

'Eh, stop headbutting the wall would be a start. Anyway,' she checks the calendar on the wall. 'According to this, tonight's your turn. You're there tonight, not tomorrow.'

'Oh.'

'Right. Away and stick two hankies up your nose. You'll live.'

He touches his nose. Feels swollen, but there's no blood. 'I'm fine.'

'No, you're not, Michael. You're absolutely not. I'm going to find someone who can help you.'

'An exorcist?'

'Nope. A doctor.'

'But I don't want people to know.'

'I know.' She gathers up his empty mugs. 'It'll be fine, Michael. Trust me.'

It's an hour and a half till he needs to leave for visiting. Good. Breathe. Euan is definitely getting better: he sighs and rolls his eyes a lot whenever Michael speaks. He is developing very eloquent eyebrows. Good. Breathe. Breathe this fetid air that is all the flakes of skin and specks of spittle ever exhaled here. Breathe the press and the ectoplasm of the Ghost who walks, freely now, in your study. The place where you walk through your brain. He needs fresh air. Yes, he's the talk of the steamie; dour locals might frown or nod, and maybe he needs that solidarity. That's why he became a minister – it was the delight he found in people as much as God, that multiplied sparkling net he fell into. He will concentrate on his goodness. Trust the ordinary goodness of folk.

The field behind the manse has been filled with sheep. The dumpy ruminants watch and chew as a middle-aged man pistons past them, feet stamping on the dark berries of their droppings. Mindless exertion feels nice. He ignores the pain in his knee. A distant, grinding clanging is coming from the head of the glen, up on the slope where they're building the test turbine. He came past the site entrance on his way home. A mess of mud and fencing, and several burly men. Michael's jealous of men who can make things.

Sweat down his back, his lungs pumping with good air. Thirty minutes and he's reached the top of Mary's Brae. It's not a huge hill, and it's becoming lush with leafed trees and undergrowth. For most of the climb, the view's hidden. There's a trench a few hundred yards from the summit, with markers in the ground, like the white plastic kind you plant beside fruit and veg. It's deep, the hole; five, six feet at least, and twice as long across. Much deeper than at Crychapel Wood. A pile of rubble, of stones and thick mud, lie on a tarpaulin to the left of the trench. Several more white labels are stuck at intervals down one side of the earth wall. A vitrified hillfort. That's what they think was up here. Rock melted and fused by intense, sustained burning.

At the top, the trees thin out. The summit opens before him until he can see as far as the loch. It is beautiful. Little choppy waves break, nodding like rocking horses. Glass-bright greens and blues paint the landscape, lit by a generous sun as it strolls over

Scotland. Through a rock behind him, more water bubbles, Mary's Well, where they roll away the stone. *Tobar Mhoire*. In front of him, the hillside shelves steeply to the valley. No traffic, no people. Just the end of the sky, arcing to touch the end of the world. One big gird, hooping through space. He lets his toes tip over the side, feeling them curl in his boots. Right at the edge now, holding tight to the mossy crag. Miles of horizon rushing in his ears, swooping years past land and rock, rippling water, polishing stones.

Michael stands very still. He feels cold, despite the sun. Along the valley floor, you can chart the clusters of standing stones, random on their own, but there's a pattern to them from up here, a definite line. His head, knee, his unused legs, ache. Perhaps this is what Hannah sees, with her artist's eye. These ancient people had thought they were important; important enough to heave huge rocks and measure time, trace orbits and harness stars. They were probably stupid and cruel, but they thought they mattered in the scheme of things. If he reaches up, he'll be able to feel the sky's blueness glide over his hand. His feet stutter, tense themselves as his belly spills into that wide, horrible dream of falling. He shuffles his toes back from the rim. Closes his eyes. Kneels.

'I am sorry.'

God only knows how much this is true. Up here, in the pitch of the wind, he can sense that sudden lust for life, the terror of it slipping. Did you feel that when you fell?

'Please Lord. Please. I'm sorry. I will do anything if you stop this.'

He concentrates harder, reaching to find the presence of God and that deep still light inside him. How much more can he do, can he give? Because that's how you make the light shine out of you, sn't it? So it shines with other lights, and joins up with all the pinpoints of light which live in the stones and the stars and the sea. You can't barter with God. Michael knows this. He feels the Ghost kneel quietly beside him. Keeps his eyes closed.

'Will you always be here?'

'Will you always pretend I'm not?'

Black and orange landscapes inside his eyes. Blue fizzles, a coral imprint of the final standing stone he looked at. Cold rock. A curlew, faintly calling. There is nothing there. He opens his eyes, stands up. As he does, a finch blurts from the undergrowth, shot-blue wings paddling air. It streaks past Mary's Well. Michael's thirsty. He crouches by the spring to jut his chin under the flow. Thin rods of sunlight glitter on the rocks above him. There's a piece of black stone wedged, like a votive, right at the back of the gap from which the water runs. Edges are chiselled, worked. His hand passes through the cascade, touches the stone, which pivots gracefully from its place. It looks like some kind of spearhead. But small. Maybe Auld Angus shoved it there after the kids chipped the rock last year. It looks old. He pushes it back in, for the archaeologists to find, or miss. There's a tumble of rocks behind it. They clatter down, deep inside the core of the hill, like falling down a well shaft.

Time to go. He starts to scramble back down the brae, taking the western side this time. From this angle, you can see where they're working on the turbine. A white scar of new road slices the green land. Yellow trucks and a silvery crane churn earth, while bobbing figures dip and rise. The barrel of a cement mixer turns, its belly flashing sunlight. He stops to watch. He hadn't thought of that. Concrete pouring down the well they've made. Stooped figures heave at something on the ground, the crane chunters, up and up, dragging a pale, long, massive spindle higher and straighter until it bisects the sky. A tattered cheer rises with it.

The thing is immense, even without its whirling rotors. A spew of concrete beds it steady. Fixed. There's a sudden chill up Michael's spine. He gets it now, gets Mhairi's rage and Hannah's fear. Everything is fluid, even his country is up for grabs; it's a thing to be 'won', no longer a simple place of sea and sky and land on which to live. Old certainties are floating away and people are being asked to choose. Which side, which direction? Whirling in his head, contradictory notions of forbearance and fight, past and future, acceptance and rejection, and he thinks his brain will burst with them. All those questions. He is so tired. The grass is soft.

He thinks the end is nigh.

Chapter Twenty-six

'A parent not living with a child has a responsibility and right to maintain direct contact with the child on a regular basis,' says the solicitor Hannah's had to go a hundred miles to find. 'You're actually obliged to have contact with your kids.'

'But I want to,' she says. 'It's him that's keeping Ross from me.'

The solicitor has John Lennon specs, marooned in the middle of a moon-face. That he's bald as well accentuates this. But Adams, Grant and Clarence have been her family firm for years. She thinks her parents bought their first house via Mr Adams Senior (deceased). And nobody here is connected to Lochallach in any way.

Mr Richard Clarence pours himself more coffee. 'As I understand it, your husband has no objection to you coming to the family home, at any time of your choosing, to see your son. According to his solicitor—'

'He's got a solicitor already?'

'According to his solicitor, he believes this is in Ross's best interests, to maintain normality. Particularly as it was you that walked out.'

'I'm sorry, but that's bullshit. He will not let me into the house.'

'I see.' He makes a note. 'But you did leave the marital home?'

'Because of his unreasonable behaviour.'

'Which was?'

She shakes her head. 'He's sleeping with the au pair.'

'I see.' He makes another note. 'This woman's name is?'

'Justine Arrow.'

'What details can you give me about this young lady?' A clipped smile. 'I'm sorry. I'm assuming that she's younger?'

'Yes.'

'So, let us build up a little picture of this Justine. Date of birth last known address, her previous employment.'

'I don't . . . I don't have any of that.'

He stops writing. 'But you were employing her as your nanny?'

'It was very casual.'

'You employed a woman to take care of your children, without doing any form of background checks at all?'

'It was Michael, really . . .'

'Just to clarify. It is your husband that takes to do with all child-care matters?'

'No! No. Just this time.'

'I see. And did he coerce you into receiving this woman? Is it your belief that the relationship may have been a pre-existing one?'

'What? No.' She thinks harder. 'No. I don't think so.'

'And have you proof of when exactly their liaison commenced?'

'No.'

'But you say you caught them, in flagrante?'

'I didn't . . . They were just . . . talking. But it looked intimate.'

'You have no evidence that any sexual intercourse took place?' Mr Clarence taps his pen against his teeth.

'No.'

'Any kissing? Embracing? Lewd intent? Suggestive comments?'

'No.'

Her lawyer turns the stiff white pages in his file. Rows of neat-typed words flash past, words about her and Michael, that neither of them have written. 'I understand that, previous to this instance, you yourself experienced extra-marital relations with one . . .' He glances down, 'Gil—'

'Christ! Did he tell you that? Did Michael say that?'

'According to Mr Anderson's solicitor, the liaison took place over a period of months, and, at termination, resulted in considerable emotional and physical upheaval, requiring the family to move home, and your husband to relinquish his professional status as a Church of Scotland minister?'

'No! That's not the way it was. Michael didn't want . . . he wanted a change. That isn't fair what you're saying.'

He takes off his spectacles. 'Mrs Anderson, I'm on *your* side, please remember that. I'm simply pointing out the information which will be led in court. As I said, if you're undecided as yet regarding how you wish to proceed with the marriage, then mediation may be the best route in the first instance.'

'I just want to see my son.'

'Which your husband says you can do at the marital home.'

'That's a lie! And that . . . he's still got that woman there anyway.'

'I take it you would prefer that contact is in a different location?'

'I want Ross with me.'

'And your husband feels it best that the boy remain with him. An impasse.' Both hands go wide, an expansive shrug like he is a

Mafia don, with his thin-rimmed specs dangling from one finge
'Ergo: we will need to take a court action for contact. I'll begin th
preliminaries right away.'

'How long will it take?'

Another, smaller shrug. 'A week? Maybe two? Both partie
require to be interviewed – and the child, of course.'

'Oh no, I don't want—'

'Your other son remains in hospital, I understand?'

'Yes. He should be home by . . . the end of this week. Friday . .
Hannah tails off as she realises the implications.

'So, we'll also need to consider what provisions he'll require
Euan, is it? He'll still be immobile?'

'Yes.'

'And you're currently residing in the spare room of your frien
Miss Mhairi Cowan?'

'Yes.'

'I see. And, is it your intention to keep the two boys togethe
or are we seeking custody only of the youngest child?'

Custody. Solicitors. Camps. How have they got here, her an
Michael, with such horrible rapidity? Is this how lawyers work
where they lob questions at you you'd never even thought of, the
package neat answers and chuck them back while you're runnin
on a moving pavement that deposits you miles from where yo
began? She just wants to lick her wounds. Michael's refusal to se
or speak to her or give her Ross is causing more pain than she ca
bear. Self-righteous, self-inflicted wounds; that's what M
Clarence is implying. But that's bullshit. She knows what she saw
How, for all these months, has Michael shared her bed? Feelin
how she feels now. How could he bear it?

'Both,' she says. 'Of course I want both my boys. Look, I ca

300

ent somewhere. It doesn't need to be in Kilmacarra, I can come back here to Glasgow: I could move in with my mother. I'm sure.' She repeats it, more firmly. 'I'm sure I could.'

She stayed there last night, so she could make this morning's appointment. And it was fine. Her mother thinks she's down for a day's shopping: big-city goodies to cheer Euan up. Her mum knows nothing about what's going on. Her mum thinks the sun shines out of Michael's arse.

Mr Clarence replaces his spectacles. 'Which action the court may then consider as deliberate attempt to deny Mr Anderson reasonable contact. He's a local-authority councillor, I understand? A man wedded to his community, no?'

'He's not stable!'

'I beg your pardon?'

'That's what I've heard. Since I left. His behaviour's become irrational.'

'On whose authority have you heard this?'

'The nanny's.'

'The same nanny who . . . um . . . ?'

'Yes.'

He rubs at the corner of his eye. 'I see. And would she testify to this? Do we have evidence?'

'He won't let me in the house, will he?'

'That's hardly proof of insanity, Mrs Anderson. Especially in a marital dispute.'

'Well, what should I do? Go to the police? Camp on the doorstep? Just tell me what to do to get my boys back. Please.'

'Leave this with me, Mrs Anderson. I will speak with the other party to, um, clarify the situation re visiting your son at the manse. I'm sure Mr Anderson's solicitor will ensure there is no confusion between what agreement his client *says* is on the table, and the actuality. I suggest you return to Kilmacarra in the meantime, and agree to the conditions your husband imposes in order to see your son. The court will view that favourably.' He smiles, revealing the tiniest of teeth. 'A little self-sacrifice is always attractive in a woman.'

'Thank you, Mr Clarence.'

'Please. Call me Dick.'

The light outside the solicitor's office is like tissue-paper. Hannah's neat leather handbag swings from be-ringed fingers. They look like capable fingers. They don't feel like they belong to her. She walks the bustling length of Byres Road, licking salt away from her cheeks. Michael has transformed into a man who will use cheap shots and tender places to get his way. She never knew that about him. He says she's abandoned her children. And he's right. She did. She did it first when she slept with Gil.

She turns into University Avenue. It teems with multicoloured students, with bearded lecturers, the odd stray OAP. The whole world going about its business, and Hannah, in it, and yet not. She is careful to hold her own pocket of air around her. Fixes her face to vacant. That way, even the casual onlooker will know that her presence is merely temporary, and that they, all this brightness, is banal. The blackened spire of the university points skywards. *Aim higher*, it intones. *Don't make your alma mater sad.* Glasgow Uni is covered in knobbly bumps. It is all curly towers and jaggy bits and arching bits and cavernous bits, like Mary Shelley had thrown a craw-stepped, gargoylicious confection into one big cauldron, flashing mortar instead of electricity. To the right, as the road curves, a small demo is assembling outside the

Union. The place where she and Michael met. A wan boy in a tammy beats time on a drum. The tartan trim on the posters gives the game away.

Scottish Students for Independence

Other students mill past; some accept the leaflets thrust on them, others decline. A girl who's all raven hair and cheekbones shouts: *In-di-pendence. Here to stay!*
In-di-pendence. Won't go away!

Hannah aches to join them, not for the protest. For the being. Certainly not for the protest. This urge to unpick; all the bad places it can lead to. Were Britons not as ancient as the Scots? Only names, words we pick to call ourselves to make more divisions. Is the wind going to stop blowing when it gets to Gretna? Does the rain change colour at Berwick? She likes to think she's a feminist, but she made Michael's branch teas and cast half-hearted votes just as she washed cassocks and hosted Bible Study in her front room. To please her husband. Now the referendum is thundering closer, she feels like she's scrabbling in air, backtracking on a cliff edge that scares her. Which is a metaphor for her life, in fact.

She envies these students their skinny vibrancy. Lives that are fresh and hectic choices. Their hips will never be this angular, their skin so luminous again. Before them lies unrippled water, waiting. From a second-floor window, a bulging bomb plunges through air, striking the concrete paving. A volcano of water douses drum and drummer. Yup. It's a condom. A slow voice follows from the window: 'Would yous shut the fuck up?'

They first kissed here, she and Michael. Up there somewhere; a Christmas all-nighter in the Union. Made love that first night too – see, no one would suspect that about him, that he could be fast. Decisive. Oh, but he was. His hand, spanning her breast. That's how they used to sleep. Did he sleep like that with Justine?

Does he? Michael's hard body is softer now. Life has smoothed their corners; it should've made for a better fit. *Are you sure?* said her mum when they got engaged. *It's awful quick.* But she'd wanted to discover him, find the truth behind his eyes. When you sleep beside another person, when you lean up on your elbow and regard the full silent length of them, stay awake to drink the contours of their face. That is love. That she thought he was destined for *God* – and, by default, her. How romantic. That he knew all the things she wondered about, was confident and quiet, that he would be her lodestone. That he was so *good*. Then, how she broke that goodness, shattered it like a mirror in which she cannot bear to look. How she see flashes of them, Hannah and Michael, still, in the pieces that she finds.

Is that how Michael's feeling? She's aware of his self flowing on without her, deep and strange, his surface altered. Beneath it, he goes to places she can't follow. She thought it was only her that did that.

Chapter Twenty-seven

East, West
Home is best

Frank's tapestry rests on the mantelpiece. It's quite big. Justine doesny really know where to put it. What if it's melted by the fire? More vibrant in daylight than it appeared in the pub, there's a border of strawberries and holly leaves; each corner has a different wee bird: an owl, some kind of hovering bird of prey and two nondescript ones with heads too big for their bodies. Man, it's ugly. She will persuade Michael to give it to Hannah as a peace offering. Hannah loves old stuff. You only have to look around this house: most of the contents are old, or cunningly crafted to seem that way.

All right, doll? I know you think I tapped your husband, so here's a scabby piece of sewing to make up for it.

The embroidered words make her think of a big starburst, or a compass, where all points gravitate to home. Sixteen hundred and something. You wouldny think thread would last that long. Fair chance it's a fake.

'How's it going, wee man?'

Ross is lying on his tummy on the floor, colouring in. They've been doing paper rubbings of the gravestones. Macabre perhaps, but he is fascinated with the way the rough shapes emerge. She's surprised he's never done it before. Now he's copying the pictures of birds and animals in his sticker book. Or doing crappy squiggles instead.

'*No*. Draw round the shape of the sticker, daftie. Put the paper on top like we did with the gravestones and draw round the shape of the birdie.'

She puts her feet up. Unwraps a Penguin biscuit.

'But I done the squirly whirlies! Look!'

A whole page of curly flourishes, none remotely like a bird.

'I made Johnny's secret sign.'

'Did you? That's lovely.'

Despite the telly and Ross's chatter, the house is hushed. Expectant. Surely Mhairi will have passed the message on to Hannah by now? It's been two days. Fuck, Duncan wasn't far off the truth. This does feel like a war zone; with Justine stuck in no-man's-land. She could text Hannah direct, or phone her. But she senses that would enrage her more. Man, it's frustrating. Now would be perfect timing too – Michael has finally succumbed and gone to see a doctor. Justine is no specialist in headshrinks, but it appears she does an excellent line in nagging. Never had the balls to nag before, not really. Not to push beyond that initial first wheedle without fear of getting your teeth to play with. She stretches out on the couch, toes pressing into soft velour. On his belly, on the carpet, Ross blethers away.

'Mhm. It is on Duncan's nice picture. He has to practise it for a secret.'

'Does he? Duncan? Duncan's nice, isn't he?' Stretches deeper. Gets a wee sparkle up her legs when she thinks of Duncan.

'*No*, silly. Johnny.' He waves a piece of white card.

'Scruffy Johnny? Johnny with-Buddy-the-dog Johnny?' Justine takes the card Ross is brandishing, turns it over. It's the postcard Duncan gave him when they were at Cardrummond.

'What is cruffy? Is it a colour?'

For the first time, she properly studies the design on the front. Three interlocked spirals. Unlocking and waving. Waving, not drowning; their black and white fronds in anemone whorls. *Le Breton triskèle* is circled round the symbol in ornate print. Copycat fronds uncurling in her stomach.

'My name is not a colour. What does annersons mean, Justi?'

'Uh-huh. What, sweetie?' Her attention is diluted. Pumping. The pattern on the postcard is the same symbol from the car. The car towed by the van that struck Euan.

'Green!' says Ross, triumphant. 'Johnny's other name is Green. Not cruffy. But his mummy's name is not. Isn't that funny?'

She flips the card again. In tiny print below Aunt Effie's hand-writing, she reads:

Dans la mythologie Celtique, le Breton triskèle peut représenter les trois éléments primordiaux: l'air, l'eau et la terre. Aussi, c'est un symbole solaire ou lunaire. Visitez Bretagne et appréciez!

You put stickers on your car to say where you're from, not where you've been. The vehicle that hit Euan was from France. In all the days since the accident happened, the same fraught thought has helixed in her head: *This is stupid. You need to tell them what you know. This is stupid. You need to remove all trace.*

All around Justine is muddle and pain; she suspects she carries it like the plague. Man, the least she can do for them is this. She has to tell the police. She turns the volume down on the telly. She'll need to get that stupid mobile off Johnny first. Where was her head; what had she been thinking? If she phones, then he phones, they'll think she's . . .

Well, they'll know she's a duplicitous cow.

Do the thing you'll regret not doing. Does that work but, if you've already not done it? This 'thing'? If Justine could sort this properly, if she finally had the balls to go: I'm sorry, I got it wrong. I was scared and stupid. I didny know yous then. To tell them, just open her mouth and say: *It was me that saw the crash. Me that left him lying there.* The relief of it being out, the relief of the hole she's smashed open to breathe, and then the rush of air coming in. She thinks beyond the saying of it, to the moment after; it's what she always does: *in five minutes this will be over. This time tomorrow, this will be past; by next week, it won't hurt.* Then she thinks past her relief, past their slow hurt faces, to the coldness and the hardening and the words she can't take back. Them, uniting against a common enemy – which might effect a reconciliation, so kudos there, Justine. But what happens after that? What always happens. The villagers drive the enemy out.

'Did you say Johnny's been practising it for a secret?'

'Mhm. To make Euan better. It is a magic spell.'

'Is it? Well, that's good. Did he tell you how he knows it?'

Ross shakes his head. Tongue out as he laboriously scribbles round a new picture. 'It's just magic. Oh! Look at the telly, Justi. Look! It's Auntie Mhairi!'

The sound is low, but if you strain, you can still hear it. Mhairi, surrounded by a phalanx of dreadlocks, plenty of flushed faces, a few dark suits. Her fist is up and pumping, her face an angry balloon. 'Breach of the peace?' she yells. 'It's them that's breaching our peace!'

Justine finds the remote, punches the volume back up. 'They're stabbing the earth!' wails a posh lady. The scrolling type underneath reads: 'Protesters arrested at Argyll windfarm site. Earlier today . . .' Then they cut to footage of a wind turbine.

'That's of our hills, Justi! That's where you can see the sheep!'

The film is shot from below, and you see immediately why the television might want to cover the story. It will become an urban myth that Mhairi made it to the top: she's only about twenty feet up – as high as a decent extending stepladder might take you, and there's a fire engine in attendance. The fireman is leaning out, trying to reach her as Mhairi hangs like a crucified Jesus, or a witch being burned at the stake. It's bright, breezy; she's wearing one of her hideous dirndl skirts, a flame-red fabric which bunches and billows over her head. Although chained, she also teeters on a tiny platform, perhaps it's just a rim where two portions of the turbine join together. You can see the folds of fat at her knees. You can see her pants.

'Oh God,' says Justine. 'Poor Mhairi.'

'*Full coverage of the windfarm debate tonight on* Newsnight,' scrolls the band beneath.

Then the next item glides on, a piece about tractor theft. '*Remember,*' rolls the accompanying text, '*you can call Crimestoppers free on 0800 111 555. All calls are anonymous, and you may be eligible for a reward.*'

Her mate Francine used Crimestoppers once. Got £500 for grassing up her ex. And a week in hospital when she got pissed and shouted her mouth off about it. Daft cow. Very daft. C'est bon d'être anonyme.

Chapter Twenty-eight

'What I hear you saying is that you try too hard; to be all things to all people?'

Bright, sharp Sally, Michael's pocket-sized psychologist, who tempers each truth with dimples. 'You see yourself as a receptacle?'

'Like a drain, you mean? For everyone else's crap?' He shouldn't be rude; it was kind of her to fit him in.

Sally considers him, with her bright bird head. 'I wonder if you think that's a little harsh?'

'Not really, no.' Michael can speak here with anonymous honesty. It is refreshing. Like a shower. Sally is all for him, just listening, not judging. Expecting nothing from him but the truth. His vertebrae shift one notch higher, clean air pumping to his lungs. This must be how it is to have confession.

'How do you feel about that?'

'About what? That nobody gives a damn about me? *Boo-hoo.* That my marriage is unlikely to recover? That I'm having visions? I'm schizophrenic?'

'As I said, Michael, many mental-health professionals no longer take the view that hallucinations are part of a psychopathic disease syndrome. How would it be if we considered them as a variation in human experience – a special faculty, if you like, that doesn't require a cure?'

'Believe me. I need a cure.'

Sally smiles, professionally. 'There are many varied circumstances, what you might call coping mechanisms, that can cause us to believe our own thoughts are separate voices speaking to us. It might be painful, overwhelming even, but these experiences can speak to us in a meaningful way about our life, emotions or environment. The imagination as illumination, so to speak.'

'There is *nothing* meaningful about my condition.'

'You tell me it's one cogent manifestation. Always this ghost. You joust with him. You say you're not experiencing multiple voices, or being told that you should harm anyone. Are you?'

'No. But he was different shapes at first.'

'Pardon?'

Michael clears his throat. 'The Ghost can . . . does, take different shapes – birds, animals, light. But it's always the same voice. Same man.'

'Ah. And you know this because . . .'

He rubs his nose. 'I just do, all right? I just know it's the same voice.'

'Is it a voice you recognise?'

'No.' His nose is itchy. Too stuffy in here. 'Just the same voice. Always the same voice.'

'I see. As you know, the orthodox treatment is with tranquillisers.'

'No! No medication. I . . . I don't want my brain fuddled. I need to be . . . sharp. For my wife. They're talking about decisions. About my sons. My children need me. And I have far too much on at work, I couldn't possibly—'

She raises her hand. 'Michael. Please focus.'

'I'm not—'

'Acknowledge your agitation, and let it pass.'

'Doctor, I'm fine.'

She smiles again. Waits for him to comply. 'All right?'

'Yes.'

Sally's office is in a pleasant Victorian townhouse in Oban. They are two floors up. Outside her window you can see the port. There's the cheery red CalMac lion on the lumbering ferry. There's a long brick chimney, reaching for the sky. It's not that high. But it is high enough. There's a squawk of gulls and the perma-smell of fish. Shadow-tails move across the wall as a lorry passes. Michael 'acknowledges' a ripping sickness in his stomach, which does not pass.

'In any case, tranquillisers do not get rid of the voices,' says Sally.

'Yes. Exactly. So what am I meant to do? I can't go on like this. My wife's gone mental. My boys need me to be strong. My eldest boy's in hospital still, and we've never even found out who put him there, and now she's wanting to take them from me. Accusing me of fucking all-sorts—'

'That aggressive language makes me uncomfortable, Michael.'

'Me too.' He gulps some of the water she poured him earlier. 'This isn't me. Why am I like this? You have to help me.'

'Is it here now? The ghost?'

Michael pauses. Listens for the sneery commentary he's been automatically blocking, but there's nothing.

'No. Not at the moment. I don't think. But he's always around. I . . . there's a weight.'

'You say these visions began before your son's accident?'

'Yes. So?'

She puts her hands in a neat knot, lays them on her desk. Fleetingly, he sees Justine make the same gesture in his car. 'Just as trauma can trigger an hallucinatory experience, so a major shift in our emotional landscape can silence it too. I'm trying to ascertain if there's been any obvious catalyst.'

'Nope.'

'I see. You seem very sure of this.'

'I am.'

'Do you accept that the ghost exists?' she asks.

'*No.*'

'What about the Devil then?'

'What? Of course not.'

'But you believe in the existence of God?'

'I'm a minister. Was. Am.'

'That's not what I asked.'

'Yes. I believe in God,' Michael replies.

'OK. And, given that, do you *see* this deity? Can you envisage a God, or is he simply a "concept"?'

'Really? Are we going to have a theological debate? Look, I'm sorry, doctor, but questioning my belief system isn't helpful. Would you ask a . . . I don't know, a farmer or an accountant if . . .'

Tell yourself the truth.

Sally puts down her pen. 'Michael, voice-hearers and visionaries seek explanations to account for what they're experiencing. Understanding where the hallucinations come from, and what triggers them, can be helpful in developing a coping strategy. In the process of taking responsibility for yourself, the first stage is acceptance of the voices as belonging to you. Do you understand this? This is one of the most important steps to take.'

313

'Yes.'

'And do you agree with this statement?'

'Yes.'

No. Do you think I encourage him?

'Voices can express what you're feeling or thinking: sadness, aggression, fear about an event or a relationship. It's the feelings that are important, not the voices. It can be very beneficial to discuss the messages, fully, with someone you trust. If you'd rather not do that with me, do you have someone else you can talk to?'

He thinks immediately of Justine, then feels ashamed. Only because he and Hannah aren't speaking. Only that.

'Not really.'

'Well then. For our next session, I'd like you to consider exactly when these hallucinations first began.'

You mean when I sat trembling in my car, examining blood that was not mine, observing the blood become snakes and the snakes become limbs?

Sally's face shades from detached to pity. Is he that transparent? 'I want you to be honest. Search deeply inside yourself for anything you think may have been the trigger. Consider all the times the hallucinations have recurred – might anything have prompted them? An event or an emotion? Unless some meaning is attributed to your hallucinations, it can be difficult to feel more in control. It's my belief that coping depends not on the *content* of your hallucinations, but on the nature of your relationship with them. In short,' her gaze slips briefly to the wall behind him, 'if you believe the voice is in control of you, you may not be able to cope. If you believe you're stronger than the voice is, you can.'

'I see.'

'Same time next week?'

'Oh. OK.'

See how she did that? Brought him neatly to a close: in time and on budget. Had the Ghost been present, he'd have joined him in a comedy-wink.

'In the meantime, I'd like to write to your GP, refer you for some tests. Just to rule out any physical causes.'

'No. I'd rather not. I didn't really want anyone local knowing.'

'I understand. But we do need to explore every possibility. And, Michael.'

'Yes?'

'One final piece of advice. In my experience, strategies of avoidance seem to exacerbate the problem.'

Michael walks downstairs. The wooden banister is punctuated with black studs, which rub his palm as he labours down. His knee aches. His footsteps echo on the stone stairs of the close, which is tiled in rippling green. It's like being in an underwater cavern. He is light and heavy, up and down. His brain has been churned, and the silt rises to the surface. *Acknowledge it, then let it pass.*

Do you believe in God?

When he used to run half-marathons, there'd come a point when, irrespective of fierce will, his legs did not contain the physical energy to maintain pace. The only way to cope was zoning-out, to trust that some residual power would pump his legs and arms, his heart. But it ceased to be a conscious effort. Same with his belief. Now, whenever the panicked ticking of his heart kicks off – Hannah's betrayal, Euan's accident, his qualms about the council, the windfarm, his sad and complex life – he bundles everything up, holds it all like a globe in his hand. Offers the globe to God.

Tell the truth.

Where do you start?
At the beginning is always good.
Even when it's bad?
Ooh. Esspecially then, pal. That's the best bit.

Chapter Twenty-nine

They find Johnny and Buddy down by the burn, poking things with sticks.

'All right?' says Justine.

'Aye?' His reply is full of bruised suspicion.

'Here, Ross tells me you've been drawing him pictures?'

'No I huvny.' Darting eyes at Ross, who is fully engaged with the collie. 'Good *boy*, Buddy.' Each word is prefaced by a clumsy pat.

'Did you ever phone the polis?'

'No yet . . .'

Her heart slows.

'How?' he scowled. 'What you gonny do? Get the polis on me?' He takes a swig from the can he holds.

'God, you're a spiky wee bugger. You don't have to be so rude.'

Ross is only metres away, holding a salt and vinegar crisp above Buddy's head.

'Give me a *paw*, Buddy.' Without making any effort to comply, the dog reaches out a casual tongue. The crisp is gone in a second.

'*No*, Buddy. Bad dog.' Ross kisses the dog's head.

'Look, I think it's best if we forget about the police, yeah? Forget our wee game too.'

'Game?'

'Aye, you know. The one where you kid on you're me.'

'So I don't get any money then?' He tosses the Irn-Bru can on the ground.

'You want to pick that up?'

'Nuh.' He begins dribbling it like a football.

'Johnny. Please can we just forget the whole thing? Eh? It was a really stupid idea? I mean, you might get into trouble, as well as me. If they found out.'

'How?'

She improvises. 'Aiding and abetting? Withholding evidence?'

He stops kicking the can.

'So. You want to give me back my mobile?'

'Canny.'

'I'll buy you another one. A better one. And how about I still give you the reward money. So you can get a new bike, eh? How's that?' She checks on Ross, to make sure he's still far enough away from the burn. He's riding on Buddy's back – if riding means squatting over a very flat dog, who's frog-pressed into the grass.

'Can I get the money now?'

Justine holds out her hand for the mobile. 'Sure. You give me phone, I give you money. Much was it again?'

'A hunner.'

'One hundred pounds? I'm pretty sure it wasn't that much. How about fifty?'

'Justi!' Ross waves at her. 'We are in a circus!'

'Good for you!'

'Seventy-five. That's ma final offer.'

'Done. Now, d'you want to give me the phone? I'll take the wee bit of paper too, if you have it.'

'I've got the paper . . .'

'And the phone?'

'Chucked it.'

'Why?'

''Cause it was fucking pink, all right?'

'Hey. Cool your jets, wee man. It's fine. Honestly. As long as it's gone.' She glances up the bank. Ross is showing Buddy how to *lie down* on the grass. Buddy is sitting upright and watching Ross.

'I *telt* you, didn't I? It's away.'

'Where?'

'I don't know – in the bin, right? In the wheelie bin at school.'

'Justi!' calls Ross. 'I need the toilet now.'

'All right. Good. So we'll say no more about it? Promise?'

He wipes his face with the back of his hand. 'Do I still get ma money but?'

'Yes. Yes. You will. I just don't have it on me at the moment.'

'Justi!' shrieks Ross. 'It is com-*ing*!'

'Right, wee man, I need to go.' She taps the side of her nose. 'I was never here, right?'

'Whit?'

'Nothing.'

''M'on boy!' Buddy bounds towards him. Johnny picks up the Irn-Bru can, lobs it in the burn, and the daft dog jumps in after it.

Chapter Thirty

A thin layer of cloud hangs, sun bleeding out in long pink threads. Hannah lets herself into the manse. 'I'm home,' she says to no one. Is greeted by fousty morning air – that and a pile of mail, which she's to slither out the way with her foot before the door will properly open. She steels herself for an onslaught: either Michael screaming at her, or Ross running into her arms. But the house is empty. She senses this, knows the long echoes of her home when there is nobody there.

Home. She scoops up the letters. Nice, small things she can control. Slitting them open, stacking or binning them. There's a simplicity to that. Perhaps Justine's references will have arrived. But she doesn't look; she dumps the post on the hallstand. Unhooks the spare key for Mhairi's house. She'll text Michael in a minute. Their solicitors have agreed he cannot bar her from her house. Briefly, she has a perfect round pool of peace. She'll make a cup of tea. Hannah's veins are full of dusty law firms and hospital disinfectant, teeth spongy from temperate air-conditioning. She spent the night in Euan's room. Mhairi has gone to ground. No idea where she is. Silly besom must be mortified. Hannah could not get in last night when she came back from the dig. The nurses are very kind; they know the score with her and Michael, so they leave out blankets and leave her be. She didn't sleep much, though. But that doesn't matter, because she was woken with wonderful news. Bright, pale sky outside, she can smell the leaves warming into the light. Her boy is coming home! To facilitate that, she'll fight dragons.

She goes to her kitchen, trails her hand over the back of a pine chair. They each have their own seat at this table: Michael at the top, nearest the window, Hannah facing him. The boys a kick-width across from one another – Hannah often has to referee their feet. This one is Euan's chair. A square of sunlight spills on to the table. Hannah sits, lays her head down on the light, so the world goes sideways. From the corner of her eye, she sees a burgundy hand towel, hanging on a hook. It is the colour of Justine's hair when she first saw her.

Her whole body hurts. Squinting up through the window, Hannah can see the church, with the standing stones behind. She focuses on her tiredness, and the squidge of her cheek on the table, and the patch of wobbling light. It feels good to be back in this kitchen. The walls aren't important. It's what fills it. Blame and reasoning do not seem useful. Her anger no longer has the strength to rail. Euan is getting home. And they have found the driver of the car. The police called her first thing.

She must have fallen asleep, because the sun's faded by the time there is a click and a thump; a scamper of feet and joyous noise.

'Mummy! Mummy!' Ross barrels into his mother's arms.

'Oh, my baby.' His hair in her face; his perfect smell of clean and goodness. She folds and folds him up, would eat him back inside her, would groom him with her tongue. Kissing his brow, his forehead. Her belly twists when she sees Michael.

'What are you doing here?' he says.

Her son burrows into her breast, pressing and pressing like a little bull, her looking from above, framing a square so it is only her swelling breast and his gold head, Hannah's black jumper and Ross's white T-shirt. They make a perfect ying and yang. The weight and shape of him is made to fit.

'Michael. They've found it. They've found the car that hit Euan.'

'Oh. Oh.' Two long, flickery blinks. They clutch hands for an instant, then back away from one another.

She tells him it's a French family that struck their child. They were driving a motorhome, wrong-hand drive on unfamiliar roads. It was the casual swing of their towed car which caught him. They didn't even know they'd dragged the bone out of his leg. He was a stutter on their journey, an uneasy bump which was a badger, a ditch, a dark nonentity for which you don't look back. There was a mother, a father, a boy and a girl. It was a female that relayed the information, said the police. Anonymously. Spoke mostly in English, but sounded French. The family are liars, then. Was it the mother or the daughter who called? Which one betrayed their family, their splinter of guilt working free until they had to tell? They are currently being interviewed, car and motorhome impounded, examined for strips of Euan's skin.

'Did the police say what'll happen to them?' says Michael.

'Don't know. They're sending a couple of cops over to France. They've still to confirm it's that actual vehicle.'

'Is that the people that hurt Euan, Mummy?'

'Yes, sweetie.'

'But I thought you said they'd found them?' says Michael.

'I know. They're pretty sure it's the right car. But the tip-off was just a description, no registration numbers. Red car, white motorhome with a French sticker or something on it. It meant the police could check the description against cross-Channel ferries and motorway cameras, though. And this family have admitted to being in Argyll at the right time.' Hannah falters. 'Right time. I didn't mean that.'

'I know.'

'They got Euan into a wheelchair today.'

'Did they? Great.' Michael's eyelids flit shut. He has long black lashes, which dance on his hollow cheeks. He leans his head into the wall behind him.

'And they want an occupational therapist to come and assess the house.'

'This house?'

She shrugs. 'How are you?' Kisses the top of Ross's head again.

'I am hippy-happy, Mummy,' says Ross. 'Where *were* you?'

'All right,' says Michael, turning away. This man would have kept them apart.

'I just had some special work to do, sweetie. But I'm back now. Where's Justine?' she asks Michael.

'Out. It's her day off.'

'Oh, so she's still an employee then?'

'Justi is at Cardrumming, Mummy. You know Duncan? I like Duncy-boy.'

'Two-timing you, is she?'

Scratch, scratch on his forearm. His eczema must have flared up. Exuberant flakes fall to the floor. You can tell Michael is desperate for her to go, but then he astonishes her; takes her hand again. 'Hannah. I want to tell you something.' It's the hollow bass of how he says this, it's warning music, bold type.

'Rossie. Do you want to watch cartoons, baby? Just for a wee minute.'

'But you will stay right here?'

She does an ET finger-on-his-heart. 'Right here. I promise sweetheart. I am not leaving you, not ever. And you can have a biscuit, OK? One.'

'But I am not hungry, Mummy. Can I have it for later?'

'Of course you can.' She rubs her nose on his. 'Eskimo kiss.'

He holds his cheek up to her eyelid, so she can flicker her lashes on him. 'Butterfly kiss.'

'I should have told you . . .' Michael begins his spiel as Ross chuckles like a wee old man. She knows what's coming next, dodges her head out the way as Ross pretends to lunge. 'Glasgow kiss!'

'Oi, you wee toe-rag!'

'I keep trying, but all our times are the wrong times.'

Can Michael not see his son's still present in the room? 'OK. Off you go, baby. I'll be through in one wee minute.'

Michael plonks down on the chair opposite. 'Where to . . . I don't know how to do this. She says I've to be honest . . . God, you know, there are times I can see inside my own veins but I can't even *look* at you properly . . .'

'Michael, please. You're going to make yourself ill.'

He looks at her, amazed. 'I *am* ill. Can't you see that?'

She takes Michael's wrists. 'What is it you want to tell me? You can tell me anything, you know that.'

Removing his hands from hers. 'I couldn't – I *can't* – bear it. You were perfect to me, Hannah, always perfect. Too good to love a boring bastard like me. But I built my world on that. You were the foundations; the point of it all. And you ruined it.' He looks anywhere but her; angled glances at walls, at hands, at light. She hears the pulse too fast in her head. 'I've tried to . . . I've been so angry. I try to forget it, you and *Gil*; I kept scrumpling it up and pushing it down until it was a hard wee lump inside me. Like cancer.'

'Why didn't you tell me this before?'

Michael ignores her. He crushes his head into his fists. 'Oh God. No wonder I see . . . My whole job was to make folk believe in a thing they'll NEVER BLOODY SEE!'

'Michael. Did you sleep with Justine?'

'No!' He is fast and wounded with his answer. 'It was . . .' He tries to shake the redness off, the way Buddy shakes when he's wet. 'It was just the night you walked out—'

'I did not walk out.'

'What would you call it?'

'I was upset. Does that mean any time we have a fight, I'd better watch in case you screw one of your waifs and strays? Jesus, Michael. How many other times? What about the woman from the Sunday Supper Club in Castlemilk? *She* had the hots for you.'

'Hannah. You're not listening to me. I did not sleep with Justine . . . I was really losing it, and she was comforting me, then she started crying too, saying she . . .' He literally raises his eyes heavenwards, and Hannah wants to slap him. Her life is a nasty joke. Some puppetmaster God is. Is there nothing good on celestial telly . . . see this, *this* is why she can't do this any more; all this being a patient dog and waiting for a pat— In the hall, their phone is ringing.

'Justine isn't a nursery nurse,' he says.

'What?'

'She's a . . . I think she ran away. I think that's why she came to Kilmacarra. Someone hurt her, and she ran away.'

'From where? Who is she then?'

'I don't know.'

'But you thought you'd kiss her better? Christ, you know nothing about her, and you let her stay here. With my son?'

'I didn't . . .' he holds his breath. 'Hannah. I didn't. But this isn't about Justine. It's not even about Gil, is it? It's about you and me. Do we want . . .' Michael waves his hand aimlessly, spinning a helix round their misery '. . . *this*.'

Air sucks from the space between them. She sees her life fall away in scales and gentle layers. Before she can speak, Michael says, 'I don't. I want to start again. With everything. I want a clean slate.'

'With me too?'

The door creaks open. 'Daddy. Mrs Ailsa's big boy Terry says to tell you she is died.'

Chapter Thirty-one

As dark outside the window as in. Michael pulls the blanket closer, the green one from the couch. Go. Please go. He should have gone. Ailsa Grey is dead. He never went; he needs to go now, her son will need succour, practical help. He will need an explanation. It is happening again, the globe slipping through his fingers. Spinning. He has let his parishioners down, his family, his constituents. Hannah has taken Ross away from him. She is furious again, about Justine. Go. Please go. Telling *him* to calm down. She will get custody of Euan too. He's let Justine down as well, exposed her to ridicule. He wanted to tell Hannah everything, but she wouldn't listen. Nobody ever listens.

I do.

Go. Please, please go.

The ache in his head pushes outwards, until it crams his breast, his bones. Michael has prayed and prayed. He has prostrated himself on stone, has bargained, reasoned. Railed. And still the dull silence rolls, still the shadow carries him. What is it that's to be revealed? More shadow, glory, the rock? Or to see the silence for what it is.

Silence.

Killing Ailsa – like she prayed – would have been murder. It would have been a merciful release. Wasted, trapped in her own misery and pain, but her lungs worked. Of their own volition, they kept pumping her with air, and she was judged fit to stay alive; until they filled with fluid in the end. And the Ghost? He chose to fill his lungs with water. His was a wilful sin.

You think?

I think.

He thinks of his friend Dennis, the padre, swilling his brandy and telling his truth. Killing and dying on the battlefield, where there is no judge and jury, only healthy, running lungs, and good rage and right. Charging wilfully into bullets. Well, that is heroic. That's what they told Johnny Green and his mum, when his daddy choked on his own blood.

Michael's head is roaring. Those two skeletons at Crychapel with their heads chopped off: a glorious sacrifice, for the greater good, so the sun would rise and the crops grow strong? Who knows? You think your thoughts. You try to make words to say your thoughts. You wonder why you have thoughts, where they came from. What you should do with them. You should *give*, of course. Give, give, give. To whom? To what? Where do they go? Beyond. You wave a hand vaguely. Outside, up there. To a tree, a rock, the sky. If you're Hannah, to a book. You make prayers of the words of your thoughts, so they have purpose as well as form. You make a purpose of your prayers, for there is a *reason*, now, for your thoughts, and you work harder and you write harder or you pray harder and you find more words to fill the gaps, the gaps and the silences and the non-sense that keeps appearing and you find more trees or stones or symbols; you pray for grace, for perfection, for escape from these thoughts, for rewards for these prayers. A wee bit higher – faster – harder, harder – you're not trying hard enough can you feel it there, just out of reach, faster, faster, higher, do you feel it? No? Pray longer. Sing faster. Give more, bleed that bleeding heart, blood of Christ, kill a goat, a kid – yes a real kid, why not, c'mon, c'mon, you're almost there, you're on the right path, harder, faster, angrier, higher you would do *anything*, anything for transcendence, for givegivegive.

Do you fake it too?

Michael's head is pulsing bigger than his body, the pressure of the Ghost bursting in and out, in and out. The dark loom of the church is only yards from here. If he sprints, he will attain it in seconds. But he thinks he's locked the door, will have to stop, unbolt, as the darkness lingers behind him. As it creeps up his spine. Where is Hannah, Justine? Any of them? They should be here.

He slips outside, unlatches the church gate. The gravestones hum with brightness, the whole scene is gently throbbing. Over by Farquhar Moray's angel, a shadow grows, pale moon-light spilling on its shoulder. The shadow is brighter than its effigy as it turns and forms its folded arms. Face carved and blank; the eyes are stony orbs yet the hair streams across and behind, giving it dreadful movement. Michael steps inside his churchyard.

The standing stones are luminous. They hurt his eyes. The gate has disappeared. The wall is huge, and rising. Michael is over-whelmed by an incandescent moon, a fierce white light flowing upwards from the ground. Another tombstone seems to answer the first, dissolving slightly as a figure emerges. Then another and another, until the whole graveyard is filled with these forms. He sees a woman wrapped in plaid, clutching the hands of two chil-dren. Staring at him. He sees a tattered man in uniform, he sees old and young, men with rifles, girls with creels. He sees winding-sheets blow in terrible sails, sees ancient pennies fall from eyes. A fellow cleric with a bandaged jaw, trails of scattered leaves blowing through him, does not move, yet Michael sees his head incline. An acknowledgment of this, of all these see-through stones that glimmer whitely, and do not look, cannot look, yet consume him with reproach. On the roof of the church, a pale figure waits. It is a young man. Translucent.

'What? What is it you want?'

Moonlight strikes the cleric, his jabot sheerest white against frock-coat black. Marble mouth, unopen. Black with pleading. On and on, they do not stare at him, begging until the heaviness of it bursts.

'What? *Please*. What?'

'This is you, Michael. This is it. Can you feel it? All those ashes crawling in your mouth? All the lies you ever told.' A distant flicker in the cleric's eye. Entirely separate; the voice snakes out, grows thicker, more unctuous as it speaks. 'You walk on their bones every day. Constantly. They have to listen to the lies you pimp. Fluffy clouds. Thrones and righteousness. Eating them out.'

'Stop it! I don't believe you.'

'No use sticking your fingers in your ears.' The slick light that is the Ghost slides on marble skin. 'No when I'm inside your heart. I'm your tapeworm, pal.'

'I can't take this any more. I just . . .'

Michael drops on to his knees. Face first over a tombstone. The imprint of the man who stands on the roof is on his retina when he blinks. Gaunt, close-cropped, he has pit-marks in his skin and a small swallow tattooed on his neck. His wedding ring is a bold half-sovereign, round his neck, a chain called 'DAD'. His eyes are missing.

'I cannot do this.'

He is prepared to die. If death is to be quiet ash, then it's preferable to this.

'You'd leave them all behind, would you? You arrogant, selfish prick.'

'You did.'

A bandaged mandible clunks off the stone he's lying on. Michael's lips are open; soily crumbs of decomposition roll into his mouth. The Ghost crawls from the cleric's eye socket. Sits up. No longer animal or bird, he is fully formed. Gaunt, close-cropped. The swallow on his neck. He is crying.

'What kind of God are you a man of?'

He feels damp fists, damp hands that seize and shake. 'You lost my soul,' it screams. 'Fuck you, you could of saved it.'

A wall of water hits him; flip from front to back to hanging, an infinitesimal hanging; then Michael is falling to the earth as he is shoved from the tombstone, except there is no earth, just the steady sucking wet screaming fall oblivious and miles and miles of rushing fall all mud in mouth and spine in air to twist and lurch and knot his belly sooking out of him, owl eyes scanning circles, sweeping past earth and stone, shock of empty breath, beer on empty breath the pale figure is falling with him, his swallow flying, black hooks and hair all ripped cheeks judderjudder jack-knifing back and whirling, twirling spinningscreamingliving.

Crying.

Falling and crying from the highest place.

Chapter Thirty-two

It is the morning after the night before. Kilmacarra's street is quiet. Respectful. Justine and Ross tramp round the side of the manse, which has sombre, half-curtained windows, past the kirk and into the warm blast of the café. A beaded plant-holder hits Justine in the face.

'Rossie! Son!'

Mhairi lunges, grabs. Squashes. 'Oh, son. I'm that sorry about your daddy.'

'Bloody hell, Mhairi! You nearly sent him flying.'

Mhairi disentangles herself from Justine's charge. Sets her hands on her knees. Pinny taut, legs set wide like she's about to pounce. 'I suppose you'll be wanting something to eat?'

'Yes please, Auntie Mhairi.'

'She no feeding you right? Away you and get a seat, son.'

Justine leans over the counter, as Mhairi goes round, busies herself at the urn. 'So. How was jail?'

'I wasny *in* bloody jail. I stayed at my friend Isla's, that's all.'

'Tut tut, Mhairi. Hiding? Isla the posh one or Mrs Dreadlocks?'

'Posh. Very posh. She's a spare room the size of ma house.' They're both waiting for Ross to clamber on to his chair.

'I was all set to tie a yellow ribbon round the door for you as well.'

Mhairi sniffs. Slides her a mug of tea. 'You're gie chirpy, given the circumstances.'

How to explain? The waiting, a long night's waiting; Hannah by the bedside, the warm scoop of Ross on Justine's lap in the corridor outside. And Euan. Euan was there. A skinny boy in a wheelchair, plaster-cast leg thrust outright, hair too long and in his eyes. Same amber eyes as Michael.

'See?' whispered Ross. 'I told you Justi was pretty.'

An embarrassed smile. A flash of metal where his teeth are bound and healing. He didn't recognise her at all. Not a glimmer on him. For as long as she stays here – for ever – she'll be safe. Michael will be cured and it will all be fine.

Deferentially, Mhairi lowers her voice. 'Is he . . . ?'

The bell over the café door rings.

'Mhairi, can I get a—' the boy stops talking. 'Justine.'

It's wee Johnny. Buddy at his heels. His mouth breaks, smiling. He begins to dart forward. Frowns. 'I thought you were coming to see me?'

'Hello, John-boy!' calls Ross. 'Justi, please can I get a cake too? And for Johnny too maybe?'

'Yes you can. Would you like a cake as well, Johnny?' She gives Johnny a wink, means to charm him later, when Mhairi is not present.

'A cake?' He sidles grubby fingers to his hair.

'Ho you, ya wee bugger,' says Mhairi. 'Don't you be getting your nits over my clean counter.'

'I've no got nits, ya fat bitch.'

'Hoi! Don't use language like that in my café, you.'

'It's a manky dive anyway. Justine,' he tugs at her sleeve, 'I need to talk to you.'

'Well, just let me finish speaking to Mhairi first, all right?'

'But this is important.'

'And so's this. How come you're not at school?'

'It's ma mum. You *said* you'd give us—'

'In a *minute*, Johnny. Grown-ups talking, OK?'

'You said you'd give me ma money.'

'What money? Away and don't be daft.' Eyebrows raised, a glaikit smile, how thick is this boy? 'Why don't you take Buddy outside and I'll talk to you later, eh?'

'He sponging off you an' all?' says Mhairi. 'You know, I caught the wee bugger pinching a quiche out the kitchen.'

'Johnny Green! What are you like? You'll be midgie-raking next.' She tries to ruffle his hair. Her smile is wider. Is what you'd term 'affectionate'. A soft space is clicking, quietly, round them; Johnny's eyes darkening, finally getting the gist. *We will talk about this later.*

'Ach, fuck you.'

'Johnny!'

'Naw, I mean it.' It comes in a fierce sob. 'Fuck off, Justine. I *hate* you.'

Boy and dog slink off.

'Charming. Cheeky wee bastard,' says Mhairi. 'Either him or his dug's got fleas.'

Justine watches the slow drag of the boy's feet. Her heart brittles. Even the dog's tail is flat. 'Och, he's all right.' Clearly, he is thick, though. But she shouldny have been so harsh. She'll find him afterwards, explain you don't discuss deals in front of strangers. Give him the cash, a cheeky wee hug, and Johnny will be good as new. Stuff it; she'll buy him a bloody bike.

'It's no wonder, with that mother of his. Bloody lazy besom. Anyroad. How is Michael doing?'

There's a dull, hard thud at the window. Feathers sheer past.

'Jesus!'

Justine's first thought is Johnny, throwing stuff. That's what she'd do if she was a pissed-off wean. A wee half-brick; the deep joy of release. Mhairi pushes back the macramé curtain. An outline of a bird in flight shadows the glass. 'Bloody pigeons.'

The splayed-shape looks bigger than a pigeon. 'Can you see it? Is it dead?'

Mhairi shoves her cheek up against the window. 'Nah. Nothing there.' She leaves a cloud of breath, which blurs the imprint on the other side. 'Right. Michael. What's the latest?'

'Still unconscious. They're keeping him sedated a wee while longer. But they think it was a success.'

Mhairi unties her pinny, hangs it by the cooker. 'Good. Christ, the thought you could have a time bomb, ticking in your head. Ugh. Makes you want to . . . ugh, I don't know. Hear you were a star, though.'

'Och, no. Not really. Kept calm, got a blanket . . .'

'Was he *mugged*, d'you think?'

'In Kilmacarra? Doubt it. They think he's maybe slipped.'

'But what was he doing out there?'

Banging his head against the stones, Mhairi. To stop the voices. She bets that's exactly what he was doing. 'Dunno. He likes to walk through the churchyard. It relaxes him. I think.'

'Hm. How's Hannah doing?'

'Hanging on like grim death. Sitting at his bed like a sentry. That's how I brought Rossie home. She says she'll phone if there's any change. Oh, plus her mum's on the way up the road. So I've instructions to gut the house.'

'Does that mean your services are no longer required? When Mrs G gets here?'

'Need to wait and see.'

Justine is a triumph of hope over experience. One day, people will need her.

'Well, you and me both. Tell you, if this bloody windfarm goes through, I've had it. Off. Bye-bye Kilmacarra. I just want a quiet life. I canny take much more fighting.'

'You don't mean that, Mhairi. I don't want to leave here – and you can't either. Here you go, Rossie,' she takes him his toasted cheese, comes back to the counter. 'Listen. I had an idea . . . it was for Michael, but it doesn't matter who does it. Why don't you play them at their own game?'

'How d'you mean?'

'Challenge them. Tell Donald John you want a public debate, a mini referendum about the windfarm. Call his bluff. If they want folk to vote for them in September, they need to show they'll listen now.'

'You think?'

'Yeah! And what about this Kilmacarra Museum you've been promising? Who's going to set that up if you go? Look, I've even brought you the prize exhibit.' She unwraps the tapestry, which was the purpose of her visit; but Mhairi's sorting plates into the dishwasher.

'Ach, the museum was just a fat old bitch shooting her mouth off. End of the day, it's only a bit of land. Stupid poles on hills. Disny seem that important, does it?' Clatter of cutlery, cursory wipe of her hands, then she has a poke at the opened-out parcel. 'What is it anyway? It's horrible.'

'It's a tapestry. A very old tapestry, from here. Look.'

'Oh, right. Very good.' Uninterested; a vague facsimile of what used to be here; like the pigeon-print on the window. *Who is this sad woman, and what have you done with Mhairi?*

The door chimes again as two men enter. Both wear yellow jackets. They nudge and jostle like schoolboys.

'All right, ladies? We'll have two rolls and sausage, and I'll take a coffee. Jim?'

'Tea for me.'

'Aye, go on then. Make mine's a tea an' all. Two teas, hen.' He winks at his mate. 'We're absolutely panting, aren't we, Jim?'

'Aye,' snickers the other. '*Panting*, so we are.' Jim appears to be wetting himself. 'Big, big pants.'

'Right. Away yous both and piss off. I'm no serving anyone fae Sentinel.'

His arms spread wide; a swaggering contrition. 'Oh, come on. There's no need to be like that.'

'Can we get it to go?' says his mate. 'Quick as a *flash* now, eh?'

'Get out ma café. NOW!'

The fat cherub holding the door chimes wobbles as Mhairi pushes, then boots the café door. She spins the sign to *CLOSED*. A crescendo of tinkles accompany her movements. Justine thinks Mhairi is going to start crying. It flickers, certainly, her face, but then ebbs into a grin. Her smile is wild. For a moment, it's just her smile and her fierce, warm eyes, and Mhairi, being almost beautiful. 'Well, at least it got me on the national news, eh?'

'And they were nice pants, Mhairi.'

'They were gorgeous scants, weren't they?'

It is her pride in this – a kid scowling, grinning: *I don't care* – that makes Justine laugh all the harder. It's a nice feeling. Smelling the baking, the outside whiff of peaty earth the men brought in. *Scants.* What a lovely word.

'Aye,' Mhairi blows the laughter from her nose. 'But I've been bound over to keep the peace. No more protests for me, I'm afraid. No, what we need is some young ones to take up the fight.'

'Mm.'

They both stare a while at the tapestry on the counter. Mhairi turns it sideways. 'Och look! See there. *Jemima W.* I wonder if that's old Effie's Jemima? You know? Oh here, she'll be that chuffed if it is.'

'Who's Jemima?'

'Jemima White in the graveyard? They drowned her, so they did.'

'Why?'

'Poor lassie was a Covenanter. Effie's very proud of her, you know. Oh, I'll need to gie her a wee phone. This'll make her day if it is her. Where was it you got this again? A junkshop?'

'Aye – *Drowned* her? On purpose? For what?'

'For sticking up for what she believed in.'

'Jesus.' The naive tapestry, with its birds and flowers and childish rhyme, has lost any appeal it might have had. She draws the wrapping across the front of it. 'Well, give it to Effie then. I don't care.'

'Why don't you?'

'Nah. Don't want to get involved.'

'Justine.' Mhairi folds her hands across her rotund stomach. 'How long you planning to be here for?'

'Until I get sorted.'

'And what does "sorted" mean, exactly?'

Justine shrugs.

'Why did you come here? To Kilmacarra? Or rather, why are you *still* here? Is it to make trouble? Because, see to be honest, that wee family have more than enough on their plates to be bothered wi' a wee hairy like you.'

'No! Man, I just want to . . .' Justine tacks her lips. Tight-stitched syllables she doesn't want to share. 'You're not from here either, are you?'

'No. I'm a Glasgow girl, like you.'

'So what made *you* stay?'

Mhairi, gruff. 'That's none of your business.'

'Look. All I do is fuck things up. I fuck stuff up, then I run away. I'm tired. And I'm lonely. I felt . . . safe here. People were kind to me.'

'The Andersons are not your family; you canny have them.'

'I know that, Mhairi.'

But she can still admire the things she can't possess. She can still want one safe place into which she can slip, that will open up and accept her. Have you never cooried under the blankets of your bed, Mhairi, put them wrapped round your head like the Queen of Sheba, and sat quiet in the dark? Staring out your window to a rain-smeared street, all the lights twinkling and you, not in it, but alone and watching through the wash of water on the glass. And how quiet it is, and how the lights come on – you can see a hall light, then a landing light. Bathroom, bedroom maybe, back downstairs. Landing off, kitchen on. You can see the buds of people – an arm, the curve of cheek, leaning in towards the blue light of their tellies, and you are not with them. But they are there, around you, and you feel the quiet, and safe. Occasionally a front door opens and you can see the warm blaze of hall, some coats hanging, and you imagine walking in. Just walking into the warm and putting up your coat, up there, beside the anoraks and the dog lead, and *come away in* and *your dinner's on the table*. For a while it stops hurting. Do you never have that feeling, Mhairi?

Then Justine comes here, to this tiny place and there's a fire and a toasting fork. There's a wee shop and a café, there are the stones, all the solid stones for ever that are like long bones of far ago. And it makes her feel safe. Even the windfarm coming and the people fighting; even that; the fact they care. That makes her feel safe. If she wanted, she could maybe join in. It would be like going to a party, not on your own, but when you walk in with someone else, and it validates you, proves you are acceptable. Oh, not to walk in with a person you are scared of; there's no validation in that; only fawning and glazed, gritted darts of smiles which fade as they form, but walking with a person, a decent, normal person-who-fits who, by their presence, says: *Yeah. Justine's all right. Look. I'll even stand beside her. Even get her drinks.* She wonders about old Frank, the tramp. Who stands beside him? And she wishes she'd been kinder to him when he came in the pub.

'I just want to settle somewhere,' is what comes out. 'That's all. I want to eat and sleep and be happy. Find a person to take care of, maybe. One day.'

'Aye, well. Good luck with that here. Unless you like shagging sheep.'

'More people will come to Kilmacarra, Mhairi. If we have the museum. I promise you. Even if they build the stupid windfarm, it's not for ever. Look at all the bits of crofts, the rubble scattered. Look at the burn, and how wee and slow it is – when it used to cover all this valley. Things change. Duncan says—'

'Oh Duncan says, is it? Ah, now I get it. You do know he's sell-ng Cardrummond?'

'What?'

'Have you no heard? Aye, Sentinel are buying it off him.'

When your guts whip and drop, too quick to even feel sick. That s being gutted. She feels it as a sore blast of wind, a creeping shock. All day yesterday, and he never said a word. She feels empty. Yet Mhairi knows?

'Why?'

'You'll need tae ask him. It's all very sudden. I think the bank's called in the loan. He's away to Oban the now. You just missed him actually.'

When you look properly at Mhairi — face her up, and not be embarrassed for her, or a wee bit scared — her pudding features change. What is creamy curds are cheeks, a chin. What are puffy pads are sills for bright, clever eyes. 'You still want to stay?'

Justine's thoughts are falling. Water over rock, lit water.

Mhairi folds her cloth, pats the dampness of it flat and neat. 'Look. See when Hannah's mum gets here, you can stay at mine. Not theirs. OK?'

'OK.'

'You know where my house is? The one on its own, by Nether Meikle. I'll see you there this evening? You can leave your bag here the now.'

'Thank you, Mhairi. That's really—'

'Och, piss off, you. Away and do whit you need to do. I think I'm gonny close up early. Take Hannah a wee bite to eat.'

Chapter Thirty-three

Cold studs press fast to the pads of his hand. Charlie Boy wrings the collar like he is owning somebody's neck, feels the actual lingering hairs of his dog, the rough tufts of bristling fur that he . . .

That he.

Cunt. Fucking cunt. The fucking, fucking cunts. He wishes there was another cunting fucking mother-fucking cunting word that was stronger, sharper. But if there are, he doesn't know them.

Some fucking cunt has put a crossbow through his dog's head. Fucking bolt, straight through the skull of a dog that couldny even run. The body lies, chained still, in the yard. He canny look at it, has got two of the boys to . . . Christ. He disny know. *Just take it away*, he was shouting. *Fucking take it away*, screeching it so he wouldny greet. His dog, his Askit, that they're taking to the dump, the incinerator, fuckknows because that's his dog that was, and now it's soiled goods. It's nothing.

But it doesn't feel like nothing. He is walking, walking, with the collar wrapped round his hand; folk'll think he's a loony, taking a collar for a walk, so he hams it up, spread tight across his knuckles, and now it's a chib.

You fucking lookin' at?

But no one asks him. No one speaks to this scary, snottery man who is muttering to hisself, who is a shambling prick that has lost the respect of his men, his community.

For who would do a thing like that? Who would dare do that to Charlie Boy?

It's just a dog. It's nothing.

Feels like war. There's a million cunts could of done it.

Fucking Justine. She started this. Once you lose your woman, you're fucked. You're cracked open to the fucking sky. *Weak*. Fair game.

Charlie Boy despises weakness. He grinds on as the rain begins to fall, past Queen's Park and the infirmary, past Shawlands and the posh fucking school where that arse from the Mearns sent his kids. The rain falls in sheets, laying over him and under him. Feels the wet inside his trainers, the damp curl of his hair which he fucking hates; you canny have curly hair; that's bent so it is, and he plasters it down with his hand and the fucking stuff springs up again and he batters and slaps it down; then there's blood, he can taste blood running; he knows its difference from the rain, knows the salty thickness of it on his skin. Fucking studs on the collar've cut him, the collar in his hand, and he chucks the thing away. Just chucks it, like they'll be chucking Askit's body, and he throws back his face and lets the rain pour in.

Durring next to his heart. *Durrr* and *durr* and *durr*; there's the throbbing as his phone rings. He does not want to answer it, it'll be one of the boys, or worse, some other bastard, someone like Gerry Kiernan going: *Heard about your* dug, *pal. Do yous need some extra muscle?* with that, with that sleekit dip in his voice that just rips you.

The smell in the air changes as he strides on, it's higher, damper. More fousty. Christ. He's walked as far as the river so he has. He's in the town; it's afternoon, he's a guy with money in his pocket and an afternoon free; so how about he goes for a fucking drink? Him, Charlie Boy, in a pub he does not own or rent or have a stake in. He can be a sodden, nameless sadsack, greetin' in his beer and so fuck, so fuck if some cunt tries to take the pish because then he will rise, and he will take his glass and he will smash it deep, chew the skin straight across in that open Glasgow grin that stays for ever and he'll taste their blood, he'll fucking lick it off his fingers. Like a dog.

So fuck. He will.

Pubs on the Clydeside are old men's pubs, tramps and jakies, and he hates jakies. Clatty bastards. He heads up George's Square. Used to be loads of flower beds there. Flowers and grass among long-columned statues of men he doesny know. And all the doos. They've cut down loads of the trees, so where do the doos roost? The Counting House is by the square, it's a big barn of a pub with no music. That would suit him fine, so it would, but there's some bloody rally on across from the Cenotaph; he can hear loudhailers as he gets closer. Fuck. His phone judders, ringing again, and he goes to chib it, fucking chib it in the bin so's no cunt can nip his ear. But he disny. Just stands and waits till it goes silent, and moves on.

Square's hoaching with people, despite the rain. A big white trailer is set along the west side, *The Referendum Roadshow* plastered all over, and each time the words appear there's a Saltire and a Union Jack painted either side. Front of the trailer's open, there's a whole bunch of people up there, like they're on a stage, and this dude in a suit and tie's poncing round with a megaphone, going:

'OK, folks. So. You wake up the day after the referendum. Just imagine how you feel? Will you be elated, relieved? Distraught? People, your destiny's in your hands.'

Charlie Boy doesn't believe in destiny. You fight for what you want, you take it. Survival of the fittest, and this shitty wee country isny very fit. It's a fucking joke. He cuts across St Vincent Street on the diagonal, carries on up the long low hill at the side of the railway station, past John Lewis car park, there's a nice wee howf near Cowcaddens, aye that would do, he needs a fucking drink, and it's pishing down, so he'll cut through the bus station and the place is jumping, fucking jumping, and there's tourists and lassies up the toon and boys heading to the football. The Tic's playing later. G'aun the bhoys; there's a nun collecting money and fat bastards eating Big Macs with their fat bastarding weans, chomp-and-belch-and-dropping-chips and there's a man with his dog, and a dosser on a bench, fucking sleeping in the day, so he is, with his big red head and his toe hinging out his shoe. Manky, lazy fuck.

Neat diagonal again, cutting through the concourse to the door at the top. He can almost smell his pint. Passes level with the dosser. Frightwig of a ginger, *ging*, as in *singer*, not juh. No, jin-juhr is too soft for this raggedy cunt whose face is sublimely peaceful. As Charlie Boy sheers by, he reaches into his pocket. Does not stop, does not slow but maintains his onward bounce as he leans in and sparks his lighter. Cunt's 40% proof anyroad. Hears the gentle *whoosh* as his hair ignites, as Charlie Boy drives onwards, out the door, out the fucking cunting door, hears a muffled scream, hears shouts, there is a split-shimmer of what you might call happiness, then a spike of ice. He feels it stab his breast, his cunting, cunting phone goes again.

'What the fuck do you want?' He roars at the phone, at the open, wet sky.

People do that Glasgow thing where they flinch and keep their eyes fixed low on the street. Away from the crazy with the moby and the soaking, curly hair. There's a whimpered, 'Sorry', then: 'Are you the man?'

Charlie's sponge-brain is whirring, all the names of all the folk that might want to gloat and humiliate him and this sounds like a wean and he canny think straight. The blue light of an ambulance flashes by, up on Cowcaddens.

'Who is this?'

'It's Johnny.'

'Who the fuck is Johnny?'

'Me. I live in Kilmacarra. She's here. Are you the man? Justine's here. Now.'

Charlie Boy sees the ground rise. He slumps against a wall. Swallows.

'She's a total bloody bitch. Are you the man that wants her? Cause I *hate* her.'

Charlie Boy steadies his voice. 'Is that right, bud? You'n' me both.'

Chapter Thirty-four

'Coffee?' It comes out: 'Caw-ee?'

Hannah wrinkles her nose.

'Tea?' Much easier to say.

'No, ta.'

'Eeght?'

'Bring me back a sandwich?'

'Plah-ic chee aw plah-ic haa?'

'What? Ah, *plastic*. Very funny. Oh, go on. Surprise me.'

Euan smiles, and it's like gold pouring. Even in his wheelchair, he seems taller than her, it's a sudden lurch skywards, as quick and inevitable as the roughness of his chin. He holds out his hand for her purse, then propels himself off. It's only one floor, the lifts are wide, but she will hold her breath till he returns. She's not remotely hungry.

Hannah takes Michael's hand. There's only one hand she can have, the right, because the left is bound and has a cannula in it; a thick needle which drives up his vein almost to the crook of his elbow. She kisses where it joins his skin. Her husband rests lightly between life and death. She and her boy wait with him. Last night, they had taped his copper eyes shut, but this morning, the nurse slowly peeled the tape off. She senses a gathering, an imminence;

it's why she flinches whenever anyone comes in or out. There
seems to be an optimum time for him to wake, though no one'
spelled this out. It's vital she stay vigilant. White wings flap, you
see them like huddled buzzards, with their pained expressions and
their nodding heads.

—*Mrs Anderson?*

—*Can we have a word?*

They've done their work, their best. Keep telling her how
lucky Michael is. If it wasn't for him battering his head on a
gravestone – and what was he doing out there, what was he *doing*
Did he fall? Did he mean it? – the tumour would never have been
spotted. Would have continued to grow. The doctor who oper-
ated spoke kindly to her. That nice young man who held
Michael's brain in his hands; the mass of fine-webbed jelly she
always wanted to possess, which is his hopes, his movement
language. His whole life.

Gently, the doctor explained how the head injury had caused a
bulging bleed. How the damaged vein must be blocked off. How
it's like a forest fire in the brain: acres of swirling fronds, scorched
clean as the damage spreads. Or a spider scuttling, casting a blood-
web. How he must open a cleft between two of the brain lobes
find and isolate the artery, bypass the damaged vein. How, when
he did, he found a cluster. Cells gone wrong, got big.

Not cancer. But a tumour nonetheless, in amongst the jewel-
bright blood.

Now they need to wait. No matter how hard she sighs out,
there's no respite from the pain in her breast. Hannah fingers her
wedding ring. It's got loose. Michael's not a dull, worthy man.
And he does not have boundless reserves. Other people might –
do – love him, and do it better than she. Her husband's not a bad

person. Not like Hannah. Michael is a man of such sensitivity that she's driven him to madness. Justine told her he sees a ghost: a man who changes shape. How do you respond to that? And then she thinks: it was the tumour, and then she thinks: no, it was you, and then she thinks: is it much different anyway, to putting on a frock, mounting a set of stairs and telling folk to talk to the sky? He must have been so lonely.

No change! the nurses say, with reassuring smiles. Hannah, china-brittle terrified. Temporal. Benign. These are soft, kind words compared to the ones on his chart.

Does not open eyes.

Incomprehensible sounds (occasional, sporadic. No obvious stimuli).

Occasional motor extension to painful stimuli.

They press on the beds of his fingernails, then. She hates it. If he twitches, though, her heart bursts. She doesn't look at the intercranial pressure readings, the cerebral perfusion readings, because these are not visible proofs and she does not want to know what volumes of fluid crash and crush inside her husband's skull. All Hannah will believe is what she can see.

She can see a plastic tube at Michael's neck. They plan to cut his pale flesh in a tracheotomy, just there, if he's not able to breathe on his own. For the moment, the tube snakes on into tape, plastic, his mouth. It's linked to the ventilator. Another thin tube is in his nose, going all the way to his stomach to drain it. She sees his skull shorn and missing, where a section of the bone has been flapped to reveal the brain beneath, and the tumour tucked in its folds. This tender place makes her think of her children's fontanelles when they were born. She sees the monitor for his heart rate, his breathing rate, his blood pressure. She sees the lines into his blood vessels: a central line in his neck to deliver drugs and nourishment and an arterial line in his wrist, to monitor blood pressure, take blood tests. If she lifts the covers she'll see the catheter in his penis, draining urine, checking his kidney function.

And she sees his breast rise and fall.

'Eugh-ya.' Euan returns, chucks her a cheese ploughman's.

'Ta.' She peels back the cellophane and a ripe sweat-smell comes out. The veins of lettuce are brown, the pappy bread white. They look obliquely at Michael. It's quiet in this room, apart from the machines. Hannah's been writing here, though the book's meaningless. She has told them she can't meet her deadline. *Not to worry*, said the TV folk. *We're going with a series about a telepathic dog now, anyway. Kind of* Lassie *meets* Hollyoaks *via* Life on Mars? *Not to worry, darling*, said her agent. *You just take care.* But she writes still, in shards, because she must do something in this fragmented yellow room. No space to grieve poor Ailsa, though. Those energies are finite. Reserved for this.

Euan pops the tab on a can of Fanta. The sharp phssh causes her to jump, any sharp noise in here elicits Pavlovian panic. Two sets of eyes slide to a bleeping bed. She has to pretend Michael's sleeping. How could she not have seen this coming? She tries to keep her mind blank. He is sleeping, that's all. His face seems mottled, but it's hard to be sure. She cannot wait until the mask is off, and he can speak to her again.

He tried to speak to her, before. Hannah curls herself into the chair. The room is very hot and she is very cold. She tries to chew. A ribbon of tomato catches in her throat.

'Hello, hello! It's the foodie reinforcements!' There's a shaft of light, and the brilliant big heft of Mhairi slips into the room, carrying warm-smelling bags. 'Och, c'mon. You're no eating thon hospital crap when I've brought you a lovely flask of soup.'

Euan leans forward. 'Hey! Muh. On't cry.'

Is she crying? Hannah gets pulled into her big boy's chest. Her cheeks go sticky on his shirt. Huh. So she is.

Chapter Thirty-five

Mouth thick. There's . . . on her face. Damp fingers.

'Euch! What you doing?'

Ross takes his finger out of Justine's nose.

'Ross!'

'I am drawing your face.'

They're lying side by side, on top of Justine's bed. 'Ouf. What time is it?' She sits. Scratches her head. Brain waking up. Duncan is leaving Kilmacarra.

'Ross? How long we been asleep?' Shakes her stupid watch. 'Did your mummy phone?'

'No.'

Duncan is going. Michael is still Godknows where, for when, with who – oh man, that's a whole other nightmare opening out; and Hannah's . . . oh, and *Duncan*'s going and he didn't say and there's no use hanging on to stuff. Ever. No fucking use.

'Did your gran phone?'

'No. And her name is Grand*ma*.'

'Grand*ma*, then. C'mon, wee man. Time to get up.'

'I *am* up.' Ross slides his beaker of juice towards him. Dips one hand in and stirs.

She'd only lain down for a moment. Lying sideways is another way you can prohibit tears, disguise them at least, with blinking and weary rubs. Why did Duncan not say? They spent a whole afternoon and evening together. It wasn't a date: she was helping him with the lambs, had held the curly wet weight of a newborn and for a fleeting, stupid instant, when he pressed close against her, it felt as if they were joined-up, and it was nothing but the two of them, not touching, not speaking. Just looking up at his eyes, at the back of them where it was warm and lovely until it felt like she was falling.

Ach, you know what? Guy's a prick. He should've said. No matter how 'sudden', he could've left a message at the manse. Man, he was in the bloody café, it's a two-minute walk. Mhairi would've told him; he must've known she was at the hospital. Nuh. No way. She won't stay here. What is the point? The instant Hannah's mum arrives, Justine's off. Up and off. Leave no trace. It is the only way to flit through life. And if Michael dies . . . He won't, it's not cancer or anything. Hannah's said they got it out. Oh man. It's nothing to do with her. They don't care about her here. She is aye making these bloody holes for herself, stumbling from one crater into another. A clean, smooth passage to follow: loads of people have that. Girls her age who've been to college, are planning weddings. Getting pregnant. They all know the right steps. She'll get her stuff, get packed right now and will not think of this little lovely boy who is carefully licking juice from each of his individual fingers.

'Can you no drink out of a cup?'

'No.'

She leaves Ross smearing the sticky residue on her bedclothes, while she lugs down her bag, starts dumping stuff inside.

'What you doing?'

Justine keeps her head inside the wardrobe. 'Packing. I'm going on a wee adventure.'

'I *like* ventures. Where are we going, Justi?'

'You've got to stay and see your gran, sweetie.'

'She doesn't like me,' he sighs. 'She only likes Euan Poo-head.'

'I don't believe that.' She peels off a hundred quid, then makes a wee nest for the rest of the money. Stuffs it in her bag, folds more clothes on top. 'Cause you are the most gorgeous boy in the world.'

'I know. Are you crying, Justi?'

'Nope. Now, we need to go find Johnny again. I've got a wee present for him.'

'Can we get a dog, Justi? Like Buddy?'

'Oh, you'd need to ask your mum, Ross. Right, let's get going, eh? Shoes on. And watch that cup—'

'Uh-oh,' says Ross. Too late. The juice spills everywhere.

On the side of Mary's Brae, the archaeologists are packing up for the day, trudging past the manse as they make their way down to the pub, with Ross going 'hello man' and 'did you find more bones?' They laugh. Say 'lovely afternoon'. It is; it's crisp and cold. There will be stars tonight. Justine can see Kilmacarra's tiny sheep, the lazy burn and Mhairi's daft balloon above it. Far up the hill across the glen, she can make out the shape of Cardrummond. From here, she could watch the ribbon of Duncan's car fumes, as he wends himself away from her. She could, except his car's not there, it's actually a grey cloud rolling in, and she has this small boy hinging on her arm.

'Swing me, Justi. Swing *meee*!'

They walk along the main street, stop outside Johnny's house. 'Right, you. Stay there. In fact, here. Swing on Johnny's gate.

That'll keep you busy.' It's a solid thing, though the paint is peeled and rusty. She goes up the path, chaps the front door. Like the gate, it's seen better days. Buddy barks. A curtain stirs. She knocks a second time. Then a third.

A snarled 'What?' behind the door.

'Johnny. Can I talk to you?'

'Nuh. Leave me alone.'

'No. I'm not going to go away. I can stand here all night if you like.'

'No!' He opens up. Eyes-wide terrified. 'Piss off away from my door.'

'Hey, Johnny. Come on. I'm sorry I was sharp with you in the café.'

'Couldny gie a fuck.'

'I was worried about Ross's dad. You know, Mr Anderson?'

'He's gonny die, isn't he?'

'Sssh. We don't know what's going to happen—'

'Then Ross and Euan will have no dad.' There's a hint of satisfaction as he sums this up. 'Billy Halliday said his brain's all pure swole up, and he'll be a mong anyroad.'

'A *mong*? What a horrible word. Do you even know what that means?'

'Aye. A spazz.'

'Oh, for *Godsake*. Does your mum let you speak like that?'

Johnny shakes his fringe out his eyes. He's a colourless wee soul; hair, brows and lashes the same dull beige as his skin. 'What's it to do with you? You've never even seen ma mum.'

Come to mention it, she never has.

'Look, I'm sorry I upset you. But you were going on and on in front of Mhairi.'

'It's ma bloody money. I wanted it. I *need* it.'

'Ta dah!' Justine wheechs out an envelope. 'Here. I've got it here. See? I hadn't forgotten. Always pay my debts, me.'

His face wavers, buckles.

'A hundred? Think that's only fair.'

Mouth twisting, like the wee soul can't remember how to smile. The smile exploding to an angry shout. 'You're a stupid cow.'

'John?' A thin voice trails downstairs.

Johnny moves on to the front step, pulls the door behind him. 'Is your mum not well?'

'She's *fine*. Just leave us alone. Just piss off, Justine.'

Ross clangs on the gate. Buddy barks louder.

'Here. D'you not want your money?' Justine reaches to touch his arm, but he jerks away. As he does, his shirt flaps, revealing a rim of pink at the pocket of his jeans. Same lurid pink as her mobile phone.

'Johnny? What the hell is that?'

'Piss off.'

'Is that my phone? I thought you said you chucked it?'

'So?'

'So why d'you say it if it wisny true?'

He shrugs. Chin trembling.

She grips his wrist. Thin, hollow as a reed. She could fracture it if she has to. 'Give me the fucking phone.'

The boy is properly weeping. She flings his wrist away. Helps herself to the mobile, which slides out easily. The kid is so skinny; she can feel his jutting hip bone.

'So. What's the big deal? You been phoning porn lines or something?' She switches it on. 'I canny see how, there wasn't enough credit on it.'

'Don't!' His shout echoes up the glen. Even Ross stops swinging and looks over. Justine waves.

'It's fine. We're just playing.' As the screen begins to glow, she sees five missed calls. 'You got a girlfriend, is that it?'

'Please,' he whimpers. 'Don't answer it if he phones.'

'If who phones?'

'It was just for the games.'

'What are you on about? I don't mind if you used it, honest.'

'I wanted to see if there was any good games on it.'

'Doubt it.' She's a little more cheerful now she has the phone in her hand. What's the big deal? 'It's just a cheapo.'

'I know. That's how I swapped the cards roon.'

'What cards?'

'The SIM card. It was in your wee pouch-thing.'

It is in that film *Sinbad* or some Hammer Horror or maybe it's *The Mummy* but there is a scene inside the pyramid where, one by one, shutters begin to slide, a square of light becomes a slit and it is snatched away, the poor sod turning, spinning desperate as long walls of granite descend to block the doors and sand is pouring. For one horrible moment, the camera pans into live eyes, and you see them flicker with the knowledge of what is happening. That is what Justine sees: it is like she is unpleating. One hank of her is watching a pyramid seal while another vague strand sees a phone crack under a bus and a third is listening. Dying.

'Soon as it went in, this man starts calling. I didny know what to do. I tried to take the card back out but the wee clicker hingy's broke on the back – see.'

His hand brushes hers.

'I was feart ma mum would find it . . . I'm sorry, right? If you just keep it switched off he canny phone. Just hide it or break it or something.' He scans the vast trough of valley. Desperate. 'But you canny hide nothing here. Folk see everything.'

'How do you know it was a man?'

Dull eyes on dull fingers as she clicks to check the missed calls. But she knows. *CB CB CB CB*.

'Did you answer it?'

'*No*.'

'Did you fucking speak to him?'

'I . . .'

'Did you tell him where I was? Oh Jesuschrist. You stupid little *fuck*.' The phone is scalding her as she throws it. Tumbling over rocket-fast, cracking through air. Off his breastbone.

'Don't hit me!' he sobs, folding in on himself. 'Don't hit me', but she doesn't, because Ross comes running up the path then, Buddy barking, leaping at the window.

'*Johnny*. Christ. What did you tell him?'

'I telt him you were here.'

Chapter Thirty-six

In the hospital Hannah takes her notebook, the fat, full pages. Tears them down the middle. She is writing an ugly nightmare. It comes in spews. She has a hundred different endings to her story. All wrong; full of black shadowy things that don't work right. She sits, in the dark, with her husband. 'I won't leave you. I promise.'

His ventilator sighs. The noise of the monitor is like a long-engaged phone, always one beat of silence more than you think. Before the beep.

Beep.

Sigh.

Clatter, car noise from beyond. Then nothing.

No trace. Just the rolling silence, like the hills. How often, if Michael's honest, has he ever heard God's voice? Oh, he hears thoughts, yes, and attributes them to God. He feels unknown joy, and attributes it to God. As a young man, fierce in love with the drama of cassocks and holy wine, pan bread from the supermarket that you bless yourself, of the fact that your words have hidden portent – and better yet: your silences have profundity. For a shy, bookish boy, that was the ultimate saving grace.

*

Hannah keeps biting the inside of her mouth, to check she's still here. Salty blood affirms she is. A rubbery callous has formed in the web of skin behind her cheek. Occasionally, she'll bite it off entirely, swallow. Start again. The ventilator makes her focus on her own breath, on the unconscious movement that is keeping it going, which becomes self-conscious, laboured. If she could scissor out her lungs, give them to Michael, she would do it. Mhairi's taken Euan for a 'wee hurl' outside. She is anxious when he's gone; and glad of the way she can let her face slip. Through the half-glazed door, she can see the room opposite. Exactly the same as this, but empty. Waiting quietly for another soul who is, right this moment, making toast or phoning home, who has no idea about the speeding car, the gun, the trip, the fall, the fire.

Michael has lived deeply, quietly. But it has been a self-conscious act. His rock has been rules and rituals, the fervent truths that leave no space for doubt.

The peace that passes all our understanding. But he doesn't understand it.

'I don't think you can, pal.'

The noise on the monitor changes gear; it is a different pitch, a glimpse of change at the edge of Hannah's vision, which is vanished by the time she reaches her husband's side. Imagined, hoped. Hallucinated. She calls the nurse, red buzzing button, thirty seconds, max.

'What? What is it?'

'Can you check . . . I thought it made a different noise. Can you check the readings? Please?'

The nurse smiles. Tired. She fiddles, presses, reads. 'Nope. I'm sorry. No change.'

'Are you sure?'

'Positive. I'm sorry.'

Hannah slumps into her chair.

'Can I get you a cup of tea?'

'Will you do another CAT scan?'

'Mrs Anderson, there's really no need.'

'What if I said I saw him move?'

'Did you?'

'No.'

The woman pats her shoulder. 'I'll get you some tea.'

Then, a tut. A scrumple.

'Is this – are these all for the bin?' Handfuls of Hannah's notes in her hands.

'Yes.'

'Budge up.' The Ghost sits on the rock beside him. He is paler, thinner. Yet the blue of his tattoo is sharp. 'You canny understand. I think that's the point. You either feel it, or you don't.'

'Did you?'

'Nah. Felt love, mind. Too much love. And I guess she didn't feel it back.'

Hannah watches the ventilator in Michael's mouth. His lungs recoil as the positive pressure withdraws, and the corner of his mouth moves with it. Automatic, but it is movement. She undoes the sidebar of the bed, so she can lean her head alongside his. It's not as if he's going to fall. With one finger, she traces the outline of his jaw, feels the stubble. 'Michael,' she whispers. 'Michael. It's me. I'm touching you, the side of your mouth. Can you feel me? Your mouth can move when the ventilator goes in and out. Can you feel it move? Concentrate. If you can hear me, can you make your jaw go tight? Feel where I'm touching you, baby. Can you touch me?'

The muscle continues to quiver in and out, synchronised with the false hope of the machine.

'Here, Mrs Anderson.' The nurse cuts between Hannah and her husband. 'There you go. Drink your tea.'

'Thank you.' The tea's sweet. 'Have you heard from my nanny yet? Did she get back to you?'

'Not yet.' She tuts, fixes the bed-guard into place.

'Could you try the manse again please?'

'Of course.'

Hannah waits until the nurse is gone. Wets her finger in the tea, smears it on Michael's lips. 'You thirsty? Can you feel it warm? It's tea.' The smell of outside seems to fill the whole room. It's green; like leaf-sap. She pulls down the bed-rail once more, so she can get as close as possible to his skin. There are seven different tubes attached to various parts of his body.

'Here. One more and you'd be an octopus.' She kisses his forehead. Careful. She has watched the nurses at their work. She knows this one is for draining, while this clear snake is what keeps his fluids up. Knows too an alarm will trigger when the oblong switch is flicked. She was there when they tried him off the ventilator. Stood watching, till they hurried her outside. Loud voices. Failure. Disobedient vitals. Attempted reintubation. Alarm bells ringing, a flurry of white, like wings round Michael's bed.

*

'Do you wish you hadn't?'

'What? Jumped? Or loved her?' The Ghost smiles. 'Both, I suppose. But I'm no sad I loved the wean.'

'Can you – do you go other places as well?' says Michael. 'To them?'

He shivers. 'I canny.'

'I'm so sorry I couldn't help you.'

The Ghost takes Michael's hand in his. The cold is spectacular, liquid; he is all chill water and that darting blue tattoo. 'Down to me, pal. You didny do anything.'

Hannah climbs on the bed beside him. Raises his sleeping head on to her breast, freeing him of as much encumbrance as she can. The wires are all the lines of a balloon, tethering him to earth. She lies with her husband in the curtained room. One by one, she strokes his fingers.

'Sing yo-ho, boys.'

Both her children love this lullaby.

'Let her go, boys.'

Gently, she soothes him on her breast, where he will smell her.

'Pull her head round. Now altogether.'

It sounds like a sea shanty, but it's not. It's a plaint, a love song for home. Hannah sings it low, in her mother's accent, which is hers when she sings, and her mother's song is her grandma's and it's not Glasgow, but the isles, those aching Western Isles that lift it up.

'Sailing homewards, tae Mingulay.'

Silence. Michael is holding on to silence. And then, it is another hand. A warm hand which is reaching down to pull him up, and he hears it, faint like birds.

*

'I'll keep singing,' Hannah whispers, and she rocks him harder and her heart is thumping. 'Don't leave us.'

His sleeping face, not sleeping. Her tears running in his mouth, and there's tears coming out his mouth, running bubbles, singing bubbles under the mask.

And he feels a weight slip off him.

Chapter Thirty-seven

Imagination is a fine thing. The way it links pictures and people you have seen, and morphs them into new distortions, more vivid and obscenely bright. How is it Justine's never noticed that rock before, the one with the eyes and the chin? How it looks right at them, wherever they move.

'Come on, baby. Just a wee bit higher.'

She has packed her clothes, her money and the toasting fork. She has left a note and then she has ripped it up, because it is a trace he could find Charlie could find them she is a headless chicken panicking hiding waiting for the bus going mental staying calm.

The cloud, which from the ground was merely wisps, begins to curl in. It's not thick, just damp. So much for stars. 'Put your hood up, Rossie.' They are scrabbling up Mary's Brae. From here, they have an excellent vantage point. There's a green canvas tent beside the soaring stones and the chambered cairn, flap open, a pile of shovels and buckets inside. The archaeologists must leave their stuff in here each night. She can see a giant sieve, a steel, dirt-crusted ladder, a grid, pickaxes, some seed trays full of pebbly finds, but no people.

'Can we have a sleepover in the tent?'

'No.'

Ross is not impressed. She's surprised the men haven't dug round the chamber itself. With its sliding man-made lid, it must be sterile ground. Done, dug and dusted. Should she have said about that tooth? Doesny matter now, nothing matters except hiding here, waiting for the bus, first bus if it's up or down, it will take them out of here. She will return the money. She would have taken Michael's car but she cannot find the keys, canny find a way to think or stop her teeth from chattering. Give Charlie Boy the money and pray for mercy; that's all she can think of to do. She's not crazy obviously, she will post it back or put it through his door or something but she needs to get him away from here, from these people who are her friends and she's offered them up as sacrifice; her stupid shield.

They move from the zig-zag path, climbing directly up the scree. Justine thinks she hears a crunch behind her. Turns. Looks.

Nothing.

She has made a bargain with fate. If Ross's gran gets here first, or if Mhairi comes back, she'll leave Ross in Kilmacarra. If it's the bus for Lochallach – which comes twice a day, and she doesn't know if they've missed it yet – she'll take Ross to the hospital, to his mum. She has tried phoning Hannah, but you canny have mobiles in intensive care, and she has tried to get the number, but they keep putting her though to orthopaedics, and Hannah's never even phoned to say if Michael's awake, and if the Glasgow bus comes first, then they'll both get on. Her and Ross. Only twenty minutes. It is due in twenty minutes. That is the most they need to hide for now. They've lasted an hour and a bit already, and nothing bad's happened. In twenty more minutes, she can take Ross legitimately. For his own good. She will be a hero. And it will not be abduction; it's just for a wee while; how can Hannah cope with Euan and with Michael; she will be saving them . . . Justine veers her thoughts from Hannah, because she's developing this skill; it's really good. You can direct your thoughts like a light-beam. If you focus intently (she does, in fact, imagine a lighthouse for this bit), you can see them fall back into darkness, and make new thoughts appear. Just like that. Or not think at all, and only focus on bright light.

'Ross!'

'Am not doing it!' Ross drops the pickaxe he's playing with.

'Leave that alone. It's jaggy. Come out up here where I am. Chip-chop.'

He skulks towards her on all fours. A grumpy little bear.

'Now sit there, on that rock. You keep watch, all right?'

'For pirates?' he says hopefully.

'Yes. Pirates.'

He nods, his wee jaw jutting out. Justine thinks again of Hannah. The mist's beginning to settle. Her eyes flit across the valley. No traffic. No stour or exhaust clouds rising. She takes a long breath in. They are fine.

Justine unfocuses her gaze. Imagines the view peopled and full of busyness. These long glens used to be full. Right behind her loom the biggest of the megaliths. Beyond her lies the church, more knots and pillars of standing stones. Beyond that, Crychapel Wood, Cardrummond, the hills, the gleam of movement. A smudgy mist. The turbines with the same white-grey as the colour of scudding clouds. But the digger which is working up on the test turbine is yellow. It makes a bright flash against the mute colours of the earth. The various clangs of metal on metal sound out across the glen; the call, the echoing response. She saw this programme once, about the isle of Lewis. Man, what a boring place. Long Sundays spent listening to the precenting: unaccompanied psalms sung in Gaelic, where each line is put out by the precentor for the congregation to join in, gradually, singing their trills and words and speeds all different so it comes like lapping waves. These researchers had done a study. The chanting on Lewis was the exact same chanting of the Appalachian Hills, and of the south, the Deep South. Worship that was remembered by settlers and by the descendants of African slaves, who were taught it by their Scottish owners, who were taught it in the distant islands, who all sang the song, kept it coming in waves.

She tries to count all the standing stones. It is impossible. And these are nothing compared to Stonehenge; or the ones in France on that postcard in the kitchen. Some pattern was working its way across the world, thousands and thousands of years ago, when folk were meant to be savages. If you spent every day searching for food, fighting to stay warm, stay alive – why would you waste your time in monuments?

Justine woz 'ere.

Her J on the church pew. The tattoo on her thigh. The war dead above the gate and the gravestones with their etched-out names which are made of absence, not presence. All the sad landscape below her, aching with what it no longer holds. In the faded distance, the yellow truck chunters back and forth. Hairy-arsed men and beating windmills. Aye, that'll add some mystery to the place. They should move further up the hill. This is too exposed; she remembers seeing the egg-rollers all the way up here from the road. But it's fine: she's being an idiot. Johnny never said he was coming. Still. He will come, she knows this. If not today, then soon; this won't be one of those times when Charlie leaves his victim to drown in paroxysms of their own sweat. There's a trench near the top; they could hide in there, till the bus comes. She needs to be under something safe.

'You want to see a really big hole, Ross?'

'No.'

'Aw, come on. A wee peek, then we'll go back down. I'll give you a coalie-back.'

'Oh-*kay.*'

She crouches by the rock, so Ross can dreep on to her back. They rise up, wobbling. The feel of those baby limbs round her neck is indescribable. Damp skin. It's drizzling. All that mist is becoming moisture, boulders glistening like jewels and oil. Justine swithers. Up or down? The further up they go, the further they'll have to scramble back. What if the bus doesn't wait? But her movements have become inevitable, like falling. Like it is not her making them. They need to climb as high as they can go.

She trudges on. Rivulets of rain down the nape of her neck. Ross's compact, pearly flesh begins to drag on her throat.

'Where is the big, big hole, Justi? Is there treasure?'

'No, pet.' She stumbles through a stony rivulet. Wet feet ugh, minging; she can feel the coldness seeping. Vainly, she shakes her ankle.

'Justi! I am falling. Save me!'

She lifts Ross higher, elbows tight into her waist to stop him slipping. They stop for a minute, till he gets comfy. Can hear the crack of breathing trees. Birch and oak. A few rowans. They are safe in the thicket. No one will see them from here. Her arms ache, thigh muscles throbbing. This is daft. Here is far enough. She looks back downhill, through a long gap in the trees. In fact . . . The world goes wee. A toytown bus is trundling along the yellow road.

'Shit. Come on, Rossie-boy. Let's go back down.' She starts to run. Ross bounces on her back, her bag swinging wide.

'Ow!' His voice judders. 'You are going too fast, Justi. And there is a jaggy thing hurting me. Why have you got our fork?'

'Whee-ee. Pretend I'm your horsey again, and you're a cowbo—'

She stops. Crumples. All the breath coming out. The bus is going the wrong way. Justine checks her watch. It is still twenty minutes to go. Yet, between the broad leaves and the coming twilight, she can see the bus like ticker-tape, leaving Kilmacarra. She shakes her wrist. Turning, pointlessly, on the spot. The bus has come and gone, and they have missed it.

'Shit!'

'You saided a bad word, Justi. A *nother* one.'

'I know. I'm sorry.'

There is a definite crack of wood.

She freezes. Deliberate. The quiet has shifted, it has curdled up behind her. Observing.

She will not turn round. Stupid. Stupid. She needs to get back. Decides to move off the path, it will feel safer inside the thickest of the trees. Won't look up, won't look down; just her tip-toeing feet, sideways along the brae. Trees all tucked round them, follow the slope downhill. Ice is emptying her out, it is scooping crystals from her lungs and throat. Is creeping up her spine. Two small, clumsy hands stroke her hair. She picks her way down the brae. Dim-lit and shivering. Roots like the rungs of a ladder. Their limbs twine like tendrils; Ross's lips touch her hair. Knowing. She locks her fists round his legs.

Another crack. Rupturing. Deliberate.

'Hello, Justine.'

Ice and lead. The voice is not it is flat it is not there notthere not keep moving.

Gut sparkling with fear. Cannot hear him.

He is not there.

'Justi,' whispers Ross, his grip tightening. The wet rocks shine up at her. Hills roll on, and the dark; the dark is coming. A street-light goes on in the village.

'Nice night for a walk, eh, doll?'

Blood gone from her fingertips. A drilling, sick cold. She will not turn round. This is not happening, she has been waiting always, sick and dreadful. Waiting since she left.

'How you been, darlin? Who's this wee man, then?'

Charlie's voice is light and dangerous. Here would be a grave. They will find her bones in a thousand years, and put her in a seed tray.

'Charlie.' Not Justine speaking, but her ghost.

She will not turn round. She loosens her hold on Ross's legs, lets him slide to the ground. Pulls him into the side of her coat.

'*Charlie.*' He mimics her lispy softness. She hears the rustle of kappa, that cheap hiss of flammable nylon that is so familiar. A hand is on her shoulder, at her neck. Stroking away the hair. Wet lips smear skin above her artery, wet teeth settle, for an instant, where it throbs. Is a dream is a dream wake up is a dream. The hand pushes her round, till she is facing him. Is inches from his sour breath. Ross still nestled behind. Tries to speak. A sob comes out. A fierce splash of urine. Hard eyes. Black; they are all pupil, with only a glaring rim of brown. He is still beautiful, like stone is beautiful.

'*Please.*'

'Please,' he repeats, more loudly than she can, and he raises his hand from her hair and strikes her brickfasthard and she is losing her vision; the mist and the rain, the roaring pain in her head.

'Hi-*ya*,' he leers. 'Surprise!'

'Run, Ross!' she screams, shoving the child away. 'Run home now. RUN!'

Charlie Boy kicks her shin, full and cracking, and she is down into the mud where their feet have churned, her heels scrabbling like little mice to get a grip get a fucking grip, she smells the earth, good earth where bad things happen she will be a bad thing, a memory that lingers like a smell a stain, where is Ross is he safe, and the ground says *there you are* organic matter wormfeed lost potential and he hits her and he hits her, she is conscious of his fairness, ensuring every bit gets a doing. And that this is the aperitif.

'Chah.' Mouth swollen, there are lumps of teeth or blood clots she must tongue through. Swallow. Spit. Air on torn scream skin-scream. Her leg is trapped beneath her. 'I gotthe . . . money. Youc'n have . . . it—'

He stops mid-slap. 'I can *have* it? My own fucking money? I can fucking *have* it, can I?'

His eyes are gone, or hers are, wet mist and pain is all there is and ringing smashing her body, thumping out a heartbeat on her flesh. Her ears schlush and boom as she tries to move her head, ankle searing, but his full weight is on her, pinning neck and arm, one arm, there is less numbness in one arm and her fingers, here, can you move, scrabble-scrabble little mouse, clagging earth to catch on, crumble through her hands as gravity shifts and her world goes spinning down and down and her fingers slide, scrabble-scrabble as he rips at her hair, her clothes the hardness in her hands, scrabble-scrabble—

'Don't you hurt her!'

She is aware of Ross, a wee hand flailing, and Charlie's arm is out to casually swat her baby; his tiny body flies *you fucking bastard* scrabble-scrabble, feel the roughness of the rock, its freight, feel some unsteady power shoot up her arm like a bullet as she smashes it down and down again. On him, on bone? He stops moving anyway.

Reverberations up her arm. Lies there. Chasing comets, blinking, blinking. Trying to see. Weight of her bloodied head, too heavy. Needs to close her eyes. Skin on her face is too tight. Feeling a squashy thing, flumped. His arm. Pain shoots up her leg as she moves. Slow dusk rolling, but it's all there, the scene is there; it's just her puffy eyes. Blink more. Fucking *move*. Stand.

'Ross!' she yells.

'Justi!'

'Oh Christ. Don't move.'

Rain smirring. Blink. Concentrate. Look . . . for points of light. Long shapes in the twilight. Charlie Boy is on his flank beside her. Eyes closed. He is in the recovery position. She does not check his breathing. 'Ross, baby. I can't see you.'

'I am here. Look!' Pale fronds wave at her. Fingertips.

'Oh, baby. Are you all right?' Hands and knees, to him. She spits out her own blood. 'Where's sore?' Wiping dirt from his hair, his eyes.

'I am fine, silly. But you are hurted.'

'It's fine. We need to get down this hill. Quick, quick, yes?' Her foot caves when she tries to stand. Shafts of bright, fresh pain. 'Let Justi lean on you a wee bit, yeah?'

'But not to squash me?'

'No,' she whispers. 'Now, big big ssh, OK? Really quiet and really quick. As fast as we can. Pretend we are on a flying carpet.'

She thinks her ankle is broken. They will never make it down. She snatches up her bag, full of those thousands of pounds which got her here. Together, they slide and stumble in the half-light. Running, running on a ruptured foot. Each sclatter of scree, each muffled, painful breath makes terrible echoes. She knows Charlie won't shout; that's not his style. If he is following, he will let them enjoy their terror. Then he'll pounce.

Emerging now, from the screen of trees. Less encumbrance here; they can slide faster. Justine blanks off the pain in her ankle. It's not part of her. She can just make out the bulk of stones by the chambered cairn. The light on the hill is fading rapidly; it does that here, the sky flicking its hood up. It'll be pitch black before they reach the bottom. Far, far away, she can see a light glowing at Cardrummond.

'You all right, sweetie?'

Ross's clear 'No' bounces off the rocks.

'Ssh. We've got to be very very quiet, remember? Like wee mice.' Sweat and rain sting her eyes.

'Justi,' he whispers loudly. 'Are you frightened?'

'No! We're just playing at pirates, OK?'

Keep turning your head. If he can walk, he will come after you.

'I don't want to play now. My legs are hurting.'

Feel the soft, damp dark enfold you. It will be like lying in the snow. Give in, and make this stop.

'I know. Uhh,' she stifles a scream, catching her foot, her ankle in a rabbit hole. Stones spew. Pain spews. There is another crash of rocks and pebbles further up the hill.

'Ah fuck!' shouts Charlie Boy. 'Fuck you, Justine! Do you hear me? Fuck you!'

She begins to topple, puts her hand out to stop the fall. Cold, tall stone. They have reached the looming menhirs which flank the chambered cairn.

'Rossie, here,' she hisses. 'Help Justi slide the lid.' She can barely see him, just feels him small against her side. They put their hands out to touch the lower rocks, fumbling against stone. Smooth metal rubs along her palm. Smooth and curved. 'Watch your fingers. Ssh, darling. Don't cry.' She shoves her hand through the iron staple on the top of the concrete cover. Grinds it slowly open. Every scrape is a flare in the dark, but there are no more shouts. 'We'll have a wee rest in here, eh?'

'No,' Ross wails. 'It is dark.'

'Man, would you ssh! For fu— look, baby, it's getting really dark out here too. Please, please get in.' She lifts him bodily, bundles him inside the chamber. 'The bad man is coming. We can curl up all cosy in here.'

'I want my mummy.'

'I know, darling.' Her throat is hoarse with rasping. 'But we just need to hide like wee mice, just for a wee while. I promise I'll keep you safe, OK?' Tries to drag the lid shut, but there's no handle on the inside. It's getting dark. All covered in rock and grass, from the outside the chamber is just a wee hillock, a bump on the brae. The lid a fallen-down slab. He won't even know it's here. She shuffles them both backwards, as far as they can fit. Dunting her bum against the earthen wall, where she knows it's weak. Further from the open lid. They are both crying. The tin taste mingles with the bloody spittle from her mouth. She coils tight against Ross, trying to stop the shivering. Darker in here than out, but it's dry. Justine wriggles and eases deeper in, trying to find the soft space in the earth. A slice of grey air flashes above them, grey light on the tips of their toes. She scrunches Ross's legs, so his feet are tucked behind him.

They wait for Charlie Boy's footfall. He is good at being silent. She waits in the darkness, gnawing on her knuckle till the blood comes. Ross's face damp in her breast.

Thinks she hears a noise to her left, to her right, circling like a cat. Waits for the pounce, the slap, the night-time games. All her skin is wet and burning cold.

There is a scuffle above, hard shoes against her thigh as he swings in legs first, using the concrete lid to give him purchase, and she counters, kicking out her leg, connecting with the underside of his chin. Too late. He is laughing, a maniac, spitting out the tooth she has loosed even as he descends on them, she is screaming, screaming for her life. There is *Fuck you* and *fuck you* and dull low keening. There is panting and wailing and a cry that is not human. Then there is an almighty rumble, a terrible, terrible slamming, of metal. Rock. A final crunching of hard-gone-soft.

Chapter Thirty-eight

Why? Hannah whispers it often. Gently. With love. Michael thinks it often, in the dull bloom of his head. He lets the whispers come.

*

In the beginning was a minister. His name was Michael, and, last summer, he'd gone down to Glasgow for a Church Without Walls conference at the Days Inn Hotel. It's not the prettiest of hotels, seeing as it's a featureless box beside a run of railway arches. The hotel sits in the Gorbals, a southern enclave of the city which derives its name from *gort a' bhaile* (Gaelic 'garden of the town'), the Latin *garbale* (sheaf), suggestive of a tithe of corn, or the 'gory bells' of lepers, depending on which Wikipedia site you read. Either way, the place that was once home to Franciscan friars (and allegedly still houses the finger bone of St Valentine himself) is now a utilitarian mix of modern yellow-brick apartments, damp local-authority housing and cuboid, stranded pubs for communities that no longer exist. Although handy for the city centre, Gorbals is neither romantic, nor a tourist destination. As he drove into the hotel car park, Michael saw a coach party descend from their bus. Immediately, he wanted to warn them. Hide your valuables, don't walk back here at night! Which was probably unfair. He and Euan frequently had debates about the nature of Glasgow. Michael saw poverty and disparity, while Euan saw vibrancy, beauty and love.

He is a fine boy, his Euan.

The conference, too, was fine. Lots of stirring seminars: 'Moving Out and Welcoming In'; 'Open All Hours: 24/7 churching' (churching – note the verb. The minister leading this workshop wore his cross on a leather thong). When the first day was over, some of the younger ministers hit the town. Being neither young nor old, Michael tagged along for a wee while. He was feeling pretty chuffed with himself. He had survived. He'd left his parish under a cloud: rumours and long sad smiles were the order of the day. But he was entitled to be here (although he had bunked off 'Consider the Lilies: Community Gardens in Graveyards'). These folk were his tribe, his people. And it felt good. He was still an ordained priest. Hannah hadn't taken that away from him. This made him really happy, until about his third pint, when it made him really sad. Then angry. Michael's not a big drinker. A gaggle of hens (a cluck?) came stoating into the bar as he was preparing to leave. In time-honoured tradition, they descended on all the male drinkers in the pub, banging their pots and demanding money for the bride, in exchange for kisses. When they discovered they'd cornered a bunch (a blessing? a muddle? a mourning?) of ministers, hilarity ensued. Feather boas were draped, some dancing broke out. Another round of drinks ordered. Most of the hens were nurses. Ample thighs, amenable shoulders. He didn't do anything. Just talked to one of them, a soft Irish lass who was good at listening.

'I mean, why's itshtill me trying to make her happy? Shouldn' it be thother way roun'? You know? I mean, I really, really love her. But she'sh ripped my heart out.'

Eventually, the nurse got bored. She had patted him kindly. 'You poor soldier, you.' Before she went, she slipped her hand along the length of his thigh. A jolt of electricity shot up his penis.

'You need to love the world again.'

'Mike!' called the thong-crossed minister. 'We're going clubbing. Fancy it?'

The nurse shook her head. 'No, this wee lamb's had enough. He's going home, aren't you, sunshine?'

He left the merry throng somewhere in the Merchant City (which *is* a lovely tourist destination) and weaved over Albert Bridge to return to the Gorbals. Halfway across, he noticed a young man, elbows resting on the parapet. Four cans of lager were beside his elbow, a fifth at his mouth. As Michael came alongside, the lad flung his can into the Clyde.

'Hoi!' said Michael.

The lad turned. On his neck was a swallow tattoo. 'Who the fuck're you talking to?'

Backing away. 'It's jusht, you shouldn't . . . litter.'

'Away and get tae . . .' But it was an exhausted aggression, one in which all the energy was spent. The young man returned to his examination of the Clyde. His hair was razored into the nape of his neck, one of those necks that is neat and branches perfectly into the supporting sinew, bone and muscle required to cradle the skull. Michael's neck has hairy clumps which the barber discreetly zipped off. He'd started doing the same with the tips of Michael's ears.

Even in the dark light, he could see the pulse running up the man's corded neck. The swallow wing of his tattoo dancing.

'Are you all right?' Michael touched his arm; the young man spun to swing a punch, his cans clattering over the parapet and into the thick-churning river.

'You stupid fuck!'

Distracted by this loss, the man's fist fell. In fact, his whole pumped-up body sagged, like it was drum-stretched over a gaping hole, and had been ruptured. His eyes hooked on to Michael. He was waiting. Waiting for something to make it right.

'I'm sorry. I didn't mean . . .' Michael's words sharpened, the warmth and softness of the alcohol receding in the desperate vacancy of the young man's stare. He played his trump card, the decider that made folk split themselves open or clam up. 'Look, I'm a minister—'

The man snorted.

Michael forged on, because thy word is a lamp. Michael and his flaming sword of truth.

'You upset? Yousheem upset.'

'Is that right?' The man took a long, slow gob into the Clyde. 'Nae offence, pal, but would you just fuck off?'

'Sure. It's just. If you wanna talk about anything, I'm a good listener. Maybe help? D'you need a bed for the night?'

A mirthless *aw fuck*. 'I'm no a fucking jakey, man.'

Michael looked at the man's pressed, short-sleeved shirt, at the muscular heft of his arms. 'No. No, of course.' He began to plan his exit, select what reassuring lump of scripture he could lob as they parted ways. The lad must have sensed this retraction, or some swell inside him shifted course, or the rind of moon slashing the face of the river spoke words beyond Michael, but anyway, there it was. A subtle change, the connection woven through them both. He started it. Michael started it, of that there is no doubt. But then the young man began to speak.

He told Michael that his name was Alan. He was a builder. Married, one wee boy, aged ten months.

'That's nice—'

'No it fucking isny. No when you . . .' His voice broke against the thin moon, a sob that hit the stars, then was swallowed almost instantly. 'Fuck, man.' He laid his cheek on the parapet of the bridge and wept. Today, he and his wife had fought. They were always fighting, ever since the wean was born. She said he loved him more than her. Today, his wife had told him that the child wasn't his. The pain was unbearable.

'I've just been walking for fucking hours. Walking and drinking and fucking greeting. I . . . I canny take it, know? I literally canny stand here wi' my feet on the ground and stay straight. I don't know what . . . I don't know.'

He let him cry, awkwardly, with Alan's face prone on the parapet and Michael's arm resting on his shoulders.

'Fucking poofters,' a passing drunk shouted.

So who gave Michael the words that night? He was contriving to fashion some message of love and hope, watching this abject soul whose heart had been broken, watching the cold moon on the Clyde with the flow of the water rising, filling up his own shattered heart which he had pretended was stuck together.

'Fuckin' cows.'

'Whit?' Alan's face came up, bleary and sore.

'Women are fucking cows.' He saw Hannah, on her knees. Her face was scarlet with . . . what? Panic? Guilt? Snot bubbling out her nostrils, her golden hair wired in a crazy halo. Her grief melting him. Making him take his own and fold it up, fold it smaller and smaller until he could tell himself that it was unimportant. Selfish even.

A clumsy pat to Alan's shoulder. 'Don't you let her see you're hurting.'

'But I have to talk to her.'

'Aye, but . . . they jus' con you. Tell you how sorry they are and how much they love you, but it's like . . . It's jus' spoiled. Like blood in milk. And then they make you feel guilty for making them stay.'

Alan pushed himself away from the parapet. He wobbled, clutched the bridge of his nose with finger and thumb. Michael noticed his knuckles were bleeding. 'Aw fuck, man. I canny listen to this.'

'Jus' you protect yourself, son. You're young. Tell her to fuck off. You think about number one.'

Alan had half-raised his arm, in farewell or a warding-off. Or maybe it was for balance. Michael likes to pretend it was for balance; that he was very wobbly that night. He watched the young man stagger off, back towards the town. Watched him turn left along the Clydeside, on to the Broomielaw where laden cargo ships would dock and laden emigrant ships would leave, once, hundreds of years ago. The boy, Alan, his name was Alan, became a misty outline, then nothing. If Michael was a good and sentient man, he might have followed him. Seen his unsteady progress all the way along the Broomielaw until it becomes a muddle of overhead motorway and pillars and shiny-façaded offices and there is a street there called Cheapside where a terrible disaster in the sixties means the ghosts of nineteen firemen haunt the spot and there is a street there called Finnieston which leads away from the river and takes you up to yet another leg of the motorway which spiders Glasgow. How it curves, this C-shaped climb. How it takes you up above the rooftops. You could be a bird up there, staring at your city. If it is quiet and dark and car-free, you could walk all the way up this soaring road. No one would stop you, not even a teary minister, who is climbing into his car and drink-driving from Gorbals to Govan (which is not far, as the crow flies). But you are a swallow. You could take your heart up there and carry it high. Present it to the sky-gods. Maybe ask again for help. Or maybe you are so, so sore that it no longer matters, and you present it to the water gods instead.

Standing alone, on the Kingston Bridge. Oh the wind, up there. Would be fierce. And the swing of it, the concrete, the cables, the graceful arc. Did you look out and across? Down? Did you shut your eyes? Was your last conscious act unconscious?

Did you fly?

With a swoop. It was Michael's words that sent him spinning.

Michael didn't know this. Not yet. He was ranting in his car, frog-hopping the gears, picking the darkest streets. Oh, he was crafty enough for that. He was arrow-sharp and straight in his momentum. *Bitch*, he was crying. *Fucking bitch. Bastard.* Six months had passed since Hannah told him, or rather, that woman told him, about Gil. And the wee folded-up piece of hurt was uncontainable. It had billowed open. It made him a sail, took him wild and furious to where it all began, to the thing he had imagined and spied on and swallowed back and had eaten him alive.

Gil.

This man that had had his wife. Gil Ashworth was very pale when he answered the door. Michael remembers that. There were candles in his flat, and a faint muzzy smell that might be incense. But he was alone. What kind of a man lights candles on his own?

Flame animated him, lent his skin a rosy glow and burned the rage deeper into Michael. He was so tired of shadows. Brief glimpses of another, possible life, dragging behind, darting in front. His lost life. Tears and anger and pleading and contrition and then closure. Do we have 'closure'? That is what she actually said. He had the strangest feeling that Hannah was close. That if he went outside and turned his head, she'd be waiting. If only she'd come back to him, properly. Extinguish this hanging-on. He'd lingered so long, burning, burning, half a man, that if she were to even breathe on him, he'd blow away. The fine dust of him would disintegrate in a line of ash.

Thinking of her was like bereavement.

The sad thing is, he thinks Gil understood. Gil would have done it too, if Hannah were his. Beaten fuck out of his opponent. Smashed his skull with wide blank fists; it would have to be fists. Was fists. Fists and feet, flesh on flesh, hammering out the flesh on unfaithful flesh you relive, daily in your head. He remembers pounding on the door. The opening of it, this packed figure which was him rushing into Gil, on him. Gil on the ground before he knew it. He remembers how the carpet soaked with blood.

The force of his fury scared him – that he was the creator of this unleashing is the thing which has unmade him more than anything else. Even when Gil's eyes were jelly, the fists, the feet, kept pummelling. As if a demon had possessed him.

With each blow, he was trying to force his demon into Gil.

Afterwards, in his car.
Tell the truth.

He doesn't know. He doesn't know if he spoke. He doesn't know if Gil was conscious, assumes he didn't die, because he'd have heard, then, wouldn't he? They'd have come looking for him then and it did, it did it came looking for him for ever, red lines of blood that twisted of their own volition, rose clean from his spattered forearm and took residence in his brain. Licked up the blood, puffed him gently on his way.

Michael slept in his car. Woke with a raging thirst and no memory.

Liar.

His knee ached: he must have banged it. Careful depressions, slow-turning wheels. Michael made it back to the Days Inn to shower, collect his bags. He did not participate in the second day of the conference. Food poisoning. Did he say that? Possibly, but it was only a message left; he was careful not to let anyone see him. Sly, and pumped. Rock-hard cock of the walk. No contrition. No memory, you see.

Oh for shame, Michael.

Swill of coffee in his room, quick flick through shopping channels to the news. Reporting Scotland, that two-minute round-up at the end before they go back to London and an interview on the couch.

Police are appealing for witnesses
Body of a young man
River Clyde
Eye for a jellied eye
No suspects
No memory, you see.

Chapter Thirty-nine

'He seems calmer now?'

'Yes.' The young man in his greeny-blue scrubs fiddles with a knob on the monitor. 'Sedation does that.' He writes quickly on Michael's chart. 'Good. Now, I'm going to have to ask you to make yourself scarce for an hour or two, I'm afraid.'

'Why?' Hannah grips on to the bed-guard. 'But he's breathing on his own now.'

'We need to do some more tests, Mrs Anderson.'

'Why? What's wrong? What are you going to do to him now?'

'Nothing invasive, I promise. We'll be doing another ECG, to read the electrical activity in his brain. And we'll need to reset his meds a tad, so he might get a wee bit jumpy.'

Hannah clasps her other hand over the first. One big knot of controlled desperation. 'What will you be looking for? Exactly?'

'I really do think it would be a good idea for you to go home now, Mrs Anderson? Yes? Get some rest?'

She stands, walks past him to Michael's bed, to the top, where his head is. She daren't touch his skull now, not even his hair in case it presses on his brain. *You cannot move the patient, Mrs Anderson!*

'Do you think he can feel it? Did I hurt him?'

The vulnerability of his skin is compounded by the hard metal that surrounds him. Machines and sensors. Monitors on his skull. Hooks and clicks, dark whirrings. There are thick, tired lines like half-moon spectacles, there is unshaven hair and long, broken planes of shadow. He's lost any trace of plumpness, which was only an illusion, because she knows the smooth skin of his belly, but that was the impression of him: plump and middle-aged, all the connotations of contentment. He is pared-away. He is all the man she married, every last bit of him, full and present in this liminal space where his copper eyes are not quite shut. The swell of Hannah's chest threatens to burst her open.

'But he's breathing now. Is he going to be all right?'

'It will take time. A long time, maybe.'

'Be honest with me, doctor. Please.'

'It's Andrew. My name is Andrew.'

'How many heads have you been inside? You seem very young. How many folk will get better from something like this? Honestly, properly better?'

'Honestly, it depends.'

'On what? What can I do?'

'Be patient.' The doctor rests his bum against the edge of the sink. 'Depending where it strikes, a haematoma can eat your memories, your speech. It can steal time. One half of your body might wither and die. Get you at the front of your brain, and your personality will morph. But I think we've been lucky here. The combination of the head injury, plus the tumour. You could say they've worked to our advantage.'

'Advantage?'

'Well, the bleed was small, we caught it quickly. The tumour was even smaller. Believe me, that makes the prognosis reasonable. Good, even.'

Hannah imagines their scale of 'good'. How many people has Andrew truly restored? He'll have seen vacant eyes light briefly, as a loved one enters. Brave men weeping at their obstinate hands. Shiny-swollen faces struggling to relearn words. Are these good outcomes? She wants her Michael back, every bit of him. Together, their pieces slot. Fit one into the other, the points touch, the edges meet and run.

'I promise you.' The doctor touches her hand. His awkwardness makes her think of Euan. 'This was a very positive procedure. Give him time, let him heal. We have a hundred million brain cells, you know – more than all particles in the universe.' Andrew smiles. 'The brain's the most beautiful structure there is. My old boss used to say we were "working close to the architecture of God".'

There's a rap at the door. A familiar perfume drifts. 'Hannah!' Her mum appears, throwing open her arms. Soft folds of love and pity, sweeping her back to infancy. Hannah climbs inside, to a wrist scented with Nina Ricci, the light glide of fingertips, the upstroke of palm. This hand has forty years' practice in navigating her heartbreaks.

'Oh, Mum.'

'Ssh.'

Breathing in her mum, slippery skin on silk. Her knotted neck being stroked. 'Where's the boys?' she asks. 'Have they had any dinner?'

'I don't know, darling,' says her mum into her hair. 'Did you not get Rossie something here? What about you? Have you eaten?' She cups Hannah's cheeks. 'Oh, darling, this is awful. How are you? How's Michael? Poor pet.' Her eyes fill up as she looks at the bed. 'Can he hear us?'

'Did you come straight here then? Is Ross not at the manse?'

'No. Is he not with you?' Her mother's bony fingers at the top of Hannah's arms. Pressing. 'I waited and waited. I assumed he must be with you.'

'No.'

'Where *is* he, then? I tried Euan's room, but he's down for physio they said.'

'But, Mum, you were supposed to get Ross at the house.'

'I know. That's why I waited.'

'For what?'

'For Ross. But there was nobody there.'

'Don't worry. Justine'll have him somewhere. Did you try the café?'

'That's what I'm saying. They're not there. I went to the shop, the café, the park. I waited in the house for ages, in case they came back. The girl's gone.'

'Mum. What do you mean, gone?'

'I mean gone. Hasn't even tidied up like you asked: dishes in the sink, crumbs—'

'Yes, but they'll be at . . . I know. Did you try Cardrummond?'

'Hannah. I've tried everyone I could think of, I'm not senile you know. Kilmacarra isn't exactly huge. That's why I was getting worried. You said she was in the basement? Which is why I'm in the wee room with Ross, and I don't mind, honestly I don't. But, when they didn't come back, well, I went down and had a proper look, you know? I wasn't being nosy. Hannah, her room's empty. Her wardrobe, everything. No note, no Ross.'

'But Ross is meant to be with her.'

'Well, where are they then? Where are they, darling? Because they've both gone.'

Chapter Forty

She won't sleep.

Just dark and quiet womb noises. A faint, persistent drip. The chamber has no time. Justine tells herself it must be night-time. There is a strange leaden warmth; Ross has fallen into exhausted sleep, as she keeps vigil. For what? They have yelled themselves hoarse, but nobody comes. She won't sleep. But the nightwatch tricks her into dreams. Of deadness and elongated hours. Of grasping hands. Of fire and stone and angry lights, of feet scuffling and a sudden-snapping wakefulness. She is thick and dark, is nowhere. Allows the gentle dumbness to fold round her. It stops the whirring from cracking out her skull.

She won't sleep, and then she has. Again. Wakes, again, to the hard-backed soreness of her neck. She's in a sticky heap. A faint and desperate thrashing. There was a struggle. She remembers.

She remembers Charlie, and his feet kicking her. Remembers falling back. A roar of wind. They are in some endless cave; she can feel rough walls, a rocky shelf, then yards and yards of empty black. Too frightened to walk out into this nothingness, they have been huddled against the jagged shelf. There's no cave mouth she can see, no light. Only panic. Air curdling. Shallow breaths, she tries to breathe slowly, quietly, listening to where they are, spreading out against the teethed walls of the cave that are screaming in her face, sucking the air from her chest and forcing it up to make her gag.

That they might not leave this gluey air. A momentary terror, sharper than the rest. She touches Ross's lips. Still warm. He stirs slightly. Charlie's body has stopped convulsing, she thinks. The noises have stopped. That was the desperate thrashing she is trying to forget. It happened so quickly. Quivering, the first shudder beneath the pressure of the hill caving in, or so it felt, not just the earthen wall falling from behind her, but the ceiling too, the whole entrance pouring in on itself, vast shards of stone and earth seething. Her, shielding Ross with her body as the rain of rock kept coming. Then, suddenly, no clattering. Deep silence, dust eddying. Blackness, sealing them in. Blind, hand in front of her face, on her knees with Ross clinging to her leg. First, she heard him. Then, she felt him: Charlie skewed beneath the debris, his legs jerking. She buries her nose in Ross's neck. The earth continued to tremble far below them, all the teetering weight of Mary's Brae above.

Justine makes slits of her eyes, tuning-in to the dark. She thinks they've been here for hours. And no fucker is coming. Her wounds throb in time with her pulse. There are layers of darkness, if you focus: velvet, silk and gauze, coal and iron and granite. She can see proximities: the compact curve of Ross's spine, the outline of Charlie's feet. The upper half of his body is hidden by the pile of rocks. Impassable pile of rocks. The dripping continues. Her throat's parched; if she follows the sound, they might find water. The notion of minutes, hours is gone. It would be cruel to wake Ross, but he'll need to drink. She will have to do this carefully. Her fingers lace his hair.

'Rossie,' she whispers. 'Sweetie. Wake up.'

'*Mh.*'

'Now, don't be scared, but it's gonny be dark when you open your eyes. Justi will be here. I'm right here. We're going to get you a wee drink.'

Immediately, he is crying. 'Muh-mee,' he beats her off. 'Want my mummy.'

'Ssh. I know you do.' Cuddling him. 'And we'll see her soon. I promise. They'll come and find us soon.'

'*Who?* How'llae,' a gulping sob, 'know we are he-ere? Mum-mee,' he shouts. 'Muuuuh-mee.'

She lets him yell.

'Just like that. What we're going to do is keep shouting. Just as good as you did there. But first, we need to get a drinkie, or our throats will be sore.'

'My throat *is* sore. And my tummy is hungry.'

'Are you a hungry hungry hippo?'

'No,' he sniffs. 'I am just awful very hungry.'

'Well, let's try and get a drink first, yes?'

With her belt, Justine ties Ross to her, looping their waistbands together. She's petrified they'll lose themselves in the dark, has no idea of the geography of this place; if the floor will sheer away or their heads batter on overhangs.

'Now you can be like Buddy, eh?'

'Don't want to.'

'It doesny have to be Buddy. The game is we walk on our hands and knees, like a doggie. You go behind Justi, and we're going to try and find where that drip-drip noise is coming from. Can you hear it?'

'Uh-huh.'

'Good. Now, let's keep close beside this rock on our left, yeah?'

'What is our—'

'This side. The hand you don't hold your pencil in.'

Slowly, they set off; a limping caravan. The ground is silky dust; it feels almost like shingle. Every so often, where you hit rock, there's a definite, twisty groove which makes her dizzy trying to understand it. Round and pointlessly round; as if the grooves are mocking their passage. Justine counts their steps – can you call them steps when it's on your knees? There's no entrance any more, but she doesn't want to become entirely disorientated. If they keep returning to where the cave mouth fell in . . . well, it's some fixed point. For when the people come. They'll come for Ross, won't they? But all the rubble seemed to fall in a sinkhole, she's no idea if there's any outward sign, if the concrete slab is split, if the menhirs have toppled and her bag's belching money into air. Or if the sliding concrete lid's still there, and no one thinks to look inside, and it must be fully dark by now.

How long does trapped air last? There will be draughts and breezes coming in, surely? But this is not a proper cave: they are locked inside the belly of the hill. The further they shuffle round the perimeter, the more she's aware how long and vast this space is. This unstable space, which has already crumbled in to meet itself. She changes hands every few paces, one to support her knees, one to reach out and feel what's ahead. All she can smell is dankness, no fresh stirrings. No rays of light, oh man, she's lost count of their steps and there's an overwhelming wave of panic rising, her throat seals shut, skin is searing, she is bone, dead bone, and who will go first? When they weaken ohgodohgod she mustn't scream. She snuffles through her nose until she can trust herself to open her mouth.

'You all right behind, mister?'

'No. It is spitting on my hair.'

'What is?' Justine pats out her hands behind her, on his head. 'Wet?'

'Or it might of been bird poo. A seagull bird pooed on my head once and Euan just laughed.'

She holds her hand a moment, cupped, until another drip falls.

'Clever boy. You've found the water. Now, stick out your tongue and catch the drips.'

'No.'

'Why not?'

'It is dirty.'

'No it's not. Don't be daft. Look, Justi'll do it first then.'

'No. It might be poisoned and you will die and you will leave me. No!' He slaps her hand away from his head.

'Ross, you're being silly.' She licks her fingers. Tastes manky, but that could just be her. 'We need to have a drink. What if we can see where it's coming from, eh? Would that make it not dirty? If you can see it's just nice clean water?' Feeling upwards, till she finds a damp, slimy patch of rock. Follows it with her fingers, her fingers hit a groove, a dent, and another, lots of gouges in the rock, standing up and spanning higher till she feels a little ledge. 'Right, there's a wee bit up here we can maybe get up on to. Then we'll see where that goes, all right?' Justine never went to Brownies or camp or any of that woolly woodcraft shite, but the water has to flow, and soak and be replenished. If they can follow the water up, to its source . . . There is the spring at the summit of Mary's Brae, there is a gap in the rocks through which water pours. She feels the slippery rockface above them. More strange cuttings.

Regular and shaped. Yes, it's desperate. Possibly pointless. But there is nothing else. Her fingers keep moving. The ledge is broad. She inches her good foot up the rockface, winces as pain builds in her injured one. Shifts her grip and her fingers bump, running from rough to smooth. Very smooth, a strange, brittle scoop, nudging out and into her palm. She finds a foothold and punts herself, springy like a kid peeking over a wall. Sees her hand on the empty sockets of a skull.

'Jesus!' Her fingers flash back.

'See? I am already saying to Jesus,' says Ross gloomily. 'But it is not working. And my daddy says it works. But it is not.'

She feels sick. The darkness is getting to him, Christ, she thinks about all the bones that might be down here, and the long lush days she has ruined of her life, the knocks and the confusions, the dragging deathless waste of it; and the sun outside, it is just outside of here, and she lifts Ross and lifts her good foot, fucking stamping on Godknows what to get a purchase, pushing Ross up with her shoulder.

'Right. Find some roots or stones, baby. Pull. We are getting out of here.'

But the side is too slippy, they sink back, tumbling, which way is up, she's on the ground, she feels the earth, the mud in her sore mouth and the weight inverts, she has Ross by the elbow and there's a firmness again at her feet.

'Rossie. Just you stay here. Just sit tight a wee minute, yes? I'm going to see if I can get up there on my own. Then I'll lean down and pull you up, right?'

He nods. Wide-eyed. Justine holds her hands in front of her. They are steady. Ish. Imagines the veins inside. Bright, gleaming blue. Her blood has been galvanised. She moves stiff limbs, pushes herself up on . . . a stone. More bones? Whatever, with the piled mud on top, there's enough springy give, and there's a big clump of root to get a foothold, to haul harder and harder till she finds the beginning of the wet sweet trickle, running over the ledge.

'Justi!'

'I will come back for you, I promise.'

Arms burning, she forces on to her elbows, dragging the dead weight of her body up until a knee hooks on to the rock. One final thrust, and she's up. From the ledge, the glimmer of her veins is brighter; how is it she can see the actual outline of her veins? There's a kind of phosphorescence coming from the thin run of water, whirls of steam rising, like coils on the stone itself, and there is the faintest stream of light above. It's a fissure in the rock, lit from within. She can see a tiny bead of white, miles over-head: a headlamp at the end of an hour-long tunnel. Moonlight? The round, distant whiteness echoes the skull, which she refuses to acknowledge, set in its niche to the left of her. By ignoring it, it seems to double and loom, teasing her that there are two heads watching from the corner of her eye. But it's the arrow of light she's focused on. The fissure is five, maybe six feet higher than she can reach, and it's narrow. If she could swing out, do a Tarzan leap, there's another point of rock that offers a foothold. From there, she thinks she could reach the gap.

'Justi?' calls Ross.

'Wee minute, sweetie. Hang on.'

The air glitters and she is reaching for it, towards the tiny shaft, and the sticky-out piece of rock, but her forehead cracks on another, unseen ledge, jerking her head back, tumbling slightly as the momentum kicks, then it is a leery, veering lumber, skittering stone.

Bright shriek as her hand flails from earth to air.

She stumbles. Kneels. One hand, one elbow, anchored on a rock stump. Afraid to look, to lean over. Scrabbling from the frayed-away limits of the overhang.

'Justi!' Ross is yelling.

'I'm all right.'

There's enough light to tempt her to lean further forward. On scree, steep scree that is sliding with her unsure feet. 'Justi!' She can hear Ross sobbing. 'Mummy!'

The long shaft is three, four feet away. Beyond is crumbling air. Can feel a draught. She stinks of animal, grasping.

'Justi! Please come back. Justi!'

The drip is wetting her fringe.

'Justi!'

Fingertip far, she stretches. Sucks at the cold splinter of air, desperate.

'Justee! I am frightened.'

It's no use. If she leaps, she won't get back. She cannot leave him.

'I'm coming down, honey. It's all right. I'm coming back.'

She fumbles her way to his voice. Much easier to lower yourself down than clamber up. She holds the trembling child in her arms. Back to black. The dark feels thicker now she knows the light is up above; it's inside her lungs, thick as mucous, webs of it catching in her ribs, her sinuses. The two of them coil at the foot of the dripping rock. Decomposing. Sand in the pyramid: she can laugh at that image now, because the real feeling is nothing like you imagine. It's not panic, not fear. It is the sucking absence of light. A speck of water hits her cheekbone. When his lips get cracked, she can moisten them with her fingers. She won't think beyond that.

Ross sniffs. 'Justi. Do you know the ho-yo song?'

'No, baby, I don't. I'm sorry. I'm so sorry.'

'Is OK,' he whispers. 'I will teach you.'

Chapter Forty-one

Dawn. Orange streaks into blue as the dark falls back. Thin shadows stretch. Trees yawn and people stir. Hundreds of people, in a slow march across the glen. They have searched all night, in gullies and in culverts, in bins and attics, rolled-up carpets, garden ponds. The police fan out in front, officers in baseball caps and overalls, stumping sticks, some on their knees. Each place that was searched will be searched again. Every so often, they bring her stuff: a piece of litter – *Does he eat Milky Ways?*; a purple scarf – *No. Not his.* Could it be Justine's? *Maybe. I don't know*; Michael's car keys found 'posted' in an envelope inside their hall bench. *No, he does that. Rossie does that.* But is it significant, they ask, that the envelope is for Justine? There's a note in the envelope: *Trouble at t'farm! Need to talk to you. Tonight?* And a squiggle that could be L or D. *I don't know*, she says. *I don't know.* The church is become an incident room, the café given over to vast urns and huddled faces stealing a quick respite before they return outside. Specialist dogs are coming up from Glasgow, the Mountain Rescue is out, and a helicopter sweeps. Sentinel Power have offered every man they have, and you see their yellow jackets in behind the cops. Others wear their bunnets and thick coats, for it's been a chill night, a braw bricht moonlicht nicht once the rain had stopped, and though you get a sweat up, searching, when the wind bites you need warmth at your back.

Men no longer chatter. The first wild surge of conviction has ebbed; there's an air of grim resolve. Clusters form, then dwindle. Folk come, folk go. Councillor McCall's been patting Hannah's arm for ages, saying it will be a tribute. A tribute for the family. It will be a beacon of local democracy, this village debate. Polling really strongly; the press are very keen. *For the people, by the people.* Or maybe *Wind in Our Sails*, they haven't decided yet. She's no idea what he's on about, but he tells her: 'It's what Michael would have wanted.' Hannah nods till he leaves her alone. 'He's not dead,' she says, suddenly, as his backside judders out of view.

She can't stop herself from rocking. When the surprise of Ross had happened to her, when it was still unshared, Hannah had sat on the toilet, rocking. Pee-stick in her hand. She'd noticed a small varicose vein at the angle where her right knee bent. It shrivelled when she pressed it; a snake shedding blue skin. What might it be like to be perfectly free? she'd wondered. Stripped of wife and mum and dutiful daughter. Just you again. Just you when you were unencumbered and intact. Because then you'd only feel what you wanted to feel, and there would be no power ever that could hurt you.

Mhairi drapes a blanket over Hannah's shoulders. 'Are you coming back inside?'

She shakes her head.

'Can I get you anything?'

A young woman offers her a mug of tea. Hannah doesn't recognise her, until she speaks. 'Please drink it. You'll think you don't need it, but you do.' It's Johnny's mum, Fiona. The young woman stands beside her for a long time. They don't speak. Hannah watches Duncan's sheep, the ewes square and plodding, the lambs leaping for the very joy of being alive. Fiona's profile is sculpted against the sun.

'Where's your Johnny? Is he safe?'

'He's out with Buddy. Looking.'

Hannah nods. She sips, doesn't taste the tea, but she feels it slip down. She looks at the mug, the liquid inside. Turns the tea out on to her hand. Although she cups her fingers really, really tight, she can't hold on to a single drop.

'Here.' Fiona takes the mug from her. Mhairi calls over. 'Hannah, that's the polis wanting a word.'

The blanket falls away as she walks towards this new inspector coming. Duncan from Cardrummond accompanies him; he's pointing out various landmarks, the inspector nodding.

'Mrs Anderson. My name's Grant. We spoke on the phone.'

'Did they find anything?'

'We've sent officers to various addresses in Glasgow: her mother, her boyfriend, known associates.'

'And? Was I right?'

'Her name's not Arrow, it's Strang.'

'And is she—'

'She has got previous convictions, Mrs Anderson, yes. Several.'

'I knew it!' The spike in her belly is fear, not vindication.

'You'll appreciate I can't disclose the nature of them.'

'I'll *appreciate*? I'll appreciate she's got my wee boy Christ-knows where. With Christ-knows who. But you're protecting *her*?'

It is the 'who', all the numberless connotations of lost infants and vacant stares and docile bodies being led, being led. All she can see is the orange light, and Ross's face. Between them, Fiona and Duncan lead her inside the café. A glass is thrust in her hands. 'Drink.'

'Mrs Anderson,' says the inspector. 'Her boyfriend is also missing. We're focusing one strand of the investigation on him. Several of his associates are currently being questioned as to his whereabouts.'

'Can you tell us anything about the boyfriend?' asks Duncan.

'I'm afraid I can't. Only that he's known to us as well.'

'Ah Duncan.' Mouth dry. The world all shrinking, all converging in a rush. 'D'you not get it?' It makes sense, the bruised grubbiness of her; Michael's fascination – not with the sex, she no longer thinks that, but with the tawdry glamour, all his flirting with power and robes, his need to *save*. *Tell me he didn't know.* She seizes the edge of the inspector's fluorescent jacket. 'When you said boyfriend. Did you mean pimp?'

'I really can't—'

'She's a hooker, isn't she? And a con artist. They're a team of predators and they've got my boy.'

'Now come on—'

'Duncan, shut up. *Please.* Stop wasting your time poking about in burns and find them. Before it's too late.'

'Mrs Anderson,' says Duncan. 'Please listen to yourself. This is *not* Justine. No matter what you say she's done, Justine loves Ross, she absolutely loves Ross. I know she wouldn't hurt him. There is no way. No way.' As if he's trying to convince himself that this is truth, and he has a lovely, honest face and it does not deserve to be hurt but she doesn't care.

'Tell him,' she says. 'Tell him what she is.'

The inspector rubs his thumb along his chin. Tic-toc, tic-toc; a half-moon dial, with the pointer, ticking off the seconds. When the tip of his thumb touches his lower lip, he speaks. 'Justine does have convictions for soliciting, yes.'

'Christ. I knew it! She's a hoor and a thief. Everything, everything of mine has fallen apart because of her.' The swirl of people around her, blurry. Dense. She swings round to catch their faces, so they will look at her. Trying to make them *see*.

'Now, Hannah.' Mhairi's soft arm is smothering. 'We all know you're tired—'

'Fuck *off*, Mhairi. Just all of you fuck off and find my boy. He's not here. She's *taken* him.'

Hannah hears a dog barking. Turns from the futility of the scene, all these static people, out of the café to the fresh air. There is mud on her face and in her nails. Grained earth pressed into the grooves and ruts of fingertips. Fingers that write stupid words that don't stain your hands and break your nails. This is just a story, she tells herself. The beginning and the end, all tied in a bow that's become unravelled. She needs to find the end. She doesn't know how, but she needs to find it.

Under the bed. Did they check, did anyone check there, in case he made a tent? As Hannah runs towards her front door, clouds come. The earth goes striped and fluttering, scuttling past the side of the house. Twisted barley-sugar light. It's beautiful. On her doorstep, Margaret Campbell has left a tiny posy of bluebells, and one of her infamous stews.

'Ross!' She lifts her face up to the light. 'ROSS!'

Hears the dog bark again, louder. A rush of feet.

'Mrs Anderson!' It's Johnny Green, filthier than usual. He flits past his mother, the cops, straight to her. 'Come on!'

'What is it?'

'In the dunny. Come on!'

'Dunny?' says the inspector.

Fiona lays her hand on her son's shoulder. He flickers; looks up at his mum, surprised. 'He means the chambered cairn.'

'The one on Mary's Brae?' The inspector signals to two of his cops. 'You've been in there, yes?'

'Aye, sir. It's about three foot across. You could just about get two folk in there, but it's totally clear. Checked it ma'sel'.'

'Aye, behind that,' Johnny is breathless. 'He was pure whimpering, Buddy. He kept going back in the dunny. See the back wall, it's all soft. Like the mud's fell in. He kept digging at it. Look! Buddy found a tooth.'

All noise and orders barking then; a great wellspring of compact, focused movement. Disembodied words come on radios, more tea, more blankets, infrared heat-seeking robots. One of Sentinel's yellow diggers rumbles into life: it is a vortex of colour. In the middle of it: Hannah, running from her blanket; seeing the fresh blood on the tooth in the barley-sugar light.

Chapter Forty-two

Grey September.

The souterrain is 'incredible', they all breathlessly agree. The people enter crouched. Ferns and moss cushion the walls on either side. Runnels of water drip between the vegetation; the light is funky green. There's a draught coming from further down, a coppery smell of earth and damp. The hole of sky behind them is the only light, and it shrinks away to nothing as they pass in single file. But all is fine, for they have torches. Hand torches, issued no more than ten at a time. There is no way cables and electric lighting are being strung on these walls. There is talk of lighting it from above, unobtrusive shafts of atmospheric colour, perhaps a *son et lumière* show; there's a plinth where a string quartet could stand. Or a fiddle band. *Fingal's Cave*: you could commission something nice; there could be a competition.

The people blink. Ease themselves to upright, surprised that they can stand. Blink again. It takes a minute until they realise that the ceiling is comfortably high, and that there is no limit to the stretch of the walls, which soar long and deeply into the hill-side, like endless dark wings.

'Now, if you look to your left. Far left . . .'

They are transfixed by the carvings on the wall. They are shown the three separate alcoves, with the marks of different Celtic tribes. Professor Tom is not tired of repeating himself, he will do this in batches, then the locals will be trained, or there will be official guides. But for now, this is Tom's domain, and he's exuberant. Arms flung wide, voice modulated to quiet – slow – BOOM as the light glides up in a graceful arc to sweep dancing animals.

'See there: we have the stag of the Creones, from Cernunnos, the horned god – which also gives us the word "cairn", of course. Creones and Carnonacae were known as Caledonii by the Romans; a tribal alliance basically. You'll also find Creones in Cornwall and Brittany. We're confident that Kelt, Galat or, in this case, Caled all mean the same thing.' He nods, knowledgeably, at the murmuring group.

'However, what we're also seeing here is evidence of tribes assembling from much further afield. There, see?' The professor points the torch beam at an angry, trotting dog. 'We have the Venicones, represented by this carving of the hound or wolf. Now, these peoples came from the area around Fife and Tayside.' He bounces the light left. 'Observe too the horse, depicting the Epidii, who covered the area from Kintyre to Jura, and here,' he alights on a three-legged cloud, 'we have the sheep of the Caeren, who stretched as far as Sutherland. We even have the cow of the Selgovae in the south-west. Note the exceptionally short horns.' The cow looks like a rhinoceros, with a long, curving tail that girdles its body.

'What you have to understand is that this is an oral tradition. For a Pict or a Celt to write all these symbols down together is very powerful – and also makes them very vulnerable. Essentially, you're laying yourself open before your enemy.' He turns to face the listeners, shining the torchlight under his own chin. Whether by accident or design, the spooky shadowlight is chilling. 'It is a mark of great faith and trust in each of these differing tribes – they are revealing their true faces, if you like. Celtic scholars among you will know the words for "face" and "honour" are closely linked.'

He frowns and pauses, so that the gathered group will realise the import of his words, that they are looking at profundity. 'You have to understand,' Professor Tom repeats, 'how incredible this place is. We know of Druids convening in Gaul to mediate disputes between tribes, but we've never heard of it here in Scotland. For all we know, this may have been an early form of parliament. And of even earlier worship too.' He flashes his big teeth, and his torch. The light leaps from his bony, animated fingers. 'Diodorus Siculus tells us the Celts liked to "fight, cele-brate and speak well"—'

'No change there, then!' shouts a voice from the gloom. There's a ripple of laughter, which reverberates round the cave.

'Indeed. They also believed that the immortal soul lives in the head: ergo the severing of the sacred skull.'

The people shine their torches up the walls, all searching for the bone-light, two niches facing east where the skulls have kept their long vigil. Two of them: an adult female and a child. The originals have been reunited with their bones, but their polished resin substitutes gleam on. Even up close, you can barely tell the difference. It's the same with dentures, when they give them arti-ficial, slight flaws to make them seem even more real. Folk shudder at the thought, the *thought*, of how they died. There is a whispery thrill at the back of people's ears, where the hard bone curves. Were the heads severed before or after? Is he talking about sacrifices? That's disgusting. Dripping walls of shifting liquid could be slime; the echoes are locked-in screams where nobody hears and nobody comes and who would *do* that; if you were human who would do that?

But the people are also searching for more recent death. There is a topical frisson that will either fade or be augmented over the years, as folk forget, or embellish, as they stand respectfully weighted under this good earth, or as they peer into the darkness and imagine ghostly flittings and sighs. They will make their own tales.

The group hear the professor speak of 'ancient democracy', but they are looking for recent blood. With a broken neck, though, you get little gore. Not on the outside. Suffocation is slower, cleaner, until the bodily fluids start to ooze. They are looking and whispering. Overawed. You canny pretend it's not good for business.

'The most common name for a souterrain was "*wamn*", meaning "earth house". What's notable about this structure, though, is the length of it. When we go to Crychapel Wood, you'll observe this "tunnel opening into a chamber" approach mirrors the same, keyhole-style. Only, at Crychapel, it's a tree tunnel, leading to a stone circle. Indeed many of the patterns throughout the glen echo this. Of course, there's also the argument that, rather than a keyhole, it is a birth canal and a "womb" ' – he does two wee quote marks – 'with which we are presented. Which leads me . . .' Tom clears his throat '. . . to the final, wonderful secret of this place.'

He swings to the right, all the bobbing heads and torches following. There's a collective gasp. Spirals. Clusters of spirals, joined in groups of three. As their torches wobble and scan, the people see a dark, square pool about three feet above the ground, uneasy at one corner where water splashes in. The stream runs freely now they've removed the blockage at the top of Mary's Well. Found a lovely wee pendant there too; serrated jet which makes you think of teeth marks round the rim. A phosphorescent glow rises from the water, sparking diamonds and emeralds. The carved spirals on the wall turn, here, to something else: beneath the slime and greenery – even, they realise, on the floor – a repeating pattern of circles within a circle, edged with carved-out dots. Outside, on the standing stones, these same patterns will make them think of the moon and sun, but here, in this musky hole, it makes them think of sex.

You can hear the tremor in Professor Tom's voice. He is done with the foreplay. 'Now, at neighbouring Dunadd, we have the famous coronation footprint, and the boar carving of warriors and kings. Here, beneath the earth – and linked in layout and design to the far more ancient Crychapel Circle – we have . . . up, please!'

Another gasp. On the wall directly facing them, water flows; the water that is agitating the pool. It flashes on rock and plant, shifting and showing, then closing over. But the shape behind the running water is big, and simple, enough to make out three concave humps drawn with double lines, joined to an elongated oval beneath.

'I give you Màthair!'

Someone flashes a camera. 'No photos please! I made that very clear at the start.'

A mumbled *sorry*.

The professor tuts. The people – who all wanted to take a photo too – tut louder. 'I shall have to ask anyone who attempts to take photographs to leave, is that clear?'

'Yes.'

'Yes.'

'*Sorry.*'

'Màthair,' he pauses. Frowns once more at the sorry snapper. 'The great mother. Possibly where the name Mary's Well derives from – and perhaps even Kil-*ma-hur*-ra itself.'

Several *ums* of approval, or surprise.

'Now, this original carving is considerably older than these Pictish tribal carvings we've been looking at. We can only presume they were basing their beliefs on a more ancient system, particularly as the skulls from this cave have been carbon dated to the same period as the bones we recovered in Crychapel.'

'So, are they the same people then?'

'We believe so. It's possible that these already revered bodies were exhumed from Crychapel thousands of years later, and the skulls repositioned here. The conditions in the cave have preserved—'

'How come she's got three tits?'

This is Johnny, the only child permitted access on account of his newfound heroic status.

'She is one goddess, and three. A trinity. She represents many things: sovereignty and political power; nature and fertility. Life and death. Maiden, mother, crone. You've heard of the Cailleach? Well, what is a witch but a goddess displaced? Only through appealing to her could a tribe succeed. So it's fitting that, in this already ancient place, our ancestors gathered to unite and form alliances. Our whole notion of nationhood is . . .'

The professor's repeating himself already. Justine takes a step back. 'You coming?' she whispers, slipping her hand into Johnny's sticky one. Flesh on glorious flesh, a wee reaching hand through the blackness.

I've found her! I've found them!

The wetness of Buddy's tongue on her face. Seeing the light.

They clamber back out of the souterrain, her and Johnny. 'Well done,' he says.

'For what?'

'Were you no scared, going back in there?'

'Wee bit. Were you?'

'*Nuh.*' He frowns a little. Justine hopes he won't cry again. *It's not your fault.* Saying it to him, over and over. He's just a baby too, like Ross; he could never have realised. She squeezes his hand. 'But it kept me safe in there as well, didn't it? Until you came for us.'

'Aye.' He beams. 'Splatted fuck outa that wanker an' all.'

'Johnny! Will you please not use language like that?'

'How no?'

It's a dreich day in Kilmacarra, but she will never tire of feeling the wind in her face. The steadiness of the sky, and how the earth is beautiful.

'You going to that stupit ceremony thing now?' he asks.

'You not?'

'Nuh. No way.' He swings up his bright new bike, from where it's resting on the ground.

'Why not? You should chain that, by the way.'

'Because it's wank.'

'Johnny!'

He laughs at her, pedals furiously away. Justine makes her way up the slope at the back of the church. Despite the dull weather, there's a festive air about the place. They needn't have worried. A crowd of people have gathered in front of the manse, where two men are putting the finishing touches to a wee stage. It's only temporary, but Mhairi has instructed them to *bloody make it strong, cause I'm no going up and falling arse over tit*. At the side of the manse, a scaffolder is erecting poles. Once the scaffolding's up, they'll fix the roof of the manse. Windows next, then, when it's watertight, they can look at insulation; proper temperature controls. Now that she's sold her house at Nether Meikle, Mhairi will keep the lounge for herself – that and Justine's wee nook in the basement. But the rest will be museum. It would be good if they could have bought the church too, with its leaded panes and its carved wooden lintel of a mother and child at peace, but its future is still uncertain. Mhairi has great ambitions since the grant came through. The money has been match-funded by the council, and Sentinel have agreed to making a generous donation. Part of what swung the vote in their favour. Only three small turbines are visible from the glen – three too many for Mhairi, certainly, but *that's democracy. And you canny argue wi' that*. The Village Votes was a firm success: people talked, and people listened. Folk are still talking about it now. There's a suggestion the model might be adopted for other decisions too, in the jam-smeared promises of 'tomorrow'. But then, there's a lot of talk about at the moment. Of commonweal and catastrophe and destiny and family ties. Everything's poised on this fulcrum. Each side of the debate shouts, then holds its breath, terrified at how the wind might blow, what will turn next. Whatever happens, things will change. Already, Scotland is tip-toeing through broken glass. Justine still doesny know which way she'll jump.

Her feet slap down into the mud, which splashes the back of her wellies. Justine Strang is wearing wellies. She has two pairs actually: green for dog-walking, flowery ones for fun. She sees

Mhairi, signalling to the scaffolder to come down. The scaffolder is Duncan. He grins at Justine, waves. She waves back. Blushes when he blows her a kiss. He looks tousled and lovely, in his nest of metal bars. The men are finished doing the platform; Señor Escobar is already up there. Him and Donald John both, two puffed-up bookends either side of the stage.

'You nervous?' she says to Mhairi. 'Oh shit. What's she doing here?'

'I invited her.' Mhairi sinks her teeth into an apple. Hannah Anderson is nearly upon them, is gliding towards them on invisible wheels. Or really nice suede boots at least; avoiding the big puddle that Justine didn't. Go away, please go away. Her hair's all gold and windswept, body swathed in a dark-grey wrap.

'Hiya, ladies.'

What do you say, what do you say? Hannah's stare feels like cold water. The last thing this woman screamed at her was *Keep away from my family.*

Mhairi nods. 'All right? Boys up with you?'

'They're over seeing one of Euan's pals.'

'Good stuff. Michael with them?'

'Yeah! We didn't know if he'd be up for the journey, but he's been doing really well.'

Hannah moves her head slightly, careful to include Justine in the conversation. 'His speech therapist says he's exceeded her expectations. The rehab's really good.'

Justine reciprocates. Equally carefully. 'And Euan? Is he enjoying being back in Glasgow?'

'Yes and no.'

'I heard wee Julie Astley hitched all the way down to see him.'

'I *know*. Her mum was livid.'

'Ach, young love.' Mhairi takes another bite. 'Is thon Julie sixteen yet?'

'*No.* Quit trying to recruit people to the cause.'

'Every little helps. We're only days away. *Days*, mind! You definitely on the electoral register, Justine?'

'Yup. Form filled in and posted ages ago.'

'Hmm.' Mhairi chews the flesh. She's been trying really hard – no cakes or pies, long walks up the hills, and the weight is falling off her. But she's still Mhairi. 'So the Big Smoke's working out OK then? Definitely no plans to come back?'

Hannah looks around her. Her gaze elides over Justine. Justine pretends she doesn't care. A big bird, a hawk or a heron or something, drifts above their heads. You can see its wingspan ripple the ground. 'No. I don't think so. We're doing all right in Glasgow.'

'Fair enough. Did you bring me some pakora?'

'There's two bags in the boot of the car.' Hannah shakes her head. 'Smell drove me crazy on the way up.'

'Aye. You canny beat a Glesca curry.'

'Mhairi! Mhairi – that's them ready for you now.' A swoop. A scliff. Johnny, on his shiny bike. He and Buddy loop round Mhairi. 'Come *on*. They're waiting.'

'Right. Come on, you two. My audience awaits.' She lobs her apple core into the long grass. The three women troop to where the stage is. Mhairi gets up beside Escobar, who puts out an arm to steady her. He smiles. She goes all girlie. Donald John moves across to join them. The whole of Kilmacarra is assembled here, plenty folk from further afield have come too. There's the photographer from the *Courier*, and another couple of reporter-looking types that Justine doesn't know. No TV cameras, not enough interest, not when the world is so busy outside. Not even if Mhairi offered to flash her pants again. There's a referendum looming. Scottish Independence. Will we or won't we? How will our hearts be doing, at that moment, in that booth? Who will we be?

Mhairi moves to the front of the platform. Raises her hands like an old pro. Big smile, arms out. Duncan winks at Justine as he slides off the stage, to the ground. She does not deserve Duncan. But then, he says he doesn't deserve her. To wake each morning at Cardrummond: that she could be allowed to have that, and it's not being greedy. The farm is safe. Bought and paid for. She would love it to have been her money that saved him, but the bastard polis put paid to that. Fair enough; it would only have tainted the place, made the soil go sour. She'd begged them to let her keep Askit, though, but they couldny find him at the house. She hopes he's being loved somewhere.

'Ladies and gentlemen. I'd like to thank you all very much for coming, to this, the official launch of the Kilmacarra Museum appeal. We've got the building, we've got the willpower and, thanks to Professor Tom Wilson and his team, we've even got some stuff to put in it! We've also been hugely fortunate to get our hands on the Covenanters' Tapestry.' Mhairi holds up the old tapestry Frank found. It's been professionally stretched, and put in a split-new frame.

'We've been advised that the quality and rarity of this wee gem is such that it could have fetched £60,000 on the open market. So we're extremely grateful to the wonderful Effie and Duncan Grey for selling it to us privately.' Whoops and cheering for an embarrassed Duncan, who half-raises his hand while lowering his head. Yes, Mhairi, she thinks. He *is*. He has given her love. Fire and warmth until she can't distinguish joy from nervous flutters.

Always, she is first. It's a concept she still struggles with, that a person can give your desires priority over theirs. But she's learning. Duncan's a good teacher.

'As you know, talks are ongoing with museums across Scotland and beyond, to see if we can bring other artefacts home, that may currently be housed elsewhere. But, of course, all of this costs money—' she slows her delivery, so they can nod and mumble – 'and that's why we're launching this appeal. We've already had generous donations from Historic Scotland' (big cheer), 'our local council' (smaller cheer), 'and Sentinel Power' (boos and cheers in equal measure). Mhairi waits for the hubbub to die down. 'Anyway. No matter what happens ultimately to this glen, we aim to build a museum that'll tell the story of *all* the people that have passed through here.' The wind catches her frizzy hair, whips it across her shining face, and she is prettier than Hannah. Spits of rain begin to fall, the clouds pulling down, drawing the hills closer.

'We are fortunate to be blessed with a unique landscape. To be *entrusted* with it. Like Scotland's people, Kilmacarra is quiet and unassuming . . .'

'Och, here she goes,' whispers a young woman behind Justine. 'We're getting the party political broadcast.'

The lassie's got a point: Mhairi is beginning to drone – they'll have no need of that piper who's waiting to round off the celebrations. The people fidget slightly, like water. But still listening. Still contained. Justine drifts away too, her mind wandering back down the slope, towards the damp, blue-grey hills, and Cardrummond.

'Hello, Justine, pet!' Miss Campbell puts her arm through Justine's. 'How's the—'

A man and a woman turn. The woman eyes her up and down,

trying to equate her face with the mugshot in the papers. 'Justine? Are you that lassie from Glasgow? The one that killed that dead guy in the cave?'

'No, Sheena. It was a love triangle, mind?'

'No. He'd been beating you up, hen, hadn't he?'

Miss Campbell draws herself to a full five foot one. 'Do you mind? This lady is nothing to do with that nonsense at all. Which was a *fatal accident* actually, if you bother to check. And her people are from here. No that it's any of your business.'

The couple mumble their apologies.

'Honest to God,' whispers Miss Campbell. 'Some people.'

But Justine doesny care. She feels Miss Campbell's bird-hand round her wrist, sees Duncan sorting the mic cable beside the stage. He mouths *I'll see you after?* She nods. Feels a long ripple. Which she likes. She backs away from all the bodies, catches the eye of wee Johnny, who is circling the edges of the crowd. He sticks his tongue out, calls: 'You coming to see me at football on Friday?'

'I am indeed,' she calls back, moving further down the slope. Relief as the distance increases. She's not so good with crowds, folk all jostling up against her, sharp voices, and the hands. She's good here, with the pillowed, wide clouds and the open land. She moves faster as she reaches the bottom; her feet keep running from her. She makes a new path through the bracken and the mud. Reaches the edge of the field, the fence, the gate, and she is definitely running. She runs past the shape of Michael and his boys, she turns, jogging backwards, and it *is* them, she's sure, she feels it certain, those distant people who are being helped from the car, those three slow figures who are making their way past the small prides and polished doorknobs of Kilmacarra's houses, the

two who are flanking the limping third, who form a single creature: Euan the head, Michael the humphy back, wee Rossie, the
mischievous tail, who are moving along the road towards the
church, and all the people. And Hannah, who yelled: *Keep away
from my family*.

She watches them limp and struggle; her Michael with his sons,
his wife. Who got their miracle. She wishes them love. She keeps
on running, over empty broad land filled with mist and rock. She
runs past the shadows of castles, past the memories of war, past
human-hefted, soaring stones. She runs past the rubble of farms
and the pastures of sheep, past road-scars and the three spears of
turbines. She runs over bones and blood and seeds and roots.
Goes fast, then slow, picking her way over the biggest ruts, the
bumps and knots, the loam and peat and stone. Then fast, faster
than she ever thought was possible, until it feels like she has wings
and her heart's too big to fit inside. Above her, another huge bird
rises like a kite, and she watches it soar. Follows it, faster, she is
running, rising up the rock and heather hills; she will run until
her muscles are buckling, glorious and full.

She won't fall, though.

Because she is pinned into the map.

Acknowledgements

Many lovely people have helped in making this book. With grateful thanks to my two midwives – my agent Jo Unwin and my editor Helen Garnons-Williams; to Tram-Anh Doan, Inez Munsch, Alice Shortland, Terry Lee, Madeleine Feeny, Sarah-Jane Forder, Greg Heinimann, Liz Woabank, Oliver Holden-Rea, my US editor Kathy Belkin, and everyone at Bloomsbury for all their enthusiasm and support; Susan Armstrong; Shelley Harris; Helen Fitzgerald and Sergio Casci; Jan and Isabella Smedh; Tom and Margaret Cassidy; Dr Neil Hughes; Stuart McHardy; Mairi Matheson; Dougie, Eidann and Ciorstan for reading, love and provision of all writerly comforts; and to the folk of Kilmartin Museum and Kilmartin Glen – a magical place in Argyll on which Kilmacarra is – loosely – based.